UNDER EASTERN STARS

HEART OF INDIA SERIES

Silk
Under Eastern Stars

UNDER EASTERN STARS

LINDA CHAIKIN

BETHANY HOUSE PUBLISHERS
MINNEAPOLIS, MINNESOTA 55438

Cover illustration by Joe Nordstrom

Published by Bethany House Publishers
A Ministry of Bethany Fellowship, Inc.
11300 Hampshire Avenue South
Minneapolis, Minnesota 55438

Printed in the United States of America

Library of Congress Cataloging-in-Publication Data

Chaikin, Linda.
    Under eastern stars / Linda Chaikin.
       p. cm.
    Sequel to: Silk.

    1. British—India—History—18th century—Fiction.
2. Women—India—History—18th century—Fiction.
I. Title.
PS3553.H2427U5   1993
813'.54—dc20   93–25160
ISBN 1–55661–366–0   CIP

July 19th, 1993

This second book of the *Heart of India Series*
is dedicated in memory of my beloved mother who is
now . . . "forever with the Lord."

LINDA CHAIKIN is a full-time writer and has two books published in the Christian market. She graduated from Multnomah School of the Bible and is working on a degree with Moody Bible Institute. She and her husband, Steve, are involved with a church-planting mission among Hindus in Kerala, India. They make their home in San Jose, California.

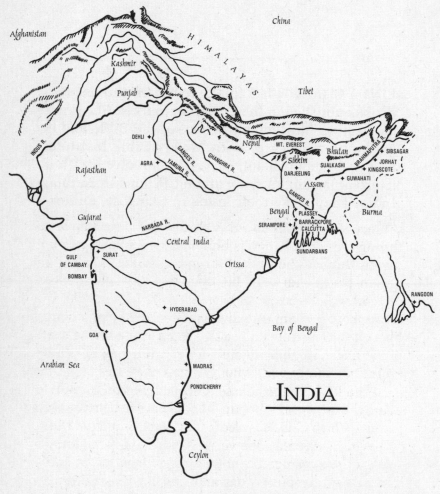

INDIA

1

Calcutta, India
1799

Jace Buckley scowled a little and ran his hand through his dark hair. His blue-black eyes narrowed under his lashes as he studied the ancient map. Wearing an Indian tunic and worn buckskin trousers, he lounged comfortably on cushions beside a low rattan table. The small private room was divided from the common area by a curtain of wooden beads. The eatery, offering some of the finest Mughlai cuisine in Calcutta, was owned by an Indian family with whom he had close ties.

As Jace waited for his servant-companion, Gokul, to bring the meal and join him, he concentrated on the map given to him by his deceased father, Captain Jarred Buckley. With a calculating eye, he traced the little-known trails crisscrossing the northeastern frontier of India along its precarious border with Burma. *The ruling warlord may be able to offer information on the attack at the British outpost of Jorhat.*

His thoughts were interrupted as the wooden beads parted with dull clacking sounds. He looked up. Gokul

9

stood there, out of breath, one hand on his protruding belly, his marble-black eyes agitated.

Jace rolled the map and placed it within his black woolen tunic. "What is it?"

"I try to stop him, but he ran like a cheetah!"

"Who ran like a cheetah?"

"Indian boy! Maybe fourteen. He disappeared in crowd. Left a message."

Jace stood. "For me?"

Gokul glanced backward over his shoulder. "Best you read it for yourself. The boy knew enough to bring this to Chowringhee address." He reached inside his sleeve and handed Jace a sealed envelope.

There was no handwriting. A letter delivered to him here was suspect. "Did he say anything?"

"He whispered a name."

Jace met his gaze. "What name?"

"Javed Kasam."

The name struck like a blow, but he did not visibly react.

"He sneak in and ask for me. When I came he whispered the name, then ran. There was no time for anything else."

Saturday, October 13
Huzoor! Javed Kasam:
I am willing to pay a worthy price for important information. Needless to say, our meeting must be kept in the strictest confidence. My ghari* will be parked by the Armenian church in the Chowringhee district next Saturday, October 20.

Signed,
Ayub Khan

---

*A glossary of Indian words is at the back of the book.

Jace frowned. It had been over three years since he had worked under the name of Javed Kasam. Who but a foe would know enough about this side of his life to send him a message at Chowringhee?

Gokul watched him with intense dark eyes. "Trouble?"

"Ever heard of Ayub Khan?"

Gokul pursed his lips. "The son of the Burmese warlord?"

"Yes. But Khan is dead. Someone is using his name."

"This Ayub Khan wishes to meet with you?"

Jace handed him the letter, then retrieved his scabbard, strapping it on. "Ask around the bazaars. I want to know who is masquerading as Khan, and why."

Gokul handed him the letter, his face grave. "Sahib, think well of what you do. This could be a trap."

Jace was thinking of the stolen Hindu idol, Kali. Did this Khan think Jace had it? His jaw set. "I shall meet with him."

"Suppose Ayub Khan comes in disguise? There may be spies waiting by the church. Do not go alone."

Jace had understood the dangers when he entered the complicated world of Eastern intrigue years earlier. His first involvement was quite by accident, the result of bumping into a sticky web of deceit and assassination in northeastern India, and becoming entangled in a plot to steal the jeweled idol of Kali from a Hindu temple, and the death of a much-venerated holy man. He had escaped by posing as an Indian guru by the name of Javed Kasam. Who had killed the holy man, or gotten away with the idol, he did not know, but there were those who believed him responsible. Since that time, he had participated in the art of intrigue on various occasions. Once for a friend; a few times for pay. It was a dangerous way of life, one he wanted to leave behind. Javed Kasam had enemies.

Gokul, who worked the bazaars, knew many informers in the south and north and had kept Jace informed, but the name Kasam had not been spoken in three or four years. Those who knew Jace Buckley to be Javed were few. Gokul was one, and the two fighters from the warrior caste—Faridul and Arif. But these were men he could count on. That only left Rawlings in London, whom he had worked for on two occasions, and the Burmese warlord. Jace had not paid Rawlings a visit since selling him the matching ivory elephant for his collection; and he knew of no one to whom Rawlings might give his name, nor did he believe that the warlord had sent someone masquerading as his slain son, Ayub Khan.

That left only an enemy. Perhaps a man hired by the royal family over the matter of the stolen idol.

"Have Faridul meet the ghari in the churchyard on Saturday. When the carriage leaves, watch to see if it's being followed. If Khan comes alone, I will ride to meet him outside Calcutta near the dak-bungalow. If we stay on the move, there can be no trap. It is I who shall trap Ayub Khan. Go at once."

───────

Coral Kendall came down the stairs of her uncle's Roxbury residence in Calcutta. Her green eyes shone beneath a fringe of lashes and her golden curls fell about her shoulders. *How can I sneak out to meet with Javed Kasam?*

She hoped her tension did not show as she saw her sister Kathleen in the entrance hall. Her other sister, Marianna, and Aunt Margaret were waiting on the porch. *If only they would leave for Mrs. Waterman's garden party,* she thought. Even now there was a possibility that she would be late for her meeting with the Indian mercenary.

The customary garden party was being held that afternoon, but Coral had managed to decline the invitation. She tried to smile pleasantly as she carried down her pink fringed shawl for Kathleen to wear with her afternoon garden dress.

"The color will flatter your chestnut curls," said Coral.

Kathleen's amber eyes shone with anything but pleasure. "I would rather not go," she said, taking the shawl. "But Aunt Margaret insisted. I would much rather work on my designs than listen to prattle."

She might have felt sympathy for her older sister, but Coral knew she *must* get her out of the house. She thought of the scrapbook that she had recently seen Kathleen carrying about in her satchel. She had shown Coral some of her clothing sketches, and Coral had been impressed with the intricate work. The dresses were organized under afternoon and evening wear, according to the seasons.

"Why not take your book with you? You might get some ideas. Just think of all those ladies wearing their afternoon dresses. Maybe you could sketch some of them for fun, then see how you can redesign them to best flatter each figure."

"Why, Coral, what a grand idea! I should have thought of that myself!"

With shawl in hand, Kathleen rushed for the stairs. "I will get my things. Everyone will be so busy milling about they will not even notice me sketching!"

Coral smiled. It was good to see Kathleen enthusiastic. Her sister had still not gotten over her disappointment over leaving the Silk House in London.

A short time later, Coral followed the others onto the lower verandah, where the carriage waited to drive them to the Waterman house. It was a bright morning, alive with sunshine and bird song, but a taste of autumn was in the air.

"Goodbye, dear. We will be home before dinner," Margaret told Coral. "Rest up from that nasty fever for the picnic next week. It is the last outdoor social of the season and will last all day and into the night."

Coral watched from the verandah and gave a wave as the white-clad servant assisted her sisters and aunt into the carriage. When the vehicle disappeared around the corner, she picked up her skirts and sped back into the house. She must hurry!

She felt a bit guilty over her secret plans for the afternoon but relieved that her family had left. She was now free for the day.

"If the family finds out what I am about to do, I shall never hear the end of it," murmured Coral nervously. She was not one to mislead, but when it came to Gem, nothing would stop her. She owed her family love and loyalty, but surely she could not be blamed for doing everything within her power to locate information on her son.

As it did so often, Gem's face appeared in her memory, and so did the haunting scream of "Mummy, Mummy, Mummy" that had pierced her heart the night of his abduction. Forever that sight would conjure up a torrent of mixed emotions. She had a fear that her family was right—Gem was dead—but also a fierce determination to find him again . . . at whatever cost.

She had one ally in the house to assist her, however small. Jay.

"I stop ghari-wallah on the street for you, missy. He there now," whispered the little servant-boy Jay.

Coral brushed a thank-you against his dark head, then rushed up the stairs to her room and changed quickly into the clothes that she had prepared for the secret meeting. She scanned herself in the mirror, frowning a little. She might be able to hide her hair color beneath the Indian head covering, but her eyes would give her away.

No matter. Once I meet Javed Kasam in person, I can explain my need for secrecy.

Coral hurried to her wardrobe and took out the traditional full-trousered Indian suit worn by Punjabi women, this one trimmed with silver ribbon. She quickly pulled on the loose-fitting trousers, over which she slipped on a *kameez*, a knee-length smock that flared out at the bottom. The long *chunni*, or head covering, was black silk highlighted with small silver bangles that tinkled. Carefully, she shielded her hair so that her tresses would not show, then wrapped the Roxbury ring tightly in a lace handkerchief and placed it in her beaded bag.

Misgivings flooded in, and Coral shut her eyes. "Forgive me, Grandmother Victoria, but my Gem is worth the family heirloom. . . ."

While Jay kept watch, prepared to whistle if any of the servants loyal to her uncle, Sir Hugo, appeared, Coral slipped from the house by a side door and through the garden.

Jay ran ahead, shimmied up the trunk of a big tree, and straddled a high branch like a leopard. All was clear. Silently as a cat, Coral made her escape from the boundaries of the house.

On the massive open park of green surrounding Fort William, she looked for the rented ghari. The driver was waiting for her, and Coral boarded the carriage. On the western side of the fort was the Hooghly River and the area called Chowringhee, with jungle paths and crowded bazaars. It was to this seamy side of Calcutta that Coral had sent her inquiry to Javed Kasam.

At the northeastern corner of the park, the ghari passed the hawkers, the sweet and tea shops, then moved toward the Old China Bazaar, housing the thriving, mysterious oriental culture. She had a glimpse of coolies wearing triangular chip-straw hats and short pants, and of black doors with red and gold markings, before the horse turned to plod on toward an even older Armenian sector of Calcutta.

Coral's eyes searched for the Armenian Church, built in 1724, and tensed as it came into view. The carriage came to a stop near the church cemetery, and Coral waited, seeing no sign of any Indian that she might take for Javed Kasam. She left the ghari door ajar for his approach and felt the dry wind stir her head covering, jingling the silver bangles. She adjusted it to shield her curls from clear view, her heart thudding.

Several minutes crept by. Her eyes scanned the church grounds and the cemetery beyond. Then she saw him. A big, bearded Indian soldier whom she guessed to be a *rajput* from the military caste of the Hindus. Immaculately dressed in warrior's garb and wearing a sword, he stepped from behind some greenery to walk toward the open door of the ghari.

Coral leaned back into the seat as he blocked the door with his frame, hand on sword hilt. She said nothing as the handsome dark eyes swept the inside of the ghari, coming to rest on the empty seat opposite her.

"Where is Ayub Khan?"

"I am Ayub Khan. . . . Are you Javed Kasam?"

His eyes, hard and black, swerved to confront hers. They narrowed, and Coral tried not to wince. She hoped she had not offended him by using the male name, and tried to explain. "You see, I did not want you to contact members of my family, and—"

The rajput said something to the driver, then before she could respond, he swung his heavy frame into the seat, slammed the door, and the carriage lurched forward, leaving the old church behind.

"Sir! I wish to speak here! Where are you taking me?"

He did not speak and was concentrating on the road behind them. Coral felt panic rising up.

"Javed Kasam, I should like—"

"Silence, sahiba."

She watched him, her alarm growing. He seemed intent on making sure no one followed them. The carriage was moving at a fast clip now, the hoofs of the horse stirring up dust. Coral held her chunni against her nose and mouth. Looking out the window, she saw that they were headed away from Calcutta.

"Where are you taking me!"

"I shall bring you to Javed Kasam."

Then he is only a contact. She relaxed a little. "Is it far?"

"Not far."

The pitted road was inches deep in fine brown dust, and thorn bushes stood as prickly guards on Coral's side of the carriage, keeping her penned. Was she a prisoner? The rajput's promise of *"not far"* turned into an hour's ride, and Coral was relieved to finally hear him order the driver to stop the vehicle.

The rajput guard exited, then commanded the irritated ghari-wallah to keep silent, assuring him that he would be paid well enough for his services.

Coral was not only furious at her treatment but nervous. Just what sort of renegade was this Javed Kasam to hurry off his prospective clients as though they were thieves out to steal from him?

The thud of hoofs sounded, and she turned in her seat to look out the window. Had he come at last? Before she knew what was happening, the ghari lurched forward again and started off at a good clip just as a man swung himself in, slamming the door after him. As he turned to confront her, Coral froze.

2

"Javed Kasam" wore a black Indian tunic belted with a silver chain. The sword was one of those curved, deadly blades called a *tulwar* that Coral had seen on Kingscote among the Indian guards. The turban, too, was black, but it was the man's eyes and handsome features that were becoming all too familiar in the guise of several different men, reminding her that if she did not know Javed Kasam, neither did she truly know the disciplined Major Buckley, nor the adventurer with the monkey on his shoulder who had rescued her at the bazaar.

Coral stared at him. He leaned over and swept aside her chunni, unmasking her golden-colored curls. The blue-black of his eyes glittered. He sank back, and she heard him mutter something in a breath of exasperation.

"But . . . *you* cannot be Javed Kasam."

He fixed her with a narrowed gaze. "And surely, madam, you are not Ayub Khan."

Coral did not know why, but she flushed. "I once heard my father speak of him."

"Which is not quite the same thing. Besides, Khan is dead."

"Oh. Actually, I was afraid you would—I mean—that

19

Javed Kasam would go to Sir Hugo with my name."

"Hardly. I would be blowing the trumpet on my own disguise."

Coral pulled off her chunni and drew in a breath. "You must understand, sir, I am rather new at this vice."

"Vice?"

Aware of whom she was talking with, and knowing how desperately she needed his help, she hastened, "I suppose that is not the proper word. Intrigue would be better."

He watched her.

This is not going the way I intended. She busied herself with the chunni, smoothing the silk with the palm of her hand.

"I must say it is a charming masquerade," came the smooth voice, and Coral looked up. He made a handsome Indian warrior.

"Imagine, an Indian woman of high fashion bearing the masculine name of a Muslim ruling prince," he said. "Do you make a practice of this, Miss Kendall—or should I call you Madam Khan?"

She could not afford to nettle him, and bridled her own irritation. "Speaking of masquerades, just who is it I am addressing? A sea captain, a military major, or Javed Kasam?"

"That depends." He smiled. "You may call me Jace."

Well, I asked for that one. Jace was the last thing she would call him, being too familiar, which of course he knew.

"I would like to know how you got hold of the name." His expression was grave again, and she felt comfortable with the safe distance between them.

"On my word, sir, I intend to explain everything."

"You do realize that there are some matters we simply do not discuss, and one is the true identity of Javed Kasam," he said quietly. "It was a risk for me to meet you like this. I prefer my head where it is. Before we part, you will swear silence to ever having known this Indian scoundrel."

Coral felt uneasy knowing she had brought him some risk. "Of course," she said quickly. "But would you tell me why you are in danger?"

"Since you have requested to see me, I will be the one to ask questions. First, who told you about me?"

She settled back against the seat and met his gaze evenly. "Director Rawlings of the East India Company. I went to see him in his office in London and he gave me your name."

At the mention of Rawlings, she noticed a perceptible glimmer of relief in his gaze.

"Who told you about Rawlings?"

"No one told me outright. I once overheard my father discussing him."

He looked surprised. "Hampton involved in the clandestine?"

Coral said nothing. She knew little of her father's contacts.

"It is not surprising, I suppose. The location of Kingscote would demand contacts in India and Burma. And the man with whom your father discussed Rawlings?"

"I am sorry. I do not recall. He was a Dutchman who came to see him on shipping business. I overheard a brief discussion about Director Rawlings knowing 'certain individuals who could gain secret information in the East.'"

"Ah. And so you went to Rawlings while you were staying at Roxbury House."

"Yes. I waited until Sir Hugo returned to India."

"Why?" he asked.

21

She thought he already knew, but explained again, "Sir Hugo insists that Gem is dead. I do not believe it. My situation in the family is such that turning to Director Rawlings offered my best chance of locating my son. I asked about a man I could hire to discover Gem's whereabouts. Director Rawlings was hesitant, but at last wrote out a name and handed it to me. He said I could find Javed Kasam in Calcutta, and that he was very good—for the right price." Coral's hand tightened on the beaded bag containing the Roxbury ring.

If she expected him to react to the hint of a hefty payment for his services, he did not. Coral felt a prickle of disappointment. Suppose he refused to help? Something warned her not to place all her confidence in the ring. She did not know where the Darjeeling tea plantation stood in his future plans, but the ring was worth any number of voyages he might risk on his clipper. She doubted little that he could bring himself to refuse.

"And, of course, now I know who Javed Kasam is," she continued. If Coral felt unsettled about anything, it was whether she felt more comfortable with Major Buckley, or Javed Kasam.

"And now that you know?" he repeated.

"I am even more convinced that this 'Indian mercenary'—one of the best in the East according to Director Rawlings—is the man to help me locate Gem."

She hoped he would respond to that, and her uncertainty continued to grow when he did not. If her previous suggestion of payment had not brought the response she hoped for, neither did her confidence in his abilities. He merely watched her, and as he did, she became more desperate.

Coral lapsed into an uncomfortable silence. She tried not to form opinions of the man in front of her, but they came nonetheless. *Independent, strong, and as untamable*

22

as the vast land of India. Just what was Jace truly like beneath his many disguises? He was nothing like Ethan. *Ethan.* Suddenly she wished he were there.

"You will permit me to hire you?" she asked, breaking the uneasy silence.

He studied her for a moment in the shadows of the ghari, and answered as though he had not heard her question. "Have you mentioned Kasam to anyone? Your sisters, your aunt?"

"No. I memorized the name and the Chowringhee address while still in London, then burned the paper Director Rawlings gave me. I did not know how long it would be until I returned to India, and three years was too long to keep the paper."

"You would do well in the world of intrigue."

She gave him a side glance. . . . Certainly he was joking.

"Then no one but the boy knows you sent a message?"

"The boy? Oh, I see what you mean. Perhaps I should not have risked the two brothers, but it seemed the only way to contact you. They will say nothing, I am sure of it. You will let me hire you?"

"No."

Startled, she urged, "But I will pay you handsomely!"

"I am sorry to disappoint you over my refusal, but I am not for hire."

"If anyone can help me find out if Gem is alive, it is you. I am glad you are Javed Kasam, because you have a clear understanding of what is involved in his abduction. It was you who warned me, and it is you who can discover the truth now."

The ghari stopped, and an uneasy silence locked them in shadows. The wind buffeted the door, rocking the carriage. Coral leaned toward him.

"He is mine. I love him, I raised him, I have poured

23

years of my life into him, and I want him back!"

He studied her without speaking.

"Major, I will give you anything you want, anything within my authority to give. You are aware that I am a silk heiress."

Something unpleasant flickered in his eyes, but she did not accept the warning.

"That tea plantation you and Michael wanted so badly, I will buy it for you."

"Indeed?" He folded his arms across his chest and regarded her with a look that seemed to make the black in his eyes more prominent, like glowing coals.

Although she noticed the familiar set of his jaw, she took this expression for interest. "There is something I want to show you. I brought it with me."

Quickly now, believing she had won him over, she opened her beaded drawstring bag and took out the knotted handkerchief. She fumbled to untie it. A minute later she extended her palm with open handkerchief, the rubies in the Roxbury ring glimmering like fire. "Find out if Gem is alive. If he is, help me get him back and this is yours. You can retire on your plantation. You will not need to brave wind and sea on your clipper to scrimp and save, not when I can easily give it to you!"

Unexpectedly, his warm, strong hand closed over hers so tightly the jewels dug into her palm. "What do you take me for?"

Confused, she stared at him. He was angry! "But, the ring is more than enough to buy your plantation!"

"I *know* what it is worth."

Her eyes searched his and found only displeasure.

He gritted, "I do intend to own that plantation. And I shall go on scrimping and saving every miserable *rupee* until I do. And when I have accomplished what I set out to do, the plantation will be mine, not handed to me by a silk heiress. I do not want your ring. I do not want anything you have as a Kendall. I will remain forever chained to my clipper before I allow a woman to turn Jace Buckley into a 'lap dog with a diamond collar around his neck.' " He lifted her hand clutching the Roxbury heirloom. "Even if it was placed there by your pretty little hand."

He let go and opened the ghari door, prepared to leave. He looked back at her. "Give it to Ethan Boswell. I have a notion Sir Hugo's nephew will have no qualms."

Ethan? The name swirled about her brain. What did her cousin have to do with this? But she was too surprised over his reaction to find offense in his suggestion that Ethan could be bought. What did he know about her cousin?

As if to add wood to the fires of her dismay, he abruptly disembarked from the ghari despite her protests, and shouted something in Bengali to the rajput, who quickly produced his horse.

Coral was leaning out the ghari door as he swung himself onto his mount, and he looked down at her, unrelenting.

"Good day, Madam Khan." Then wheeling his horse, he rode off.

Coral sat there gripping the seat. The thud of horse hoofs disappeared, and wind struck the side of the ghari. She pondered his reaction to the ring. Had she been too glib about it? Had it seemed a bribe? Or was there something more that motivated his actions? Her brow furrowed, she fell back against the seat.

On the way back to Calcutta, weary and dejected, Coral wondered what had gone so badly.

Javed Kasam, according to Director Rawlings, was a mercenary soldier who accepted dangerous missions for precisely one reason: high pay. Then why had he been offended? She rehearsed in her mind what had happened, deciding that unlike the other men she had met in London, whose motives Granny V warned of being suspect, her position as a silk heiress was nettlesome to Jace. The ghari wheel hit a bump, and she was thrown to one side, hitting her shoulder. It was not the pain that made her wince, but a sudden realization.

"Coral Kendall! Why, you have behaved positively brutish! You have waved the ring before him as though baiting a bear! Offering to buy without difficulty the very thing Jace Buckley has struggled to attain for the last several years!"

Coral groaned at her folly. Her desperation to locate Gem had made her insensitive to Jace.

I should have known better.

But just how well did she know this man? Hardly at all. And now what?

When they arrived at Fort William, the ghari-wallah climbed down from his seat, his expression showing sullen displeasure over the afternoon. She carefully paid him, adding a tuppence.

I will not give up, thought Coral fiercely as she watched the ghari leave. *Jace Buckley is the most knowledgeable man in India. I will try again.*

Next time, she would know better than to offer him an heirloom, or flippantly promise to buy him a tea plantation from her bulging purse.

Evidently she had riled the territorial pride of a cheetah, a cheetah who staked his own prize and refused assistance from anyone—especially Coral Kendall.

3

Margaret Roxbury squared her shoulders as she paused outside the door to the suite she shared with her husband. She touched her brunette chignon, her brown eyes sober. Taking in a small breath, she opened the door.

Hugo Roxbury stood before the mirror, his broad back toward her as she shut the door.

"Good morning, Hugo."

He slipped his jacket over the watered-silk waistcoat and his black eyes met hers in the mirror. He smiled, his even teeth showing beneath his close-clipped mustache. His beard was well-groomed, and she was reminded of how striking her husband was in his outward appearance.

"You are up early after waltzing the night away," he said evenly.

She stiffened. "I waltzed little, actually. Lady Carlton had an attack of asthma and had to be rushed home. I took her place in the receiving line." She walked across the thick indigo rug and opened wide the doors to the upper verandah.

He tapped his well-manicured nails along the front of his waistcoat, and the ruby ring glinted. "I was remiss

in telling you how lovely you looked at the state ball."
He turned toward her. "The colonel occupied much of
your time."

"I do not call a waltz or two occupying a good deal
of my time. He was merely being polite." She looked at
him, remembering how his appearance had first at-
tracted her to him when she was a young girl in London.
Sir Hugo Roxbury had been an exciting mystery, a distant cousin with charming manners and fair speech, convincing her that with his moral support her talent in
design could be carried to the heights of success. He had
won her from the attentions of the young ensign John
Sebastian Warbeck, a man who was adamant about her
becoming a military wife in the Company. Warbeck, in
his youthful pride, had refused to bow to the pressure of
the family silk dynasty and yoke himself to the will of
Lord Henry and Lady Victoria Roxbury. In the end, it
had been the family's disapproval of John Warbeck more
than her love for Hugo that had brought about the marriage.

"What does the governor-general want to see you
about today?" she asked.

Hugo's meetings at Government-House were growing
more frequent. Working with the governor insured
greater prestige within the confines of the Company, and
so did the upcoming engagement of their daughter, Belinda, to Sir Arlen George, a relation to the governor. It
was about Belinda that she wished to talk to Hugo.

"It is not about the northern frontier again, is it?" she
pressed.

"I fear it is. The attack on the outpost at Jorhat was
only the beginning of renewed trouble with Burma. The
governor-general is keeping the incident quiet, but there
was an attempt to kill the nephew of the raj at Guwahati."

"Hugo, must you get involved? It is so dangerous."

He took hold of her shoulders. "It is for the good of both England and India that I serve the governor. Do not worry. There are others in more precarious situations than I, including Hampton."

"Hampton!"

His expression turned grave. "If Hampton were wise he would change his mind about working with the Company. Kingscote is located dangerously close to Jorhat. He may soon need our help."

"Hampton Kendall is too independent to sign away control of the plantation. The Kingscote Plantation was untouched by Assam's previous trouble with Burma. Why should they be in danger now?"

"Burma's determination to possess the northern frontier, especially Assam, is not over. New fighting can break out at any time. Someday there may be a full-scale war, and we'll be fighting for the first time inside Burma!"

"Forget all this, Hugo. Let's go back to London. You have work to do there, and Victoria needs you."

His smile was faint. "Someday. There is too much to do in India now. And it affects the silk. Now that we have some manner of treaty with the king of Assam, penetration of the East India Company into the Himalayas with an objective to opening up trade with Tibet is progressing. I have expectations of working with Hampton to double, even triple, silk production."

Margaret knew there was little she could do to induce him to return to London. Year after year she waited for something to turn up that would convince him to run for Parliament.

"Opportunities in the northeast are too great to ignore," he was saying.

"Speaking of Hampton," she began casually, "I think you should speak to him about Alex and Belinda."

29

She saw his black eyes flicker with impatience. He was determined his daughter marry Sir George. His hands dropped from her shoulders and he turned back to the mirror, adding the finishing touches to his appearance. "We have been through this before, Margaret. Belinda's girlish infatuation with her cousin Alex will pass with maturity."

She sighed. "I am not so certain it is infatuation."

"Nonsense. She is only seventeen."

"I was only a year older when we married."

"You were different than Belinda, my dear."

"Not so different, Hugo. I see so much of myself in her these days."

He gave a short, amused laugh. "I am Arlen George, and Alex is Colonel Warbeck, is that it?"

"This has nothing to do with our past, or with the colonel. I do not want to see Belinda forced into a marriage she does not want."

"The way you were?"

"Hugo, please." She walked over to the verandah and looked out. Jay and two other servant-children were hauling buckets of water to fill the trench around the orange tree. "Hugo, she is our only child."

"Belinda is spoiled. She needs someone like Arlen George who can put up with her tantrums."

"If I have been easy, it's because you were too hard."

"Let us not get into child rearing now. It is too late to go back."

"But it is not too late where her future is concerned. Marriage is too important, and I will not have her rushed into something she is so upset about. Belinda is all I have."

"You are forgetting me, my pet."

Margaret turned her head and looked at him, feeling a throb of dull pain. "Did I ever have you, Hugo?"

His brow arched, and he eyed her curiously. "Strange remark, Mrs. Roxbury. You have always had my attention, my devotion."

Margaret looked out across the verandah. "I just left Belinda. She spent a good deal of the evening last night with Arlen. He is insisting a wedding day be set at the Christmas ball at Barrackpore. She is very upset."

"Upset? I would think she would be elated. It is not every young lady in the Company who is so sought by a man like Arlen George. Marriage to him secures her future in India."

Margaret tried to keep her exasperation veiled. "She does not want Anglo-Indian life. You know that. She wants to go back to London."

"Belinda did not seem unduly concerned last night. She looked to be enjoying herself with any number of young officers whirling her about the floor. You will admit that Arlen was mature enough not to interfere with her gaiety. He spoils her. He knows she has this infatuation with Alex Kendall, and he is willing to let her grow out of it. Arlen is the best possible husband for Belinda. Alex is temperamental. His music is his life. I doubt if he knows Belinda exists."

"He does. He wrote her while he was in Vienna."

Hugo grew still and searched her face. "This is rather sudden, is it not?"

"It is not sudden at all. They are cousins. They have corresponded since childhood."

"Alex has been writing her, and I am only now learning about it?"

"Belinda did not think it a deep, dark secret, nor did Alex. She wrote Michael, too, when he was alive."

His mouth turned grim. "I never thought Alex would lead her on this way."

"That is completely unfair. One would think Alex was

a penniless scamp. I do not understand you. You want your nephew Ethan to marry Coral, yet Alex is also an heir of Kingscote. Why not marriage to Belinda?"

"For a number of important reasons, my dear. One of them is Arlen George himself. He is an ambitious man with good sense. He'll amount to something in India. Who knows? He may one day become the governor-general himself. Now, tell me about these letters coming from Vienna."

"There were not that many from Alex."

"Has Belinda been throwing herself at him?"

"Hugo!"

"Then you did not know about the letters?"

"No. But if I had, it would not have upset me. Belinda tells me the letters had nothing to do with romance. In his last one he congratulated her on her upcoming engagement, and spent the rest of the letter discussing music and Vienna. But Belinda seems to think Alex does care, and I promised her I would speak to you about him."

"This is all sentimental nonsense, Margaret. I doubt if Alex *cares*, as she puts it. But if he did, it is surface romance. He is not the manner of man for her." Hugo came near, taking hold of her. "If Assam eventually becomes a raj state under British rule, Arlen could become commissioner. Her marriage is as important to the silk enterprise as Ethan's marriage to Coral. The Roxbury family needs them both."

"And the Kendalls?" she asked flatly. "Is it important to them?"

His face was smooth. "We are all in the silk business together, are we not? Margaret, do not look at me that way." He gave an unexpected laugh and drew her into his arms. She was so furious with him that she trembled, and she knew he felt her shaking, for his embrace tightened.

The amusement over her anger had left his voice, and it was quiet. "Darling, you are angry."

Her voice shook. "Yes, Hugo, I am angry. You are like a stubborn bear. You charge forward, trampling underfoot anything or anyone who opposes your plans."

He was silent, and she did not pull away as he held her.

"Am I to understand that you will never forgive me if I do not speak to Hampton about Alex?"

The change in his voice took her by surprise. She raised her head and searched his face. "I would like you to speak to Hampton, yes."

"Then, my dear Margaret, if it will make you happy, I will do so."

Stunned, she could not speak or move for a moment. "You mean that?"

"Yes, but I think the entire matter about Alex is a waste. You speak of my being hard on Belinda; the truth is, I would worry about her if she married Alex. He is a young man of dark moods."

"Alex?" she said with a laugh.

"I have heard—well, perhaps I should say nothing."

"About Alex? What is it?"

"I did not want to say this, but perhaps the girls were called home not only because of Elizabeth, but Alex."

"Alex, but why?"

"Do you remember back some years ago when he shut himself in his room at Kingscote? His mood was such that he refused to eat or talk to the family for days."

"Yes," she said quietly, a sense of wariness stealing over her. "He wanted to pursue his music in Vienna. Hampton wanted him to concern himself with silk. In the end, Elizabeth talked to Hampton and he relented.

Music means so much to Alex. I can understand how he was depressed."

"He was more than depressed. He tried to commit suicide."

She sucked in a quick breath. Young, handsome, sensitive Alex? "But Elizabeth never said anything; she never told me—"

"Your sister thought it best for his future that she say nothing to the family. I would not know about it if Ethan had not been acquainted with the physician treating him in Vienna. He told me about Alex when we were in London."

"He was ill again while in Vienna?"

His hands tightened on her shoulders. "He never fully recovered, even after he was encouraged to go to Vienna. Last year he collapsed during a recital and was incapacitated for months. There was a time when the physician thought he might never recover."

Margaret struggled against what she was hearing. It seemed inconceivable.

"Alex is better now. He has come home to Kingscote. But there is uncertainty over his state of mind, over what his future holds. Elizabeth does not know of this recent problem. . . . She is too ill, and Hampton kept it from her. But he thought it best that his daughters come home. He needs their help. I would have said nothing, except I cannot bear the way you looked at me now, as though I cared nothing for my daughter's happiness, or yours."

Margaret felt dazed. "If Belinda finds out, it will devastate her."

"I am sorry I had to tell you. But if you do wish to postpone Belinda's engagement to Arlen until spring, I will speak to him about a delay."

She shook her head with confusion. "I do not know! This changes everything. Poor Alex. Hugo? You are quite certain this is true? There might have been some mistake."

"I can swear to nothing, nor would I, yet Doctor Schuler is a friend of Ethan's, and neither man has cause to exaggerate the state of your nephew's mind." He sighed. "You could write to Hampton, I suppose. But you must be careful. We would not want to add to your sister's unhappiness. Elizabeth has had more than her share of sorrow. First the child—what was his name?"

Margaret's heart swelled with pain as she thought of her sister. "Ranek," she murmured dismally, thinking that she too had once lost a baby boy, but she had been only five months along when she miscarried.

"Then, there is the tragedy of the Indian boy's death, not to mention Michael."

"Hugo, hold me."

"Darling Margaret." He embraced her. "You mean everything to me. I would do nothing to hurt you. You know that? I did not want to tell you."

Margaret swallowed back the desire to cry. She was past those early days of her marriage when she had cried too much. At times she could vow that Hugo loved her; at other times he seemed as driven as Alex was with his music.

Her mind went back to her sister. Elizabeth remained strong through her emotional losses because of her confidence in the Scriptures. She relied on God's promises as her light and source of hope. *What about the foundation of my own faith?* Margaret wondered. *Is it there?* She had believed in the teachings of Christianity as a child, and yet . . . Elizabeth was able to approach God in a way that she could not, for Christ seemed far removed from her world, an impersonal force.

At the moment, the only thing that was real to Margaret was her husband's strong arms around her.

Through the twenty years of their uncertain relationship, he had not held her enough.

"I want to believe in our marriage, Hugo."

"Believe me, because it is true. Someday I will make you happy, Margaret. I will take you back to Roxbury House. You will see. I promise. But I have work to do here in India that I cannot walk away from. Perhaps you can go back to see Victoria again next year, and I will join you as soon as I can. You would like to go back, darling?"

"Yes, you know I would."

"Victoria would be pleased if you would oversee the Silk House for a time."

She looked at him, her breath stopping. "Hugo, do you mean it?"

"Darling, I have felt badly taking you away, knowing how much it means to you. Perhaps if Belinda and Arlen's wedding day were announced this Christmas, Arlen could take both you and Belinda to London. Your mother would want to meet him before the wedding next year."

"Hugo, are you certain about Alex?"

"I regret the necessity of having told you. You are right. Belinda will be hurt if she finds out. It may be more merciful for her not to know. Perhaps if she thought that Alex had already married the young lady in Vienna. What was her name?"

"Katarina Fredricks," said Margaret. "But Hugo, it would be a lie. How could we do that to our own daughter?"

"If he returns to Vienna next year, no doubt he will end up marrying her. We must do what is best for Belinda. We must think of her children, and of the entire family. Believe me, she will get over this girlish infatuation with her cousin. And Arlen will be good to her."

"I do not know, Hugo. . . . Maybe you are right, and yet, I do know she wants to go back to London."

"And if you and Arlen went with her, I am confident matters would turn out for the best."

"Yes, perhaps. Let me think about it, Hugo."

"Take all the time you need. But the matter must be settled before the Christmas festivities at Barrackpore." He kissed her forehead. "Sir George is pressing me for a public announcement."

———————

"War!" The echo of voices around the breakfast table joined Coral's alarm. If the clouds of renewed war with Burma gathered in the northeast, then she must get home before all travel was cut off!

Sir Hugo's dark eyes circled the table. "The outpost at Jorhat was attacked by Burmese soldiers. A British officer named Selwyn was taken prisoner, interrogated, then butchered."

A sick moan came from Marianna, but Hugo seemed not to notice. "The governor-general asked Colonel Warbeck to send reinforcements. He has managed to get his son back in uniform. Major Buckley will be leading a troop north."

Coral knew of Assam's past skirmishes with Burma, but an all-out war? Coral glanced about the table, and all the faces were somber.

It was Marianna who asked the question that was hovering like a ghost above Coral's head. "Then how do we get home to Kingscote?" Her light blue eyes were wide, and her delicate features were so pale that her strawberry curls seemed even brighter.

Coral reached across the table and squeezed her younger sister's hand. "We will get home. We have Seward, remember? He can hire Indian guards to join our safari."

"I am afraid not, Coral," came Sir Hugo's firm voice.

She looked at her uncle across the table. The dark eyes beneath the heavy brows were fixed upon her.

"It is too dangerous to journey now, even with Seward. I discussed this with him yesterday. For the sake of safety, it is best you and your sisters wait until the matter at Jorhat is settled." He turned to his daughter, Belinda. "I suppose you will be pleased to have your cousins here for your engagement party during the Christmas holidays?"

Belinda paled at the word engagement and said nothing. Margaret said quickly, "For a wedding gift, your father wishes Sir George to escort us to London. While your grandmother becomes acquainted with Arlen, I will be overseeing the Silk House. You will like that, will you not, Belinda?"

Belinda's sultry dark eyes came alive, and she looked from her mother's tense face to her father. "Truly, Father?"

"I thought an interval at Roxbury House with Arlen before the wedding would make you happy. You may marry in London if you wish. Your grandmother will plan an extravagant ceremony, inviting the Duke and Duchess of Sandhurst. And it is no secret how your mother has longed these years to return to her silk design."

Coral's mind remained on Sir Hugo's announcement that she could not return to Kingscote. Her stomach muscles tightened. *She had to get home!* He was her uncle, but what right did he have to order her to stay in Calcutta when her father had sent for them to come home immediately?

"Seward can handle most anything." Coral found her voice interrupting the discussion of London. "With mother so ill, I am compelled to risk the safari. There may be others at Kingscote who are ill, including the children. I want to talk to Seward. Where can I find him?"

Silence fell upon those seated around the table. She was aware of the flicker of impatience in her uncle's eyes, but it was Aunt Margaret who spoke, her voice tense but calm. "Dear, we never know what these natives will do next. Your uncle has experience in these matters. We had best listen to him. Try not to worry. You will get home to your mother as soon as it is safe to travel."

Coral pushed back her plate and stood, but Sir Hugo's voice cut through her actions. "As your guardian while away from Kingscote, I am forced to act. Hampton would expect it of me. Seward and a few hired Indian mercenaries are hardly a safe vanguard for a two-month safari. Not with the risk of fighting." He smiled. "Besides, my dear, you are in no condition to be nursing a passel of children on Kingscote. You must set aside your sensitivity and look upon these matters with the eyes of a realist. India is a mother with a million squalling children. There is little any of us can do about it. Do sit down and finish your breakfast."

She heard Margaret's cup clatter on the saucer and became aware of the awkward silence holding the others to their chairs. Margaret was hoping she would not respond. . . . Coral knew that. But if she gave in now, what possibility would there be of returning home unless Hugo permitted it?

The fear of being manipulated against her will made her react promptly. Coral's calm voice surprised even herself. "I understand, Uncle. But I know tropical fever. I know what my mother is going through, and I cannot risk a year's absence waiting for the East India Company to settle their differences with Burma." She glanced at her sisters, who stared at her with surprise. "I will not put Kathleen and Marianna at risk if they wish to stay here. I will go alone if necessary."

The silence grew heavier. *Will someone please say something?* Her heart pounded.

Sir Hugo unexpectedly gave a short laugh. She saw what seemed to be a slight flicker of respect in his eyes. "You have always been a stalwart young woman, Coral, despite your problems with illness. I do not mean to question your liberties, nor to suggest you cannot go home if your heart is set. But you must understand my concerns. A raid on the safari could mean your captivity. I blanch at the horrendous difficulty Hampton would have in bargaining for your release."

Coral found his presence overpowering, and it could intimidate her emotionally if she let it.

"Really, Hugo, I do think we should wait to discuss this," said Margaret.

"You are right." He sounded sympathetic now. "Ethan's arrival will brighten your stay in Calcutta, Coral."

Taken off guard, she sat down quickly, staring at him. "Ethan? Coming here?"

"You did not know? We discussed it before I left London. He was to catch a Dutch ship from Dover a month after we sailed. He will be here before Christmas . . . in time for Belinda's engagement."

"No. He said nothing."

"He must have assumed I had already told you."

"I did not see him for several weeks before we sailed," Coral admitted. "He was at Oxford on medical business."

"Then that accounts for the little surprise," said Hugo good-naturedly.

"It is a surprise," Margaret said brightly, obviously trying to cheer Coral. "I must say though, I am as confused by this as Coral. Was not Ethan to be elevated to some position? Research, was it not, Hugo?"

He looked intently at his wife. "You are mistaken, dear."

"I am certain he told me so. He was looking forward to the position. Pass the tea, darling."

"You know how sacrificing Ethan can be." Hugo refilled her cup. "Nothing is too great for the medical cause. Like Coral, he has a concern for the Indian people."

Caught by the turn of events, Coral tried to sort through her emotions. *Ethan is coming to India . . .*

"But he will continue his research," said Hugo. "Hampton has been in correspondence with him about setting up a lab in the jungles around Kingscote."

Margaret turned to Coral. "With Elizabeth ill, it will come at a good time."

Anxious to be alone to think, Coral rose from her chair too swiftly, and a wave of dizziness threatened her balance. Sir Hugo also stood, looking alert.

"It is nothing," murmured Coral. "I often get dizzy; it passes."

"Send for Doctor Harvey."

A doctor! "No, really, I do not need a physician," argued Coral.

Less than an hour later, Coral sat in a high-backed armchair, submitting to the lecture of the retired army physician.

"A bit of rest, and a spoonful of this before bed, and you will be up dancing again by Christmas."

"A few days in bed will do her well," added Sir Hugo.

Coral started to protest, but Doctor Harvey plucked nervously at his silver goatee. "Rightly so, Hugo, rightly so."

"I would hate to write a letter to Hampton telling him you had a relapse," said Hugo.

Coral glanced at him. Memories of her long stay at the summer house in London brought a cold feeling of panic. *No, God, not that again, please.* The very thought of being placed under strong medication caused her to give in, but once in bed and alone with her sisters, she bolted upright, tossing aside the covers and confronting Kathleen.

"Why did you not stand with me against Uncle?"

Kathleen turned her back, staring out the window, but Marianna wrung her hands, and her voice quavered when she spoke. "I fear Uncle. I am sorry, Sissy."

"I was not speaking of you, Marianna, but Kathleen. She is the eldest, and she should have stood with me." Coral groaned, walked to the rattan settee by her vanity table, and sank down. "In Calcutta till after Christmas! Mama's ill and Papa needs us! I am not about to stay!" She stood again. "I know what you are thinking, Kathleen! That if we stay, you can somehow return to London with Aunt Margaret and Belinda!"

Kathleen whirled, her eyes snapping. "Yes! I am the eldest, and I have even more right to a life of my own than you. Working with Jacques at the Silk House means as much to me as the school you hope to build on Kingscote."

"Oh do, *do* stop!" cried Marianna. "I do hate for the two of you to argue! I hate it! Oh, Coral, what do you intend to do about Uncle's wishes?"

"What can I do? I am confined to bed till the picnic. Aunt Margaret will see to that. She will be watching me. They both will, just like they did in London. Five days in bed! I must get a message to Seward."

Kathleen eyed her dubiously. "What can Seward do? You heard Uncle. His 'suggestion' was more like a warning: 'Stay in bed, my dear, or you will be here till spring.' "

"Mama may be in heaven by then," sighed Marianna.

"Will you stop that!" Kathleen winced. "Uncle wants

to keep you here until Cousin Ethan arrives at Christmas," Kathleen said thoughtfully. "I was surprised you dug your heels in as long as you did."

"Uncle may be guardian, but Papa sent Seward to bring us home," said Coral. "I know Seward. He is loyal. After I explain everything, he will cooperate and arrange the safari."

"Against Uncle's concerns for safety? I am not so certain. He cannot be making it up about the danger of travel." She took a letter from her bodice. "You said I did not back you up, but I could have given Uncle more reason to delay our journey if I showed him this."

Suspicious, Coral walked toward her. "A letter?"

"From Captain McKay. It arrived from Plassey this morning by delivery boy."

"Plassey is on our way north," said Coral cautiously.

"Yes, and it is the reason Gavin was not at the ball. He was transferred to the 82nd regiment there. He wrote that they expect trouble. Not from Burma, it is too far away, but from India—the kingdom of the Maharattas."

Marianna wrinkled her nose. "Ma-ha-what?"

"A central Indian state independent of the Company. Captain McKay says they have had trouble with them for years. When we travel, we will pass near where there is fighting."

Coral was more doubtful than her determination showed. War . . . would it ever end? She thought of Major Buckley. So he, too, was back in the military and leading a troop to the outpost at Jorhat. *Jorhat!* She caught her breath.

Kathleen scowled at her, and Marianna came out of her pessimistic mood long enough to fix her with a curious stare.

"What is it?" Kathleen asked.

"I have an idea," said Coral.

43

"Oh, no. I do not want to hear it," said Kathleen, walking to the door. "Come, Marianna, let Coral rest."

"Wait," said Coral, her eyes gleaming. They both looked at her—Kathleen, dubious; Marianna, expectant.

Coral was thinking of Jace. How long would he be in Calcutta? A plan was blazing through her mind. What if—what if she could get Major Buckley to bring them to Kingscote? Sir Hugo's argument about the risk of danger would be annulled. English civilians often journeyed under the protection of the East India Company.

"I know what you are thinking," said Kathleen. "That we could travel under military escort. I heard what Uncle said about Major Buckley. But that still leaves the problem of Ethan. Uncle will insist we wait for his arrival so we can all travel home together."

"Coral, you will not have a relapse, will you?" asked Marianna worriedly.

Coral smiled brightly, even though she did feel tired. There was hope again. And again, like discovering information on Gem, the hope rested on Jace Buckley.

"Do not worry about me. I can survive the safari to Kingscote. And as for Ethan, he did not expect to travel with us. He will need to journey slowly to safeguard his medical equipment. Oh, I am glad he is coming! He will be able to help Mother the way he did me. See, Marianna? Everything is going to turn out well. The Lord is directing our paths."

"He is? I thought it was Uncle Hugo," said Marianna.

"Suppose Uncle discovers what you are up to?" warned Kathleen.

"He will not," said Coral with confidence, thinking of her clandestine meeting with Javed Kasam.

"Hugo is not one who enjoys being thwarted," said Kathleen. "Do you know he used to be a corsair?"

Marianna sucked in her breath. Coral stared.

"Belinda told me," said Kathleen.

"Why would Belinda say a thing like that about her father?" asked Coral.

"Because a few weeks ago she overheard him talking to an Englishman. They scuttled a Portuguese ship off the coast of Pondicherry when they were young."

Coral could believe her.

"Belinda says the man was unusual in his appearance. His eyes were pale, and his skin was unusually white-looking. Even his hair looked platinum."

"An albino?" asked Coral.

"A pale-eyed ghost," whispered Marianna.

"Nonsense," said Coral. "But whatever you do, say nothing to Aunt Margaret. Her relationship with Uncle is already strained because of Belinda and Sir George."

"I do not blame Belinda about not wanting to marry Sir George," said Kathleen. "The man is as cold and domineering as Hugo." She took hold of Marianna's arm, pulling her sister reluctantly to the door with her. "And do not repeat a word of anything I said to Aunt Margaret."

"Of course not, Sissy," Marianna replied. "What do you take me for, a silly goose?"

Kathleen smiled too sweetly, patted her sister's red curls, then shut the door behind them.

4

The next day Coral sat in the rickshaw holding on to her wide-brimmed hat, its trailing ribbons matching the yards of blue organdy of her dress worn over a layer of petticoats. The delicately puffed sleeves and tailored bodice were decorated with tiny white shell buttons.

It was the day after the picnic. And again, with the help of little Jay, she had managed to get away from the house without being noticed. Holding to the seat, Coral looked about, a little dazed by her surroundings. There were people everywhere—so many that it was inconceivable to view them as individuals with hopes and pains of their own. Shoppers and beggars ignored one another, keeping to their castes. The untouchables were at the bottom, most of them without hope, destitute of the compassion of their fellows.

Calcutta sprawled north and south along the Hooghly River. Children scampered everywhere, some of them naked except for worn loin cloths. Numerous ox-drawn carts and meandering, unattended cows blocked the movement of traffic. One old cow stood munching the fresh goods from a cart while the merchant stood by passively. Not far away beggars were chased away with a ring of curses. *The paradox of Calcutta,* Coral thought.

There were various costumes among the people, each color and style belonging to different castes. Wealth and destitution met in a strange kind of coexistence, as the caste system led the majority to accept their state as divine will. Death was seen as only one more event to bring yet another reincarnation. Perhaps after ten thousand reincarnations freedom might come. Maybe. It was doubtful for most. In the meantime, to break one's caste was unthinkable.

Now, in the center of this metropolis of humanity, her own human frailty obscured spiritual vision. A multitude of faces blurred, and voices lost their distinction. She felt deluged by the need around her, and for a moment felt nothing but a sudden desire to escape it all.

How can God care for so many? she wondered. But He did. She thought of the children of Israel in bondage to Pharaoh in the book of Exodus. *I have heard their groaning,* God had told Moses.

Her eyes moistened; her palm clenched into a damp fist on her lap. *Oh, to see these as you see them, Father; to feel as you feel for their souls.*

Was it possible? Would not such love and compassion break her heart?

Then grant me but a drop of your compassion in my cup. And even then, I can only carry it by your grace.

Surely this place, however destitute of spiritual life, however miserable, is where the Lord wants me to be. In the end it will be worth every moment of sacrifice.

"And soon, I shall have a portion of Scripture in Hindi," Coral murmured with a smile. She would spread that light from one end of Kingscote to the other! She would teach the children in their own language.

Would she be able to convince Seward to proceed with the planned safari? And what would be her father's reaction to starting a mission school?

Pray, she thought. *I must pray about the school, about Kingscote, about Mother recovering from the fever.*

At times Coral felt overwhelmed at the impossibility of it all, as if she were but a tiny pebble on India's vast continent. She was not only up against Sir Hugo and the Company's displeasure, but she had no guarantee that even her parents would consent. The fire set by the sepoys at the time of Gem's abduction had frightened her father. Could she blame him? He had poured his very life into building the silk plantation into its present success. One tiny flame tossed to the caterpillar hatcheries could mean its end.

She shuddered, remembering her dream. The search for Gem among the flames was so vivid that she could almost smell the smoke.

The rickshaw found a path in the throng, and with a jolt began moving through the marketplace. Next to Government-House, Coral caught sight of St. John's Church, and it was here that she had the rickshaw boy stop. Inside, she sat in a pew and spent several minutes in silent prayer.

When she returned to the rickshaw, she heard the clatter of hoofs behind her on the stone. Turning, she saw a young man astride a Company horse. The man looked vaguely familiar. Where had she seen him before? He wore a knee-length coat and tan breeches, and as he walked the horse toward her he removed his hat and smiled.

"Why, good afternoon, Miss Kendall."

"I am sorry. The fault is mine, but . . ." her voice trailed away.

"The name is Franklin Peddington. I met you the other night at the state ball. I believe you know my brother Charles."

"Yes, of course, hello, Mr. Peddington!" She recognized the secretary to the governor-general. "Perhaps you can help me. I am looking for a friend of my father. A Mister Seward."

He glanced at the rickshaw and seemed surprised that she was without a chaperon. Coral hastened, "It is most important that I talk to him."

"By all means, Miss Kendall. I shall send someone to locate him. He is probably at the military quarters."

The court building was set back into a square, with the clerks' offices on the south and the jail on the north. There were a number of native troopers about, their scarlet coats standing out and their shakos all neatly in place upon their heads. An Indian in a blue turban stood by one of the doors. Behind him were several orientals, known unflatteringly as coolies, and these served as errand boys. He called, "*Koi hai!*" and they came running up, offering the bow of honorary greeting. "*Huzoor, huzoor, burra-sahib!*"

"Send word to find Sahib Seward at the garrison. Miss Kendall is here to see him. *Ram! Ram!* Hurry."

They ran off, and Franklin Peddington stood with her in the shade of the building, waiting for Seward. When she asked about Charles, he explained that his younger brother was still with Master Carey at Serampore, but that he would be coming to work for the Company soon after the new year.

She had not forgotten Charles's invitation to show her around William Carey's mission compound, but it would not be as easy to accomplish as slipping off for a few hours as she was doing now. Visiting Serampore meant a trip up the Hooghly by boat and would be an all-day excursion.

"I believe that is Seward now," Franklin said, politely taking his leave of her.

Seward was a giant of a man, broad-shouldered, with a full wide face to match his size. A stringy thatch of graying red hair was tied at the nape of his neck beneath his hat. At the age of fifty, he could best any man younger than himself. He had served her father on Kingscote well, arriving soon after the birth of Gem, but had left with Michael to sail on the *Madras* with Jace Buckley to Macau and Cadiz. Just how much he was involved in the Darjeeling tea project, she was not quite certain. She supposed that he had a percentage in the future plantation. Recently Seward had agreed to serve Hampton by seeing Coral and her sisters home to Kingscote.

Seward's past was a mystery, and Coral never inquired into it, but she rather suspected it might have something to do with smuggling in China. Yet she had no concern for her safety with Seward near. He was now to be her coconspirator in bringing her to meet the major and insure her safari home, although he was likely to disapprove of her plan.

His brows hunched together as he came up, his eyes searching her face. "Something wrong, lass?"

She faced him for battle, hands on hips. "Wrong? Not if Sir Hugo's attempt to keep me in Calcutta under lock and key is foiled. Where have you been?"

Seward scowled when she mentioned Sir Hugo. "Aye, I understand how ye feel, but 'twas Sir Hugo who insisted you and your sisters stay. And I've been keepin' me ear open here about any fightin' in the north. Since Sir Hugo be your uncle, there waren't very much I could do about it. His word be law now, lass."

"Trouble in Jorhat or not, I want to leave next week as scheduled."

"Now, ye wouldn't be expectin' me to risk the rage of Sir Hugo by going against his clear commands, would ye? He be an orn'ry man, and maybe he's got something about it not being wise to travel to the northern frontier. Neither Mister Hampton nor Miss Elizabeth would be wantin' me to risk their comely daughters to dangerous trekking."

She sobered, thinking more of the danger to Kingscote than to herself. "Do you think it was soldiers from Burma who made the attack on Jorhat?"

He rubbed his bearded chin and hedged. Coral's lashes narrowed suspiciously. "You do not believe Sir Hugo?"

"Not for me to say till Jace—I mean the major—looks into it."

She pressed. "Does Major Buckley think otherwise?"

"Now would he be telling me that?"

"I have a feeling he tells more than you are willing to share with me. By the way," she said cautiously, "where is the major? Is he about?"

He grinned. "He be on the *Madras*. A bit of coddling before he rides north."

"Then it is true? He will command the troop at Jorhat?"

"Aye, and not a bit pleased about exchanging the sea for the British cavalry. He be leavin' on short notice, as soon as the colonel gives the word. I be expectin' to ride with him on my way to Kingscote."

Coral offered her sweetest smile. "I thought you might intend to ride with him, Seward. That is why I'm here now. I am going with you. What safer journey could I have to the northern frontier than with you and Major Buckley's troop?"

For a moment his expression was blank. Then as he became aware of the full import of her words, the rugged lines creased above his shaggy brows. "Now look here, Jace won't be liking that, I can tell ye so right now. You're wastin' your time and breath. I be sure of it."

Coral smiled, and her eyes challenged him with good humor. "Indeed? Suppose you let him decide?"

He cocked his head and scanned her suspiciously. "I hear ye was up all night waltzing with the major at that ball."

"I could hardly refuse him. He was Michael's friend, was he not? Besides, he saved me from a batch of crows in the bazaar the day we arrived. Nevermind, I will explain later. Now, Seward, be the dear that you are, and take me to see his clipper."

He scowled and folded his muscled arms across the wide expanse of his chest. "Ain't worthy to be wastin' your eyes upon, lass. 'Tis a ship. That be all."

She gave a laugh. "Now I have heard it all. A lover of the sea telling me the *Madras* is unworthy of my inspection?"

He lowered his eyes. " 'Tis the ship we lost Michael on."

Coral had forgotten that. Her smile faded. Memory of her brother swept in like the wind across a deck. Seward's feelings for Michael were obvious, and she laid a hand on his arm. "He is with the Lord. We grieve for the loss of him, but he knows only joy."

He sighed. "Aye, that be true, little one. Sure ye be wantin' to walk aboard?"

She straightened her shoulders. "Yes, Seward. I do. And it is important I meet with the major before he leaves."

Seward gave her a wary glance as though he read the shift in her thinking. "Pardon me saying so, but I put nothin' past Sir Hugo. If he thinks you be stirring up trouble, even godly trouble, by starting some school for the little ones, Sir Hugo will swoop down on your father like a crow on a ripe mango."

She took his arm and propelled him toward the rickshaw, all the while smiling. "Let's not discuss it now. First I must get home. Now, Seward, this matter with the major is going to work out well indeed, just you wait and see."

"I don't like this. And I got a feeling Jace won't like it either."

Coral remembered her unsuccessful meeting with Javed Kasam. Would this be another cause doomed to failure? She had no doubt that the elusive captain could be difficult, but she refused to accept defeat without at least trying.

"Then if you are so certain he will refuse, there is nothing to worry about. Take me to his ship."

———————

As they rode toward Diamond Point on the Calcutta harbor, Coral asked him about Jace. She learned for the first time that Seward had known Jace's father, Captain Jarred Buckley, and that he had sailed with him to China. As a boy, Jace had been raised at his father's side, sailing with him to the rich and mysterious trading ports of the East.

Seward's walnut face, creased with sun lines, settled into a scowl. " 'Tis too long a tale to embark upon now. But his father and me were traders in tea . . . and well, some other commodities that isn't fit to mention. Captain Jarred could be orn'ry at times, but he doted on Jace."

Her suspicions grew. "You mean to tell me his father was a smuggler, and you were his partner?"

Seward's hardened face reddened a bit. "Jace was but a lad at the time and he had no mother. He had nothing to do with piracy." Seward cleared his throat and glanced at her sideways. "He went wherever his father sailed. If ye feel sorry for these untouchables, lass, then you ought to feel for Jace as well. His own fate as a lad in China 'twas far worse than what may befall these untouchables. Why, after his father died, he was left alone on the beach of Whampoa and saw the Buckley ship go up in flames—taking many good men with her. Captain Jarred was beheaded by Chinese warlords before the boy's very eyes, and for a few years Jace was a child-slave. He still carries some scars on him, and they be not all on his flesh, I can tell ye that."

A child-slave . . . Coral's understanding of the captain of the *Madras* softened against her will. Jace was more vulnerable than he appeared.

"His father and me—" he paused and cleared his throat, "we owned a ship licensed by John Company."

Coral tried to recall the vague conversations that her father had engaged in with Seward when they both thought that she was not listening. Her father must already know of Seward's unscrupulous past. "John Company is like the East India Company?"

Seward let out a breath. "Aye, but John Company is merely another name for the East India Company herself. John Company handles, well, less honorable trade. They issue licenses to independent ships to haul cargo. They're better known as China traders, sailing the Eastern ports—Singapore to Pearl River in China." He glanced at her. "Most times our cargo was legitimate, as you say—tea and chinaware. But we was into dark contraband too." Seward shifted his position.

Coral felt his eyes gauging her response, to see if she was offended. She straightened her hat. "Do not forget I was born and raised in India, Seward. Father has mentioned the horrors of opium. Is that what you and Captain Jarred Buckley smuggled?"

Seward sighed. "I had nothing to do with the ugly stuff. I was against the idea of messing with it from the beginning. Jarred, too, was against it. But he got into some deep trouble, and his ship came into debt. He was afraid he'd lose her, and he got involved with the China traders."

"So he compromised."

He paused. "He did. But he was no God-fearing man, lass. He loved his son, but that was about all he did love. The opium was made here in British Bengal and sold to the Chinese mainland. We got caught in something that was dark indeed, and in the end it took his life. I escaped from the attack on the beach by swimming out to a Chinese junk. I tried to save Jace, but in the fighting I couldn't find him."

"He was left there?"

Seward's face became dark and he stared straight ahead. "Aye."

Coral digested what she was hearing about Jace's unpleasant childhood. What he must have gone through as a child-slave to angry Chinese warlords, especially as the son of an English captain! "How did he escape China?"

Seward obviously took pleasure in telling of Jace's wit. She found out that he had eventually escaped by route of the Old Silk Road across the Himalayas, a passage once used by the ancient caravan traders bringing silk from the Chinese dynasties to Persia and Baghdad. He told her that upon crossing through Sikkim and into the area of Darjeeling, he had met a so-called *munshi*— a teacher and writer—by the name of Gokul.

"But Gokul wasn't any of that, not really. He knew the ins and outs of the bazaars—the world of intrigue— and Jace learned it too."

Again, Coral remembered Javed Kasam. "Yes," she murmured. "He did learn it, and well."

By the age of fourteen, Jace had already embraced the life of an adventurer. With Gokul, they toured India

and Burma. It was in Bengal that the colonel John Sebastian Warbeck had fought with a British-held outpost.
A village was taken, the raja fled with his remaining soldiers, and the colonel had taken Jace with him back to
Calcutta, adopting him as a son. There followed another
interval when Jace entered military school in London,
then returned to serve with the British forces. But he
always had a love of the sea.

"Learned from Captain Jarred. He be considered by
the Company to be one of the best captains about, but
an interloper."

Coral vaguely recalled the word being used by her
father. "Interloper?" She hoped the word did not mean
anything of ill-repute.

"It means he be in business for himself."

Thinking of contraband, Coral stirred uneasily and
glanced at him from beneath her hat. "How did he manage to get the *Madras*?"

Seward rubbed his beard. "I don't know. But he was
hauling tea down the Pearl River from Canton, and he
could have gotten the clipper that way. He's smart
enough. While he's a bit of a wild one, he's not a black-
guard. Least not like Captain Jarred was."

"He is going back into the military to save his ship?"

Seward unexpectedly chuckled. "The colonel be a determined man. The two of 'em butt heads at times, yet
they have themselves a silent agreement of respect. The
colonel, he be doin' everything to keep him in the Company. Right now Jace has got little choice in the matter.
But as for the sea—well," he boasted with a grin, "there
ain't an Englishman in India who knows it better. Knows
the Hindu mind, too. Speaks Bengali like a native, some
Marathi too, and he knows their religions like a man
knows the back of his hand."

Religion. . . . Again, she wondered about Jace Buckley spending his formative years with "Gokul the mun-shi."

"Is he inclined . . . ah, toward the Hindu belief?"

"He knows it well, but he has books from John New-ton, too, and knows the old man himself."

"He knows John Newton!"

"But that ain't to say he be a devoted Christian," he warned, looking at her.

Did her pleasure show too much?

Seward gave her a thoughtful glance. "You need to ask Jace about what he believes. He don't talk much about it. You like him, lass?"

Coral busied herself with her hat. "How can I say? He is an enigma. As adventurers go, I suppose he can mingle comfortably with the best of them, and the worst."

"There ain't no excuse when it comes to the past way of things, but a man ought not to be marked by the sins of his father. As far as Jace goes, you won't find a man with an inch more of courage, and it's my thinking that he ought to stand on his own merit, not his father's past sins."

Seward was right of course. She turned her head and cautiously scrutinized the side of his hard brown face. So this was the background of her father's most trusted friend and servant. It proved a man could change, that the grace of God was sufficient for the worst of black-guards, for Seward now claimed to adhere to the name of Christ.

When they arrived at the East India docks at Dia-mond Point, people of all nationalities jammed the har-bor. Strange dialects mingled in Coral's ears, exotic scents floated on the light breeze that ruffled the sails of many ships, and the steps leading to the water were filled with Hindu bathers seeking religious cleansing in the holy Ganges River.

With precarious footsteps, Coral followed Seward's lead down the quay. Her eyes skimmed the ships and fell on an impressive white-masted clipper farther down the dock with the name *Madras*.

Seward stopped. "Sure ye be wantin' to do this?"

"Yes, Seward, I am certain."

"Aye, then, ye wait here a minute."

Coral watched him intercept a lean, bronzed Indian sailor known as a *karwa*, and a moment later Seward climbed the plank and disappeared. She felt a tightening in her chest. How would Jace react to seeing her aboard his ship? There was no denying that he had been upset with her offer to buy him with the Roxbury ring.

Her eyes scanned the ship. Strange. . . . He was willing to go back into the military in order to save his vessel even when the idea irked him, but he would not accept the ring from her and walk free.

She waited, rehearsing in her mind what she would say to him. Could she convince him of her desperate need to reach Kingscote? Did she dare offer to pay him for his service, this time not with the ring, but perhaps a cargo of Kingscote silk?

It seemed an endless time had crept by before she saw Seward's rugged frame walking toward her.

He hesitated and rubbed his bearded chin. "Lass, if I were you, I'd not go barging into his cabin. The captain's in a riled mood."

For a moment, she feared that he was still angry over their last meeting. "He refused to see me?"

"Nay, nothing like that. He don't know you're here, but he be a mite vexed, and nursing one black headache."

Headache. . . . Coral tensed.

From Seward's expression, she could see that he was

hoping she would turn back. Coral drew in a little breath and picked up her skirts. She had too much to gain to turn back now. She slipped past him. Riled mood or not, she was going through with the meeting. "It is all right, Seward. I want to see him."

Seward shrugged, then walked behind her as she made her way up the plank to the deck of the *Madras*.

5

Jace touched the bloody bruise on the back of his head and winced. His lack of vigilance embarrassed him. Who would have thought that after escaping harrowing expeditions from China to Sumatra, he would naively allow himself to fall prey to a common thief in Calcutta?

He had left the ship late last night with the prized Moghul sword in his scabbard when he was struck. The club must have weighed a ton, he decided sourly. His vision was blurred, his head throbbed, and he did not have a rupee left. Far worse, the magnificent sword belonging to a fifteenth century Moghul king from Agra was lost. The sword could have bought a wealth of information on what had really happened at the outpost in Jorhat.

Sprawled on his cot, donned only in worn buckskin breeches, he felt in a miserable mood when the tap on his cabin door sounded. It rattled through his head like a twelve-pound cannon. He winced again.

"No need to break it down, Seward! Just come in!" The door opened abruptly, and a shaft of bright daylight flooded the cabin. Jace turned his head away to avoid the painful glare, and snapped, "Get Jin-Soo to dig up

61

some snake cure for this miserable headache. I am desperate. Bring the coffee?"

"The kansamah says you're out of coffee, lad. So Jin-Soo be brewin' tea." Seward cleared his throat. "You have yerself a visitor—"

"Tea! I am sick of thinking about it, smelling it, bartering for it. I must be insane to want to grow the stuff! Remind me of this if I ever get out of uniform. We will go to the West Indies for coffee beans."

"Your kansamah be ready to mutiny against his cookstove, lad. Says he needs a bag of rupees for supplies."

"I am leasing the clipper to the Company for a voyage to the Spice Islands. They can buy their own supplies."

"Aye, but the karwas are threatening to hire onto another ship. Seems the colonel didn't pay 'em when they arrived from Singapore."

"Tell them I was robbed last night. No one gets paid aboard ship until I get back from Jorhat. Here, help me with these, will you? I can't bend over." He threw the boots in the direction of Seward's voice. "Did you send men to check out the taverns?"

"Aye, nothing. No scoundrel boasting a Moghul sword."

"It is worth a fortune! I doubt if the thief even knows what it is."

"Lad, ye've got a visitor—"

"No visitors!"

Coral drew in a little breath, ignoring his words, and decided Seward was not doing enough to announce just *who* the captain's visitor was. Mustering her courage, she stepped through the cabin door just as the boots landed with a thud near her silk slippers. As her eyes collided with the bare-chested masculine form sprawled on the cot, she went mute and blushed.

So! He *was* a rogue, just as she had first thought at the bazaar! There was no telling where he had been during the night! And his polished manners at the state ball? Another of his masquerades!

Coral found her voice at last. "You were right, Seward. It looks as if the captain of the *Madras* is in no condition to discuss the reason for my visit. You had best take me home."

Jace abruptly turned his face toward the open doorway where she stood, and she saw him squint against the light. She stared back at him piously, hoping her blush did not show, and self-consciously touched her wide-brimmed hat.

For a moment he said nothing. "Well, Seward. Remind me to clobber you later."

Seward cleared his throat again. "Aye, Cap'n. Sorry, I'll . . . ah, wait outside. Pardon me, lass, but I'll let ye two talk this one out alone."

Coral stood with false dignity, feeling herself shaking under her armor. Nevertheless, her expression was unreadable.

A golden monkey suddenly jumped from a bookcase to swing on the lamp chain above the desk.

"Get off there, Goldfish!" Jace commanded. "You'll break it."

The monkey leaped to his cot and snatched Jace's tunic, intending to run off with it. Jace grabbed it back, and the monkey squealed and took refuge on the bookcase.

"He has no manners. I do not know why I keep him. Would you like a new pet, Madam Khan?"

Her blush deepened. *Madam Khan!*

He stood up with a slight smirk, swaying a little, and

she stared at him. He gestured with his tunic. "Would you mind?"

Her eyes widened a little at his temerity, then she quickly turned her back, arms folded.

"I assumed you would not mind, since you barged into my cabin," he said.

"I apologize. . . . I was desperate, afraid you would refuse to see me."

"Now why would I do that, my dear Madam Khan?"

"Sir, would you please stop calling me that?"

"In fact, had I known you would grace my ship with your company, I would have had dinner ready. Do you like Mughlai cuisine?" came his lightly mocking voice.

"I am not hungry, thank you." She glanced about for any signs of Hindu relics. There were none. When she turned back, he had slipped his tunic over his head, and she watched him stand unsteadily while the blood surged to his temples.

"Do you mind if I groan? It makes me feel better." He grasped the edge of the bunk and steadied himself.

Coral laughed softly. "I am usually prone to sympathy where suffering is concerned. For some reason," she said airily, "your discomfort brings me satisfaction."

"No doubt I deserve every bit of it. The natural harvest of my undisciplined appetites."

"Your description is quite appropriate."

"But your assumption is not." He made his way to an oak desk, and throwing open a drawer, rummaged through the contents. "I was robbed last night. Someone clobbered me. Nothing more."

Robbed? For a moment she was too embarrassed to answer. "Oh, I see. . . . I am terribly sorry." Coral threw off her hat and hurried toward him, taking hold of his arm to ease him into the captain's chair. "Can I . . . ah, help you find something in your desk drawer? You see, I thought—"

"Yes, I know what you thought. Well, think nothing of it. I was not exactly prepared to receive visitors. I do not care to sit down."

She dropped his arm, and he leaned against his desk. Folding his arms across his chest, he studied her intently. He seemed in no mood for compromise, so Coral walked back to her hat, picked it up, and self-consciously put it back on, tying it firmly beneath her chin.

He raised one brow but remained silent.

"I must talk to you. However, since you are in pain I can come back tomorrow."

He smiled. With relief, Coral smiled too. "I—"

"How can I help you, Miss Kendall?"

At least he had stopped saying "*Madam Khan.*" She wondered how she could make amends and approach him about going home to Kingscote, and finding Gem. She felt a tug at her skirt and looked down. It was Goldfish. She stooped and picked him up, and he clung to her, his thin golden arm going around her neck.

"So you intend to open a mission school?"

His question jolted her. It was the last thing she expected him to say. "Who told you?"

"Seward."

She tried to read his thoughts, but he was inscrutable.

"William Carey, at least, would approve," he added.

That Jace would know of the missionary translator surprised her. She remembered what Seward had told her about John Newton. What books had Newton given to him?

"You know Master Carey?"

"No. Gokul told me about him." He threw open a second drawer and searched the contents.

"I am equally surprised your munshi friend would

know about the Bible translation work," she said, watching him rummage through the drawer and wondering what he was looking for.

"Carey knows a few brahmins in Serampore," said Jace. "Right now, he's looked upon as a mere oddity. They respect his interest in India, and in Sanskrit. Carey is quite a scholar for having been a shoe cobbler. But once he gains a convert to Christianity, matters will change. He will have not only the displeasure of the Company, but also the anger of the brahmins."

She was surprised Jace understood. He also knew about the Company's policy toward missionary work.

"Master Carey will never retreat in the face of opposition," she said.

"From what Gokul has said, you are right. The man is dedicated to his cause. And what of you, Miss Kendall? Are you also prepared to brave the lion's den? A mission school on Kingscote will be enough to set the ghazis on edge."

As always, her thoughts raced back to Gem's abduction. Had it been executed by Hindu religious zealots opposing his upbringing?

"The untouchables are under my father's jurisdiction," she said. "I never approved, but he bought them. And my uncle's wish to bring Kingscote under the control of the Company will be met dourly by my father. With or without the support of my uncle, I intend to help these children."

His voice was smooth. "I have little but applause for anyone who wishes to embrace orphans. But you must know that the danger to yourself is real if you ignore the ire of the Hindus. Does your father agree to the school?"

Coral was cautious. He did not yet know. Her task to convince the great Hampton Kendall would prove difficult. *The first giant to fell. . . .*

"I am certain that in the end I shall prevail. Father has always had a heart for the children, and I intend to convince him the school will meet a desperate need. The untouchables will learn to read and write, as well as discover a God who will not abandon them to tigers, or throw them to the river crocodiles as meaningless sacrifices."

His gaze swept her. "Well said. Noble causes are not without their sacrifices, however. Sometimes they are quite costly. I should loathe seeing you become an offering to the river. Seward seems to think you are starting the school in the memory of Gem."

At the mention of Gem she became alert, studying his face, but saw nothing to convince her that he had changed his mind about letting her hire his services. But when she remembered that he would soon become a major again, she wondered if his refusal had partly been due to his obligations to the military. She took courage and, seizing the opportunity, said with a rush, "I offended you by offering the Roxbury ring. It was not my intention." She moved to where he leaned against the desk and sought his eyes.

"That morning so long ago . . . the morning of the monsoon when I walked to the wagon carrying Jemani's son, you said something to me that I have since thought of a thousand times. In London I went to sleep with the hope of your words on my heart, and when I awoke, I was still thinking of them. Do you remember what you said to me, Captain Buckley?"

Holding her gaze, he reached over and sent Goldfish scampering away. "Suppose you tell me."

"You told me you knew Rajiv. That he had been your friend."

"He was."

"You said you knew his family. That his uncle was a raja."

"The maharaja yet lives."

Coral's heart began to pound. She sought for some flicker of hope in his eyes indicating he would reconsider.

"Since you know the maharaja, you could discover if Gem is alive. He would tell you." She waited. The moments of silence seemed long.

"A school for the untouchables is not enough to challenge your spirit, is that it? You also want to alert the maharaja."

"I want my son back."

"If he were alive, and you had him back, you could not keep him at Kingscote for long. It would demand your constant vigil. Would you have him surrounded with a bodyguard until he was man enough to carry his own sword?"

"Yes, if that is what it takes to secure his freedom. I could send him to London, even Spain. Jemani died in peace believing that her child would be taught the truth. As long as he is kept from me, and wrapped in the darkness of falsehood, the vow I made that night is but a mockery."

"Consider the idea that Rajiv was killed by his family, or someone hired by them. That should convince you of the zeal of those involved. The maharaja's nephew does not break caste without penalty. Gem would pay a high price to bear the Kendall name."

"I think he would bear that name proudly and insist on his position. And whatever price I need to pay for his return, I will pay."

"Do you think Rajiv's enemies will bargain with a woman who is dedicated to the Christ they do not own?"

"I must try. I have to know if he is alive!"

"And if he is? What makes you think he would choose to come back to you?"

Not come back to her willingly? It was unthinkable! Gem was her baby, her beloved. . . . She had held him, fed him, laughed with him, cried with him. . . .

Her thoughts were interrupted as a frail, old Chinese man with a silver braid entered with a tray and, seeing Coral, bowed at the waist.

"No evil coffee, Captain; only honorable Chinese tea."

Coral turned away to conceal her emotions. What was Jace trying to say? That Gem—if alive—had adopted his Indian ancestry to her exclusion? But he was her *son*. She had experienced Gem's devotion too long to believe he would not return to her if given the chance. Still, Jace's suggestion troubled her.

As Jin-Soo poured the tea, and bandaged the captain's bruise, Coral worked to calm her emotions by focusing on the various treasures from all the ports. There was jade from China, rice paper from Japan, and Indian ivory. A rugged but costly mahogany chest from the Spice Islands stood with a drawer open, and her eyes fell upon a glimmer of black. Absently, she picked up a miniature cheetah, noting that the piece was designed well. Its left eye was missing, but that made it more intriguing. The cheetah, the Indian panther, a symbol of freedom and strength, was in reality vulnerable. Her fevered emotions took mental solace in the cool ebony stone, and she ran her thumb over the smooth piece.

The cabin was enclosed with silence, and realizing that Jin-Soo had left, Coral turned.

Jace leaned against the desk, cup in hand, watching her.

"The Indian mercenary I met nearly two weeks ago could not be bought," she began. "But I was not trying to *buy* him."

His eyes grew remote, and she could feel the impenetrable barrier between them.

"Very well. I accept the idea that he thinks a silk heiress is a spoiled damsel demanding her way. I doubt if I shall ever see him again."

He drank his tea. Was his mood of indifference affected?

"I have not come to your ship to offer you anything, Captain, but to seek your help, to appeal to you as a friend." She walked up to him. "You are the only one left who can help me! Sir Hugo insists Gem is dead." She turned away, the pain rushing through her. "And my father accepts the same decision." She looked back at him. "But I do not. Every beat of my heart tells me he lives."

His eyes were alert. "Why did Sir Hugo insist he was dead?"

"He was there the night when Gem was abducted, and the fire—"

"He was on Kingscote?"

"Yes. It was not long after the adoption ceremony. My uncle was soon to leave for London to address Parliament."

"What exactly happened that night? Seward could not fill me in on everything. Do you remember?"

"Most of it. I was ill afterwards. It was then that my family decided to send me to London to be treated by Doctor Boswell. I told you about it at the ball."

"Yes. Go on."

"I awoke that night on Kingscote and heard horses and shouting below the verandah. I saw my father and some members of the family. There was a fire in the direction of the hatcheries. I do not know why, but I suddenly remembered what you had said to me about Gem, and I was afraid. I ran into the nursery and—" Her voice broke. "I saw a sepoy climbing over the verandah. He had Gem! And Gem kept screaming *Mummy! Mummy! Mummy!* I tried to save him but I couldn't! And ... I couldn't—"

She was sobbing, and unexpectedly, she felt the side of her face against his leather tunic, his hand on her back.

Coral stopped crying almost at once, and for an infinite moment stood there in the shelter of his arms, unable to think of anything else. He did not say a word. Slowly, awareness of his embrace crept over her. She stiffened and pulled back, turning away. Fumbling, she took a handkerchief from her purse, her face hot.

But his voice was casual. "Was Sir Hugo with your father when you noticed the fire?"

"Yes. They were all there. And my father was shouting orders, and the guards arrived on elephants."

"Why does your uncle insist Gem is no longer alive?"

A ripple of pain ran through her, and she opened up her bag, taking out the tiny cross. She brought it to him, extending her palm. "Because of this. I placed this on Gem the day of his adoption. He wore it always ... he was wearing it the night he was abducted."

He took hold of her hand, staring at the emblem. "Yes, I remember. Sir Hugo gave this to you?"

"No. My father sent it to me. My uncle and some servants found a child's body on the ghat steps. He had been attacked by—" She could not go on.

"Sit down," he said gently. "Would you like some of this tea?"

She shook her head and remained standing.

"Then Sir Hugo found the child?"

"Yes."

"And brought him and the cross to your father?"

"Yes." She looked at him, wondering if he was thinking the same thing that she had thought. "The little boy

71

could have been someone else. An untouchable from the village, perhaps."

"Perhaps," he said.

"My ayah wrote me while I was in London. She prepared the child for burial and said there was a scar on his left heel, and that she did not recall seeing a scar on Gem."

His eyes left the cross now hidden within her knotted fist. "When I rode up to the hut where Gem was born and saw you coming out the door with an Indian baby, I thought, 'Now here is a spoiled silk heiress who wishes to collect human toys as a child collects dolls for her play nursery.' Then I saw the look on your face when you came to the wagon, holding him to your heart. You were not much more than a child yourself, but your eyes said everything that needed to be said."

For a moment she felt his look, and it seemed to contact her soul with an understanding that brought renewed tears to her eyes.

"You have not changed much," he said softly. "You still want that Indian baby. You are willing to make him a Kendall heir to a silk fortune."

"Yes, I want him . . . enough to pay any price to get him back. Enough to send him away to Europe, to hire guards if necessary until he can walk freely—as a man who knows his own heart, and is not ashamed to bear the name of his God. And if he must, he will wear a sword to protect his life. And I have every reason to believe Gem will one day stand alone. He is worth any sacrifice. So are the hundred children working in the hatcheries. You see, when I was in London I made a vow to God. If I should regain my health enough to return to India, I would seek the welfare of the children on Kingscote, and I intend to keep my promise."

She could not tell what he thought of all this, for a

breath escaped him, and he fixed his attention on the teapot and empty mug. He poured a second cup.

"I want to make sure you understand. Someone on Kingscote betrayed Gem's whereabouts to the family of the raja. Someone who silently disapproved of his upbringing."

"That cannot be true. No one knew Gem was related to the maharaja, not even my parents."

"Someone did." He looked at her. "The same person who arranged for Rajiv's ritual killing."

"You think someone on Kingscote was to blame for that too?"

"Yes, and whoever it was is still there."

Coral masked a shiver. "Why not someone from the village who may have recognized him?"

"The two may be linked. There could have been contacts with any number of people in the village and elsewhere."

Elsewhere? What did he mean by that?

"I think I told you before," he said, "that whoever told Rajiv to meet his killer in the jungle was trusted by him. Your return home to start the school—if you convince your father—will set you up as a target."

Coral stared up into the handsome face that showed little but calm concern.

"But, Captain Buckley, you must be wrong. The Indians who work there are like part of our family. And those serving within the house have been there since before I was born. I have often wondered about Natine, but he has served my father since they were both children! He is crotchety, and he is a devout Hindu, but he would not hurt us; I cannot believe it about him. In fact, I can vouch for all the house servants. Not one of them would desire to hurt me or Gem."

He folded his arms and gave her a slanted look. "Not

all the villains in India are English, Miss Kendall. You know about the ghazis. You know their aims, do you not?"

She tensed, but tried not to show it. "Yes. They have bound themselves with an oath to rid India of every last *feringhi*."

"Foreigners, especially with English accents. It is my opinion the fire in the hatcheries was a warning to your father."

She had thought the same thing, but to blame one of their own for setting it?

"It was meant to frighten your father, to show him how easily Kingscote could be destroyed if he pursued Gem's abductors. And so he did not pursue. For he, above everyone else, knows how vulnerable Kingscote truly is."

"What! Why, you are saying my father yielded to threats, that he did not look for Gem? I know for a fact he did. He stopped because he thought they had found him."

"Oh, I am quite certain he did search, but not in the right places. You told a *certain mercenary* that your father knew Rawlings. May I suggest, he could have hired a man to track down Gem?"

Coral did not know whether she should be insulted. "Are you saying that my father deliberately—"

"I am not accusing him of anything except an understandable fear of the ghazis. And, a love for his plantation. We cannot fault him for that. By saying all this, I am trying to convince you to leave it alone. I warned you from the beginning."

"Then you will not help me?"

"I doubt if I could successfully bargain for his release, even if he is alive. Whatever the price, you can count on it exceeding anything your father or Sir Hugo is willing to pay."

"My uncle has nothing to do with it. Kingscote belongs to the Kendalls."

"Quite. But the silk enterprise is a family dynasty, is it not? The Roxburys and Kendalls are very much intertwined, as your engagement to Doctor Boswell explains."

"I am not engaged to my cousin."

"Not yet. But Sir Hugo is determined. You will have little to say about who you marry."

The idea that she would have nothing to say about it, or that she would capitulate against her will, was irksome. "Nevermind my marriage, Captain. It is the last concern I have. And it does not matter what my uncle may think, since my future is not his to bargain with."

"He will beg to differ. And if you truly intend to go your own way, you had better be wise enough, and strong enough, to walk through his traps. He is both ambitious and clever."

Coral thought of her stay in London and her experiences with her uncle. She was never quite certain whether they were traps, or merely coincidences.

She refused to show alarm, for fear it would give Jace reason to avoid looking for Gem.

"I have my father and Seward to help me avoid any traps, and my own determination. Not to mention my faith in the guidance of God. I ask only that you find out from the maharaja if Gem is alive."

He said nothing, and yet there was some change that encouraged her to think that he was beginning to relent.

"I will be leaving for the northern frontier soon," he said. "Did Sir Hugo mention the attack on the outpost?"

She recalled the second reason that had brought her to the *Madras*. Perhaps it was unwise to press him with two requests at once.

"I am commissioned to look into matters," he continued. "A friend of mine was assassinated in the attack."

"Major Selwyn?"

He was alert. "How did you know his name?"

"My uncle mentioned it. I am sorry about your friend. Did Seward know him too?"

"We all did." He massaged the back of his neck. "All right. While I am there on business, I will see what I can find out about Gem."

Coral felt so relieved that her knees went weak. "How can I ever thank you? I shall not forget your kindness, Captain Buckley."

"I am not certain my motive is kindness. I will be in touch with you here in Calcutta when I learn something."

"Ah . . . I will be at Kingscote."

He looked up from pouring another mug of black tea. "Seward said Sir Hugo arranged for you to stay here with your aunt and cousin."

"Yes, and that brings me to the other matter I wish to discuss with you." She drew in a little breath. "I do not want to stay a day longer than I must. Despite Jorhat, I intend to safari home." Aware that he watched her with veiled curiosity, she snatched up her hat and toyed with the brim. "You see, I want to ride under the protection of your military troop as far as Guwahati. From there, Seward can bring me home to Kingscote."

He did not mask his surprise. Coral hastened, "Such things are done frequently. Why, I heard of an English party traveling with British troops all the way from Bombay to the border of Burma. It is not nearly as far to Guwahati."

When he said nothing and only looked at her, she added, "I will be no trouble, Major. And I will pay you, say . . . a cargo of Kingscote silk?"

He folded his arms across his chest. "A handsome reward, but hardly acceptable since I am under military orders. As for not being any trouble—I think you will prove a good deal of trouble, Miss Kendall."

"My health will pose no problem. I am stronger than I look. I am not above riding in a howdah on the back of an elephant, or crossing rivers with crocodiles. I can handle the trek to the northern frontier as well as anyone. I am not the fainting kind."

He smiled. "Why not remain in Calcutta until the trouble in Jorhat is taken care of? While I disagree with Sir Hugo on a number of things, he is right about the journey being risky."

"And so I wish to travel with your troop and Seward. My uncle will have no reason to argue against my returning home."

"Very clever."

She smiled and put her hat on. "I thought so. With my mother ill, it is imperative I get home soon. And, I do not like to say this, but there are times when I wonder about my uncle's motives."

"About Gem, or Boswell?"

"Gem, of course. My cousin is trustworthy."

"Would your marriage to Boswell benefit Sir Hugo in any way? Say, give him greater control of Kingscote?"

Coral knew the direction of his question, and it made her uncomfortable. "My uncle might think that way, but not Ethan."

"What is the relationship between Sir Hugo and the good doctor? That is, if you do not mind explaining."

"There is nothing to hide. Ethan was my uncle's ward, a nephew, they say. He looks upon Sir Hugo as a father."

"I see."

She wondered how two simple words could suggest so much.

"What you are thinking about Ethan is not true. He is sacrificial, a man wholly devoted to medical research. His interest in Kingscote concerns a scientific lab that my father is permitting him to build in the jungle."

"If Sir Hugo wishes for you to stay in Calcutta, he is not likely to approve of your journeying north under my command. How do you expect to convince him?"

"He can hardly refuse. Not when I will be accompanied by soldiers. If you would speak to your father the colonel, I think he could alleviate my uncle's misgivings."

"I do not doubt your determination to get to Kingscote, but the journey will be hard. Are you quite certain a few more months, regardless of Sir Hugo, will not be best?"

She smiled. "I am quite certain."

He was silent, then, "As you wish. How could I turn down a young woman of such conviction? I will tell Seward to arrange your travel. We will leave in five days. Can you manage?"

"I shall be ready. Major, I do not know how I can thank you enough for your assistance."

His mouth curved slightly. "I will give that some thought, Miss Kendall."

She felt her face grow warm under his gaze. Quickly she scooped up her bag from the chair and went to the cabin door.

"Oh." She stopped, aware that she still held the ebony cheetah. She felt foolish, as though he might think that her action had been deliberate. She walked over to the half-open drawer and put the miniature back.

"Good day, Captain—I mean, Major."

He laughed. "Back to that again. Why not try Jace? It really is not that difficult to say, and less confusing."

"Yes, so it is."

He walked up, retrieved the cheetah, and turned it over. "Would you like a cheetah with a missing eye?"

"How did he loose it?"

"Right now, I cannot remember. Maybe he was born that way."

"I rather like him with a missing eye. He looks vulnerable. But, Captain, I could not take it."

"Consider him a gift from a 'certain mercenary' who was rude to leave you stranded an hour outside Calcutta in a broken-down ghari. He'll be pleased to know you got home safely. As for the cheetah, he will be happier in your custody." He pressed it into her hand with a slight smile. "He will soon be purring. Good day, Miss Kendall. I will have Seward get in touch."

Her lashes lowered, Coral slowly turned toward the door to leave. "Good day, *Jace*," she murmured softly.

6

Coral softly shut her bedroom door and leaned against it with exhaustion, closing her eyes and feeling a steady headache throb in her temples. Alone at last, she was able to release her guarded feelings without the necessity of keeping a smile of composure while affirming to Aunt Margaret that she felt "quite well, actually," and that her trip with Seward to the *Madras* had neither been tiring nor anything less than "perfectly proper." Soon she must confront the family with her decision to return to Kingscote escorted by Major Buckley's troop. But her health, already strained to its frail limits, could take no more without rest.

In the deep afternoon silence of the room with its tall windows opening onto the verandah, she absently fingered the cheetah that Jace Buckley had given her. Vaguely, she wondered if she should have accepted it.

She walked tiredly across the room and out onto the verandah, letting her wide-brimmed hat flutter to the matting as her skirts whispered with her steps. Below her, the orange garden of marigolds ended near the tangle of brush that crowded the banks of the Hooghly. The rank river masqueraded beneath rays of the sun, offering the illusion of shimmering golds, but the afternoon air was realistically harsh, housing many different sounds and smells. She saw paddle-steamers churning up the Hooghly, and the indistinguishable voices of boatmen using bamboo poles to wend their barges back down the river after a day's business at Barrackpore.

Coral sighed. It did not matter that she must yet confront Uncle Hugo with her trek to Kingscote, or that in the next several days she must find some way to travel upriver to Serampore to visit William Carey's mission station. The Scripture portion in Hindi that Master Carey might be able to give her was worth withstanding any scowl of disapproval from Hugo. She would send a message to Charles Peddington that she wished to pay Serampore a visit.

It was at this point that she thought once again of Major Jace Buckley, and was surprised that she began to make excuses to herself of why she had accepted the ebony cheetah with one missing eye, or why she felt a warm sense of satisfaction in knowing that she had won him to her side—at least in the matter of Gem. But she swiftly reminded herself that while he had agreed to look into the matter upon arriving at Jorhat, that fact did not suggest his continued involvement. Jace Buckley was puzzling; a little dangerous perhaps. His masculine appeal was indisputable, but she would not let such things turn her head. She dismissed the memory of that brief moment in his arms. She must never think of it again.

With determination, Coral went to her desk and sat down to write Charles Peddington about her wish to visit William Carey at Serampore.

———

Jace walked the path that fronted the Hooghly. In the shadow of the trees, mynahs were arguing loudly, and far in the distance pariah dogs barked. The banks of the river were crowded with narrow boats, the lean Indians in short white pants slicing their bamboo poles through the water.

His thoughts were not pleasant. Roxbury had attributed the attack on the outpost to Burma, and like the colonel, Jace nurtured his suspicions. His best source of information would be the Burmese prisoner now being held in confinement. But even interrogating the prisoner was not enough. He needed someone to wander the bazaars in Jorhat and pick up bits of information that only the watching eyes of India would see, eyes that were avid and intent, belonging to stoic faces who spoke only with Indian comrades in their mother tongue. A trusted Indian spy was needed. With the right incentive, he might convince his old friend Gokul to ride north and masquerade as a traveling merchant in the mountainous village bazaars.

He thought of the Kendall daughter, and ducked his dark head just in time to keep a mango branch from knocking off his seacap. He frowned as his boots crunched the dying grasses in his way. Whatever had possessed him to agree to help her locate the boy? He was either dead, or a eunuch. In irritation he yanked his cap lower.

He reminded himself that he had the entire journey to Assam to fill Coral Kendall's ears with shuddering tales of the ghazis. Instinctively, however, he guessed that she would not easily relent, regardless of his warnings. Behind that innocent facade, he believed there lived a woman of cool nerves. He had already discovered as much when she refused to step back from her confrontation with the guru and his crows at the bazaar. When it came to Gem and the mission school, he believed her convictions were unshakable.

Entering the bungalow that he shared with Gokul along the river, Jace drew aside the split-cane curtain that opened into his room. Outside on the courtyard the lean shadow of Gokul lay long upon the sun-warmed stone.

A strange cackle greeted him: "Major Buckley. Major Buckley. Major Buckley."

Mischief, Gokul's lime green parrot, lumbered across the rail, cocking his head and repeating the new phrase that Gokul had taught him: "Major Buckley. Major Buckley. Major Buckley."

Jace winced. In sobering agreement, the military uniform was stretched across the bed as if to salute his arrival. The black and silver was spotless, the boots were polished, and the saber gleamed.

Goldfish smacked his gums and jumped up and down.

Gokul came from the courtyard oven carrying a hot urn. His black eyes sparkled beneath thick gray brows. "Ah, sahib, time for favorite coffee!"

Jace tossed his weathered cap onto a chair, his eyes fixed on the familiar uniform. In exactly two hours he would abandon his casual buckskin and Indian tunic, and emerge as Major Buckley, the new commanding officer of the 21st Bengal Light Cavalry. And in three days he would be on his way, with twenty sowars in uniform, to Jorhat.

"How did you manage?" he asked casually of the coffee.

Gokul rolled his eyes toward the roof and smiled. "The ways and wonders of Gokul are beyond explanation." He set the urn down on the hot bricks, and rushed at Goldfish, shooing him away from the uniform. "Be gone, or I make monkey stew!" And he flicked an imaginary speck from the sleeve, and held the jacket across

84

his chest and protruding belly for display, like some prized heirloom prepared for Jace's inspection. "Everything ready, sahib, Major!"

"Major Buckley. Major Buckley—"

Jace poured his coffee and scanned Gokul dubiously.

Gokul whipped a cloth from his tunic and gave an extra wipe across the boot, then scrutinized the shine. Jace took a swallow of coffee and looked down at his new uniform with a blank expression. The last emotion he felt was anticipation. He changed the subject, even though he began to remove his tunic and ready himself to become a major.

"Any word from your contact in the thieves' market?" His scabbard reminded him of the Moghul sword.

"Word passed. Expect news soon."

Jace continued to methodically put on the pieces of his uniform. It was an asset to Jace that Gokul not only knew a few brahmins, but also certain thieves in Calcutta, and the wealthy Chinese and Indian merchants who wittingly bought stolen booty to sell to the rich but unquestioning English. If the thief who had robbed him was from the Calcutta brotherhood, there was a chance that Gokul's contact in the bazaar would know of the sword. As though in answer to his thoughts, there came a rap on the door, and Gokul answered it.

A young sowar spotted Jace in uniform and saluted. He stepped forward and handed him an envelope. Jace read as the cavalryman waited outside the door.

Maj. J. Buckley, 21st Light Cal., B.L.C.
Sir:
The Governor-General's new Resident to the princely state of Assam in northern India, Sir Hugo Roxbury, requests that you meet with him in his office at Government-House this afternoon no later than 2 o'clock

P.M. *November 11th, at Fort William, Calcutta.*
Yr m.o. servant
P. Barton, Daffadar, 21st B.L.C.

Jace stared at the message. *The Governor-General's Resident!* Sir Hugo Roxbury was to represent the British government at the maharaja's palace at Guwahati!

The idea that Roxbury might want the newly vacated position had never crossed his mind. This meant that Roxbury would soon be leaving Calcutta for the northern frontier. Jace would have Sir Hugo to contend with at the outpost.

"Something wrong, sahib?"

Jace placed the letter in his sabretache, the small leather case that hung from his saber belt. Stepping to the door, he closed it on the sowar, then turned back to Gokul.

"Roxbury's been appointed ambassador to the raja at Guwahati."

Gokul gave a low whistle. "And he calls for you? The burra-sahib is interested in your new command at the Jorhat outpost. Why, I ask?" His expression was grave. "Caution, sahib. I do not trust the man."

"When will you meet with your friend at the bazaar?"

"Tonight."

"Good. There is something you must do. I need you at Jorhat. Go as a traveling merchant. Inquire about the assassination of Selwyn. More specifically, see if you can discover any connection Roxbury may have had with members of the royal family."

While Gokul stood there contemplating, Jace's mouth curved in a grim smile. He reached beneath his jacket and handed him an envelope. "Your share in the tea plantation."

Gokul smiled and placed palms together to his forehead. "Sahib most generous. I will depart before the sun rises, as soon as I negotiate meeting at the bazaar. I will bring Jin-Soo with me, and Goldfish. Yes?"

"Yes."

"You will return here tonight?"

"Yes, see that no one follows you."

"It is done."

Jace opened the door to find the sowar standing too close. Was he trying to listen? A servant of Roxbury, no doubt. The sowar turned and led the way to a waiting horse-drawn ghari.

Around Fort William a massive expanse of jungle had been cut down to give the cannons a clear line of fire, but Jace recalled that the fort had never fired a shot in battle since reclaiming Calcutta from Suraj-ud-daula in the famous Black Hole incident of 1757. Since that uprising, a massive new fort had been built with deep fortifications and trenches fronting the impregnable walls. The grounds around the fort where the jungle had been cleared were a green expanse of lawn known as the Maidan, and was bounded by the river on the west, and the bazaar to the east. The botanical gardens were in the northwest, and on any Sunday afternoon one could see a number of Company families in carriages out for a ride around the Maidan. The Company had installed a cricket field, and there were ponds, trees, and a winding strollway that led through the gardens to the banks of the Hooghly. On the bank were several ghats, landing places with stairs leading down to the river, with Indian boatmen waiting to ferry customers across, or up the river toward Barrackpore and Serampore—the Danish center for trading holdings in India.

At Government-House the sowar escorted Jace to Sir Hugo's office. Jace dismissed him, knocked, and entered. Roxbury's office turned out to be a luxurious apartment, decorated and furnished for the use of British visitors. From the window, Sir Hugo could look out across the Maidan to the river.

Upon his entry, Jace paused; Sir Hugo was not alone. Hugo sat behind a large desk, and to his right stood an Indian officer, the dark eyes measuring him with keen interest. He wore the black and silver uniform of the 21st, but Jace did not remember him from his days at the outpost. He was a rissaldar-major, second-in-command to the British officer.

He is too young, Jace was thinking when Roxbury's voice, tinged with deliberate friendliness, interrupted.

"Stand easy, Major." Roxbury pushed back his chair and stood, a large handsome figure in black. Jace noticed that the two men bore one thing in common; they both had deep-set dark eyes that observed him with the sharpness of a hunting fowl.

"Major, this is Rissaldar Sanjay from the outpost at Jorhat. He arrived a few days ago, bringing news to the colonel of the Burmese attack on the outpost."

From the taut expression on the rissaldar's face, Jace thought he appeared ill at ease, as though concerned with other matters.

"The colonel is pleased to have you back in uniform, Major," Sir Hugo was saying. "I, too, find myself in agreement with your decision to return to the honorable East India Company. Excellent soldiers are a rare breed here in India."

There followed a moment of silence in which Jace was expected to acknowledge his compliment and agree that it was also his pleasure to be back. Jace was neither pleased, nor did he find the Company altogether honorable. His gaze was hard. "A worthy captain of a ship is also a rare breed, sir. Am I to assume, then, that the death of your nephew aboard my vessel is no longer questioned?"

Sir Hugo leaned across the desk with a humorless smile. "One must never listen to rumors, Major. I see no reason why I should question Michael's death at sea."

So he wants to let the matter drop.

"If I did not have the highest regard for your abilities, I would not have spoken to the governor-general about you."

Alert, Jace noticed for the first time the official paper on the desk.

"I have heard of your reputation in the northeast. It is noteworthy that your conduct was awarded a brevet for courage and a promotion just before you left the colonel's troops."

Jace was expressionless, and the compliment made him suspicious of Sir Hugo's intentions. But Roxbury appeared not to notice the silence, although Jace believed he knew of the extreme measures used by the colonel to get him back into uniform.

Jace responded in a level tone. "There are many in India who deem themselves to be courageous and more dedicated to the cause of the English presence than I. The incident in the northeast was merely the exercise of duty."

Sir Hugo raised his brows. "I do not believe a word of it. Duty is a precious word in my ear, Major, and not a trait to ignore, and it is the reason for my request to the governor-general. Colonel Warbeck is displeased with the change in your mission, and yet I am sure he will recognize that my request to a higher authority was necessary."

Sir Hugo sucked on his pipe and seemed to be gauging his response, but Jace affected military discipline. Higher authority? A change in his orders?

"I will be truthful with you, Major. When my niece informed us that she hoped to be traveling under your protection to the northern frontier, I was prepared to forbid it, until I realized the decision was a wise one. As Rissaldar Sanjay here has informed us, anyone traveling north at this time will encounter grave risk."

Jace looked at the rissaldar, who quickly shot a glance toward Sir Hugo.

Sir Hugo stood and paced, his hands behind his back. "I will come to the point, Major. My own circumstances changed quite unexpectedly. I will not be serving the Company in Calcutta for the next few years, but the province of Assam, as the resident of the governor-general."

This position placed him in a seat of authority in rich northern territory previously independent of the Company, including the vast Kendall holdings. Jace remained silent.

"Of necessity, your orders have been changed by the governor-general. You will not command the 21st at Jorhat, but accompany me to Guwahati as commander of my security guard."

What!

"Your position is a sensitive one, Major, and it demands the best of skilled fighting men to be chosen, not only in order to protect me, but perhaps, the royal family."

Jace was furious. Outwardly he remained unreadable.

"I regret our journey cannot embark as soon as your previous orders called for," Roxbury continued. "I will need to clear up some unfinished business here in Calcutta for the Company, and then there is the matter of my family. My nephew Doctor Ethan Boswell will arrive in December and will journey with us as far as Guwahati. I would prefer to leave at once, but the first week of January must suffice. Will that suit you?"

Whether it did or not he was certain that Sir Hugo found his opinion irrelevant. Their departure was nearly two months away! Jace curbed the anger swarming over his soul like a battalion of army ants. "As you wish, sir. But what of sending reinforcements to the outpost at Jorhat? Has the governor-general decided to let the 21st sit there without a commanding officer?"

His objection was waved off by Roxbury. "Military matters are out of my jurisdiction, Major. Colonel Warbeck is looking into that now. He is expecting you on the cricket field."

The colonel had betrayed him. *Security guard for Roxbury!*

"Believe me, Major, there are valid reasons for the change in your orders," said Sir Hugo. "Rissaldar Sanjay has reason to believe the outpost at Jorhat is not the intended target of Burmese forces, but rather, Guwahati. Correct, Rissaldar?"

"Yes, sahib, that is so. I hasten to add that it is the opinion of the nephew of the maharaja that His Excellency's life may be in danger from the ghazis. They are displeased with the treaty signed with the East India Company."

The nephew of the maharaja? wondered Jace. He wanted to ask about Rajiv's brother, Prince Sunil, but did not wish to alert Sir Hugo that he knew him; nor was he certain whether Sir Hugo knew of Gem's connection with the maharaja.

Sir Hugo shot a glance at the Indian officer. "Explain."

"Since an assassination attack on Prince Sunil, the maharaja is not trusting anyone except his bodyguard."

Jace was alert. Sunil was ruthless and could not be trusted. Had he truly been attacked?

"The maharaja's nephew was fortunate. He was only wounded," continued Rissaldar Sanjay.

Roxbury turned to Jace. "It is our lone opinion that an assassination attempt will be made on the maharaja himself."

"By 'lone opinion,' are you saying Prince Sunil is the only one who agrees with you?"

Sir Hugo walked to the window. "Do not misunderstand. I mean in no way to cast your father in a dubious light. We all know his record to be above reproach. It is also true to say that the military worries too much over a handful of British soldiers at the outpost, when the palace of the raja may be the real target." He was staring in the direction of the cricket field. "I have been unsuccessful in convincing the colonel, so I was forced to go directly to the governor-general. I believe the military underestimates the danger in Assam, Major." He looked at Jace. "There is fierce determination to undermine the English presence on the northern frontier."

Jace was well acquainted with the north and knew this. Many independent nawabs and rajas feared that the East India Company would eventually try to annex all of northern India, including Darjeeling and Kashmir, by making independent treaties with the princely states as they had just done with the royal family at Guwahati. Despite any pretext of renewed hostilities with Burma, the annexation of India to British rule was a festering sore even among those native soldiers who wore the uniform of the British. There were, in fact, more Indians in English uniforms in India than there were British. The native soldiers enlisted in the Bengal ranks were commanded by British officers in regiments belonging to the East India Company. The Indians numbered in the thousands, and few of the British officers had reason to doubt their absolute loyalty. Jace had known many such sepoys and sowars. Some had enlisted for employment, others for opportunity, perhaps even to spread sedition in the army, although that possibility was unthinkable to the British officers.

"I agree," said Jace, "that the colonel is fully committed to the loyalty of Johnny Sepoy, but I am not."

The rissaldar's eyes flashed momentarily. Jace wondered if Sir Hugo was using the resentment among the sepoys and sowars for his own purposes.

"Rissaldar Sanjay has made it clear to the colonel that Prince Sunil fears worse than the recent attack on the outpost," said Sir Hugo. "We suspect the ghazis of plotting with the Burmese warlord to dispel any British presence in the north."

Jace asked smoothly, "You suspect ghazis tried to assassinate the prince?"

Sir Hugo shrugged his heavy shoulders. "Who else? What is your opinion, Rissaldar?"

"Perhaps, sahib, Major Selwyn knew something and was silenced. There may be some plot to mutiny within the ranks at the outpost itself."

Jace wondered if they were feeling him out, trying to discover what he thought. He remained silent. It remained of interest to him that the Indian officer appeared ill at ease.

Did Sir Hugo know of the Burmese prisoner taken in the raid on the outpost? Jace did not mention him.

"Your new orders were issued from the governor-general himself," Sir Hugo said. "The time may also come when you will be called upon to protect the royal family. Your task is crucial."

Jace did not trust him. What was the man up to? Why would he even want him around?

Sir Hugo lifted the paper from his desk. "Your new orders, Major."

Jace bridled his irritation. A moment passed; he took the paper. The signature of the chief representative of the English government stared up at him.

Just what had prompted Sir Hugo to go to such extremes to have the orders of Colonel Warbeck changed? Jace did not believe for a minute that his military reputation had anything to do with Roxbury's action. Jace had warned the Kendall daughter of traps, but perhaps it was *he* who needed to be on guard.

7

Jace took leave of Sir Hugo, and it was with restrained anger that he walked across the Maidan toward the cricket field. Indian servants walked about in white knee-length coats with polished brass buttons. The native military wore yellow, red, or blue coats, with white crossbelts, cuffs, and collars. A few English carriages passed on an afternoon ride toward the gardens. With them came a rush of feminine gossip, a show of curls, lace, and coquettish glances that Jace ignored. Ahead he saw the colonel. He was not on the cricket field, but in a game of croquet with several other officers, including the portly General Basil. A dozen or so other English military and civil servants stood about in lazy discourse. Jace stopped a few feet away.

The colonel, upon seeing his adopted son, showed neither concern for his mood nor pleasure at his presence. He tossed his mallet to the grass and excused himself from the game. Jace fell into step beside him, and for a moment neither spoke. The massive walls of the fort enclosed the world of England within, while outside its gates, India silently resented their presence.

"You knew all along I would be sent as a security guard at Guwahati."

"No. I underestimated him."

That his father would admit to being outwitted was surprising, and had a consoling effect on Jace's irritation. He turned his head to glance at the rugged face and found the colonel undisturbed by his admittance.

"The fact that Roxbury went over my head convinces me my suspicions are correct."

"He was involved in the attack?"

"And the assassination of Major Selwyn." The hard gray eyes turned to him. "I need proof. The question is, for what reason? And that is for you to find out."

Colonel Warbeck motioned toward a cluster of trees. "You may dislike the change in your orders, but it could prove the opening we need to learn what Roxbury is up to. At the maharaja's palace, you will have opportunity to pry about, and keep Roxbury in view. You are aware he asked for your service from the governor-general only because he wants to keep an eye on you? Make it mutual."

"I thought it was because of my military valor."

Only a slight twist of the colonel's mouth responded to Jace's light sarcasm.

"What of the 21st? They are sitting ducks. Roxbury will not leave until his nephew arrives in December."

"Major Packer's 34th is being sent from Plassey. You will be given men from the 17th Lancers."

"Then give me Rissaldar Nadir. He is a friend. I can trust him. Roxbury also talks of mutiny in the blood of the sepoys. I rather agree with him on that."

"Johnny Sepoy will never mutiny. Oh, yes, I know, emotions run high when it comes to their religion and dispossessed nobles, but mutiny against their British officers? Never! I have served with them too long. If there is talk, you can wager it's being propagated by men like Roxbury. They are in this for their own gain, though what it might be where he is concerned, I have no idea."

"Kingscote perhaps. But just how a mutiny would help him is unclear. Kendall himself may have ideas on that."

The colonel, seeing an Indian servant in a blue coat and turban, gestured him forward.

The servant salaamed and produced a satchel, then departed. Colonel Warbeck handed it to Jace.

Jace felt a hard, cold object meet his fingers. He slowly brought it into the light, and it sprang up like multicolored fire. The stolen idol of the Hindu god Kali!

His questioning gaze met his father's.

The colonel smiled, his gray eyes glinting with satisfaction. "Merry Christmas," he said, and chuckled.

As they strolled back across the Maidan, the colonel told Jace how he had obtained it. Sir Hugo had unexpectedly appeared at his bungalow the night before, explaining that he only recently discovered that the object had been stolen from the raja. Sir Hugo could only imagine the embarrassment over the situation if the royal family in Guwahati discovered it in his collection!

Jace would bring the statue of Kali with him to present to the raja. With it, he could gain the audience he needed.

———

Coral was startled by the news. Uncle Hugo, the resident at Guwahati? Aunt Margaret had never hinted of the possibility; had she known about it? Yet her aunt did not seem surprised.

Seward had arrived that morning with the news that Jace would take up a security post in Guwahati.

"We'll not be leaving Calcutta until January," Seward

told the small feminine gathering in the Roxbury residence that morning.

"Two months," moaned Coral, "but why so long a delay, Seward?"

"As for the major, he's all for leaving by week's end. 'Tis Doctor Boswell. Sir Hugo won't leave till he arrives."

Coral knew Seward well enough to distinguish the veiled irritation in his voice, but the others did not.

"Well, I am all for the delay," announced Aunt Margaret. "I would prefer the family to spend the holidays together. One never knows how long the separation will be." She changed the subject. "Lady Isobel's invitation arrived this morning from Barrackpore. We are to spend the holiday week there."

Barrackpore was a resort and military station to which the fashionable and affluent of the East India Company in Calcutta flocked for relaxation and entertainment, especially during the holiday season. Margaret took delight in pointing out that it was a favorite of the governor-general himself. The traditional week-long celebration would begin at their arrival in mid-December at the grand house of Lord and Lady Canterbury where they would room until after the New Year.

"There are seven absolutely wonderful balls to attend," explained her cousin Belinda. "Plus late-night suppers, house-to-house desserts, and if the weather holds, an outdoor party. You will absolutely adore Barrackpore; it is so European."

Margaret arose and, coming behind Marianna, put her arms around her neck. "Do not look so downcast, darling. A few more weeks in Calcutta will pass quickly, and you will be home to your mother soon enough. And it will be so much nicer with Ethan arriving and taking the safari with you. Elizabeth's illness will be treated, and your uncle will be only a short journey away at Guwahati."

Marianna raised her childish face and the wide eyes looked hopelessly up at her aunt. "Do you think so, Aunt Margaret? Will everything be all right with mother?"

"Certainly, and she would want you to enjoy the holiday festivities while you are here. I noticed that young Charles Peddington has taken quite an interest in you, Marianna."

Marianna blushed. "Oh, we are just friends. He loves to discuss Master Carey and his work."

A servant entered with a small platter in hand. On top of it lay a letter; he brought it to Coral.

"For you, missy."

Coral read the return address: Charles Peddington, Serampore. She glanced up to see the others looking at her expectantly, but was hesitant to open it in front of them.

"I suppose it is from Major Jace Buckley," teased Cousin Belinda.

"Major Buckley has no reason to write me," said Coral calmly, and ignored the little smile that passed between Belinda and Kathleen.

Coral opened the envelope and removed the contents. Her heart wanted to stop, then throb, with a surge of emotion that brought moisture to her eyes. On a sheet of paper was written in Hindi the words of Matthew 19:13–15:

Then were there brought unto him little children, that he should put his hands on them, and pray: and the disciples rebuked them. But Jesus said, Suffer little children, and forbid them not, to come unto me: for of such is the kingdom of heaven. And he laid his hands on them, and departed thence.

"Coral, what is it?" asked Aunt Margaret.

Coral handed her the Scripture portion and saw written on a second piece of paper:

Dear Miss Kendall:

Master Carey and the Marshmans will be most honored to receive you at Serampore on the date you requested. A ghari will arrive at Roxbury residence at Fort William on the morning of November 14th.

Your friend in service to our Lord,

Charles Peddington

The fourteenth . . . that is today, thought Coral, and looked toward the window facing the carriageway.

Margaret was frowning at the writing. "It is Bengali, isn't it?"

"Hindi. It is a Scripture verse, from Charles Peddington," explained Coral. "Isn't it wonderful to behold? Matthew nineteen, the verse on children!"

Margaret's brow furrowed. She continued to gaze upon the verse. "Yes . . . it is nice."

"Oh, dear, I have been so taken up with Uncle's news and the change in traveling plans that I forgot I might hear from Charles today," confessed Coral. "Where is Seward?"

"He left," said Marianna.

"What does Mr. Peddington want?" asked Margaret, handing the Scripture portion back.

Belinda and Kathleen moved to the front window at the same time, drawing aside the sheer curtain. "A ghari is arriving."

"We are not expecting anyone," said Margaret.

A moment later Coral stood as a servant entered. "A ghari-wallah is here to take Miss Coral to Serampore."

Margaret turned abruptly. "Coral! Not William Carey!"

The disappointment in her aunt's voice almost made Coral feel guilty.

"You promised me you would do nothing to anger Hugo," said Margaret. "And you know how upset he gets when you mention the religious dissenter Carey."

"Aunt Margaret, that is not a fair description," said Coral. "The men and women you call dissenters have merely left the cold formality of the Anglican Church for a personal relationship with Christ and the Scriptures and—"

"Coral, please, not now." Margaret sighed. "I have never been one to argue the finer points of religion, and I would rather not get into a debate."

Coral felt the puzzled gaze of Belinda studying her. Kathleen had turned her back to look out the window, and Coral guessed that she was embarrassed. Marianna stared at her plate of cold waffles.

"I do not wish to appear rigid," said Aunt Margaret, "but a trip to Serampore would mean your absence for two or three days. Without a chaperon you cannot possibly go."

"Perhaps Seward—" began Coral, already feeling it was a lost battle.

"No, dear. Seward is involved with Major Buckley. Your uncle would be furious if I permit you to go. Try to understand. Recently Hugo has been so tense. Another of his black moods, and he may wish to cancel the holiday trip to Barrackpore."

A groan went up from Belinda, and Kathleen said crossly, "All we need is for you to spoil everyone's holidays. Do not be so selfish, Coral. A visit to Carey can wait. You know enough Hindi to do your own translation of the Scriptures anyway."

"Sissy, that is not so," defended Marianna. "Charles said you need to know Hebrew and Greek, too."

"Girls!" said Aunt Margaret.

Belinda swept up to Coral and took hold of her arms, her dark eyes pleading. "Oh, Coral, you will not ruin our holiday, will you? I shall die if I cannot go to Barrackpore! You should see the houses where the balls are held; they are huge! With crystal chandeliers! And we will dance to large orchestras, and the ballrooms are decorated with a thousand candles and green sprigs—"

"No, my sister will not ruin our Christmas," said Kathleen, hands on hips. "Because I will not let her."

Margaret moved at once to settle the matter. "Where is Pande?"

No one had noticed the servant standing near the doorway, his brown face immobile. He salaamed. "Here, sahiba."

Margaret looked across the room. "Coral?"

Coral stood with quiet dignity. She could see that her aunt wanted her to be the one to decline. Despite the unpleasant moment, Coral felt a strange peace. She desperately wanted the Scriptures in Hindi, yet somehow she felt prompted to not demand her way. *Lord, I leave the matter to you to work out.*

She walked to the desk and sat down, briefly writing a note to be delivered to Charles Peddington. A moment later she stood and handed it to Pande.

"Give this to the ghari-wallah, please. Thank you, Pande."

When he had gone, the room was quiet for a moment. They heard the wheels of the ghari, and the plop-plop of the horse's hoofs on the stone, then silence. The front door closed again behind Pande, and he passed down the hall to attend to work.

Marianna stood from her chair at the table, her expression glum, and walked out of the dining room, up the stairs.

Margaret broke the silence. "Girls, we have shopping to do for Belinda's trousseau."

When Margaret and Belinda left the room, Coral picked up the paper with the Hindi translation.

"Go ahead," said Kathleen. "Call me a traitor."

Coral glanced up at her older sister. "I do not care to argue, Kathleen. I am not upset with you, really."

"Do not be so sacrificial. That attitude makes me more upset than anything you could say."

Coral studied her, surprised. "Why, whatever are you so dour about? We are going to Barrackpore. I should think being able to dance the night away at seven balls would sweeten you."

"Oh, pooh! Sometimes you are impossible!" Kathleen snatched up her skirts and flounced out.

"I am not the only one," muttered Coral.

Calcutta had a reputation to keep up in the way of holiday gaiety, and there were party invitations arriving almost daily. These were greeted with profound glee by Belinda, who insisted to her mother that for the sake of her cousins, they *simply must* accept them all.

In the weeks following, there were not only social gaieties to attend in Calcutta but preparation for the holiday season, keeping the girls in a state of excitement over silks, satins, and brocades. The cousins also received a flattering amount of attention from the garrison, and young Marianna was overwhelmed when Mr. Charles Peddington wrote her from Serampore.

Coral had never seen Kathleen so happy since they had left Roxbury House. Young Diantha Waterman had gained her mother's permission for Kathleen to design the girl's main ball dress, even paying Kathleen several pounds, and there was great excitement when the goods arrived in four boxes carried by solemn-faced Indian servants. "For the memsahibs," they announced.

Aunt Margaret loaned Kathleen her private fitting room with a long cutting table, trestle, pins, threads, thimbles, and special cutting scissors that she had long ago ordered from Lyons, France. The excitement mounted as Diantha came to spend a week for the pinning, and careful assessment of the bust and waist design.

As departure for Barrackpore drew nearer, the preparations increased, with a great deal of shopping to do for gift-giving.

Dressed in bonnets and carrying palmetto fans to ward off troublesome insects, Aunt Margaret, Belinda, and Marianna poured excitedly into the ghari, followed by Coral. Kathleen had opted to stay behind with Diantha to work on the dress.

By afternoon the ghari was piled with boxes and packages, many of them to be toted upriver when they left for Barrackpore. Coral made a few purchases for herself and her sisters, items that they would need on the safari.

As they were returning home for afternoon tea, Coral caught a glimpse of Major Buckley coming out of the governor-general's palace in the company of two sepoys. He looked very much the disciplined officer, and his face showed no emotion when Margaret saw him and called out.

Major Buckley was the essence of propriety as he came up to the door where Lady Margaret greeted him. After bowing, he proceeded to offer all the appropriate words expected from a precise officer and gentleman, inquiring as to their well-being and to the Christmas shopping.

Margaret explained about the two weeks in Barrackpore, and insisted that he was invited to all the balls, and that she was pleased to know her husband would be

in such capable hands while serving his new post in Guwahati, not to mention the safety of her nieces on the
journey. And again Major Buckley made the correct reply,
but with a faintly contradicting gleam in his eyes, which
no one noticed but Coral. Excusing himself, he departed
without so much as a second look her way.

He is quite annoyed over the turn of events. She
doubted if he would bother to show up at Barrackpore.

The Dutch ship *Kron Princess Maria* docked ten days
earlier than expected, and the entire household turned
out for Doctor Ethan Boswell's arrival. Coral was relieved to see him, although she was not able to tell herself
why that should be. She was perfectly safe in Calcutta,
and the upcoming journey north was still several weeks
away. She was also reminded that Ethan was a striking
man. He had gotten sun aboard the ship, causing his hair
to glint like ripened wheat, and his eyes were easy to
look into—she felt strange that she would think of that—
they were like still, gray pools. She was struck with the
wide variance between Ethan and Jace Buckley, whose
presence set her on guard. Despite Jace's role as the restrained and coolly observant major, she knew there
lived a different man beneath that affectation.

In mid-December Coral arrived in Barrackpore by
boat in the company of Ethan, and the Canterbury carriage had been waiting to bring them to the house. To
her growing excitement, she discovered that Serampore
was located across the river and appeared quite close.
Would it be possible to visit William Carey's mission
station after all?

It occurred to Coral that Ethan could meet Doctor
John Thomas, who had first interested Master Carey in
coming to India. Had not Charles Peddington mentioned

to her that Thomas was in Serampore?

As if borne on angel's wings, an idea of how she could manage the visit to Serampore stirred within her mind. The Dutch settlement under General Bie was close enough so that a visit could be made by leaving in the morning and returning by dusk. And if Ethan accompanied her in order to see John Thomas—well, the family could hardly be upset.

As they made their way through Danish-controlled Barrackpore, Coral was reminded of a European town with fine houses situated on avenues of trees, the air from the river fresh and crisp. Coral's heart felt at peace, and she planned to enjoy the Christmas Ball in the magnificent and gaily decorated Canterbury House, now ablaze with lights.

8

Governor Bie took the elbow of the Countess of Denmark, who was a glitter of jewels and white satin, and escorted her away from the others in the direction of the stairway leading down to the ballroom. Their voices faded into the majestic strains of the waltz as they descended the circular staircase.

The small group of men who were left in the upstairs anteroom smoking expensive cheroots began to break up.

"I wish a private word with you, Arlen," stated the governor-general, who left the anteroom and walked out onto the extended railed hallway overlooking the crowded ballroom.

Sir Arlen George, an angular man with hawklike features and a flair for fashion, walked up beside him. "What is on your mind, Excellency?" asked Arlen. "You were not serious just now about me going to London to speak with His Majesty?"

The governor-general smiled at him. "Assuredly! Hugo has every confidence in you, and why shouldn't I?"

Arlen looked down on the crowded ballroom floor to

watch Belinda Roxbury waltzing with a Danish soldier in handsome uniform.

"Blasted French!" said the governor-general. "War with France will bleed the king's regiments from India! I shall be left with few white-skinned officers in a sea of native soldiers."

"I have always thought," said Sir George languidly, "that a spell of duty in India while the king's men make their colonial rounds is a curse of the English government. But I believe Governor Bie is correct. Napoleon has tasted too much defeat by Nelson and the Duke of Wellington to venture into India, although he knows breaking England commercially and industrially is the only way to defeat us."

"You may be right, Arlen. But I am serious in my decision to send you to His Majesty."

"A forthright decision. And I shall do my best to persuade the king of your concerns with France. A voyage should be safe. With Nelson's navy patrolling the sea, the French warships will soon drink their own gall."

"When can you sail?"

Sir George watched the swirling color of crinolines and uniforms beneath the glittering dazzle of chandeliers. The waltz came to him on a crescendo, and he saw Belinda standing off to one side with several young officers about her. She was laughing and talking, tossing her ebony curls like some coquettish minx he had seen in Paris. His lips narrowed. He was accused by Belinda of lacking jealousy where she was concerned, but it was a damnable lie!

"I am at your disposal. Name your convenience."

"Hugo said his wife and daughter are to voyage to London after the new year, and that you would be inclined to accompany them."

"I had not made up my mind until this night," his

eyes glittered, "but London will prove the best place for the marriage ceremony to take place."

"Ah! Then it is settled."

"By all means. Anything, Your Excellency, for the good of England."

"An honorable spirit. When you and your bride return, Hugo believes you will make a worthy commissioner for Guwahati. Between the two of you, I shall sleep more soundly in Calcutta."

Colorful lanterns decorated the balconies and widespread branches of the trees, casting bright festive colors through tinted glass along the front yard and entranceway. Inside the house, festoons of tropical flowers and plants decorated walls, doors, and tables, and were hung with ribbons from the chandeliers. The buffet tables were laden with delicacies fit for royalty: English and Danish pastries, huge silver platters of various smoked meats, fruits, cheeses, and a variety of drinks served from crystal bowls by richly attired servants.

Coral, dressed in a deep burgundy silk gown, left Ethan to go upstairs in search of Marianna. Her sister was not in the chamber, and Coral was returning to the ballroom when voices caused her to stop. She stood in the wide, columned hallway, with one of the private anterooms off to the side. Aunt Margaret, lovely in her personally designed amber-colored silk ball gown, stood alone facing Colonel Warbeck. He was leaning in the doorway in a stance that reminded Coral of his son, and Margaret could not pass.

"Let him accuse me. I would find it a pleasure to defend your honor."

"Please, I must go. We shall be the pinnacle of ugly gossip if you keep this up."

He laughed quietly. "I am always the topic of gossip. I shall come to London. When do you sail?"

"No. Do not come. If Hugo—"

Coral bit her lip and stepped back into the shadows. The colonel moved aside, and Margaret went past him toward the stairs. The door shut behind Colonel Warbeck. Coral stood there without moving. A minute later, she walked to the balustrade and saw Margaret below, moving off in the direction of Belinda and Kathleen.

Coral heard nothing but the waltz. How long she stood there she did not know. She walked toward the landing just as a familiar officer in the black and silver uniform of the British Cavalry was coming up the staircase. Jace appeared to have more sober contemplations on his mind than the Christmas festivities. He took the last steps two at a time, then stopped as he came upon her.

Coral wondered if her expression showed her feelings of distraction over coming upon the colonel and Aunt Margaret, for he studied her, then looked past her into the hall as if expecting to see someone else.

Coral was curious whether he had any suspicion about his father and her aunt, and found that the idea brought a tint to her cheeks. She turned away from him and walked back to the balustrade, her gaze on the dancers below.

"Hiding from someone? It must be your physician." He smiled and walked up beside her to lean against the carved stone pillar.

She smiled in spite of herself, then looked below again. A quick sweep of the dancers reminded her that Marianna was not to be seen. *Where has my little sister gone?*

"Seward said you would be too busy to come tonight," she said casually.

"And miss all this food? You do not know how I suffer from Gokul's cooking." He glanced across the room. "Your cousin?"

She followed his gaze to Ethan who stood where she had left him, but was now in conversation with several men, including Lord Canterbury.

"Yes. He arrived a week ago."

"How fortunate that he will set up his *mosquito lab* on Kingscote. When he is not busy cutting up bugs, he should be interesting company."

Her fingers tightened on the balustrade. "I gather, Major, that you do not like my cousin. Isn't this a rather hasty judgment? You have not even met him yet."

"I confess I do sound a little dour. When I was lured back into uniform, I was not informed that I would also be responsible to lead a safari of novice English civilians on a jungle trek north. Somehow, Boswell looks the sort of man who will everlastingly complain of dust and sweat."

So his dislike of Ethan has nothing to do with jealousy. "You will be surprised. Ethan labored in the jungles of Burma for several years before returning to London."

"Interesting. Perhaps I underestimate him."

She looked at him, but Jace was not watching her. "He is not above showing his displeasure, I see."

She again followed his gaze across the room. Ethan had looked up and seen them standing there. His eyes were riveted upon the major. Even the distance could not diminish the hard expression on the usually quiet face.

Coral felt a rise of uneasiness. If Jace did not like Ethan, it was evident that the feeling was going to be mutual.

"I seem to have irritated your cousin," he said casually. "If you will excuse me, the colonel is waiting down the hall. There is something we need to discuss."

"Yes, of course," she murmured, and tore her eyes from Ethan to meet the major's gaze. There was a slight glimmer of amusement in the blue-black of his eyes as he made his way across the hall.

Ethan was waiting for her when she came down, but his hard gray eyes were looking behind her and up the stairs. "I must say, I am surprised to see Buckley in uniform after what happened."

"After what happened? . . . Oh, you mean Michael."

"You are a gracious woman, Coral, yet I do not think a man like Buckley deserves your slightest indulgence. I was disturbed to learn from Aunt Margaret that the man will be in command of our journey to Kingscote. I think I should appeal to the governor-general."

"Ethan, the reported incident on the *Madras* was in error. I only recently found out."

He looked at her with skepticism. "I suppose he told you that. I would not accept his version of what happened."

"He tried to save Michael's life."

"Can we expect him to admit his stupor?"

"Ethan, please, do not speak so, especially in front of him. I fear he would—"

He gave a short laugh of scorn. "Call me out as a gentleman? Then let him. It so happens, my dear, that I am a crack shot."

She did not remember seeing him in such a hostile mood while in London. Was he jealous of Jace, or did he truly dislike him because of Michael's death? "I asked Seward about what happened, and he bears witness to the major's story. He even injured himself trying to save Michael's life."

Doctor Boswell's hard expression remained. "Seward is a friend of his. Naturally he would back up his tale. I think there is more truth to what we heard than your generosity is willing to admit."

"I am not being generous. I think you best discuss this matter in private with Uncle Hugo."

"I intend to. And do not worry, Coral, I will say nothing to Buckley—yet."

"There is no need to speak to him about it at all. I have already done so and am satisfied."

His restless gray eyes met hers. "He is not a gentleman. I have heard of his reputation. There is more than the incident aboard the *Madras*. Uncle mentioned an avalanche in the Darjeeling area. It is quite curious how Buckley returned safely to the hired servants, but Michael was left for dead."

Coral's mind darted back to that night on Kingscote when Michael had mentioned his near mishap in the avalanche. He had never explained what happened, and she had never asked. She tried to ease the matter by taking Ethan's arm and leading him toward the ballroom floor. "You need not concern yourself with the major. Uncle Hugo trusts him explicitly."

"You do not mean it?"

"It was Uncle who went to the governor-general to ask him to appoint Major Buckley as commander of the security force in Guwahati."

He stopped. "Hugo arranged it?"

"He will explain his reasons to you if you ask. He will be here in Barrackpore tomorrow afternoon."

Ethan turned and looked up toward the balustrade, a thoughtful expression on his face. "Uncle did not tell me. Then perhaps I should be more cautious in my judgment."

She let out a silent breath, relaxing.

After the waltz, Coral set out to find Marianna. In the main floor hall, it was quiet. She was about to take the side stairs to the room she shared with Marianna when something caught her attention. The door into a salon that led into an enclosed garden stood ajar, and she felt a cool draft. Her suspicions were alerted. Lady Canterbury's servants would never be so remiss. Had Marianna gone into the garden? But the December night was chill, and it was no place to go without a chaperon.

Nevertheless, Coral entered the salon and found the double doors leading into the garden open. She stepped out into the shadowed evening.

For a moment she stood there on the flagstone. The chill fingers of evening ran along her shoulders and arms. She waited, letting her eyes adjust to the darkness.

The stars were a silver glimmer in the black sky, and after a minute or so she began to see the silhouettes of tropical plants and vines standing like an arsenal of soldiers guarding the red flagstone walk that wound farther into Lady Isobel's garden.

Coral took the walk, her slippers making clicking sounds on stone, and headed briskly toward the end of the far side; Marianna was not to be seen. A gate stood open. "Marianna? Are you out there?" she called.

Marianna would never wander so far alone—unless she was not alone. . . . Becoming more chilled by the minute, she hurried ahead and through the gate, discovering that it led outside the garden to a narrow stone alleyway.

Coral was on the verge of turning back when a small figure with trailing skirts came flying toward her. Marianna ran into her, gasping for breath. One glance at her face told Coral of her fear.

"Mar—" began Coral.

Marianna's trembling fingers were cold and shaking as they pressed against Coral's lips. She glanced backward over her shoulder toward the alley.

"Shh! It is Uncle Hugo!"

"He is not in Barrackpore tonight. What is wrong?"

"Yes, he is!" Marianna's nails dug into Coral's arm. "Hurry, Coral, the man he is with saw me!"

Confused, Coral saw no reason why they should run away like two thieves; nevertheless, she acted on her sister's alarm. Together they sped through the gate back into the cloistered garden.

There was not enough time to make it to the house. From behind them Coral heard running footsteps on the stone alleyway. She grabbed Marianna's arm and pulled her aside into the thick shrubs and vines, snagging her skirts and losing a slipper. She heard Marianna stifle a moan. Together they ran toward an arbor bordering a pond. Ahead there was a shed that looked to be made of split cane, and beside it a stack of baskets. Coral pushed Marianna inside and ducked in after her, pulling the door shut. The smell of moldy earth and rotting plants filled her nostrils.

9

They waited, crouching in the darkness, and Coral heard the sound of her heart pounding in her ears. A moment later they heard footsteps stop uncertainly, then start in their direction.

Lord, prayed Coral, alarm gripping her emotions like a vise. *What is this? What is going on? Do not let him come here, please!*

From behind them in the garden there were voices. The footsteps that had followed them from the alleyway stopped, then darted off into the trees.

Whoever it was had not wished to be seen, so Coral crept out of the shed looking in the runner's direction in time to catch a glimpse of a yellow turban, then he was gone.

Was Marianna right? Had he been meeting with Uncle Hugo in the alleyway?

Marianna came up behind her, grabbing her arm. "It is Cousin Ethan and Kathleen calling us. Whaa-what shall we say?"

"The truth. I came looking for you," said Coral.

"No! Say nothing, not until I explain. Please!"

"But—"

"Coral!"

"Very well. Come, they will be worried."

A few minutes later Coral stepped onto the pathway with Marianna behind her. "We are over here," she called, surprised her voice sounded calm.

Ethan hurried toward them with Kathleen. "Are you all right?"

Marianna looked embarrassed and turned her head away.

"Yes, we are just fine," answered Coral cheerfully.

"What are you doing out here without a chaperon?" Kathleen asked with a frown.

"Oh! I went for a walk," said Marianna lamely, smoothing her curls back into place.

"In this cold?" said Kathleen accusingly.

"Yes! It is cold," agreed Marianna too quickly. "Let us go inside and get some hot, mulled punch. Coming, Coral?"

"Ah . . . yes."

Coral saw Ethan's gaze flicker across her mussed hair and then to the slipper in her hand.

"What happened? Did you fall?"

"Oh, I just lost my slipper." She managed a smile.

He took her arm. "This is dreadful. Come, dear, let me get you back to the house. You might have sprained your ankle."

At the house, Coral managed to get away from Ethan, explaining that she wanted to look in on Marianna.

When Coral entered the bedroom and shut the door, her sister was sitting on a stool, the flounces of her skirt spread about her. Marianna looked up at her, white and shaking.

Kathleen stood, hands on hips. "I want the truth. What were you doing out there?"

"Kathleen, not now. Marianna is not feeling well. The

best thing you can do is go back down to the ball. I will take care of her."

"What *happened* to you, Coral?" Kathleen scanned her.

"I was in a hurry and lost a slipper."

Marianna burst into tears, covering her face with her palms. Coral rushed to her and knelt, drawing her head against her shoulder. "Kathleen, will you please let me handle this?"

Kathleen's eyes narrowed suspiciously. "Since when do you two keep things from me?"

"Trust me. I will explain later."

"Oh, very well. I could almost believe the two of you had beaus waiting out in the garden if I did not know you better, Coral. Whatever you do, do not let Aunt Margaret see you like this."

"Keep her busy for a while, will you?"

"You have a lot of explaining to do in the morning." She looked down on Marianna. Then turning abruptly, she flounced toward the door and went out, shutting it firmly behind her.

Coral let out a breath and soothed Marianna's mussed curls. "It is all right. Here, blow your nose like a good girl."

"I . . . I do not feel well, Coral. I think I am getting ill."

"Here, let me help you get out of your clothes and into bed. I will send down for something hot to drink. After you gather your wits together you can tell me what happened."

Marianna was in bed when there came a rap on the door. Her wide eyes darted to Coral. Coral found herself glancing at the door. Marianna's nervous behavior made her feel cautious. "It is just a servant," she said. "Or maybe Aunt Margaret."

"Remember your promise," she whispered. "Do not say anything until we talk first."

Coral paused before the door, her hand on the knob. She brought her features into composure before she opened it. "Yes?"

She gulped. Her stomach flipped.

Sir Hugo stood there, with a cloak over his evening clothes. His eyes were solemn, the bearded face unreadable. His stare confronted her, making Coral wish to step back. She denied being intimidated and managed a slight smile. "Oh, it is you, Uncle. Good evening. We did not expect you to arrive tonight."

"I had a change of plans. I took a shortcut through the garden. I was informed that either you or Marianna tripped and was injured."

She felt, rather than saw, his eyes taking her in.

So . . . he does not know for certain just who saw him. "Yes, I was in the garden, Uncle. I am fine."

"The servant, Piroo, was with me. He thought you might have injured yourself. He went to find you, but you had already come back to the house."

Did he come here to tell her this so she would think the man in the yellow turban was a servant? That his running after them had been out of concern? Coral suspected differently. "I was in the garden. But I did not fall."

He looked past her toward the bed where Marianna lay with the covers pulled up around her throat. Would he ask if Marianna was with her?

"Marianna is not feeling well. I noticed it early this evening. I think she may be coming down with a raw throat."

"Indeed?" He stepped inside, and Coral had no recourse but to step back. He walked up to the bedside, gazing down. Coral came up beside him, hoping Marianna would not show alarm. To her relief, her sister's eyes were shut, and she lay motionless.

Coral tensed when Hugo reached a hand to touch Marianna's forehead. Would she jump? She remained still.

"I will ask Ethan to come up. He can give her something to help her. We must have her well and happy again before your cousin's engagement party to Arlen." He stood there for a moment longer, watching Marianna, then walked to the door. Coral followed him.

"You must not wander in the garden at night, my dear. There are vipers about."

When he had gone, Coral shut the door and listened until his steps died away. She turned the key in the lock, then hurried back to Marianna. Her eyelids fluttered open, and she tried to sit up. "I do not want to see Cousin Ethan!"

"Uncle will be suspicious if you do not. Say nothing about your being in the garden, do you understand? He thinks I was alone. It is just as well." Marianna nodded, and with her teeth chattering she lay back against the pillow.

Is this a nervous reaction, or is she actually getting ill? Coral wondered, feeling edgy.

Ethan arrived a few minutes later. Coral unlocked the door and let him in. She had expected Aunt Margaret to be with him, but he was alone. As he felt Marianna's pulse and touched her forehead, Coral remained seated on the side of the bed to assure her sister.

"Well, little cousin. I see nothing to worry about," Ethan told Marianna cheerfully. "Stay in bed tomorrow for good measure. You should be up and singing for the rest of the festivities."

He handed Coral a packet of powders. "Mix this with something hot, then let her sleep."

Coral followed him to the door while the Indian servant girl entered with a hot cup of tea for Marianna.

"You know how young girls are," Coral assured Ethan, "the excitement of the ball, the holidays, and the upcoming journey home has merely proven too much."

Ethan smiled and gave her such a searching look that Coral felt her face turning warm. She was afraid he would ask again why she was in the garden, and said swiftly, "Ethan, there is a physician you should meet. Doctor John Thomas is staying at Serampore. He has worked in India for many years. If you like, we could go to Serampore in the morning. I have a friend who can bring us to see him. You remember Charles Peddington from London?"

"Your music teacher? Ah, yes, he went to work for the Company. He knows Doctor Thomas?"

"Yes. Thomas is an associate with Master William Carey."

"The minister from Kettering? The one who wrote the pamphlet?"

"He is now a Bible translator with a mission station at Serampore. They have a printing press. He also started a school. Lady Isobel has spoken well of it. A number of English and Danish here in Barrackpore send their children there."

"Marvelous. I would like to go as soon as possible. Can you arrange it with Peddington?"

"I will send word ahead. We can take a boat first thing in the morning and return before dinner at the commissioner's."

"Splendid. How good of you to have thought of this."

"Well, actually, Ethan, I do have a motive of my own. I want to see the Marshmans' school, and Charles has reason to believe that Master Carey will have some Scripture in Hindi to give to me."

He smiled. "Then, by all means, we shall go."

"I will meet you at the ghat early . . . say, around dawn?"

"Very well, dawn it is. Then we both had best turn in early."

"Good night, Ethan, thank you."

Coral shut the door behind him. As her smile faded, she frowned and walked over to the bed. The servant girl had already poured their tea. "Anything else, miss-sahiba?"

"No, that will be all. Thank you."

The girl salaamed and slipped silently from the room. When they were alone, Coral locked the door again and lit a second lamp. Quickly she was beside the bed, and Marianna sat up against the pillows.

"All right, tell me what happened."

"I went into the garden as I said, because I thought I saw Uncle through the window where I sat by the hearth. I knew he was not supposed to be here until tomorrow. I would have thought nothing about it except he looked as though he did not wish to be seen. And when Cousin Belinda also slipped away into the garden, and did not come back—well, I decided to go look for her."

"Belinda?" asked Coral surprised. "Are you certain?"

"Yes. I never did locate her."

"But Belinda was waltzing with Arlen George when I left to find you. I thought you were here in the room."

Marianna shrugged. "Then she must have come back another way. But I did not know that, and I went through the gate because I thought it led to the pond, but I found myself in an alleyway with a garden wall. There were stairs leading up to a lemon orchard. I heard two men talking. It sounded like Uncle Hugo, so I thought nothing of it and walked toward the steps. Two men were standing there. One was Uncle; the other was an Indian with a yellow turban. I started to say, 'Good evening, Uncle, where is Belinda?' when something the Indian said stopped me." Marianna's eyes grew wide, and she plucked at the coverlet.

"Yes? What did he say?" Coral urged.

Marianna gave a shiver and glanced toward the door.

"It is bolted," said Coral.

"He said to Uncle, 'An accident of one so great is not easily arranged. Not like the first time. He has many friends, even among the Hindus.' "

Coral stared into the pale face and found her own heart suddenly pounding. "You are sure, Marianna?" she whispered.

Marianna swallowed and nodded her head.

Coral tried to keep her self-control. After all, the words could mean almost anything, couldn't they?

"Anything else?"

"No. It was then that I think I made a little noise, and they both turned in my direction. I think Uncle ran up the steps and disappeared into the lemon grove, but the other man, the Indian—he started toward me, and I was afraid and ran. I could hear him chasing after me! Then I ran into you. Oh, Coral, what could it all mean? Do . . . do you think Uncle Hugo has done something wrong?"

Coral did not know what to think. "We must not rush to conclusions. But you must say nothing of this to anyone, do you understand?"

"Not even Aunt Margaret?"

"Especially her. You must promise me not to breath a word of this until I tell you it is all right to do so, understood?"

Marianna frowned. "But if something is wrong—"

"We do not know that. Even so, all the more reason to keep quiet until I can speak to Major Buckley. We do not want anyone to know what you overheard, least of all Uncle Hugo."

"But, Coral, if that Indian man did something wrong, and he knows I heard—"

"That is why you must say nothing. Once Uncle Hugo is convinced no one overheard, it will pass."

"What if he asks me?"

"I do not think he will. I will talk to the major and see what he suggests about the matter." Coral stood, masking the alarm she felt, and prepared the medicine to add to the cup of tea.

"Oh, dear, I shall never get to sleep!"

"Try not to think about it. Here, drink this."

Marianna looked up at her with wide, frightened eyes. "What would have happened if he caught me?"

"He had no intention of catching you, or us. He could have easily outrun two women in silk slippers. I am sure he wanted to see who had overheard them talking. And you can rest secure, because he does not know."

Marianna frowned. "What makes you think so?"

"I am certain that was the reason Uncle came here to our room tonight. He wanted to find out who was in the garden. He thinks it was me."

"Oh . . ." said Marianna with a small voice. "I did not mean to get you into trouble, Coral."

Coral managed a smile. "Do not worry. Here, drink your tea."

"Coral, I wish you would not go to Serampore tomorrow."

"There is nothing to worry about. Kathleen can keep you company, and so will Aunt Margaret."

"But do you really intend to go with Cousin Ethan? Suppose Uncle Hugo finds out?"

"He will eventually. Ethan will most likely mention it to him. By then I should be back in Barrackpore. Look,

Marianna, I must get a copy of the Scriptures in Hindi. I will not get another chance soon. And it is important that I visit the Marshmans. I know so little about starting a school."

Marianna's reddish brows came together, even though her eyes began to grow sleepy from the medicine. "You are still going to start that mission school. . . . I wish you would change your mind; not because I do not think what you want to do is good, but I am afraid for you."

Coral smiled and sat down on the bed. She took the empty cup and set it aside, then covered Marianna.

"Say hello to Charles for me," her sister murmured.

"I will. Now I want you to say a verse over and over until you fall asleep. Are you willing to try to learn it?"

Marianna nodded.

" 'I will both lay me down in peace, and sleep: for thou, LORD, only makest me dwell in safety. Psalm 4:8.' " Marianna closed her eyes and repeated it softly after Coral. Within a few minutes she was asleep.

Coral lowered the lamp, having no inclination to go back down to the ball. She would be up before dawn to wait for Ethan by the river. Tomorrow night at this time, if God blessed her endeavor, a copy of the Scriptures in Hindi would be safely within her hand.

Uncle Hugo . . . and the Indian with the yellow turban . . . what had they been planning? She must inform Major Jace Buckley. But after his meeting with the colonel, he may have left. She wished to take no chances of another conversation with Sir Hugo tonight.

Coral wrote a quick note, explaining what had taken place and that she had learned something while in the garden with Marianna that might be important.

I will give the message to Seward to deliver before leaving for Serampore in the morning.

And just what would Jace Buckley think of her uncle's clandestine meeting in the garden?

———

As Jace came down the staircase with the colonel, he noticed that the Kendall daughter had left. Ethan Boswell, too, was gone. He sampled the dishes of food, and was about to leave, when he became aware of perfume and turned his head. Belinda Roxbury smiled.

"Why, Jace, how good of you to come. And to think my cousins have disappeared. No matter, I shall have you all to myself. I believe you owe me the next waltz."

He smiled. "My pleasure, Miss Roxbury."

She swished her fan. "Belinda." She glanced about. "I wonder where Ethan and Coral are? I saw them go off alone into the garden. . . ."

A brow arched. "Did you?"

"You do know, do you not, that they will marry at Kingscote?"

"I was not aware."

"Coral says she is madly in love."

"Did she?"

"With her health, isn't it grand she can marry a doctor! Of course, do not tell her I told you so."

"I shall be certain to keep your secret."

10

Danish-controlled Serampore stood on the banks of the Hooghly River, which flowed past the front gate of the mission house. Charles Peddington greeted Coral and Ethan warmly.

"I'm pleased you were able to come before I left for Calcutta to work at Government-House."

"Charles, you remember Doctor Boswell?"

"Most certainly. Good morning, sir. Welcome to India."

As Coral explained that he hoped to meet Doctor John Thomas, Charles brightened. "Yes! Doctor Thomas is here now. He has brought an Indian friend who wishes to inquire further of Christianity."

Coral glanced toward Ethan to see his reaction, but he seemed to be absorbed with his surroundings and the botanical garden that Carey had developed on the grounds of the mission.

"How many acres?" Boswell asked.

"At least two," said Charles. "Master Carey was able to come by it at an excellent price from a relative of Governor Bie."

Ethan looked surprised. "How fortunate for you to

find a friend in the Danish government."

"Indeed, sir. Had it not been for Governor Bie, we would have been sent back to London by the Company. The Lord has supplied the needs of the mission. We have a meeting hall large enough for a chapel," Charles went on, "and we all take turns preaching and holding meetings in Bengali. We have several outbuildings that we use for our residences and business needs, and of course—" he turned to Coral with a smile, "we have the Marshmans' school."

While Charles brought Ethan to meet Thomas, Coral was taken on a tour of the school by Hannah Marshman.

"How did you come to concern yourself with India?" asked Coral.

"When we heard of William's work here in India, my husband knew with a great certainty that this was his calling. He has not regretted the decision, and neither have I," Mrs. Marshman said with a smile.

Hannah Marshman was a capable woman. Her inner strength was balanced between her zeal and a practical outworking of her prudence shown in the many duties she accomplished around the mission.

Hannah had not only taken up the management of the communal affairs of the mission household, but she taught both in the school and the church, and devoted a great many hours cultivating a friendly relationship with the Hindu women who had surprisingly begun to open their doors to her.

"When I heard about your school I knew I must see it, and talk with you," said Coral, and explained her plans to start a mission school on Kingscote.

"So Charles has told us. William will be delighted to know that a young woman of your character is dedicated to making Christ known among the children," said Hannah.

"We arrive at the school at seven," Hannah told Coral as they walked along. "Classes usually run till after two each day."

"I suppose what I worry about the most is how to get the children to attend," said Coral. "How difficult was that for you?"

"Actually, our students are quite different from those you will have. Most of our boys are from English and Danish families here in Serampore and across the river in Barrackpore. We also have some from Calcutta. When the families heard of our curriculum they were immediately interested. We are noted for high instruction, and soon we had a number of students enrolled. Actually, it has become a slogan that 'everyone sends his son to Serampore.' We can see God's working and timing. The fees we must charge and the profits from Mr. Ward's printing press are able to make the mission self-supporting. This is important to William, who does not want to burden the Mission Society in London. We board Anglo-Indian boys, and I've been able to open a school for young ladies—another extremely important task. We charge forty to fifty rupees a year, depending on whether the students receive Latin, Greek, Hebrew, Persian, or Sanskrit lessons. Of course, the school at Kingscote will not need to be so involved."

Coral smiled. "I was thinking of simple reading, writing, and Bible instruction. I also hope to feed them one hot meal a day, perhaps breakfast."

"Then I must show you the free school. We have started with the Bengali boys and have forty enrolled. At first the children were certain we were going to abduct them and send them to England, but we soon made friends. What about your supplies? I suppose you brought them with you aboard ship?"

"Not nearly enough," Coral confessed. Getting her

meager supplies shipped from London to Calcutta had proved difficult. Getting them safely home to Kingscote would prove even more troublesome. "I have one trunk of teaching materials. First I must convince my family of the need for the school."

"By God's grace you will. Come, let me show you our new supplies from London. They arrived only yesterday."

Coral went through the Marshmans' material, some of it still in shipping cartons. There was Gibbon's *Rhetoric*, Hornsey's *Grammar*, Milton's *Paradise Lost*, Cowper's *Poems*, many quills, ink made for hot climates, and a box of well-bound New Testaments in English.

"It is the Hindi New Testament that I hope to buy."

"I am sure William will present you with the Scriptures as a gift, dear. He will be so pleased with your efforts. You should also visit Mr. Ward and the printing press. William's son Felix works with him."

"I look forward to it. Charles has told me so much about it."

"Charles . . . poor boy. He was so faithful while aiding Mr. Ward. We shall miss him. But the fever takes its toll. We have lost several missionaries."

"Yes, Charles told me about John Fountain."

"Not only John. We have lost Mr. Grant, also Mr. Burson. I am afraid Mrs. Carey grows worse with the passing of time. I have enormous sympathy for her, but William carries on. He is a plodder, you know. He is not a man to let difficulties and hardship hold him back from the work."

The translation work of William Carey challenged Coral to new earnestness of purpose. She discovered that upon his arrival in India he had set out to master the languages and dialects. While he gave himself to long, arduous study, Mrs. Carey was in the very next room, sometimes wrought up to heights of great neurotic frenzy because of her mental disability, and yet he patiently handled her needs, while plodding ahead in the translation work. Coral was certain that most other servants of God in those circumstances would have given up.

Coral was graciously received by William Carey, who explained more of his work.

"My goal, as the Lord enables, is to see the Word of God in every language and dialect of India," he said.

Coral felt overwhelmed with the prospect, but Carey believed it was possible. There were others involved. Marshman, Ward, a Mr. Gilchrist, Doctor John Thomas, and at various times, native Indian munshis were engaged to assist with the finer points of the language. He had received worried criticism from the Mission Society for using the munshis, but Carey was certain of what he was doing.

"Whatever help we employ I have never yet suffered a single word or a single mode of construction without having examined it and seen through it," William Carey said. "I read every proof sheet twice or thrice myself, and correct every letter with my own hand. Brother Marshman or myself compare it with Greek or Hebrew, and Brother Ward reads every sheet. Three of the translations, mainly the Bengali, Hindustani, and the Sanskrit, I translate with my own hands, the last two immediately from the Greek and Hebrew Bible which is before me while I translate the Bengali."

Coral was delighted to discover that he intended to translate the Bible in whole or in part in the Assami language, and also in Burmese. A missionary named Chater would be sent to Rangoon, and William's son Felix intended to go with him to start a mission station.

After a full morning of touring the mission, and seeing the translation work, Coral joined the others at the dinner table where the ten missionaries and nine children, four of them Carey's sons, all ate their meals in common.

Coral quietly told Carey that she had decided to start the mission school on Kingscote after reading his pamphlet on world missions.

"Then God be the One praised, my dear child."

A prayer was offered before they ate: "May this endeavor wrought in order to share the power of the gospel with the untouchables be blessed of Him a hundredfold. Yea, let an orphanage be established as God enables."

It was now after the meal, and approaching the hour of their departure to Barrackpore, but Ethan had gone off on some excursion with Thomas. As she awaited his return, Charles led her into the chapel.

"Before you go, we have something for you," said Charles, with a warm glow in his eyes.

Coral's chest tightened with emotion as she guessed what it was. There on the communion table in the chapel, resting beside the elements that they were to share together, was a Hindi New Testament. Coral swallowed back the cramp in her throat.

William Carey led in communion, and then presented her with the Scriptures. A marker had been placed at Matthew nineteen, the portion of Scripture about Jesus and the children.

Coral stared at the words of Christ until her eyes blurred with moisture. "How can I thank you, Master Carey?"

He smiled quietly, and said: "Teach it. And when you do, never speak of William Carey, but speak of William Carey's God."

After the others left the chapel, and the last goodbyes were given, Charles walked her in the direction of the river. She stopped him, and they stood in the wide avenue of mahogany trees.

"I will meet Ethan at the boat. He may be there now waiting for me. Goodbye, Charles. I do hope your work at Government-House goes well."

He sighed. "It shall never bring the satisfaction that I received today when I saw the expression on your face." He looked at the New Testament that she held, and his face sobered. "To have experienced that moment, Coral, was worth every testing we have undergone. I shall never find at Government-House anything to bring me such joy."

His hand closed about hers as it enfolded the Scriptures in Hindi.

"I will come to see you and your sisters at Kingscote when I can. And may a school stand to His honor when I arrive."

"Goodbye, Charles, and thank you again."

With the Scriptures in her bag, Coral walked down to the ghat. The boat was there, but neither Ethan nor the river guide was waiting. She shaded her eyes and glanced about, seeing no sign of their presence.

It was still early afternoon and the December day was chill, but the sun was out, and the birds were chattering noisily in the overhanging branches. Thomas had mentioned that a Hindu temple was located not far away, and she wondered if that was where they had gone. The area was a botanist's dream, and Ethan may have wanted to take some samples back to Barrackpore to occupy his time of study.

Coral left the ghat and made her way down the tree-lined road, which soon narrowed. *A missionary must learn to do things on her own*, she told herself. *I cannot be leaning on a male chaperon all the time. Once I arrive at Kingscote I will need to depend on the Lord and take responsibility for my own actions, so why not now?*

She came to a wall and followed it. The weather was moist, and she pulled the hood of her long cloak up over her tresses.

Serampore was noted for its luxurious trees. The embankment along the Hooghly River was thick with bamboo and feathery coconut palms. There were flocks of brightly colored parakeets and the long-legged cranes that served as Calcutta's scavengers. Monkeys swung from branches, and to her dismay, poisonous snakes were abundant. As she made her way precariously in the direction of the ancient temple, she felt the familiar weakness come to sap her strength and mock her independence. Despite the moist coolness, it did not take long before she was wet with perspiration. She stopped to catch her breath. Ahead was a narrow gate and the entrance to a secondary ghat that may have belonged to the temple grounds.

Coral noticed that a number of people were gathered on the bank, and a man who looked to be a Hindu priest was speaking. Were Ethan and Doctor Thomas with them? Perhaps Thomas was engaging the priest in a discussion of the Scriptures.

Coral passed through the gate and walked along the bank toward the small crowd. She did not see Thomas, but she did get a closer view of the priest. He was a thin, older man with a shaven head and a white caste mark painted on his brown forehead. The so-called sacred thread was across his shoulder. But to Coral's horror, she realized that she had come upon a ceremony that her father had forbidden to take place on Kingscote, one that sometimes occurred in the village. It was the *suttee*—a woman who had become widowed was preparing herself to be burned alive with the body of her husband on his funeral pyre.

Why, the woman is young, no more than fifteen or sixteen.

Coral's heart thudded in her chest. She wanted to turn and run away in revulsion, but her feet would not move. The girl was throwing her life, and her soul, away.

Coral's voice surprised even herself. "Roko! Roko!" she shouted.

They turned and looked at her, wondering who would dare tell them to stop.

Coral took a hesitant step forward and confronted the immobile eyes of the priest. She walked toward the small gathering feeling as though her knees would buckle. Their expressions were indomitable, the dark eyes cool.

She floundered, wondering what to say, and her gaze fell upon the young widow standing by the pyre. There were several large bundles of wood, about two and a half feet high and four feet long. As her eyes darted to the top, she saw the body of the deceased ready for burning. Coral felt sick.

As though in a move to protect the widow, her nearest relative came to stand beside her. In the girl's hand was a basket. Coral recognized the contents as sweetmeats that were used as an offering to the god Shiva.

"W-what are you doing?" Coral managed rather weakly.

"We have come to burn our dead."

"Yes. But—but his widow is alive."

They did not reply.

Coral grew bolder. "Why, she is little more than a child!"

"This is her choice. No one forces her."

"Is this true?" Coral asked her.

The young face of the girl met hers. "It is, sahiba."

Coral tried to reason with her, then with those gathered, but they soon grew angry. Coral became desperate.

"This is no less than murder! You have forced her to this, for if she does not go through with it, her family will have broken caste, and you will denounce them! Do not do it," she told the girl, and extended a hand toward her, but several men stepped between them.

"Be gone, sahiba."

The priest stepped toward her. "You interfere in that which you do not understand. It is not your affair. You are a feringhi. You intrude where you have no right."

"I was born and raised in India; I am not a foreigner. But whether I am or not, sir, has nothing to do with the matter of life and death. The living and true God forbids human sacrifice, and it is my responsibility to speak against what you are doing. It does not please Him! He has given no such commandment."

While Coral was talking, the widow had been led six times around the pile, and now she scattered the sweetmeats while the others picked them up and ate them as a holy offering.

"Stop!" she cried. "Please! God has given His very Son as the one and only sacrifice to atone for sin. Though a Hindu be born a thousand times, and dies a thousand deaths, it is of no avail; burning is wicked in His sight—"

"Is sahiba one of those pestilent Christians from William Carey's mission?" the priest demanded of her.

"They have turned Krishna Pal into a European," said another. "He was a brahmin, yet he has eaten with them. Now they baptize others in the holy Ganges!"

"I am not of Master Carey's mission, though I would find it an honor to be one of them. For they have come in love and compassion. Is it so wrong to be concerned for the life of this girl?"

"Be gone, sahiba!" he warned, and several from the funeral group took a step in her direction. Coral refused to turn and run. She called to the girl, "Come with me.

No harm will befall you if you do. They dare not force you. They admit the decision is in your hand! Fear nothing, I will take you with me to Barrackpore. I promise to care for you for the rest of your life if you will come with me now!"

To Coral's horror, the girl suddenly climbed up onto the pile. As if to show her willingness to burn, she began to dance, her hands extended.

Coral stared with horror. "No—wait!"

The girl lay down with the deceased, placing her arms around his neck. Coral took a step backward. *Oh, God!*

The others poured dry cocoa leaves and melted butter over the two bodies, then two bamboos were pressed over the pyre and held fast.

"This is murder!" shouted Coral. "Take away the bamboo! You do it to keep her there! She cannot change her mind once you set it aflame! Murder—"

Unexpectedly, a strong hand grasped her arm and whirled her about face. Jace stood there, his eyes sparking with frustration, his jaw set. "Coral! What are you doing here!"

Before she could answer, the dry kindling crackled, then exploded into flame. "Hurree-Bol, Hurree-Bol!" The loud shout of invocation from those gathered smothered any protest that might have sounded from beneath the pyre.

Coral's hands flew to cover her ears, and her eyes shut tightly. She wanted to scream.

Almost at the same moment, Jace stepped back from the heat, swung her up into his arms, and retreated down the bank of the river. Ducking beneath the overhanging branches and avoiding the tentacles of creeper that reached to entangle them, the awful shouting was left behind as the smoke curled upward like vile incense to the Hindu god.

11

Jace did not stop until they neared the ghat where an empty boat waited. Here he set her lightly on her feet, and Coral drew away, walking weakly to the platform. Steadying herself, she sank down in a daze, sickened.

"Oh . . . I feel ill."

"Do not faint on me. I have no smelling salts."

"It is vile! It ought to be outlawed!" She looked up at him, scanning his uniform accusingly. "The East India Company should do something about such wicked practices in Calcutta."

"Ask your uncle to speak to the governor-general. He managed to change my orders," he said dryly, "perhaps he can halt widow burning. As for you, Miss Kendall, I gather you need a little more excitement in your life? A midnight excursion in the garden was not challenging enough for your rare spirit, so you must confront a Hindu priest during suttee!"

"Do not say it, Major, I do not want to hear it."

"You might have gotten yourself into a great deal of trouble! Does your father know you are wandering about Calcutta without Seward?"

No, of course he did not. And Coral knew that Major

141

Buckley was correct. Her father would have exploded had he come upon her just now.

"I did not go in search of this sickening experience if that is what you think."

"I hardly know *what* to think. You are certainly not the typical English girl. And I have met a few in my time."

Coral fumed. He sounded as if he had been around a generation before her entry into the world, as if she were a child who had wandered from her nursery.

She cast him a defensive glance. She said nothing and looked back at the river feeling emotionally exhausted, too weary to do anything but watch it flow past, its murky swells conjuring up fresh images of the girl dancing on the funeral pyre. The memory would long be etched upon her mind.

"A word of advice, Miss Kendall."

"I have received nothing but advice since I arrived in Calcutta. First from my aunt, then Sir Hugo. I do not particularly care to hear any more, Major."

"You have my sympathy, but I will give mine anyway since it is born from a lifetime of experience with unpleasant situations. For your own emotional well-being, Miss Kendall, learn to shield your heart with armor before you look upon a land retching with pain. You might have been born here, but you do not know the mass of humanity that is Calcutta or Bombay. Kingscote is hardly the face of the real India that I have lived and suffered with since a boy."

She found in his words something of the real Jace Buckley. When they had first encountered each other at the bazaar, he had intimated the same outlook, suggesting she not meddle with the culture of India, that she would receive nothing but trouble for her involvement. She turned her head a little in order to study his face. Beyond the obvious good looks was a resolute hardness that refused to yield to critique. Was his armor a genuine rebuff to tenderness, or a ploy to shield vulnerability?

How much pain had Jace actually experienced since seeing his father beheaded in Whampoa? And what actually was his feeling toward her willingness for personal risk? Did he think she was wide-eyed and innocent, out on a personal crusade to better India's morals? Or did he understand that her commitment went far deeper?

"You will not stop the practice of widow burning by confronting the act," he continued. "You will get nothing for your pains but spiritual exhaustion. Your revulsion means nothing to a culture rooted in religious convictions, however dark, and if you seek to interfere you will only hurt yourself, or cause a riot. Get in the boat. I intend to take you back where you belong—Canterbury House."

Coral's frustration mounted, and somehow it seemed suddenly important that he understood, that he believed as she did, that he cared for India's pain, its grievous chains of satanic bondage. She stood, her eyes searching his for some small measure of compassion that could rise to her own height for a people in anguish.

"Are you as detached from the reality of suffering as you imply? Is that how you look upon the multitudes, Major? As a mass of humanity without a face, a name, a soul? You wish to not hear the smothered wail of one girl burning in the flames, but the voice of a multitude shouting in ignorance to Shiva, an idol of death and destruction."

"Are you speaking as a follower of Christ, or as a prideful European nauseated by heathenism?"

"The gospel is not cultural, Major."

"I am pleased you are wise enough to know the difference, Miss Kendall. Many do not. The East India Company is filled with the civilized who deplore not only the Hindu rituals but also the people. I have often contemplated what Christ would do if He were on earth walking the dusty roads of India."

"He would have stopped the suttee. He would have done something, something that revealed His compassion and authority. I know He would!"

"Compassion and authority make good kinsmen, do they not? He bears them both like the sweetness of a well-watered garden. Compassion for the multitudes, authority to break the chains that bind, and His answer to Shiva? What is it, Miss Kendall?"

Somehow she knew that his question was not asked in ignorance, for his words had revealed that the person of Christ was not a stranger to his intellect. She stared at him, surprised. Why then did he probe her, sounding quiet, yet so challenging? He was not asking as a Hindu. Of that she was certain.

"I was a boy of eight when I saw my father use a scimitar to lop off the head of a pirate aboard our ship," he said matter-of-factly. "I distinctly remember being splattered with warm blood—you find that offensive, I know. I only mention it that you might understand that human suffering was part of my daily ration. But I remember something else as well, even more distinctly. Some man, I do not even remember who he was, was shouting that it was murder. *Thou shalt not murder,*' he shouted. *'God will hold your soul eternally responsible. Mercy and forgiveness of sin are found in His Son, but if you reject Him, you will surely die.*' "

He looked down at her, his features unreadable. "I never forgot that. I remember washing the blood from my face in the cabin, and my father came in. He glowered down upon me, looking like some giant in a rough blue coat and hat. He grabbed me by the front of my tunic and shook me until my head snapped. 'You must never do as I have done,' he told me. 'If I go to hell, I do not want to see you there.' "

Coral felt a spasm of raw emotion, yet Jace spoke calmly, with detachment.

"It was not long after that," he continued, "that I saw my father killed. I remember retching in the sand and feeling the salt water roll over me. I could hear Seward calling me from the distance on a small boat. I knew I should swim out to him while I had a chance to escape. But I could not. I was too sick."

Coral felt the warm tears seeping from the corners of her eyes, and her throat constricted.

"I came here to India when I was around twelve; I really do not know how old I am. I watched mothers throw their infants to crocodiles on holy days, and heard their wails. I have seen men hang themselves on flesh hooks, and indulge in other self-inflicted tortures to appease Shiva's wrath. No amount of reasoning or anger on my part has ever stopped any of it."

There was silence. Coral wanted to say something, but her mouth was dry; she knew her voice would break off before she completed her sentence. She knew why his emotions were encased in armor, and she wanted to remove it and heal the wounds. The features of the man looking down at her masked what he was thinking or feeling. She sensed that beyond that hard facade was another Jace, but there would be a personal risk in discovering him.

So wrapped up was she in her own response, she did not see his, not until she felt his thumb brush the tear from her cheek. A faint smile warmed his features.

Aware that his light touch had awakened her senses, she stepped back, and gathering up her skirts, climbed down the steps of the ghat to the boat, leaving Jace standing there in silence.

A moment later he followed, frowning to himself. "I should not have said all that to you. I am not sure why I did."

Coral did not look at him. "I am glad."

The silence grew.

"Does Boswell have enough sense to get back on his own?" he asked flatly.

Thinking of Ethan brought William Carey back to mind. It was only then that Coral remembered.

"Oh, no!" she gasped, and whirled to look at him.

His brow went up. "Now what?"

"I must have set my bag down! I cannot leave without it, Major."

He folded his arms. "Most women have dozens of bags and parasols. A silk heiress can afford to lose one."

"But not this one. Master Carey gave me a copy of the Hindi New Testament. It was the reason I came today."

His eyes flickered over her with subdued impatience, and he turned his head to look down the river. "Do not tell me, Miss Kendall. Let me guess. You set it down by the funeral pyre."

She swallowed, and her voice quavered. "Well, yes."

"This is turning into one of those long, well-remembered days. Wait here. I will see if I can retrieve it from the lion's den."

"Oh, thank you, Major Buckley."

He gave a deep bow at the waist. "Your servant, Miss Kendall." And he took the steps upward.

Coral waited for him, pacing. She was confident that he could take care of himself, but as the minutes crept by, her anxiety increased.

At last she saw him coming down the steps with her bag in hand. He seemed in a hurry.

"Any trouble, Major?"

He took her arm and propelled her quickly toward the boat. "Let us just say, I would prefer a more desirable location to continue our conversation."

12

Jace assisted her onto the boat and took up the oars, then began moving swiftly down the Hooghly. For a few minutes they were silent.

"Seward delivered your message. I believe you have something else to tell me about last night," said Jace.

"Last night?"

"In the garden."

Coral tried to ease her emotions by lifting her face toward the sky and shutting her eyes. She listened to the slap of the water against the sides of the boat.

"Is that the reason you came to Serampore?" she asked finally. "Because of last night?"

"Yes and no."

"But how did you know I was here?"

"Seward warned me you were coming at Peddington's invitation."

"Is *warned* the right word, Major?"

"To my mind, yes, Miss Kendall."

"It seems I have a number of guardians keeping track of my whereabouts."

"With your eagerness for adventure, you will need them. Now, what happened last night?"

As the river swept past and monkeys chattered in the trees, Coral felt his alert gaze studying her reaction.

"Will you promise to say nothing of this to my aunt?"

"I have no reason to inform Lady Margaret, but I need to know exactly what happened."

"Marianna is quite certain that she witnessed a clandestine meeting in the garden last night between my uncle and an Indian."

He was alert. "Did she see the Indian's face?"

"No. I caught a glimpse of him running away, but I noticed nothing distinctive except a yellow turban."

"Did your sister overhear anything?"

Coral tensed. "Yes. The words, 'An accident of one so great is not as easily arranged as the first. He has many friends even among the Hindus.' "

"Who said it?"

"The Indian. I could tell that Marianna was not exaggerating. She was quite upset. Later, Sir Hugo came to my room. He said that he had been in the garden with a servant. He called him Piroo."

"Piroo," he repeated thoughtfully.

"Yes, have you heard of him before?"

"No. But if your uncle volunteered his name, it is not likely to be helpful."

"Major? You do not think this means that my uncle was involved in someone's accident?"

"You mean, what must have appeared to be an accident."

Coral's stomach tensed, but she tried to remain calm. "Who could they have been talking about?"

"One must be careful about making accusations until there is proof of wrongdoing."

His answer was too mild to convince her that he meant it. He had been willing enough to share his suspicions with her in the past. Coral had been watching him too closely to not recognize the change in his mood.

"I wish you would not keep secrets from me, Major."

He looked at her with surprise.

"Speak your mind, please," she said. "Do not forget you nearly accused him of Gem's abduction when I was on the *Madras*. There is little you could say about him that is worse than that."

"It was not my intention to hurt you, only to warn."

"I understand. I would like to know what you think."

She listened without comment while he explained about the outpost at Jorhat, of Major Selwyn, and a suspicion that Sir Hugo might be involved.

"I would not mention this at all, except it may eventually have some consequence to Kingscote. I will speak with your father after I arrive at Jorhat. So, you see, there is another reason why you must be cautious about starting that orphanage. It could be just the excuse Sir Hugo needs to bring trouble down on your father."

Coral wanted to reject his analysis of her uncle and the school, but it was difficult to do so.

"It is all so confusing," she mused. "The outpost, the talk of mutiny, and now last night. I will admit that I do not trust my uncle. But I cannot believe he would deliberately harm someone."

"Are you thinking of Major Selwyn?"

Mention of the man's death came as a start. Coral had not been thinking of him.

"I do not know—is that what you think? That he was involved? Or the man with the turban?"

"I intend to find out. As for Sir Hugo's ability to harm anyone, you must know by now that I am rather cynical. I once told you that ambition and greed can quickly become devilish masters. I think your uncle has an appetite that is not easily satisfied. You must be extremely cautious. Say nothing of our conversation to anyone."

She nodded, for words would not come. What would Aunt Margaret do if she knew her husband was suspected of being involved in a mutiny against the British at Jorhat?

"I do not know why I am telling you all this. The less you know, the better. Can Marianna be trusted to keep quiet about what she heard last night?"

"Yes, I have already spoken to her about it. You need not feel badly about speaking like this, I have long suspected my uncle of plotting to own Kingscote."

"Have you told anyone about our discussion of Gem?"

"No."

"Considering all things, do not. It may ruin any opportunity that may come my way. Sir Hugo will be watching me."

Jace rowed in silence for a while as Coral watched him from beneath her hat.

"Somehow, Major, you do not remind me of a man interested in raising tea."

"No? I suppose you think I am too unsettled to do anything but captain a ship. Maybe you are right."

"Your father must think a great deal of you to go to such difficulty to get you back in the Company. No doubt he hopes that you will one day serve willingly."

He was quiet. "I owe the colonel for my education. He did more for me than anyone else could have. But one day I shall get back to what I believe in—the *Madras*, and Darjeeling."

Coral studied him and said nothing for a moment. "Five months aboard the Red Dragon was quite enough for me. I will not miss a topsy-turvy cabin if I never see one again."

"You should sail on the *Madras*; she is quite stable."

"If that is an invitation," Coral said with a laugh, "I must decline. Only my sister Kathleen would be willing to sail to London again so soon after our return to India. She is expected to marry Captain McKay, but her heart is set on working at the Silk House."

"How did a future silk heiress get matched with a mere Company captain?"

Coral detected a slight barb. She turned away and watched the trees on the embankment slip by. "It is a long story, Major. You will find it dull. You see, Captain McKay is our cousin on my father's side of the family in Aberdeen. Father can find no wrong in any man with Scottish blood, or a fighting spirit."

"Ah . . . but of course. A relation. That explains everything."

She cast him a glance. He was scanning the embankment. "And Boswell is related to Sir Hugo. That makes for a very happy, well-knit family."

Her face felt warm. She settled her skirts to show she no longer wished to discuss the matter.

Unexpectedly he laughed softly to himself. "Gavin married to a silk heiress."

Coral felt uncomfortable. "Do you, ah . . . know him?"

"Rather well, in fact."

His smile was disarming. She could not tell what he was thinking but was reluctant to press for more information, believing that it might prove embarrassing to Kathleen. She said quickly, "Oh, look!" and pointed to the bank of the river, trying to draw his attention away from her. "A flock of parakeets," her voice trailed off. "Are they not lovely?"

He looked, and studied the familiar sight with intensity, as though he had never seen them before.

"Enchanting," he said.

153

13

Gokul's mission to the bazaars of Calcutta had turned up information Jace wanted on the Moghul sword. While Gokul had already departed for Guwahati to discover what he could about Sir Hugo, Jace walked the cluttered streets of Calcutta amid the noisy throng and waited for his contact. Several of the hawkers spoke to him, willing to engage in bartering, but on this day Jace was not interested.

After a time, weary of waiting, he started back to the bungalow.

A beggar approached him for alms. When close he whispered, "O Great One, what you seek is no longer in Calcutta. But the answer to many questions awaits you in Burma!"

Later, all was dark and still when he neared the bungalow he had shared with Gokul. Jace drew his blade and, entering his room, searched until he was certain of being alone; then he sat on his bed where he could not be seen and lit a candle.

Who is the man whose accident can not be easily arranged? The maharaja?—or himself?

Roxbury had gone to the governor-general to have his

155

orders changed, but Jace did not believe that Roxbury truly wanted him as security guard at Guwahati. Did he have a convenient accident planned for the long safari north?

Jace could not concentrate, and finally he lifted his mattress and removed a small black book. An ancient trader on the caravan following the Old Silk Road through the Himalayas had given it to him when he escaped China. Jace had hid under the old merchant's bundles of blankets for days, coming out only at night when the old man shared the broth he boiled over the campfire.

The old one could not read and had come across the book after rummaging through the remains of water-logged goods left on the wharf at Pearl River. A ship from England had been captured and the cargo pirated. After the booty had been stripped of its precious contents, a second group of looters had taken everything else of value, leaving the litter for the beggars to rummage through. The old one had searched and found the book.

The pages were warped in places, and the name of its original owner, written in ink, was blotched by salt water. But some of the pages of the New Testament were readable. The gospel of John, parts of the book of Acts, Romans and the other letters of Paul. Jace had read the words many times as a boy traveling with Gokul. Life had been rough and difficult. Gokul had been acquainted with more thieves than munshis. After the battle in the village between the English and the local Muslim ruler, Jace had ceased to read it. The translation had been authorized by King James of England, and that much alone had turned him against further reading.

He could smile now over his ignorance. He had learned a great deal since the colonel had taken him in and sent him to London. There, Jace had completed his education at the East India Company's Military College at Addiscombe. He had seen many fine King James Bibles, but he had always kept the worn edition the trader had given to him on the Old Silk Road.

The next morning Jace set about making sure the arrangements for the journey to the northern frontier were in order. Two days later, the security troop he now commanded waited for him on the parade ground, standing at attention. Some distance away, Sir Hugo, the governor-general's new resident, waited with his civilian party in two gharis. Seward and a half-dozen private Indian orderlies guarded the baggage train.

Jace caught a glimpse of Coral Kendall and her two sisters in the second ghari, just behind Sir Hugo and Doctor Boswell. Jace looked away to see the colonel riding to meet him, the image of British military at its best.

Before meeting his father, Jace rode up to the troop. At once he saw that the native officer he had personally requested from the colonel, an Indian soldier whom Jace trusted with his life, had been replaced. A stranger stood at attention, his face a military mask. *No*, Jace thought. *He is not a stranger—it is that wretched Sanjay from the outpost at Jorhat.* The officer who had been in Roxbury's office!

His surprise rushed to a feeling of anger. Who had dared to replace Nadir?

For a native Indian to become a high-ranking officer in the Bengal army took many years of proven faithfulness to the British officers. One hardly ever saw a young native officer, least of all a rissaldar-major! Yet Sanjay could only be in his early thirties.

The clop of horse's hoofs drew his attention away from Sanjay. The colonel rode up to him, and Jace turned the reins of his horse to face him, saluting, his slate-blue eyes rock hard.

The colonel responded. "At ease, Major."

"I do not understand," Jace gritted. "I want Sanjay removed. Where is Nadir?"

The colonel sat rigid. "Nadir took ill last night. Severe chest pains. It is not certain if he will live. A number of other sowars are down with dysentery. Yes, I know. Very convenient. But the orders to move out this morning stand."

"Are you certain Nadir is ill? Roxbury must be behind this. I told you what the Kendall daughter overheard at Barrackpore."

"The matter is being looked into. I called on Nadir this morning. There is no question that he is ill."

Jace gripped the reins in his gloved hand.

"Colonel, I cannot be expected to lead civilians across the northern frontier with men whose loyalty is in question. Are you certain of Sanjay?"

The colonel's eyes flickered, and he retorted, "I am certain of nothing but orders from the brigadier-general himself."

"Sir! I am responsible for three women!"

The colonel's jaw set like an iron trap. He breathed between his teeth, "You have your orders, Major. I will be in touch at Guwahati. Proceed as scheduled!"

Jace crisply saluted. He turned from his father to face the troop. His eyes scanned them: their black shakos were smartly in place, their uniforms at their best, their swords gleaming. How many of them had kissed the sword of loyal oath to the British? Jace shouted brusquely for the native officer to come forth. Nadir's replacement, Rissaldar-Major Sanjay, saluted Jace precisely.

"Major-bahadur!"

Jace studied him with a cool challenge before slowly returning the salute.

"Ram, ram sidar, Rissaldar-sahib." Jace clipped the

traditional greeting of honor with a cool voice. "Your report!"

The dark eyes were muted in the bronzed face. "Huzoor, Major Buckley, sahib! The ammunition in reserve is in the baggage train with rations and medical supplies. Resident Roxbury and the other civilians wait with the civilian gharis. All is ready."

"Fall in!"

Sanjay saluted and marched to his position.

Jace shouted, "Company! Form! Right! Right wheel, quick march!"

14

The horizon was awash with a flaming sunset. Coral sat by the ghari window, masking her growing feeling of illness. In her nostrils was the all-too-familiar smell of sunbaked soil. Her skin, too, felt clogged with dust particles, and damp tendrils of her hair stuck to the back of her neck.

Was it possible that they had left Calcutta only days earlier? The long days and even longer nights crept onward like some damaged three-wheel trap led by an uncooperative mule. It would take *two months* to get home! And the more difficult part of the journey was still ahead when they entered the jungle.

Outside the window she could see the mounted sowars, with Seward riding just behind and to the side of their ghari, his tricorn in contrast to the dusty black shakos of the native cavalry. Riding some distance ahead to alleviate the dust, Coral could just catch sight of the standard-bearer, followed by six sowars, then Major Buckley. Altogether, Coral counted some twenty men riding in pairs guarding the civilians, and behind the small column, a half-dozen well-armed men hardened by travel rode to protect the military baggage train carrying food, supplies, and ammunition for the troop.

Despite her fatigue, the excitement of the journey home to Kingscote made the discomfort bearable, and she had long since failed to hear the complaints of Kathleen, who spoke endlessly of the ordeal ahead of them. Marianna appeared detached. Coral knew that her little sister had not forgotten the clandestine meeting that she had stumbled upon between Hugo and the Indian in the yellow turban. Marianna whispered to her on several occasions that she was certain Uncle *knew* that it had been she, and not Coral, who had seen him in the alleyway.

Coral was not certain what her uncle thought. For the present, she felt relief that he appeared to have forgotten the incident.

"I do not know what could possibly be worse than spending all day in this miserable coach breathing dust," groaned Kathleen. "I dare say, my skin is positively ruined. I shall never get clean again!"

"Once we arrive at Plassey, we will be able to rest a few days at the garrison," Coral reminded them, trying to bring cheer. "There may even be a ball. You will be able to see Captain McKay."

Kathleen's lips turned at the mention of Cousin Gavin, and it was not clear what she thought of seeing him after three years. Marianna, however, appeared to have something more dreadful on her mind. Coral saw her shiver in spite of the perspiration on her forehead, and she plucked at her handkerchief.

"I prefer dust to the journey we must take upriver," Marianna said. "Do you know what?" She leaned toward them, trying to keep her balance. "I overheard Seward say the crocodiles are *over twelve feet long!*"

"Oh, look at the sunset," said Coral, changing the subject to distract them. Her sisters looked westward where the twilight held the sky with shades of violet.

Crocodiles, shuddered Coral. She would not mention that tiger country also awaited them.

Ahead the dak-bungalow came into view. There would be a place to rest for the night, and the kansamah would prepare what he had available to serve the evening guests. At the two previous dak-bungalows they had stayed at since leaving Calcutta, chopped meat was served with *chuppati*, an Indian unleavened bread. At the moment, feeling nauseous and with her head throbbing, the only thing she could think of was a cup of hot, steaming tea.

The previous year's monsoon had damaged the road in places, and they bumped along for several minutes, gripping the sides of their seats. The vehicle swayed precariously, followed by a well-rehearsed complaint from the lips of the Indian driver seated on the front box. Coral's stomach did a flip. The ghari lurched to the side and off the road, throwing her against the door. Her head crashed with a sickening thud. Dazed, she became aware of the weight of Marianna and Kathleen keeping her pressed against the side of the vehicle. Then she heard voices and shouts.

Coral felt Kathleen trying to pull her to a sitting position. "Coral!"

The ghari rocked as someone climbed onto it and flung open the door. Seward's rugged frame leaned in, looking down at them. "Ye be unhurt, lassies?"

"I don't know. Coral struck her head," said Kathleen.

"I'm . . . not hurt," Coral tried to mumble, and felt the weight of her sisters pulled from her as they were lifted out of the ghari. Coral tried to sit up, and Seward leaned in and lifted her out, then gently lowered her to the dusty road. For a moment she thought her legs would go out from under her.

Jace rode up. "Get Boswell," he commanded a sowar.

"I am not hurt," Coral said, wishing to avoid the fuss, but her brain spun dizzily.

"The doctor be coming now, Sir Hugo with him," said Seward.

Coral, still holding to Seward's arm, turned her head to see the massive figure of her uncle step down from the other ghari. "Anyone injured?" he called.

"Only a bad bump, Sir Roxbury," shouted Seward.

At the same instant, Ethan stepped out of the ghari behind Hugo, medical bag in hand. The expression on his face testified to his displeasure, and his mouth creased tightly when his eyes swerved toward Jace.

"Major!" came the condescending voice. "Your driver is to blame for this. I offered a warning of the hazards of this so-called *road* when we stopped only an hour ago."

Coral glanced at Jace, who remained mounted, and she guessed what his cool response might be. Yet his outward restraint remained impeccable. Could there possibly be two men inside that now dusty uniform?

Ethan hurried forward, coming between her and Seward.

"Dear, you might have broken a bone!"

Coral ducked her head to hide her embarrassment. She wished Ethan would not publicly use words of endearment, when she had not yet given him that privilege. She said with a rush, "I am quite all right, Ethan. And the ghari-wallah handled the mishap quite well."

"I have my doubts of that."

The frustrated driver was pointing to the road in self-defense. "Mercifully all is well, sahib. There is no damage. My apology, miss-sahiba."

Ethan interrupted. "Your apology is not enough. Miss Kendall might have been seriously injured." He turned toward Jace. "Well, Major? You do agree that something must be done about your driver?"

164

"Please, it is no one's fault," said Coral. "The road is terrible. It could have happened to your own ghari."

"Hardly," said Ethan.

"The doctor is right," said Jace.

Surprised, Coral looked at him. She had not expected him to agree so easily with Ethan. He gestured to the driver to go back to the baggage train.

"For the rest of the trip you will help the kansamah." Jace turned toward one of his sowars. "Lal! I am holding you responsible to see that the Kendall daughters arrive safely to Manali."

Manali! Coral turned in Jace's direction. They were to travel to Plassey. Manali was located southeast in the area of the Ganges Delta, and more than two day's journey out of their path! Jace knew that! But he did not respond to her questioning look.

Ethan had produced a clean handkerchief to blot the small cut on Coral's temple, while Seward and several sowars, with a heave, set the vehicle back on the road.

The aftermath of the ghari incident was setting in, and she no longer cared about anything but getting off by herself.

"Do come sit down in the carriage while I treat that cut," said Ethan.

As Ethan took her arm and turned her in the direction of the ghari, she saw Rissaldar-Major Sanjay leave Uncle Hugo, who had not yet walked up. The officer rode toward Jace and saluted.

"A rider has come from Plassey, Major-sahib. There's trouble. He awaits to speak to you."

The name Plassey arrested Coral's attention, and brought her confused thinking back to why Jace had said that they must backtrack to Manali. She followed the direction that the rissaldar indicated. Near the outer rim of the secondary jungle—terrain once cleared but now marked with dense undergrowth—a troop horse, sweating and breathing hard, waited, bearing a British soldier.

Jace rode to meet him, and Coral saw the young soldier salute and hand him a letter.

Kathleen must have wondered about the trouble at Plassey where Captain Gavin McKay was stationed, for she walked to her uncle, and Coral heard her asking about the reason for their detour to Manali.

Coral heard no more, for Ethan interrupted and steered her in the direction of the ghari. "You are holding up heroically, I must say."

"Heroic?" Coral gave a small laugh. "I feel anything but that."

Ethan's face was hard. "I find the major's behavior on this journey nothing less than arrogant. The sleeping quarters in the inns, not to mention the victuals, have been dreadful. Flies, heat, the smell; this is a most unhealthy locale we must submit ourselves to, and the major seems to take a special delight in my discomfort."

Coral winced from the sting of the ointment. She could not help feeling sympathetic toward Ethan. Although a physician, and rigorous, he was not accustomed to India. She agreed, however, that Jace did seem to be hardened against showing any consideration toward him.

"Our stay at Manali shall prove welcome," he was saying.

"Then you know about Manali?" she asked quickly.

"Uncle intends for us to stay a few days at the residence of an acquaintance. The food and rest at Manali will do you good."

For a reason she could not explain, Coral found that the mention of her uncle's *acquaintance* brought her thoughts darting back to the night in the garden at Barrackpore.

"This acquaintance of Uncle's," she repeated. "Is he an Englishman?"

His gray eyes came to hers, and for a moment she felt their scrutiny.

"Quite. I believe his name is Harrington. Why do you ask?"

For a brief moment she considered telling him everything. "I wondered if I had met him during our stay in Calcutta."

"Hugo says the man retired from the Company, so you might have."

"Why does Uncle wish to go to Manali? A delay is ill advised at this time. We are in the best season for travel."

"Uncle suggested Manali only after the major requested a short delay."

"The major requested it!" she said, surprised.

"Yes, there seems to be some risk if we journey now. I thought you knew," he said. "There was fighting near Plassey."

"Fighting, here! With Burma?"

"No. I believe they were called *Maharattas*."

Coral remembered Kathleen's letter from Captain McKay warning of trouble. Coral had only a vague idea of who the Maharattas were. She knew only that the East India Company had been at war with the strong warriorlike kingdom for years.

"The major received a message last night from Captain McKay," said Ethan. "McKay informed him that a patrol from the garrison at Plassey was ambushed. None were left alive, I am told. I dare say, the ambush is the reason for the soldier speaking with the major now."

Coral's thoughts were suddenly averted. She was not thinking of Plassey, but musing over the attack on the military outpost at Jorhat near Kingscote, where Jace's friend Major Selwyn had been assassinated. "We are too far from the northern frontier to have trouble with Burma," she said. "This skirmish at Plassey would have nothing to do with the royal family at Guwahati."

"Have you met the maharaja that Uncle will represent for the Company?" he asked.

"No, that is—" she stopped.

"Kingscote is near Guwahati, is it not?"

"Yes, fairly close, but I have never met the royal family."

She said no more, unexpectedly remembering a long-forgotten incident that had occurred years earlier when she had visited Guwahati.

Her heart thudded. *No, it could not be true*, she thought.

"Ah! Seward is returning from the inn. Perhaps he was able to get you a room," Ethan said. He had turned from the ghari door to look out across the dusty road toward the dak-bungalow. Coral was absorbed in her thoughts. *I must talk to Jace about Guwahati!*

15

The dak-bungalow had extensive stables for travelers, and tonight they were not only filled with packhorses and mules but also with merchants and their coolies camping outdoors. Small fires hovered in the darkness, reminding Coral of swaying yellow ghosts. The smell of food mingled with woodsmoke.

The common room was sparsely furnished with long, low wooden tables, benches, and a few chairs made of worn cane. She was hoping to speak with the major alone. Although she knew that the sowars would remain with the horses and supplies, and sleep outdoors, she expected Jace to appear in the common room for supper.

The thought of food turned Coral's stomach queasy. Despite the open windows, the room reeked with the smell of unwashed bodies. Coral felt sympathy for an unhappy English family huddled in one corner. The haggard mother was trying to change her baby, wetting a cloth from a canteen to wash him.

"This is horrible, Sissy, I want to go home," whispered Marianna, holding her handkerchief to her nose.

Kathleen leaned toward her with a fierce little smile.

169

"You and Coral should have paid heed to me and stayed at Roxbury House!"

"Everyone is in the same situation as we are," said Coral. "How would you like a crying baby to attend? Think of all the underclothes you would need to wash!"

"Which reminds me," whispered Kathleen, wrinkling her nose. "I do hope the washroom has something to dry my hands on this time instead of my petticoat. I don't want to go alone. Are you two coming with me or not?"

Marianna nodded, looking dolefully about, but Coral's attention had been diverted. She looked across the packed room to where the split-cane curtain opened onto the stone courtyard, and saw the major.

———

Jace had entered through the courtyard with his thoughts on Captain McKay and the skirmish near Plassey. In his sabretache was the letter that had just been delivered to him by the trooper. Jace had been ordered by the commander at Plassey to join forces with McKay and track down the marauders.

The attack on Plassey compounded matters for Jace. The land routes north were presently unsafe for civilian travel. Since Roxbury had an acquaintance in Manali named Harrington, who owned and operated a large indigo plantation, he had assured Jace that he and his nieces would be well taken care of until the trek to the northern frontier was advisable.

Jace did not like the turn of events. Manali was two days out of their route. If Roxbury and his nieces must journey so far, then why not return to Calcutta? Roxbury, however, had business with Harrington and assured him the plantation was a pleasant place for Coral to recuperate. Ethan had agreed.

Jace was looking for Seward as he entered the common room through the courtyard. He had been correct in warning Coral against the journey. The incident near Plassey proved it—not that the Kendall daughter would admit it. Unruffled as ever, as an ivory blossom survives the relentless pounding of the wind, she would insist that she was "doing well enough, thank you," and nothing would alter her decision to reach Kingscote and build the school. Children. A hundred of them needed her—no, they needed her Shepherd, she said. Jace found her dedication both admirable and exasperating. She would kill herself trying to accomplish her goal.

He saw her seated on a bench across the packed room, talking to Seward. She was the outer expression of all that he had miscalculated her to be upon seeing her in the Calcutta bazaar, wearing a trail of white ribbons and silk, and smelling, he supposed, like a French perfumery. The Kendall daughter had proven to be more than mere beauty under her frail facade, but now the outer shell appeared to be in danger of shattering. She was pale and worn, her bonnet crumpled in her lap, her curls in disarray, and her expensive frock smudged with dust. The cut near her brow on the otherwise lovely face only convinced him that she was a dove stalked by a lean, hungry tiger—one that he was not in a position to stop. Under the present circumstances, he could do nothing but warn her. His lack of authority annoyed him.

Jace carefully guarded his expression as he stood in dusty black and silver, watching her. He accepted a tin of water from the barefoot boy-servant. She saw him, and he guessed that she wanted to converse. He did not wish to engage her at the moment. She would press him about the detour to Manali, and he had no answer yet. He would be riding out later that night with the 17th, leaving her and the others to be guarded by Seward and several sowars.

Jace felt restrained by military discipline to mask the annoyance he felt churning inside. If he could shed the uniform of Major Buckley to retrieve the tunic that served him on the deck of the *Madras*, he would tell her that she was too frail to be on this journey.

He handed the tin back to the boy and, looking away from Coral to Seward, gestured with his head that he should join him outdoors.

Seward looked down at Coral. "Wait here, lass. I'll be but a minute."

Coral only half heard Seward's remark as he left her side. She watched Jace leave the room and Seward follow after him by way of the split-cane curtain that led onto the court. They disappeared into the evening shadows.

The major's lack of response nettled Coral. At times his arrogance affronted her; at times she felt sympathetic toward him because of the insensitivity he had endured from others as a child. She must be cautious of being too sympathetic. She remembered a tiger cub that she and her brother Michael had supposedly rescued when they were children. Coral had felt sorry for the cub and had brought it home to the back porch of the large kitchen—until a roar from the mother had sent her father and half a dozen workers outside to turn the cub loose. The analogy between the cub and Jace Buckley might not be the same, she thought dryly, but nevertheless steeled her sympathetic inclinations from getting out of hand toward the major. *Beneath that uniform of respect and restraint there lives a man quite full of himself,* she thought. One who could not wait to retrieve his golden monkey, his Indian friend Gokul, and a clipper ship. A vessel that, like its owner, was being held unwillingly at harbor, unable to sail for ports unknown.

There were other times when she felt that beneath his outward confidence there lived a young man who was not at all sure of himself, one who was more afraid of expressing feelings, and becoming vulnerable, than he was of any outward danger. He could almost appear sensitive and caring—how else could she explain his willingness to try to locate Gem? But she had to admit that most of the time he appeared anything but that.

No matter. Wishing to ignore her or not, she would find some way to talk to him tonight, for it was essential to do so.

Aware that Ethan had joined her, she turned to him, thankfully accepting the hot cup of tea that he had brought her. He sat down beside her, and she sighed, enjoying her tea. The Hindi New Testament was beside her, and he picked it up.

"Hugo was disturbed that I brought you to William Carey's mission station."

Coral already knew as much. Thankfully, in the rush to leave Calcutta, and the weeks of hard journey, her uncle had not found time to speak to her.

Ethan frowned to himself, staring at the small book. "There is much to say about a man of William Carey's unselfish devotion."

Surprised, and even impressed by his admission, she smiled. "I am pleased you changed your mind about him."

His eyes came to hers, searching, eager to respond to the noticeable change in her voice. "Your own devotion is equally unselfish. Say nothing to Uncle, but I think your idea of a mission school for the children is noble. I shall do what I can to help you."

There was a slight pause in which her breath stopped. She stared at him, overwhelmed. "Ethan, do you mean that?"

"I do." He thumbed through the New Testament. "I, of course, am only a beginner of the language. At Kingscote I hope you will help me to learn it better. Once your school is constructed, there will also be opportunity to medically assist the children you are so concerned about."

"Ethan! How marvelous of you to think of it! I confess I've thought about your skills and what they could do. Between my school and your practice, we could do so much for the children."

He handed the Testament back to her, and when he looked at her, she read the warmth in the gray eyes. "You are right. We could do so very much together. Hugo, however, is very much set against missionary work in India, as you know. We must handle the entire matter with wisdom."

Seward strode up, ignoring Ethan. "The major's spoken to the headman. We be settin' up a shamianah for you and your sisters."

Coral was delighted. A large tent. This one, Seward told them, would have carpet and mats to sleep on, and there would be complete privacy.

Outside the shamianah, Coral talked with Seward alone while her sisters were inside delighting over the spaciousness and comfort of the tent. After two weeks of arduous outdoor travel, it did indeed seem luxurious.

"The major be ridin' out tonight," he told her quietly. "Ye'll stay at Manali until it be safe for civilian travel."

"Then the major is riding to Plassey?"

"Nay, he be meetin' Captain McKay on the way. There be word of more fighting on the road north, and they must be careful."

A chill of uncertainty enveloped her, fear of being alone. How foolish! She was not abandoned. Was not the Lord to be her vision and strength? And her father had sent Seward to escort them safely home. Yet knowing this did not remove the nagging feeling of doubt. How long would Jace be gone, leaving them at Manali?

"Does Sir Hugo know about the fighting?"

His expression darkened. "Aye," he grunted, "he does. And that be what bothers me."

She glanced at the shamianah to make sure her sisters were not listening. "You do not think he was involved!" The idea seemed incredulous.

"Pardon me sayin' so, lass, but I not be knowin' what to think of your uncle."

"Have you said anything to the major?"

He smiled. "Ye don't need to worry about him. The lad be a born cynic. He don't trust nobody. 'Twas Sir Hugo's idea to spend time in Manali while the major is gone, and that's what vexes me. Not that there's proof of anythin' going on. And Manali seems a logical choice for you and your sisters."

Coral's alarm grew. "Seward, must the major go?"

"He has his orders, lass, and he cannot ignore them. I be not likin' matters meself, but he'll join us at Manali when he can."

If there is fighting on the road north it might mean an indefinite delay, thought Coral. If they did not travel soon, the weather would turn on them, and it would become miserably hot.

"The major wouldn't like it if he knew I'd troubled you. It's rest you be needing. And the major be kind enough to have seen you get the shamianah. Took some bickering, it did."

"It is important I speak to him before he rides out tonight. Can you send him a message to come here?"

"Aye, I'll tell him."

What is delaying Seward? The lantern had been extinguished to discourage insects, and Coral heard the soft breathing of Kathleen and Marianna. She lay on the edge of the straw sleeping-mat wondering if she could slip out of the tent without awaking them. She was all but fully dressed except for her outer garment and shoes. Suddenly in the distance she heard the rise and fall of voices. She guessed the hour to be some time after ten. If she was to speak to Jace before he left, it must be now. She sat up and edged herself away from the straw mat.

Shafts of pale moonlight fell across the tent floor, and Coral slipped on her shoes and found her cloak on the cane stool. Her sisters' steady, deep breathing continued without interruption. She moved quietly to the edge of the shamianah, pushed back the veil, and stepped out.

The night was without a breath of wind and the black sky was sprinkled with white gems. She stood without moving, not expecting Seward to be nearby, but finding it necessary to make sure.

"Seward?" she whispered hopefully, and waited, then: "Seward!"

Silence greeted her in the stillness. A rustle of wind swept along the tops of dry elephant grass near the secondary jungle.

Lifting her hood up over her hair, she moved softly into the shadows of the bordering trees, hurrying in the direction of the camp where the troop under Jace's command was located for the night. It could be no more than four to five minutes away from the dak-bungalow. There was always the possibility of snakes, but other than that, she wasn't likely to run into trouble.

The path leading along the edge of the secondary jungle became an arcade of secretive shadows, with branches from the trees interlocking into moving silhouettes as a wind came up and played among them. Coral hurried along, instinctively casting a glance over her shoulder and keeping to the shadows, her slippers making no sound in the dust.

Ahead, beyond the supply wagons, the clearing was deserted. Jace's troop had already pulled out! She stood motionless among the shadows of the trees. And Seward? Where was he?

Several sowars were gathered near a fire. A myriad of night insects buzzed about the firelight. The men's voices were low, the words indistinct, and they came to her ears along with the odor of smoke.

Two of the sowars were seated around the fire gambling. Their backs were toward her, while the other stood watching the road in the direction of Plassey. With a throb of disappointment, Coral understood that she had been too late. Jace had left. She pushed aside her disillusionment. After all, his first responsibility was to obey military orders, and he did not need to explain them to her. He had sent Seward to tell her he was leaving; he had even managed to get them a shamianah. What more did she expect?

And yet . . . he must have known that she wanted to speak to him. Surely Seward had time to bring Jace her request before he rode out.

A vague uneasiness stirred within. She hesitated to announce her presence to the sowars and began to retrace her steps without a sound. Perhaps Seward was back at the tent by now. Perhaps he had been there all along, weary after the long day's journey, and had dozed off. And her lantern had been out; perhaps he had decided not to awaken her.

The night hovered with stillness. She could hear the unwelcome sound of someone approaching the wagon from the path behind her. Had Kathleen or Marianna found her gone and awakened Seward?

But she heard the footsteps hesitate in the shadows, then approach haltingly. Seward would not approach with such caution. His tread was purposeful, and he would be bold enough to be calling out for her whereabouts with a booming voice.

Coral's heart skipped a beat and she shrank backwards into the shadows, into the stillness of the shrubs and overhanging branches, less alarmed over the possibility of snakes than with being discovered by the owner of those cautious footsteps. . . . Marianna? No, never her. Kathleen perhaps . . . no, Kathleen, too, would be calling out. She caught her breath. *Two* people were coming, one from behind her, the other from the direction of the wagon.

A man emerged from behind the supply wagon and walked up to the fire. He said something, and the two gamblers were swiftly on their feet, then hurried off, leaving the man standing by the fire. As he turned to glance in the direction where she had stood only moments before, Coral saw his harsh face in the dancing firelight. It was Rissaldar-Major Sanjay! What was Jace's second in command doing here, when the 17th had ridden toward Plassey?

The footsteps that had stopped on the path, coming from the direction of the dak-bungalow, were now approaching. From the wagon, Rissaldar Sanjay walked forward, and waited.

Through the screen of the drooping branches, the moonlight fell upon the trodden path, and a moment later Coral was not surprised to see Sir Hugo. But the two men spoke in a pitch that was difficult for her to grasp.

" . . . Plassey . . . severed . . ."

" . . . the colonel's son?"

The wind rattled the dry leaves of the overhanging

branches. Coral took a tiny step forward, straining to hear. Sir Hugo's low voice was sharp, questioning. The rissaldar's tone was muffled, then came in sharp contrast to the strained silence.

"I am certain!"

Again Sir Hugo's words were mere sounds.

She stiffened. From behind her there came a whisper of movement like a viper slithering through the dried grasses. A quiver ran up her back. *Lord, no, please!*

16

Caught between Sir Hugo and Rissaldar Sanjay on the path, and the movement in the thick darkness behind her, Coral stood riveted in the trees.

Sir Hugo and Sanjay were still talking, but their voices lost all meaning as her mind focused on the danger of the reptile in the dry grass.

A moment later their voices fell silent as their footsteps faded into the dusty night. Stillness wrapped about her. Slowly the moments passed. Had she imagined it?

She inched forward in the direction of the path, then in a moment of blind fear she panicked and bolted toward the clearing. Her slipper gave way to a small avalanche of leaves on the embankment. A ruthless hand latched hold of her dark hood, catching her hair in a solid grip. Coral winced as she slid backwards, down the small incline into dry elephant grass. She landed hard, her breath knocked from her. She stared with wide, frightened eyes into the face of Jace, his pistol pointed at her head.

He sucked in his breath sharply and quickly released his grip on her hood, drawing his arm away. He moved back and neither of them made a sound.

Then his breath released in a rush of words. "What are you doing here! I could have struck you with my gun before I—" he stopped and shoved the pistol inside his jacket. He lifted her gently to a sitting position. "Coral, I am extremely sorry."

His voice was suddenly apologetic, and for an indulgent moment she gave in to the temptation to enjoy his self-incrimination.

"Are you hurt?"

"Yes . . . I mean, I don't know." Dazed, she stared at him in confusion. "What are *you* doing here? You are supposed to have ridden out!"

That did not seem to bother him at all.

"You haven't answered my question. I left you in the tent, and I told Seward to keep you out of trouble. And just where *is* Seward?"

"I thought he was with you."

He looked at her, alert. "I have not seen him since supper."

"I spoke with him at the shamianah when he brought us back. He explained about Plassey Junction. He went to tell you that I wished to speak to you before you left. You have not seen him?"

There was a pause. "No. I wanted to give the impression that I had ridden off with the troop. But I had no time to tell Seward. He may have—"

"Impression, but why—" She stopped short, recalling what they had just overheard between Sir Hugo and Rissaldar Sanjay. Her eyes came to his, questioning. "You suspected trouble earlier?" she whispered.

"Yes," he admitted reluctantly.

"Then you knew they were going to meet on the path?"

"My rissaldar's loyalties were in question even before leaving Calcutta."

Coral tried to digest what this could mean but still felt dizzy from her tumble. "You heard what was said a minute ago? What does it mean?"

"The fighting near Plassey has something to do with the northern frontier. I may know more after I meet with Captain McKay in the morning."

"Then you are riding to meet him now?"

"Yes. Somehow it all ties together—Plassey and the outpost at Jorhat. Here, let me help you up. You are certain you are not hurt?"

She was tender where stones had gouged her back, but she continued to sit there, her brain swirling.

"Can you walk?"

"Yes."

He glanced toward the path. "My guess is that Seward learned about the meeting. He would have ridden to warn me."

"Then he is hoping to catch up with your troop, thinking you are with them. When he discovers you are not there . . ."

"He will come back." He drew in another breath, and she guessed that he was putting a clamp on his emotions. "I sent a galloper back to Calcutta to report to the colonel."

"It appears from the meeting," she whispered, "that it is you who may face trouble at Plassey."

"Yes," he said thoughtfully, and again glanced toward the clearing. "I could almost believe . . ."

She waited. "Yes?"

He did not reply but lifted her to her feet. "Are you certain you are not hurt?"

"Perhaps you should not ride to meet Captain McKay."

"I must. My men are riding in that direction now. Let me carry you back."

"That will not be necessary," she said quickly. "Anyway, you must not be seen."

"Do not worry about me. You will be leaving for Manali in the morning. Seward should be back by then."

"Oh," Coral said, lifting her foot, "I lost my slipper."

"Here. Sit on this rock."

Coral sat there in silence, still shaken, while he searched in the brush for her slipper. She watched him in the moonlight, his dusty black and silver uniform blending into the shadows.

"Who did you think I was?" she asked.

"A guard for the rissaldar. I thought he saw me take cover here and was on his way to report."

It must have been several minutes before he returned with slipper in hand. The familiar, crooked smile was back, a smile she found disconcerting. He shook out the dirt with elaborate fanfare and wiped the slipper clean, then blew on the silver buckle, polishing it with his sleeve. "Permit me." He stooped before her.

She hesitated, then extended her foot, watching the moonlight fall on his dark head as he replaced her slipper. She stood, somewhat shakily, and he steadied her. She looked up at him to find his mood had swiftly altered. He wore a slight frown. "What were you doing here?"

"You asked me that already. I told you. I was looking for you."

He folded his arms. "Why?"

She raised her chin. "I wanted to speak to you about Gem, but when I neared the camp I realized your troop had already ridden out except for a few guards. I was going to return when I heard someone coming. I do not know why, but I felt compelled to hide."

His voice was cautious. "What about Gem?"

Coral drew in a breath. "It was something that Ethan

said this evening. He asked me if I had met the royal family at Guwahati. I told him no." She stopped.

"And?"

"But then something I had long forgotten came to mind. I did go to Guwahati with my father once when I was girl." She searched his face. "You once told me that Rajiv's uncle was a raja. But you did not say from which province."

He did not speak, and Coral breathed, "Is it Guwahati?"

Still he made no movement and only looked down at her in the pale moonlight.

Coral swallowed. "I was twelve when I visited the city with my father. There was a religious celebration going on, and I remember seeing the maharaja riding an elephant."

"Yes?" he said quietly.

"He had the members of his family with him at the time. There were two boys, perhaps sixteen years old— no more than that. Thinking back to what they looked like, I could almost insist that one of them was Rajiv."

He stood very still, and the moment seemed to stretch out.

"Tell me the truth," she whispered. "Was Rajiv the maharaja's nephew?"

His voice was quiet but even. "I warned you that you would get hurt when you took the baby. You insisted on keeping him. The fact is, the maharaja has two nephews—Rajiv, and a younger brother named Sunil. Sunil is ruthless."

Suddenly she wished she had not asked. "Somehow I always hoped what you said about the maharaja was a mistake. And after Gem's abduction, I told myself that if he did exist, he ruled far from Kingscote. But Guwahati, then it is true—Gem does have royal blood."

"Yes. But the raja does not have Gem. Coral, I do not even know if the child is alive. You must not think because I said I would help that I believe he is. Do not allow yourself to—"

"Hope?" she asked.

He said flatly, "Our hopes are often built without foundation."

Meaning that mine are. Coral felt numb. Gem, was he truly the great-nephew of the maharaja?

"I do not understand about Rajiv," she said. "What was he doing masquerading as a peasant? He told my father he came from Rajasthan."

"Rajiv was banished by the family when he broke caste and married Jemani. I do not know how he met her, or who she was. I am inclined to think she was only a girl he met and fell in love with. Rajiv was that way. He was nothing like his brother, Sunil."

"Then you think the maharaja will know where Gem is?"

"It is my guess that he will know. But I can promise you nothing, Coral."

"Yet, you will try, Jace?"

His eyes fell momentarily upon her face. "I made you a promise. I intend to keep it. I know the raja and I have something important to return to him. In exchange, I expect to be favored with the information I want. But I cannot guarantee it will be joyous—even if he is alive."

"What do you mean? Why should I not be happy?"

He turned. "Let's go back, Coral."

She let out a breath, stilling the trembling in her body with effort. He was deliberately avoiding explanation. "You are keeping something from me."

"No. I have no facts. Can we forget it? I simply would hate to disappoint you. That is all."

She did not answer him, and he said softly, "When

you arrive at Manali, make use of the opportunity to rest. There is a long journey ahead."

"And you? You heard what the rissaldar said to Sir Hugo."

"I am always careful. Why do you think I am still alive?" he asked lightly.

"The Lord has something to do with that."

"Agreed. I also do not fall into traps easily."

"No, I do not suppose you would."

"It is part of my ignoble character."

"It is your nature not to trust yourself to anyone."

"A profound deduction, Miss Kendall. Shall we go?"

"I will find my way back safely enough."

"Sorry. But it is also *your* nature to fall into one grave difficulty after another. Come, I will escort you."

In the shadowy premises near the tent, he paused to let her go on by herself.

"Where will you go now?" she whispered.

"To find Seward. I want him with you when you and your sisters ride to Manali."

She watched him until his silhouette disappeared into the darkened trees.

17

Manali

Sir Hugo's acquaintance was indeed English. Mr. Harrington turned out to be the owner of several large and productive indigo plantations, the smaller of which happened to be the one in Manali. When they arrived at the residence, they found a miniature estate, white with a blue roof, sitting back in the jungle.

Harrington himself was an unlikely candidate to manage his own indigo plantation at Manali, and looked anything but a farmer. His skin was the pallor of bee's wax; his pale eyes, almost a pinkish tone, reminded Coral of a lashless rabbit. He could not endure the bright sunlight nor the heat of the hot season, he had explained; therefore, he managed his Indian servants from a huge desk in the front parlor overlooking green rice fields and pools of water. He had one particular Indian servant whom he trusted to handle his important affairs, a man by the name of Zameen.

Upon seeing Zameen, Coral visibly relaxed. Her uneasiness over the possibility that he could be the Indian in the yellow turban proved unwarranted. Zameen was five feet tall, with a broad brown face that bore scars from smallpox. A glance at Marianna revealed that her sister's fears were also alleviated, and for the first time since their arrival at Manali she offered a smile. Perhaps their stay, thought Coral, would not be so terrible after all, especially since they were all given private rooms. Her own adjoined Kathleen's, and had wide double doors that opened onto the front court. In the distance she could see the rice fields, hemp, and indigo.

On the morning after their arrival, Coral watched the white-clad Indian workers flitting about their work, and the quiet plantation life brought brief reminiscences of being home on Kingscote. The memory sent Coral's prayers heavenward, upholding her mother.

"For I know the thoughts that I think toward you, saith the LORD, thoughts of peace, and not of evil, to give you an expected end." Coral's favorite verse emerged from the recesses of her memory, bright and vivid, like stars appearing after the wind blew away the mists.

The comfortable days of rest at Manali were passing all too swiftly without the arrival of Seward. Jace had told Coral to expect Seward the morning they had left the dak-bungalow, yet there had been no word. Without Seward to turn to, and with the major gone, Coral fretted over whom to go to with her concerns. *Ethan?* After all, he was probably the one man she should turn to before all others.

By the next morning she had decided to speak to him on the matter, only to learn from servants that he was with Sir Hugo and Mr. Harrington preparing for the upcoming tiger shoot.

Hunting for "hunt's sake" had always been revolting to Coral. She respected the magnificent jungle creatures

190

of India, and while the cats were obviously dangerous, she saw no point in slaughtering them on a holiday just to relieve Sir Hugo's boredom.

She knew the process well. Toward dawn the *beaters*—hundreds of men on foot—would move out to encircle an area of jungle to be purged of the tigers previously held in pits or cages. By sunup, Sir Hugo, Mr. Harrington, and other hunting associates would arrive with their rifles, seated on the back of the great gray elephants, while the driver, known as a *mahout*, would guide the elephant using a long stick to prod the beast forward.

While the hunting party on elephants moved forward, the Indians would wait in the trees with ropes, to open the traps holding the tigers. From the noise of the approaching beaters, the half-starved, frightened and angry tigers would seek escape in the opposite direction, toward the line of elephants moving through the tall yellow grass.

Coral found it all quite cowardly. But she was not surprised that Mr. Harrington was staging the hunt to satisfy the appetite of her uncle.

The morning was still. The fragrance of grasses and jungle growth filled the early air. Coral shaded her eyes against the glare and walked briskly in the direction of the clearing, toward the tall elephant grass and the overhanging branches of teak.

Ethan stood with Hugo and Mr. Harrington, while Zameen went over the orders of the next morning's hunt. A handful of Indian servants in turbans and loin cloths stood by. Coral tensed when her gaze fell on Rissaldar Sanjay. It seemed inappropriate for the Indian officer to be involved in the event when his commanding officer was delayed in an area where there had been fighting. The snatches of conversation that she had overheard on the road brought unsettled feelings.

Coral paused, holding her hat, and frowned to herself. Not even Ethan appeared to be concerned about Seward. He saw her and left the others.

"I must say, you are looking fair of face today," he said, but she noted that his attempt to show a light mood appeared forced. It brought her some relief to know that he too could be concerned.

"The rest has done you good," he said.

Coral was watching the others. "Uncle Hugo appears to be in no hurry to get on with the journey."

He followed her gaze, the smile leaving his face.

"Yes. This is all a bit of a circus, I agree. Tomorrow is the hunt, and Hugo is elated."

She was bolstered in seeing his concern, hoping it was over the delay in the journey.

"I doubt if you would care to join us?" he was saying.

"No, Ethan, I am concerned about Seward. We should have heard from him by now."

"I quite agree. I was asking Hugo about the man this morning. However, he is inclined to believe that Seward decided to stay on with the major at Plassey." He looked at her, as though judging her response to the idea.

"That is not what the major told me," she assured him. "Seward was to escort us here to Manali. I was concerned when he did not show up the morning we left, but now it has been three days."

"A bit troubling. But try not to worry. Seward and the major are men who can take care of themselves. Something must have come up." He offered a smile, obviously hoping to brighten her mood. "They will arrive soon."

Coral frowned, wondering if he believed his own words. "Ethan, I am *sure* something dreadful has happened to delay Seward and the major."

"Why do you say that?"

Coral's growing doubts over her uncle nagged persistently, but her trust in Ethan had always been unwavering. She decided to take a small risk. "The night we were at the dak-bungalow, I overheard a conversation between Uncle Hugo and the Indian officer." She said nothing about Jace also being there.

"You mean Sanjay?"

"Yes, I could not hear everything that was spoken, but what I did hear brought me alarm. There was talk of fighting at Plassey, and Major Buckley's name was mentioned in terms that could only be described as threatening."

The muscles in Ethan's face tightened, and he glanced toward the others. "Did they see you?"

"No. But, Ethan—"

"Have you mentioned this to anyone else?"

"No." She felt her chest tighten at the strained look on his face. Was he frightened, or angry?

"Say nothing. Do you understand?" he said in a low, urgent voice, and when she did not answer immediately, his fingers clasped tightly about her wrist.

"Coral—"

"Yes, Ethan. I understand. I mention it to you now because I am worried."

His grip on her wrist loosened, and his face softened. He ran his fingers through his hair and tried to smile. "I do not want to add to your alarm, but I do not trust Sanjay. You must not let anyone know you saw him with Sir Hugo."

So Ethan also doubted the Indian officer even as Jace did. It made her feel better that the two men agreed.

"I will look into the matter about Seward," he said, his eyes searching her face. "Perhaps you misunderstood their conversation. Suspicions grow in darkness, my dear. Whatever the truth, let me handle this. Do not go to Hugo."

Coral had no intention of doing so but assured him that she would not. Jace had already warned her to keep silent. Snatches of conversations heard in the night were easily cloaked in mischief. Yet—neither Seward nor Jace had returned.

"I will ask Hugo to have someone ride toward Plassey," he said. "If there was more fighting, we will know soon enough."

"And if he does not agree?"

He squeezed her hand. "Trust me. I happen to be a fine horseman. I will go myself if necessary."

She believed him. His own concern was obvious.

"We have a long and difficult safari ahead of us," he told her. "You will need all of your strength. Promise that you will leave the matter to me."

Sir Hugo's voice called: "Ah, Coral, my dear, good morning. I have been wanting to talk to you."

Ethan whispered, "Say nothing," and gave her hand another squeeze before letting it go.

Sir Hugo looked cheerful as he walked up and laid a heavy hand on Ethan's shoulder, the ruby ring on his finger winking in the sunlight. "Might I suggest, dear boy, that you get some practice with that rifle? Sanjay is waiting."

Ethan looked down at Coral and smiled, his gaze reassuring. "I will see you at lunch, Coral. And do not let Uncle talk you into going on the hunt. I know how you love those golden beasts."

Ethan walked away and joined the rissaldar and Zameen, leaving Coral and Sir Hugo alone in the clearing. The warm wind tugged at the brim of her hat, and she reached up to hold it in place.

Hugo smiled down at her. "The color has come back into your cheeks. The small delay was worth every moment of frustration." He placed an arm about her shoulders and led her toward the white bungalow. "I know how worried you are about your father's good friend Seward, so I shall inform you at once that I am sending the rissaldar to Plassey in the morning."

She was surprised and pleased. Maybe she was wrong about him.

"Ah, that is better. A light has sprung up in your eyes. The major is well guarded with troops, and Seward no doubt stayed on with him."

He stopped on the road to gaze out across the field that was busy with workers, and Coral stood beside him. "My good friend Harrington tells me he wishes to sell his indigo plantations and go back to England. I am contemplating buying him out."

Coral turned her head to watch his profile. "Somehow I cannot see the Roxburys interested in anything but silk."

He laughed. "Nor can I, my dear Coral. But Harrington has made me an excellent offer. One I would loose sleep over at turning down. What do you think?"

"Are you perhaps wondering what I believe Margaret's response would be to this?"

"I was thinking of Belinda and Ethan. A string of indigo plantations might make good wedding presents. So, I was wondering what *you* thought of it."

Coral knew where his question was leading and wondered how she could avert a trek down the wedding path.

"Indigo is a most interesting product," he was saying, watching the workers bend to their task. "They gather the plant in bundles; then, I am told, it is permitted to ferment in great vats. It takes special skill to know just when the appropriate hour has come to run the green liquid into secondary vats. The coolies must beat the water until it turns a rich deep blue—much like the color of your frock. When the water has settled enough and granulated, it is drained off. The indigo dye is left on the bottom of the vats, where it is dried and pressed into bars to be shipped to England."

He turned to gaze at her. "Silk, indigo, and tea, they are the life-blood of the East India Company. When you marry Ethan, you might add this little venture to Kingscote. Who knows? The weather here is good for mulberry trees. You might even try to start a few hatcheries and expand the silk production."

Does Ethan know about this? "Ethan and I agreed in London that the test of time will not risk a relationship, if it is genuine," she said, hoping her uncle would not try to exert pressure.

Although Coral believed Ethan's Christianity was genuine, she knew that time alone would prove it. Somehow she felt compelled that the man she married must support the idea of the mission school. Yet, even she could do nothing unless her parents agreed. Was it fair to hold Ethan to the fires that burned within her own heart?

Without intending to do so, her mind wandered to Jace Buckley, and she felt an uneasy qualm. She had not meant to think about him now, but it was as if he barged into her mind without apology—much in keeping with his character, she thought grimly.

The real Jace Buckley, Coral suspected, may or may not be of genuine Christian faith, although he had intimated he believed when he had whisked her away from that dreadful suttee in Calcutta. But even if he did, she was quite certain that he did not take those beliefs seriously enough for her to feel comfortable. She wanted more. More than either he or Ethan offered. Perhaps, she thought wistfully, she was being unrealistic. But then she remembered William Carey's zeal, and Charles Peddington's sacrifice of health to serve the Christian cause in India.

When it came to Jace Buckley, she was hesitant to admit the truth: His handsome, rugged features and his energetic personality had caught her interest from the moment she had set eyes on him.

"He is falling in love with you; do you know that?"

Coral jerked her head in her uncle's direction, startled. Then she gave a short laugh. "Of that, Uncle, I am quite sure you are wrong. I do not know him well, but I am certain of one thing. He would never permit himself to be so vulnerable. He knows, as well as I, that our goals and beliefs are incompatible. He is an adventurer. He wishes to have no bonds or ties, and as soon as he can he will go back to his clipper—"

Coral stopped. Her face turned warm with the realization that Hugo had not been speaking of Jace Buckley, but of Ethan.

Sir Hugo gave her a searching look. "You speak of the major, I gather. Evidently our minds have gone their separate ways. It is Ethan who is in love with you."

Hugo's tactic of concern for her future took Coral off guard. It was far easier to resist a cold and unfeeling schemer than a fatherly confidant.

She looked away from his bright gaze, at the workers bending white amid the green, and tried to keep matters light. "Ethan has only one true love, and that is medical research."

"I fear that he was left alone too much and took solace in his studies," Hugo responded. "A lonely life, I suspect, dwarfed his ability to show much warmth to others."

"Oh, I do not think so," she said, thinking it odd her uncle would show such fatherlike concern. "Ethan has proven both thoughtful and dependable."

"I am glad to hear that much. I dare insist that he

does care for you. He will make a good husband, Coral. You are not so unlike him, after all. Illness and religious pursuits have shut you into a room of your own that few others are permitted to enter."

Coral gave an uncomfortable laugh. "I hope I am not as isolated and infertile of thought as you make me sound. I might as well cut off my hair and wear dutiful black."

"Ah, never do that, you are far too lovely for the monastic vow," he replied. "But it is true, you are a serious young woman. Thankfully lacking Belinda's frivolous nature. It is safe to say that unlike my daughter, you will not be happy in a relationship that is all emotion and no intellect. Hampton and Elizabeth realize that as well. They do want you to marry your cousin."

Yes, she thought. *My future, at least where my family is concerned, is already decided.*

"May I suggest, Coral, that you not permit sympathetic notions for the Indian children on Kingscote to turn you aside." He smiled and slipped an arm about her shoulders, walking her back toward the bungalow. "One must learn to keep religious philosophy within certain bounds. A balance is necessary for realistic judgment. Life, after all, is lived not in the sanctuary, but on the street."

"Oh, you are right. I think we are expected to live our beliefs where our feet are soiled—by walking amid the harshness of humanity. And what better place than India?"

Coral stopped and searched his bearded face. "Uncle, I want to show you something." Slowly she opened her blue lace bag, removing her Hindi New Testament. Her eyes pleaded with his to understand her joy.

"Look, Uncle! Hindi, of all languages! Who could have guessed God's plan for spreading the Scriptures, when at one time even English was outlawed."

Hugo took it and opened its pages, saying nothing. Coral fervently hoped he would be somehow touched by it. She longed for, if not his enthusiasm, his reluctant respect for men like William Carey.

His voice was quiet, and had she been less hopeful, she might have recognized the look in his eyes. "Where did you get this?"

"William Carey," she said softly. "Ethan told you of our visit to Serampore?"

"He did."

That was all. *He did.* "This translation, Uncle, is a testimony to a God too great to be confined to English, or to the small locked rooms of our lives."

He tore his eyes from the book and searched her face. "A fine work to be certain. Men like Carey have their place. But it is not every heart that wishes a god so big, or so demanding. I realize you have been taught this from childhood by Elizabeth, and even Hampton has his moments—such as when he risked Kingscote to the ghazis by allowing you to adopt Gem. But your father had the good sense to know when to stop." His black eyes stared down at her, unflinching. "I do hope you are not thinking of risking Kingscote to ashes for William Carey's translation in Hindi? Get it out of your mind, Coral. A mission school for the Hindu untouchables cannot be borne."

Her disappointment was acute. "Why must I get it out of my mind? Because the East India Company's vision is blinded to anything but its own interests? The rich are made richer, and the powerful go uncontested— is that it? What of India's greatest resource, her children?"

"Religious sentiment always sounds sweet when wrapped in the sanctimonious garb of the missionary," he scoffed. "But the premise is entirely false. The honorable East India Company was not built to propagate Christianity, but to do business. Are we to be faulted for pursuing our goals?"

"No, of course not, but—"

"Is it not reasonable? Life must go on! The Company has done much good in India. The maharajas would be the first to admit it. England has brought stability."

"That is so, Uncle, and I will be the last to fault the governor-general. Yet a higher authority also has interests in India. And I dare say that He will hold little patience for rich merchants who stand in the way."

Hugo waved a hand at her words as though they were annoying insects. "Do not misunderstand me. Religion has its place in any society, but the Company will not stand by and see an Indian uprising in order to coddle men like Carey. But enough of that. It is the family silk business I am interested in. And Hampton will agree with me that it cannot be held ransom to the torch of a mutiny. And now," he firmly took hold of her arm, looped it through his, and smiled. "One thing about you, my child. You do give your poor uncle a run for his wits."

He led her inside the house. "We will leave the greater cause of India to statesmen and maharajas. As a Kendall daughter—and a silk heiress—I have no doubt you will be practical in these matters. I might add that Hampton has already made it clear to me in a letter received at Calcutta. Your husband will either be Ethan, or you will eventually be packed off again to London to become the bride of some lord that your grandmother has in mind."

Coral said no more. She had already disclosed too much.

18

Jace drew rein, and the horse's nostrils shuddered, breaking the stillness. He peered into the darkness, where light from the silent white stars above cast an eerie glow over the road ahead. He waited, listening, but the only sounds he heard were the night creatures stirring through the jungle and the fingers of the wind rippling over dried cactus leaves.

The road that Jace had traversed for miles now opened onto a clearing sketched with clumps of dried grasses and thirsty thorn trees. Jace strained to pick out their bleak and misshapen dark forms under the stars. Somewhere out there he would meet up with his 17th and Seward, who by now had made contact with McKay and the sepoys from the outpost at Plassey.

All his instincts as well as his military experience warned him there was no time to lose. The night was oppressive, and he wished desperately for the first light of dawn. He prompted his horse forward across the padding of dust, its hooves making little sound. With caution, he saw that he was riding toward a black outcropping that loomed against the lighter skyline. A perfect trap. Then he saw him, his daffadar, a young man he had known for too long to doubt his loyalty and personal friendship.

"Hut! Sirdar-sahib! It is I!" called Jace.

The man ran toward him, saluting. "Huzoor! Major-sahib! I have been waiting!"

"Where is the jemander Rajendra?"

"He waits for you ahead. It was necessary to make camp and wait for the morning."

Jace was immediately on guard. "What happened? Where is Captain McKay and the 34th?"

"There has been a delay, Major-sahib. I do not know why. Captain McKay is still at Plassey but will show in the morning. The 34th will remain at the garrison."

"By whose orders?"

"That, Major, you will need to ask the jemander. Seward has ridden ahead to make his own inquiry."

So . . . Seward did arrive safely. Jace felt some relief, but remained tense. Something was wrong. Why would the 34th stay behind at Plassey when there was fighting between the outpost and the village?

He rode with his daffadar into the darkness. He saw no light nor smoke from the small camp belonging to his 17th, and approved of his jemander's carefulness. Automatically, Jace rested his hand on his sword hilt. "Send for the jemander," he ordered. The daffadar rode ahead and disappeared. Jace turned his horse aside toward the shrubs and waited.

A few minutes later his jemander and a sepoy rode into view with the daffadar. Jace rode to meet them, and scanned the face of the sepoy. He did not recognize the man, who wore the blue and white of the 34th.

His jemander quickly saluted. "Major-bahadur. Captain McKay will not arrive for the meeting as planned. The commissioner has sent word that you and the 17th are to report to Plassey. We have made camp for the night."

"Who delivered the message?"

"The sepoy."

Jace looked at him, and the sepoy saluted. "Under orders from the commissioner, the captain-sahib has sent me."

Jace held out his hand, and the jemander handed him the message. He could tell nothing from the jemander's face. And the sepoy from Plassey stared at him, obviously tense.

Jace could barely read it in the starlight, but he recognized Gavin McKay's handwriting.

An attack against Plassey is expected by rebel Mahar-
attas. The 34th is ordered to defend the junction, the
17th with them. Report at once. Seward is with me.
Captain G. McKay, 34th Infantry, N.N.I.
Plassey Junction

"Shall I return to Plassey, Major-sahib?" the sepoy asked, seeming only too anxious to ride off.

Jace placed the message in his jacket. "No. You will ride out with the 17th at dawn."

Was he mistaken, or did the sepoy look nervous? The Indian saluted, then turned his horse out of the way.

At dawn, Jace readied the 17th to ride toward Plassey. Well into the afternoon they came to a fork in the river, where a dusty white road ran along a ruined wall of an old fortress once belonging to some forgotten raja. In the sun's glare a temple appeared to stare down at them with disdain. Jace heard dismal bells and saw priests with shaven heads moving about.

They were still some distance from Plassey when Jace saw the small rise of dust from the contingency of the 34th. He drew up and waited, watching McKay drawing nearer. Suddenly, Jace became conscious of his jemander at his right, and glanced at him, noting the man's expression. Sweat stood out on his forehead, and his gaze darted nervously toward a red fort in ruins, long abandoned since the British had come to Plassey. Jace followed the man's gaze to the trees at the left of the ruin. His breath stopped. Sepoys were waiting in ambush! And both the 17th and McKay's 34th were about to be skinned like rabbits!

He unsheathed his sword and swerved his horse toward the jemander. "Traitor! I shall have your head for this!"

The jemander looked frightened, then his face set into contempt.

Jace jerked his head toward the trees. "Who waits there? Maharattas?"

The jemander's eyes hardened into granite. He drew his sword and spat. "No, sahib. Not Maharattas. The entire 34th Native Infantry, except for those few fools who ride with McKay. You will all be food for vultures by afternoon, followed by all the British, including your stupid commissioner!"

Suddenly a rushing wall of mounted Indian sepoys and sowars, boasting the standard of the 34th, came thundering down the rocky slope.

Captain Gavin McKay, leading twenty sepoys from the regiment, had only a flash of warning. He saw that both Jace and the 17th were ahead, and the troops he had thought to be guarding the outpost were emerging from the trees near the ruin. They approached in a cloud of red dust, the sun glinting off their drawn swords and bayonets.

McKay's dark brows lowered, and his greenish brown eyes snapped. "What the devil—" McKay turned in his saddle and shouted to his rissaldar: "Mutiny! Warn the sentry! Shut the gate!"

As though in painfully slow motion, McKay was aware that his rissaldar had turned toward him, his face that of a stranger, full of something loathsome. He lifted his rifle and aimed it at McKay's heart. A shot fired, followed by a puff of white. For a moment McKay thought he was dead, yet he felt nothing. Then he saw his rissaldar fall forward in his saddle, the rifle slipping from his hand. Out of the corner of his eye, McKay saw Seward gripping a pistol still aimed at the fallen rissaldar.

McKay's sepoy was riding toward the gate to sound the warning. One of their own thrust him through with a sword. A rifle exploded. The ball smashed into the head of the British soldier bearing the company flag. McKay felt the splatter of blood on his face. Within seconds, swords, bayonets, and rifles were unleashed. The few remaining loyal sepoys drew swords against overwhelming numbers. Seward shouted at McKay, who turned to see his daffadar coming at him. McKay had a glimpse of bared white teeth just as he parried his blade, thrust and thrust again, ramming it through the daffadar's chest.

"To the 17th!" shouted Seward, racing in the direction of the river.

The jemander drove at Jace fiercely, demanding all of Jace's skill to ward off the attack. Jace smashed his sword into his attacker's blade, swerving the blow and setting him off-balance with its force. The jemander hesitated only a second, time enough for Jace to swipe a final blow against his skull. Jace glanced about. All around him fighting raged. Plunging horses, confusion, and blood. Loyal sowars of the 17th fell in the onslaught, and he caught a glimpse of his handsome young Indian standard-bearer being plunged through with a bayonet. Still he gripped the flag, refusing to let go as his other hand covered the wound in his chest.

The sight of his sowars fighting valiantly despite the inevitable tide only hardened Jace. The blue and white of the 34th crashed through their meager line of forces. His own blade crossed sword upon sword, cutting a swathe around him, and still they came. Blood ran in his eyes and seeped out from a wound in his side. Inevitably he was knocked from his horse. A wave of riders swung around him, and a sepoy on horse came at him. Jace grabbed a rifle and hurled the bayonet through the man's chest, but the rush of his horse slammed Jace back to the ground, knocking the breath from him. Struggling to rise, he glimpsed his daffadar choking in a cloud of dust, and then the daffadar threw himself against Jace, knocking him back down.

Weeping, the daffadar rasped in Bengali: "Be still, sahib!"

Smothered by the human shield of his young daffadar, Jace fought against the heat, the darkness, but instead sank deeper into the pit of unconsciousness.

───────

"He still suspects it was me in the garden, Coral. I just know it," whispered Marianna. "Sometimes I look up from the dinner table to find him watching me with that probing look of his; you know the expression I mean?"

Coral said nothing. She did not want to feed her sister's uncertainties.

"It makes me feel like one of Cousin Ethan's dissected bugs," Marianna said, plucking at her handkerchief. "Like Uncle Hugo is trying to rummage through my mind. Even Mr. Harrington watches me."

Coral looked at her. "Mr. Harrington? Come, Marianna, now you *are* imagining things."

"I am not. And I overheard Mr. Harrington talking to that Indian man named Zameen. Did you know Zameen used to be the dewan at Guwahati?"

Coral tensed. "The chief minister?" she whispered.

Marianna nodded, nervously tying her handkerchief in a knot.

"And Mr. Harrington used to live there. I heard them talking about it."

"When?"

"Last night. They were below on the verandah, drinking something and smoking cheroots."

"Was Uncle with them?"

"It was only the two men."

"Did you hear them say anything about Plassey or Guwahati?"

Marianna shook her head.

Coral digested this in silence. Zameen, the maharaja's dewan! What was he doing in the subservient role of a secretary to Harrington? Was it genuine?

Kathleen poked her head in through the bedroom door. "Not dressed yet? Oh, do hurry. I am starved."

"Coming," Coral called and turned to Marianna. "Say nothing to anyone."

The dining area opened onto a wide garden with Harrington's prized tropical flowers. He was in the process of discussing them with Ethan when Coral entered with her sisters.

As evening settled over the garden and the fragrance of flowers became almost too sweet, Zameen appeared from another room to draw the drapes. Coral discreetly studied him. A retired dewan? He was dressed immaculately in a knee-length blue tunic tied at the waist with a fringed sash. She found herself mulling over Marianna's startling disclosure. Zameen did look more like an important Indian official than Harrington's personal secretary. Coral wondered why he now accepted the menial task of going about the salon shutting out the insects.

"So lovely, yet bent on her own destruction," Harrington commented.

Coral glanced up. Was he speaking of a person? Her gaze followed his pale eyes to a huge yellow and blue moth that beat its wings hopelessly against the lighted lantern.

"I shall be pleased to have little more to swat at in London than a fly," Harrington continued, looking across the table at Coral. He ran his fingers over his gold mustache. "You do not mind insects, Miss Kendall? You will find the indigo plantation most comfortable otherwise."

Before Coral could reply that she was not interested in indigo or insects, he went on: "The only thing I shall regret saying goodbye to is my collection of graceful kings and queens."

"Kings and queens?" Coral repeated.

Ethan leaned toward her with a smile. "Harrington collects spiders. You are not squeamish I hope? He has one to show us after dinner."

"Zameen, old boy, is it safely enclosed?" asked Harrington.

"It is, sahib. Right here." He held up a glass box filled with green leaves.

Coral could see only leaves, but a moan came from Marianna.

Harrington did not appear to notice. "Spiders are the most captivating creatures. My latest specimen is beautiful, velvet black with just a blush of crimson."

Marianna drew palms to her face.

"I think we better change the subject, or we shall have poor Marianna losing her appetite," said Ethan.

"Poor child, I do apologize," Harrington said. "I forget that not all look upon my hobby with equal fervor.

208

Away with the queen, Zameen. I shall show her to Ethan later."

Harrington turned the conversation to the jungle lab that Ethan planned to build on Kingscote. As the discussion progressed to tropical diseases, Ethan became totally absorbed in his discourse. Coral accepted the cup of tea that Uncle Hugo offered her with a smile. He had put too much honey in it. She drank it anyway, and listened to Ethan and Harrington without comment.

As time passed, Ethan's voice began to sound as wearisome as the hum of insects outside the beaded curtain in the garden. Coral felt exhausted. The meal was finished and the desert served—a fresh fruit mixture of sweet mango, bananas, and shredded coconut—but Coral had lost her appetite. She tried to stifle a yawn, and wondered what time it was. She felt relaxed, almost hypnotized by the flickering golden lantern light, the mammoth moth flapping its delicate wings, and the droning voices of Mr. Harrington and Ethan. Insects. Their voices buzzing in her ears were becoming dull and more distant as she grew more sleepy by the moment. She tried to brush a mosquito from her ear, but her hand felt heavy and wooden. Her eyes moved tiredly around the large table. Kathleen looked bored, Marianna was staring at her, and Uncle Hugo . . .

Coral's eyes sought his and they looked bright in the lantern light, almost like a cat's eyes. He leaned across the table, his heavy brows furrowing, his mouth moving as though addressing her, but she heard nothing distinguishable, only the buzzing in her ears. *These insects must be exceedingly large to drown out human voices*, she thought without feeling.

Sir Hugo was on his feet now. So was Marianna, looking pale and frightened. Kathleen frowned and spoke to Ethan. Coral did not hear what was said, but she felt

Ethan's hand take hold of her arm. Sir Hugo was standing beside her at the table, his face bent inquiringly to peer into hers. His dark eyes and brows, his meticulously clipped beard and rugged features filled her vision. His expression turned to alarm, and she responded by trying to stand to her feet. The chair fell over behind her, making no sound as it struck the polished wood floor. Coral tried uselessly to pick it up, and Ethan took hold of her shoulders. She stared up into his anxious face and heard her name, but it came as a distorted whisper: "Corrr-alll!" Her knees would not hold her up. She seemed to be in a room with grotesquely shaped shadows that loomed like the swaying heads of cobras. She tried to scream, but as she struggled, the darkness receded into a pinpoint of light until . . .

———

A sullen rumble sounded from the jungle, and Coral awoke, sitting up in the large bed. At once she regretted that she had moved so quickly, for a wave of nausea swept over her.

The yellow glow from a lantern on the table illuminated the bedroom at Mr. Harrington's house. Her brain felt thick. It proved tedious to think, to wade through the questions demanding answers, and she sank back to the goose-down pillow. Trying to ease the fear that wrapped its tentacles about her heart, Coral closed her eyes, allowing the fragments of what had happened to her in the last few days to filter through her mind. *Days?* Her heart pounded. How long had she been in bed? The spinning in her head had ceased, and at last the buzzing noise was gone from her eardrums. Perhaps she had been in bed for weeks!

The low tigerlike rumble echoed again in the distance beyond the house. *There cannot be any more tigers*, she thought numbly. *They shot them all. Poor tigers. Poor magnificent beasts. So strong, so free . . . like Jace. No, he was a cheetah, and he was not free. He—*

Coral started back to reality. It was all coming back now, even as her mind swam.

What had happened? There were insects filling her ears with a terrible noise. Ethan had caught her as the strength of her legs melted.

When she awoke, she was in her bed and found that Ethan had been seated in a chair beside her, his usually quiet gray eyes watching her with concern. He had tried to hide his alarm with a smile. Uncle Hugo came into the room, and she thought he looked like a giant warrior arrayed in black armor. "I've killed the enemy. . . ." he had said, lifting up a glass jar.

Through blurred vision Coral saw a dead spider.

Remembering, Coral shivered under the cover and closed her eyes. The house was quiet. If she could just regain her strength long enough to get dressed. She must find her sisters. Where was Seward? Was there news from the major? But she discovered that she was too weary to concern herself.

"Lord, you never slumber nor sleep, be our high tower, our keeper, our shield. . . ."

———

"Ethan's quick action saved your life," Sir Hugo said when she awoke again.

Ethan.

"This is the second time he has done so. First in London, and now here in Manali. Had it not been for his quick thinking, we would not have suspected a spider bite in time to treat you. He went searching under the table and found it beneath your chair."

"M-my chair? How—" she stammered weakly.

"A most interesting question. How the horrid thing escaped the glass box is a mystery we have all been trying to solve. Zameen swears he put the box away as Harrington ordered him to, but no one seems to distinctly remember him doing so. Zameen is upset, as you can imagine, and Harrington is threatening to destroy his entire collection. You are on the way to recovery now. You owe him your gratitude, Coral. Be kind to him, will you? He loves you so."

Be kind to him. He loves you so. Had it not been for Ethan . . .

19

For a confused minute Jace lay there in the blackness, unable to move. The weight holding him prisoner must be the piles of rock upon his grave. *No, my body feels too much pain to be dead,* he thought. He stirred and opened his swollen eyes. A tiny speck of silver shone. As he tried to focus, he realized that it was a star in the night sky, and the weight on top of him was flesh and blood—his daffadar!

Jace struggled to crawl out from under him, and as he did, he saw the bayonet in his daffadar's back. The loyalty of his sergeant had shielded him from certain death.

Lord, he thought. *How can I be worthy of this man's allegiance?*

His skull throbbed with pain. He wanted to vomit as he moved, causing the blood to surge in his temples. His fingers were swollen and stiff as he brought them to the side of his head and felt the gash. Somehow between dizzy spells he struggled to one knee and sat there in the darkness, smelling death all about him.

He squinted. On the horizon, the village of Plassey was barely visible, speckled by a few points of light. Jace

213

struggled to his feet, took a few unsteady steps, and with the last of his fading awareness, crawled toward the faint sound of a snorting horse.

He became aware of movement near him, and a harsh, low whisper. He struggled to clear his blurred eyes, wondering if the enemy had returned.

"Ye be all right, lad, just hold on," came Seward's voice.

The next time Jace awoke it was light, and the ground was moving beneath him. He was lying uncomfortably across a saddle, on his stomach. There was a cloth tied about his nose and mouth, and he immediately knew why; dust rose in clouds from beneath the slow plodding of the hoofs. Again he lost consciousness.

"He is coming around. Hand me the canteen." It was the voice of Captain McKay.

The wine was strong, and he felt it burn all the way down to his stomach. Its warmth spread through his body. He tried to shove the canteen away and turned his head, choking.

"Easy, lad, ye'll be all right now," he heard Seward say. "Drink some more. You be needing it. Take it easy! Stay put! Got yourself a severe concussion, but the gash is bandaged up nice. The village near Manali be the closest place, and Gavin and I will get you there by night. Then I'll be going for Boswell at Manali. Never thought I'd be thanking the Almighty for his being about, but I'm sure thanking Him now. All right, that's it. Nice and quiet, lad. We got to keep moving, even though it's mighty uncomfortable on that saddle. No time to camp here."

"Where—" Jace murmured.

"Say three more hours from Manali."

"17th?"

"Don't think about 'em now lad, may Christ have mercy on *them*."

"Too late," Jace whispered, and in his delirium saw the caverns of hell open wide to suck him into its jaws, to suck them all into an avalanche of burning flame. "Too late."

"Nay, lad! Don't say that," Seward choked, bending over him. But Jace could not see him, he could only feel his heavy hands patting him awkwardly, and felt something hot and wet drop onto his face. Jace blinked.

"Ye'll be all right now," Seward said. "God has His ways of mercy. I am counting on that! And I'll be getting Boswell to come and help you, even if I need to drag him all the way there!"

———————

Coral stirred from a light sleep. Something had awakened her, and she sat up, listening in the direction of the open verandah. As she strained to decipher the noise from the chirp of crickets, she caught the unmistakable echo of horses' hoofs below.

Kathleen's bedroom opened onto the same verandah, and the sound must have awakened her, too, for a moment later she hurried into Coral's room and stood in the moonlight.

"It is Seward!"

Coral threw aside the cover, the soles of her feet touching the coarse matting. She snatched up her dressing gown, putting it on as she ran toward the verandah. *Oh, thank you, Lord.* A surge of warm wind sent the leaves of a tree rustling, while somewhere in the shrubs a peacock let off with a shrill call. Coral leaned over the railing and looked down into the stone courtyard in time to see a young boy taking charge of Seward's lathered horses. Without actually seeing his face, Coral knew that Kathleen was right. In the speckled moonlight sifting its way through the leaves and branches, she recognized the broad build of Seward in his buckskin jacket and tricorn hat. She started to smile, but concern gripped her when she noted the quick, purposeful stride. And his arm was in a sling!

"Seward!" she called down breathlessly. "Seward!"

He stopped and looked up.

"You are hurt! What happened?"

"A mutiny, lass. A damnable one! The fair and honorable sowars of the 17th are dead. All of 'em!"

Coral was certain that her stomach dropped to her feet. *Jace.* Her icy hands gripped the rail.

"Lass! I be needing that cousin of yours. Can you rouse him up?"

Cousin—what cousin—?

"Lass? Are you hearing me now?"

Coral felt Kathleen's hand grip her arm as she leaned over the rail. "What is it, Seward?" Kathleen called.

"I am needing the doctor. The major be hurt and in the village."

"Yes, I will go waken him now," Kathleen cried, running through the bedroom and out the door.

Coral became alert. "Seward! Are you saying Major Buckley is not dead, but wounded?"

"He is injured, badly."

"Where is he?"

"In the village with Captain McKay."

"You should have brought him here!"

"He ought not to be moved more than be necessary. We've moved him too much already. Don't worry, lass, he's a strong one. He'll live."

"Wait for me, Seward. I am coming with you."

Coral did not stop to think. She lit the lantern with surprisingly steady fingers, dressed quickly, grabbed her

216

hooded cloak, placed the Hindi New Testament in her bag, and ran out into the hallway.

Doctor Boswell had his bag in hand and was at the stairway. Kathleen stood near the landing and turned as Marianna poked her red head out her bedroom door. "What is it, Sissy?" she asked Kathleen.

"Go back to bed!" said Kathleen. "Coral, wait! Where are you going?"

"With Ethan," Coral called over her shoulder, rushing down the stairs after him.

The library door opened and Mr. Harrington stood there in his smoking jacket, book in hand. He looked at Ethan who had stopped near the door, then at Coral.

"What the devil is going on? Did I hear Seward?"

"There was a mutiny at Plassey," came Ethan's firm voice. "Many are dead, and there are injured to care for. I will be in the village." He threw open the door, and hurried out into the night.

Coral picked up her muslin skirts to follow after him. She cast Mr. Harrington a quick glance and said, "He needs my help. I shall be fine. We will send word tomorrow!"

She closed the heavy door behind her, hurried down the porch steps, and ran across the courtyard to where Seward waited.

As though only now aware of her, Ethan turned and scowled. "Good heavens, Coral, there is no need to wear yourself out like this. I can handle the major."

"I need to go," she stated firmly, grasping her bag. "If the major is dying, I need to speak to him."

Ethan stared down at her, and in the moonlight she could see his incredulous expression turn to thoughtful suspicion.

"It is not the way you think," she whispered.

He studied her, and she saw his mouth twist in mockery. "Are you only worried about the major's soul, my dear?"

She felt irritation well up in her chest, and whirled around just as Seward strode up with furrowed brows.

"Lass, it be best if ye stay here."

"No, Seward," she stated. "I am coming with you and Ethan." She turned to the young groom. "I will need a horse, please."

"At once, Miss-sahiba," he said and ran toward the stables.

Ethan had already mounted and was waiting in chilled silence, but she did not care. He needed to understand that she would not be treated like a child, or insulted because she insisted on seeing Major Buckley. It would do no good to tell him that she would feel this strongly about anyone else. He assumed, so she guessed from his behavior, that she was infatuated with the major, and making a fool of herself.

She turned to Seward, hoping for his support, but prepared to contend if necessary. He was staring down at her with an odd expression, stroking his mustache.

"All right, lass."

She laid a hand on his arm. He understood. A minute later the groom trotted toward them, leading a saddled mare, and Seward helped her to mount. They galloped off toward the narrow, tree-lined road, and Coral felt the wind cooling her, blowing through her hair.

"Severed to the bone," Ethan told her in a clipped, professional voice. Coral did not wince as she held the lantern close to Jace's head, nor did she look away as Doctor Boswell worked tediously to clean the area of dried blood and cut away the matted dark locks, washing the area with a strong ointment. Her eyes went to Ethan as he worked. His expression was professional, and he seemed not to be aware of who she was or, for that matter, who his patient was. He worked unceasingly, his slender fingers steady. Now and then he ordered her to hand him this strange-looking tool or that one, all of them having been boiled over the small fire that Seward kept going in the hearth.

Coral's nostrils burned from the strong smell of the ointment Ethan was using, and she now watched Jace, seeing him wince in his unconsciousness. She tried not to notice the way his hair curled near his ear, or the black lashes that she usually saw in a familiar, challenging squint over slate-blue eyes.

"That is the worst of his wounds and will do for a few days."

"Aye, and he has a wound in his side," said Seward.

There were numerous cuts and abrasions. While Ethan and Seward removed his shirt, Coral worked on his right hand. The knuckles were swollen and stiff, and discoloration had set in. She cleaned and applied the foul ointment, then wrapped his hand carefully. Ethan bound his side with strips of white cloth.

The sun was already high in the brazen sky when Coral stepped wearily outside. The village was small, consisting mostly of a few farmers and fishermen. The men were already out on the water in their barges, and the women were about their duties of washing the family clothes, or working in their gardens.

The small mud hut that Seward had brought Jace to the day before belonged to the tehsildar, the village headman, who had obligingly moved in with his son's large family for the payment in rupees Seward had offered him. The villagers seemed to ignore their presence, and only the large, curious eyes of children stared at them.

The tehsildar's daughter-in-law, dressed in her sari

and carrying food, walked up to where Coral stood. "Jai ram, sahiba."

"Yes, thank you for the food. You have been very kind."

The woman smiled shyly and left, and Coral brought the basket into the hut. She proceeded to hand out the chupatti bread and pieces of vegetable root, and pour tea from the urn.

Ethan absently smiled his thanks, and Coral waited until his eyes met hers. She smiled tiredly, but hoped her gratitude showed. It must have, for he looked surprised, flushed under his growing tan, and his gray eyes brightened. She laid a hand on his.

"What would we do without you?"

He said nothing, but seemed moved by her appreciation. He walked outside with his meager breakfast and lunch combined while Coral waited on Seward.

"Only time will do the rest. And the grace of God," murmured Seward.

Coral looked over at the cot where Jace slept, and silently thanked the Lord that it appeared as though he would improve. While Seward walked outside to speak to Ethan, Coral went to the mat and stared down at Jace, studying his unguarded sleeping face for a moment. There was nothing boyish about him, for he looked just as rugged when he was unconscious as he did when he was in command, and she knew that in his unhappy childhood, he had never been permitted to be a boy. Yet, in that moment with his face relaxed, he looked far younger than she imagined. *He cannot be much older than Alex!* she concluded, surprised.

An odd feeling crept over her as she looked at him, something that wisdom warned her not to toy with. Understanding came in a flash of awareness. *He could bring me pain. As much as Gem.*

How long she stood there she did not know. Perhaps only a minute, perhaps three or four, looking at him. From outside, she heard the muffled voices of Ethan and Seward discussing the mutiny and Jace's condition.

". . . at least several weeks until he will be strong enough to be about his business," came Ethan's professional voice.

Weeks, thought Coral. She must not even think of the safari to Kingscote. Her mind wandered back to Ethan, and she pondered that professional-sounding voice. Ethan did not like the major, she concluded. And yet he had come. Immediately and without question. Ethan was committed to his medical work, and with that blessed knowledge he did good. He was also kind to her, and quite satisfied with the thought of settling down. Nothing prompted him to set sail for the horizons of the world. More importantly, he was sympathetic toward her desire to reach the untouchables. He had even suggested working with her to help the children. He had attended church with her in London. . . . He had saved her life twice. What more could she want?

She scanned Jace's face.

Ethan . . . Nothing about him hinted of emotional risk.

Coral turned away and, snatching up her cloak, walked briskly out of the room, lifting her head as she went.

The sun was warm. "I am ready now, Ethan," she announced.

Something in her voice made him turn and look at her, as though she had intimated much more. Ethan walked toward her, a lean, handsome figure in his riding clothes. She noted how the sunlight on his hair made it appear golden.

"I am sorry, Coral," he said very softly, his eyes tender.

A little startled by this confession, she searched his face. "About what?"

"About not understanding the kind of woman you are."

She hesitated. "And you now understand?"

He said nothing at first. "Yes, I think I do." His smile disappeared, and he stood looking at her with a warmth in his eyes she had not seen before. "You were good to come with me, Coral. To put a friend first, even though you have been ill yourself. I was suspicious because I know my own heart. I have never known anyone to be simply *kind*. Forgive me?"

Coral felt a rush of guilt pierce through her. *Perhaps I did have other reasons.* But they would not be allowed to surface again.

She searched his gray eyes, noting that they did not make her too aware of herself as a woman. She felt more comfortable with those emotions. She smiled and nodded, allowing him to walk her to where Seward had their horses ready.

Coral was aware of Seward's eyes watching her as he assisted her into the stirrup. She avoided his eyes and turned her head to look down at him only when he took hold of her wrist, handing her the reins. His stark blue eyes were piercing.

"I'll keep you posted on how the major is doing."

"Yes, thank you, Seward. I am quite certain he will recover." She smiled. "The major will be his old self again before you know it."

A reddish brow shot up in question, and she smiled and leaned over to lay her palm against the side of his bearded face.

"Dear, faithful Seward," she said simply, but the affection of those words were not lost on him. She saw him grin beneath his mustache.

"Watch that road on the ride back. There be some dangerous holes in it. Could break a horse's leg."

As she and Ethan rode out, Coral did not look back.

———

Colonel Warbeck:

Good men of the 17th killed in ambush near Plassey. Rest of sowars have mutinied to the side of the 34th. Land travel to northern frontier may soon be cut off, leaving the Maharaja at Guwahati and the British outpost at Jorhat near Kingscote in danger. I suggest Plassey be taken at once. I am sending Captain McKay back to Calcutta for reinforcements. My Rissaldar-Major Sanjay is suspected of arranging the ambush. Intend to complete my orders to see the Governor-General's Resident to Guwahati. If I cannot journey by land through Plassey Junction, then will go by boat. I need to return the idol of Kali to the Raja. Also intend to see that Sanjay answers for death of the 17th.

J. Buckley Warbeck, Major,
17th Lan., B.N.I.
2 o'clock P.M.
February 22, near Manali

The colonel's expression was stone when he turned from the window to look at Captain Gavin McKay. He tapped the letter against his palm.

"How badly is my son injured?"

Captain Gavin McKay stood with feet apart, and hands behind him, his expression revealing none of his frustration with the military.

"That he lives at all, sir, is attributed to the death-loyalty of his young daffadar. And to the major's own determination." The greenish eyes were cool, and he said bluntly, "He intends to find Rissaldar Sanjay and see him

223

shot for treason. When I left him three weeks ago in the care of Seward, he was flat on his back and dictated the letter to me. I suggest, Colonel, that by now he is making his plans."

The colonel said nothing and walked to his desk. He picked up a sheet of paper and handed it to him, his gaze level.

"And our plans go on, Captain. We have a treaty with the raja of Guwahati. Troops will be sent north. First, I want information on the family of Daffadar Ramon Singh. It is fitting he be properly rewarded for saving the major's life. Second, my advice to the brigadier is to send another company of cavalry and standby artillery. I have ordered Major Dalaway to lead the 13th to secure Plassey. Your orders are also changed, Captain."

Gavin McKay had been afraid of this. Like Jace, whom he had known since the unfortunate decision to attend the Company Military Academy in England, McKay also kept a calendar of his last day, hour, and minute in uniform.

"Once Plassey is secured," said the colonel, "you will proceed north to join forces with the troops at the Jorhat outpost. When Major Buckley arrives at Guwahati, you will work with him to guard the maharaja and the royal family."

Captain McKay was expressionless, but his thoughts were on Kathleen Kendall. He crisply saluted. "As you say, Colonel."

––––––––

The frustration that Jace felt clamped about his insides. The 17th had ridden into a death trap, the 34th had mutinied, and until Plassey could be retaken by troops from the Calcutta garrison, the land route to the northern frontier was cut off. The motives of those involved remained as misshapen shadows in Jace's mind.

Jace thought of his daffadar again, of all the sowars of the 17th. They had represented some of the best of the native troops in Bengal. They were not only men of courage, but for the most part, were men of military principle, who had been wasted in a battle for a cause promoting someone's political ambitions and greed.

Now, the 17th was food for jackal packs and insects. In his mind he could see the battlefield stretching on before him in a long profusion of fallen men. The wind seemed to carry to his hearing the indistinct sounds of the dying, and his daffadar. . . .

Jace steeled himself against the emotion trying to resurface. The realization that the native daffadar was proud to die for his British commander tore at his insides. A rush of emotion welled up within his chest, and for a moment he thought he could not stand it. *No*, he determined, clenching his jaw. *I will not allow myself to care this deeply*. He had not even wanted this ragtag band of sowars called the 17th! He did not want to belong to any part of the military. But it was not the military alone that he wanted to reject, it was emotional risk. It could hurt too much.

Jace put a clamp on his emotions as Seward came through the hut door. He raised himself to an elbow.

"Well?" Seward wore a dark scowl. "If he be anywheres about, he be a magician, that one. I ferreted about Harrington's residence for the past day and night, and there be no trace of him."

Jace looked down at his hand. He had removed the bandage days earlier, but the joints were still swollen and painful. His rissaldar-major would pay for his betrayal. If it took the rest of his days, he would track Sanjay down and bring him back to Calcutta to be shot as a traitor.

Seward was watching him. "I be thinking the same. It be months before the old fortress near Plassey be taken again, no matter how many reinforcements the colonel sends back with McKay. The temple be standing in the path, and they won't dare use the cannon. Smart move on their part, the priests be in on the mutiny, I say. Face it, lad. There be no hope of getting through to the north now. Maybe we should go back to Calcutta."

Jace watched him boil water for tea in the hearth. In Calcutta the brigadier had replaced his trusted second in command with Sanjay, but at whose orders? Who had been behind the change? Certainly not the colonel.

"Roxbury be in on this. I be sure of it," whispered Seward darkly.

Just how much had he known in advance about the ambush and mutiny of the 17th? "He wanted me dead," said Jace.

Seward's head jerked in his direction. "You, lad?"

"Yes, I think the entire motive for going to the governor-general about my orders was because he already knew about the plans for mutiny near Plassey. Sanjay was also in on it from the beginning."

Seward's eyes hardened. "I believe it. But we need proof for the colonel."

"And I intend to get it."

Seward looked at him with a granite stare. "From Roxbury?"

"Sanjay. Roxbury can wait until we reach Guwahati."

"Sanjay may still show at Harrington's," said Seward.

"Or he may come here looking for me."

"Aye," said Seward. "Let him. I'll be waiting."

20

Coral prepared for the dinner party, choosing an emerald-green satin frock with numerous flounces of matching lace. She held it up against her, and then for no particular reason she exchanged it for a white moire with small puffed sleeves, trimmed in Brussels lace.

She swept her golden tresses up and spent longer than usual fussing with the stylish side curls.

An hour later Coral took an anxious glance at herself in the mirror, wondered who would be at Harrington's dinner, and crossed the hall to the stairway, starting down.

She paused. Across the wide hall, Captain Gavin McKay was leaning against the double doors of the drawing room, back toward Coral. He was silently watching Kathleen at the other end of the hall peering cautiously out the window onto the front yard.

Not wanting to interrupt the first meeting between them, Coral pressed her palms against her skirts to keep the silk from rustling on her petticoats, and tiptoed down the remaining stairs, escaping into a small anteroom that opened onto Mr. Harrington's prized garden.

Kathleen stood on tiptoe at the window, watching Mr. Harrington greeting dinner guests who had just arrived in a ghari. She wrinkled her nose with boredom. So these were the dinner guests for the grand evening.

The man who greeted Mr. Harrington was short and portly, heavy-jowled, with ruddy cheeks and bulging eyes. *Looks like his gaudy cravat is too tight*, she thought.

Zameen assisted an elderly woman down the ghari step to the yard, her skirt descending behind her. She stood as if to sniff the atmosphere like some English hunting dog, then raised the lorgnette resting on her ample bosom to one sharp eye. She scanned Zameen, and her voice, although muffled through the windowpane, reached Kathleen. "So, Charles! You have got yourself a new man, have you?" she said, addressing Mr. Harrington. "What happened to the other? Do not tell me he died of cholera? My, but you *are* having terrible luck."

Kathleen heard a sound from the doorway behind her, and straightened.

"If you are waiting for your French couturier, Jacques Rollibard, you will be disappointed. The poor chap is still in London kissing the hands of rich widows."

The lazy voice tinged with mockery belonged to Gavin McKay. She turned her head with tilted chin and scanned him with what she hoped was indifference. He was leaning in the archway with a smile she did not like, and the green-gray eyes in the handsome face looked her over, taking in the blue ruffled dress and the cascade of chestnut-colored curls piled high on her head.

Kathleen prided herself that she did not blush the way Coral did every time a handsome gentleman looked at her; but then, she must not compare Captain McKay with a gentleman, she told herself. He was brash, spoiled, and if that was not enough, positively rude.

"Oh. It is you."

"My apology," he said dryly.

Kathleen turned her back to him and gazed out the window as if expecting someone important. The truth was, she had expected Gavin McKay to ride in with the major by way of the front drive.

Gavin came in and closed the doors behind him. "Well, do not let me stop you. The fact I nearly had my head walloped off obviously means nothing. But since I will be leaving for Calcutta in the morning, I thought I had better warn you in advance."

At that, she turned and looked at him suspiciously through her lashes. "Warn me of what?"

Gavin smiled lazily. "I am to escort you and your sisters back to Lady Margaret's. Plassey Junction is cut off. Travel to Kingscote is too dangerous. It appears as if you will be forced to delay your return home. But that should make you happy. Marianna tells me you have been wanting to go back. London, it seems, is still on your mind, or should I say heart?"

Kathleen smiled too sweetly and walked over to where he stood. "It seems little Marianna feels quite comfortable in sharing her heart with you."

"Why, Kathleen, do not tell me you are jealous?"

"Quite a presumption, Captain! Why should I be jealous of my sister? And one hardly out of braids at that."

He laughed. "Your feminine ego resents my attention on any female but yourself. Someone ought to tell you that you are too conceited. I do not suppose this Jacques would dare to presume."

Kathleen felt her quick temper ignite. She tried to swallow back the rush of words that would put him in his place. But she had lashed out at him many times before, and it only gave him the advantage, for he never appeared to be daunted by her. Instead, she smiled again, her prettiest smile, and took a moment of satisfaction when he laughed at her attempt to throw him off.

"Now, Gavin, do not be an impossible bore. After two weeks in that ghastly ghari, breathing and eating dust, the least you can do is waste a little flattery on me. The night will be horrid enough spent in the company of that old stick Mr. Harrington and his friends."

"What a nasty little tyrant you can be sometimes, Kathleen. How is it you inherited none of your baby sister's sweetness, or Coral's honor?"

Kathleen knew that he did not mean to sound malicious; she had grown used to his barbs, as he had her own, in the years they had known each other. Now, for some reason unknown to Kathleen, the words stung. Was she truly as hard-nosed and selfish as Gavin made her out to be?

Coral's honor . . . Marianna's sweetness . . .

"But for you, Kathleen, anything. Tonight I shall feed your conceit and play the charming military gentleman. You will be surprised how I can exceed your gallant but empty-headed French designer."

It must be my mood, thought Kathleen. Gavin was no more satirical with her than usual, but lacking in her customary ability to banter, tonight she felt out of step with his irony, even uncomfortable.

One would think I was the most selfish thing that ever walked in shoe leather, she thought, and for a brief moment envied both Coral and Marianna.

She realized that he was scrutinizing her. She turned away and walked over to the window. Another ghari was arriving with more of Harrington's dinner guests. Kathleen turned when she felt his hand on her shoulder, and his voice was oddly kind. "Something wrong, Kathleen?"

"No. Nothing is wrong. Why do you ask?"

"I expected you to come at me with claw and fang, and you looked instead as if you had swallowed a camel."

"You are gallant with your compliments."

He laughed. "You expect too many. But I will be generous," he said when her brows came together. "You look both charming and delectable tonight, and one would never guess you had braved the dust and insects of India to make it this far to Manali. As I said, a pity I will not be staying in Calcutta for more than a few days after I escort you there."

Kathleen's curiosity was baited, and she wanted to ask him why, but she also tried to pretend her disinterest.

"Oh, you mean your tour of duty will be over? And where will you go this time, Gavin, to London perhaps? Did you not say your aunt lived there?"

"She does. A sprightly little woman in her eighties. A friend of your dear Granny Victoria, I believe."

"I do not want to belittle your kindly old aunt, but Granny V happens to be a horrible snob. She would not hobnob with your sprightly maiden aunt from Aberdeen. Besides, she has little regard for the Scottish side of Papa's family. The Scotch," she said with a smile, "are known savages. Why, they used to be cannibals."

"They still are in the woods. I'll take you to visit them on our honeymoon."

Kathleen wrinkled her nose. "I shall never go to Scotland."

Captain McKay changed the subject. "Major Buckley hopes to gain your moral support in convincing Coral to return to Calcutta. Since it is known that you wish to return, this is your opportunity. Do you think you can do it?"

"And if I may ask, just why will you not be in Calcutta?"

"Duty is the honorable reason. The colonel transferred me to Jorhat. I cannot say that I am pleased about it. Buckley and I agree on a number of things, especially the avid desire to shed our uniforms."

"Oh, then you will be stationed at the Jorhat outpost?"

He grimaced. "Afraid so. If you were going home to Kingscote, I would be near enough to ride over and brighten your evenings. But it looks as if you will be going to Calcutta instead. Worst luck!"

Kathleen said nothing.

"Do not frown," he said. "You look so much lovelier when you laugh. Is my company that awful?"

Kathleen did smile, her dimples showing, and her curls sparkling under the light of lanterns. "After weeks of being starved of anything fun, Captain, I am not likely to complain of your company. Were you telling the truth? Did you almost get killed at Plassey?"

"Almost. But Jace was the lucky one. If it had not been for the loyalty of his daffadar, he would be dead."

In the salon, Lady Amelia's voice rang out: "Mutiny! Not one of us is safe in our beds with the natives on the loose. Gives me the vapors! I dare say, the military ought to be doing something to put a stop to this rampage."

There was a distraction in the entryway, and the clear, determined voice of Major Buckley was heard telling Zameen that he was expected by Sir Hugo and would show himself in.

Coral, who stood between Sir Hugo and Doctor Boswell in the salon, heard the small ruckus and looked toward the door to see the major enter. She paused, as did the others, taking note of both his countenance and his new spotless uniform, no doubt brought by Captain McKay from the Calcutta garrison. Except for a small bandage on the side of his head, his other wounds were inconspicuous.

"Ah, Major, good of you to show," said Sir Hugo. "Ethan has kept me informed of your progress. The news of your rissaldar-major has come as a shock. Am I to assume he is wanted for mutiny?"

"He will be tried and executed in Calcutta," replied Jace.

Coral glanced from Jace to Sir Hugo to see his response. Her uncle's expression was one of appropriate disdain for the betrayer. "A nasty business, this. Captain McKay informs me it will be sometime before we are in control of Plassey again. This loss of life is most regrettable."

Coral felt her heart thud. Would Jace call her uncle's deception now, in front of the guests? But while his expression was hard, it showed no accusation. In fact, if she had not been certain of running into Jace at the dakbungalow that night when Hugo spoke with Sanjay, she could believe that he had heard nothing that would in the slightest way incriminate her uncle.

"Then travel through Plassey is delayed indefinitely," said Ethan. "Our journey north is out of the question. This is most disappointing."

Coral tensed. *Indefinitely!* "There is the river," she said, speaking for the first time. She noted that Jace's jaw set, as though her observation, forgotten by the others, was an unwanted intrusion.

Jace replied, not looking at her, but at Sir Hugo: "Travel by way of the river is possible but not recommended for civilians. Much of it is delta, infested with crocodiles and tigers. I advise that you send your nieces back to Calcutta."

Coral turned sharply. *He is deliberately avoiding me.*

"I do not know what your plans are, but now that Plassey is under siege, you also may wish to return," he said to Hugo.

Her uncle appeared entirely self-possessed, and he said thoughtfully, "Then do I gather, Major, that it is your intention to go on to Guwahati by river?"

"I intend to warn the outpost of another possible mutiny."

"If there is any way to continue the journey, I, too, wish to leave at once," said Sir Hugo. "My duty to the governor-general demands it."

"As you wish. Our travel will be by small boats through the delta. Eventually we will join up with the Bramaputra River."

Ethan looked skeptical. "I do hope, Major, that you will have an appropriate river guide? I should loathe getting lost in the jungle."

"Seward and I have traveled it before."

"What of boats? I have my medical supplies to consider."

"Seward is seeing to the matter now. I cannot vouch for your supplies. We will need to travel light. I would advise that you return to Calcutta with Sir Hampton's daughters. You can travel by land route as soon as the problem in Plassey is taken care of."

Coral pressed her hands tightly against her skirts. She found her voice all at once, and it came as a breathless declaration. "I beg to differ with you, Major Buckley, but I am able to survive a river journey as well as anyone."

Jace turned to look at her for the first time. Meeting the blue granite stare, she knew that he would do everything possible to see that Sir Hugo sent her back.

"I would not advise the boat trip, Miss Kendall," came the smooth voice. "I am certain Sir Hugo will agree that the risk is too great."

So. He would even go so far as to use Sir Hugo to thwart her purpose, although they both distrusted him!

She knew that he already understood her reasons for wanting to get home to Kingscote, and the formality between them was a pretext, and yet his expression was set.

Ethan interrupted, speaking to his uncle. "Coral is right, Hugo. Her heart is set upon returning home, and I, for one, cannot see her disappointed. If we continue the journey at all, then she should be permitted to travel on with us."

Surprised by his support, Coral turned and looked at him. He smiled down at her. "If you are dauntless enough to brave crocodiles and tigers, you shall hear no complaint from me. Seriously, Hugo, I quite agree with her about Elizabeth. As a physician, I can hardly turn my back and scurry to the safety of Calcutta."

Sir Hugo seemed pleased, and Coral believed his satisfaction was because she and Ethan appeared to be getting on together.

"I do not see how I can refuse the both of you. Well, Major Buckley?" he said. "It appears as if Coral shall be coming with us. I will speak to my other nieces. It may be that they will wish a military guard back to Calcutta."

Coral glanced at Jace. He said nothing more, but his gaze riveted upon her. She felt a nervous qualm and smiled, offering a little laugh. "My! Won't this be an adventure?"

"Yes," said Jace flatly. "It will."

Ethan extended his arm. "Shall we go to dinner, Coral?"

"Ah—yes, of course. Mr. Harrington is waiting for us." She walked with him across the salon toward the dining area. From behind her she heard Sir Hugo speak to Jace: "You will join us, Major?"

"Thank you, no. Good-night."

Coral glanced to see him walk past Captain McKay

and Kathleen. He did not stop to speak, but continued on, brushing past the guests. Jace paused in the entryway, looked at Zameen for a moment, and then went out. The door shut soundly behind him.

21

The morning sun dispersed rays of light along the river, while thread-legged pelicans stalked the shoreline in search of their breakfast. The boatmen, called *manjis*, had arrived from the village to load the supplies. The river safari into the northern frontier of Assam would begin that morning. Coral glanced about for Seward. Did he load her trunk of school supplies?

Coral turned in the direction of the road to see Jace with Captain McKay. Whatever they were discussing prompted a glance in her direction. Confronted with a steady stare from the major, Coral tore her eyes away and pretended to be looking for Seward. In order to thwart any new plans that he may have had to stop her from going on the journey, she had spent hours last night talking her sisters into returning with her to Kingscote, knowing that it would give Jace less justification to oppose her independent action. Evidently it had worked, and she felt rather smug to have outmaneuvered him.

"Are we trusting ourselves to those miserable little boats?" said Kathleen. "One misstep, and we will be swimming with crocodiles."

"Oh, no," moaned Marianna. "Coral, there are only

little boats—six of them. I thought we would all be on one *big* boat!"

Like her sisters, Coral had anticipated a larger river vessel. Those waiting at the ghat were the shallow-draught country boats with square sails that she was familiar with in Assam. She tried to appear confident and offered her younger sister a bright smile.

"Now, do not worry, Marianna. The boats are more secure than they look. And think of the view we will have."

Kathleen opened her pink parasol, its fringe dancing. "Maybe I *will* go to Calcutta."

Coral took firm hold of Kathleen's arm. "Oh, no. You promised me." She looked at Marianna. "Both of you did. We are going through with this. Do not look so squeamish. Major Buckley is hoping you will both faint before we leave so he can go to Uncle and tell him it is a dreadful mistake." She looked from Marianna's gloomy face to Kathleen's scowl. "We prayed together last night, remember?"

"Yes," murmured Marianna, "but you implied the Lord would give us a big boat. I thought we would have a cabin, at least. Where will we sleep at night?"

"On land, you goose," said Kathleen. "But cheer up. The major will build a fire to keep the crawling things away."

"Oh! Coral!"

"You want to get home to Mother, do you not?" Coral pressed. "And there is the mission school to start before the monsoon. If I do not arrive in time to see some kind of structure built before the ground turns to mud, I will need to wait another six months."

"You do not even know if Papa will allow the school," cautioned Kathleen.

"I shall leave that obstacle to prayer, just the way we

committed our boat trip to Him last night. Now then . . ." Coral let out a breath and smiled at them. "It is all settled. No more questions, no more fears. We must appear strong and capable before Major Buckley, or he may try to send us back with Captain McKay."

"Oh, very well," said Kathleen. "I shall never understand you, Coral, but since I do not even know my own mind sometimes, I shall go through with this."

Despite Kathleen's cynicism, Coral felt that there were times when her sister understood more than she would admit.

"Kathleen, you go say goodbye to Captain McKay. He is waiting for you. I want to talk to Seward about my school supplies."

"What about me?" said Marianna with a hopeless expression on her young face, almost as if she were an abandoned kitten.

"Wait here by the ghari until Uncle Hugo and Ethan arrive," said Coral. "I will not be long."

Kathleen looked toward the barge. "Ethan is already here. That is him squabbling with the boatmen." Coral followed her gaze to the overloaded barge where Ethan stood wearing a hat and knee-length coat, waving his arms at the manjis. She guessed that he was frustrated trying to communicate his concern over his medical supplies.

Coral made her way toward the riverbank. The morning sunshine and the feel of baked earth beneath her slippers proclaimed the beginning of another hot day. She was only occasionally aware of the weakness due to the poisonous bite at Harrington's house, and she looked a pale but pretty figure in the blue calico dress with its yards of skirts over crinolines. It was not one of her best dresses, for she knew the rigors of the safari, and yet she would have preferred a more suitable frock. She had, however, opted to omit a parasol, preferring the freedom of a wide-brimmed hat that tied beneath her chin.

The slight breeze from off the water was muggy and smelling of dead things. Already she felt her garments sticking to her flesh. Insects buzzed, and she waved her gloved hand before her eyes. Nearing the bank she saw Seward. A waft of air greeted her from off the murky water, which was stagnant in places, and dangerously low. But Jace had sailed to far distant shores, including the Spice Islands, and she did not question his ability to navigate northward toward Assam.

She walked toward the edge of the river, where pelicans prowled the oozing dark mud. Seward looked up from beneath his tricorn and saw her.

"Morning, lassie. The mud be slippery, so watch your step."

"Good morning, Seward." She smiled. "I see you have permitted Doctor Boswell to safeguard the loading of his supplies."

"Permitted?" He scowled in the direction of the ghat. "Aye, and neither me nor the major be taking the blame for 'em not arriving in one piece either. The man be smart when it comes to helping the sick but a mite lacking in river sense."

She felt uncomfortable and a little protective of Ethan. "I take it there is some trouble?"

"You take it right. The major knows these rivers. And if the doctor were as wise as he makes out, he'd listen to a man who knows the sea. The doctor be insisting on taking the big barge, but shallow water be ahead, mark it down, lass. He be in trouble."

Coral was thinking of her own trunk. "Are you saying Major Buckley will not permit us to take the baggage?"

"Nay, I didn't say that. But the doctor arrived last night with an order from Sir Hugo to the major. The doctor will haul his medical supplies on his own rented ferry barge, and he won't be taking no for an answer."

"Do not be too harsh on him, Seward. I can understand his apparent stubbornness. If we wait to have our supplies hauled, it could be close to a year before we receive them at Kingscote. The school cannot wait, and neither can his lab. We have so much work to do. And we want to build before the rains. Where is my trunk? Do you have it loaded?"

"The doctor be having it tied down now."

"Good. Then I will see how he is progressing."

Coral walked toward the ghat. As she neared the steps leading down to the boat landing, she found Ethan engaged in an ongoing dilemma of explaining his wishes to the manjis in halting English. He saw Coral and threw up his hands in helpless despair.

"Coral, thank goodness! Would you please explain to them that the crates must be handled with delicate care? They are worse than the bellicose seamen on the East India Company docks!"

Coral laughed and called down to the men in Bengali: "You must treat them gently, please. Tie them down well. When you are done, see to that blue trunk over there by the crates. It is mine, and I want it secured."

Ethan stood guard over the process like a hawk above a field of feeding mice. Coral was still smiling when she turned around to find Jace standing behind her.

In place of his uniform he wore a loose-fitting tunic and rugged jerkins. Once again he appeared the arrogant young adventurer, his hat low to keep the sun out of his eyes. The only thing missing was Goldfish.

He cocked his head and surveyed her blue dress. "Ah, I see you have already changed your mind. A wise decision, Coral, or are we back to the *Major Buckley and Miss Kendall* routine?"

"Changed my mind?" she repeated, confused.

He flashed a devastating smile. "Your ball gown."

Ball gown! She looked down at her calico, far from an elaborate dress, but obviously he wanted to pretend that it was.

"Since it is more suitable for a ball at the East India Company than a pitiless river journey, I assume," he said good-naturedly, "that you have already decided to return to Calcutta."

Coral gave him a wry smile. "Captain Buckley, do you ever give up?"

He encountered her gaze. "No."

"A commendable virtue when invested properly. However, I simply refuse to let you nettle me out of my amiable mood this morning."

"A difficult task, I can see. Are you always so angelic? You do have me curious."

He could not actually think that she was *angelic*?

She said airily, ignoring his question, "I suppose that I could try to please you and don a military uniform, if you have one to spare."

He lowered his hat and regarded her, then looked over to where Kathleen and Marianna stood beneath parasols, looking like pink and white froth on a cool summer's drink. "Do your charming sisters realize the river will be infested with smiling crocodiles?"

She folded her arms. "They were also born in India."

"But apt to swoon more often, is my guess."

"Not Kathleen. When necessary she has nerves of steel."

"Good. Because I will not have time to meander about with smelling salts."

"My, my, but you are in a nasty mood this morning, are you not? I assume the mosquitoes must have kept you awake all night. As for those crocodiles you hope to frighten me with, it will do no good. I will not go back to Calcutta. And, Major, do not forget to mention man-eating tigers and snakes."

"Pythons."

"I am sure we will run into a few of those also."

Jace folded his arms and gave her one of his familiar slanted looks. "I could say you never cease to amaze me, my dear Miss Kendall, but I will not. It is enough that I can depend on you to not swoon at the first roar of a tiger."

Swoon! She laughed. "I have never seen a Bengal tiger yet that caused me to drop into a heap of petticoats."

He smiled, and it was deliberately disbelieving. "As you wish." He lowered his voice. "But we best not tell your sisters that the tigers can swim to our little boats."

Coral refused to show alarm because she suspected that he wanted to jolt her. She also gleaned an amused hint of challenge in the slate color of his eyes. "Are you sure you are not making that part up?" she suggested.

"You might ask the several hundred fishermen in the area. However . . ." and he glanced about. "I fear that many are no longer able to explain."

Coral's stomach did a flip. "Well, I will take your word for it. The truth is, I did feel quite safe until I caught sight of those boats."

He followed her gaze. "Miserable, are they not? And to think I left the *Madras* for this." He mocked a groan. "Let us hope they stay afloat."

"With crocodiles? Indeed! Where did you get them?"

His mood changed. He looked back in the direction of the residence. "Harrington arranged for the boats. I keep thinking I have seen that man somewhere before."

"You might have."

His eyes swerved to hers. She explained quietly: "Mr. Harrington once lived in Guwahati. You may have seen him there when you served at the outpost. And Zameen was the maharaja's dewan."

"Ah! That accounts for it."

"Becoming secretary to Mr. Harrington is a humble step down from one who served as chief minister, you agree?"

"My guess," said Jace, "is that he is more than a secretary to Harrington. Interesting. I wish you had told me this sooner."

"Why? Is it important?"

"Maybe. And Zameen. It now makes sense."

"Not to me. Whatever are you suggesting?"

"I cannot prove it, but I do not think I will need to search further for the one who helped my rissaldar escape into the black of night. I also think I will find him at Guwahati."

"For that matter, we know little about Harrington," said Coral. "Except he is said to be a friend of my uncle. I hope Sir Hugo is up to nothing worse than minor disagreements with my father over Kingscote and the Company."

"In the meantime I will have McKay alert the colonel to my suspicion."

"I wondered about Zameen myself," Coral admitted. "I do not know why, but when I first learned that Uncle wished us to stay at Manali with an acquaintance, I had an odd feeling. As though Marianna and I would come face-to-face with the man we saw in the garden at Barrackpore."

He looked at her. "You are sure it was *not* Zameen?"

"Quite. The other man was tall with a yellow turban."

He smiled. "I doubt if he goes around wearing a yellow turban all the time. We will give him credit for laundering his garments and changing them."

"Regardless, the man I saw was not Zameen. And

Marianna showed no recognition when she saw him. We cannot both be wrong."

"You are quite sure he *was* an Indian?"

"Yes, well—" She stopped and bit her lip. "He wore a turban."

A brow slanted.

"And he spoke Bengali," she said with a note of defense.

"You and I both speak Bengali. Many English do. The turban and dialect could have been a deliberate disguise, just to be sure no one at Barrackpore could possibly recognize him."

Coral felt a prickle of her skin as she understood where his thoughts were leading. "Mr. Harrington?" she whispered. "Is it possible?"

"Why not?"

"Then, Uncle may have—" She paused.

"Brought you here deliberately. Just to see if either you or Marianna could identify him. And I was unwise enough to let you come."

"You could not have known."

"I should have."

For a moment they said nothing. Coral stood remembering Mr. Harrington and breathing a thankful prayer that Marianna did not perceive who Harrington was.

All those weeks at Manali without the major or Seward. She shuddered. And illness had kept her deaf and dumb to the situation around them.

"I think we have unwound the yellow turban and discovered our garden intruder. I will alert Colonel Warbeck. Say nothing to your sister about this. Sir Hugo is convinced that you are blind to Harrington's masquerade."

She glanced over her shoulder to see the arrival of a

ghari. "It is Uncle. At least he now has confidence in you. He suspects nothing."

"He is putting on an act. He does not trust me anymore than I do him. He expected me to die by the hands of my jemander near Plassey. I think it was the reason behind the change in my orders."

Coral felt sick. *No! Her uncle would never go so far in his plans!*

"Now he is stuck with me as the head of his security guard in Guwahati." He gave her a scrutinizing look. "You have not mentioned what you overheard between him and Sanjay to your sisters?"

She hesitated, thinking of Ethan. "No."

He looked relieved. "I do not want them involved. And I do not want Sir Hugo to know I overheard him and Sanjay. I can learn more of what is going on by playing his way. I only wish you did not know so much. What about Boswell? Did you tell him?"

His look evoked a feeling of guilt, and she turned defensive. "Oh, come. He is not a conniver." She rearranged the ribbon beneath her chin. Beneath his alert gaze, she turned toward Ethan, who was still inspecting the loading of his barrels and crates, as though they held the jewels of the Taj Mahal.

"Then you did tell him," he said softly.

"Why not? I trust him," she said defensively.

"I do not."

"He will not say anything to my uncle. I will ask him to remain silent."

"No. Say nothing. The less you bring up the subject, the better. What makes you so certain of your cousin?"

"He has done nothing to warrant my suspicions, and he intends to help me with the school. Besides," she reminded him, "he did doctor your wounds after the mutiny. If it is true what you think about my uncle, then

Ethan was not involved. He might have let you die. We rode to the village with Seward the moment he told us what had happened."

"We?"

She had not intended to let him know that she had felt compelled to go with Ethan and Seward. She said simply, "I went with Ethan. He needed my help."

There was silence, and she could feel his gaze. She busied herself with her hat, and when the moments continued to pass without his response, she said too abruptly, hoping to interrupt his thoughts, "Ethan's devotion to medicine is not practiced to put others in his debt. He is a man of honor."

"I can see your cousin is the embodiment of your most noble crusader."

She gave a short laugh to throw him off track. "It so happens I am a trifle more sophisticated than *that*. I hardly go about mooning and cultivating romantic notions of heroic knights sweeping me away to unknown isles aboard stolen ships."

He smiled. "A knight rode a horse, my dear; he was not a sea captain."

She turned away, glancing down the river as though impatient to be off. "I do not know how we got onto this silly subject."

"Ethan is misleading you."

"You seem to know a good deal about other people's motives."

"Regardless of the doctor's gallant intervention the other night with your uncle, I would like to insist that the man knows nothing about the dangers of the journey. You and your sisters would be better off to return to Calcutta."

"There is no need to be angry with him," she said. "I would have discovered some way to proceed with the journey without his moral support."

Her defense of Ethan seemed only to evoke Jace's impatient glance down to the ghat steps, where her cousin hovered over his crates of books.

"He is making a mistake taking the barge. Which reminds me, your contraband would be better if left to McKay than to the inexperience of Boswell. Follow his advice, and you may end up with nothing."

Coral was taken off guard. "Contraband?"

"Your *mission supplies*, being smuggled to Kingscote under the nose of Sir Hugo. McKay will see your materials are delivered when he arrives to take up his position at the outpost."

She let out a sigh of gratitude. "Why, the idea is perfect. And they will arrive in time to set up a temporary structure before the monsoon. What about Ethan's medical supplies?" she asked. "Can you ask Captain McKay to see to their safety as well?"

"I could," he said dryly. "But the doctor's great scientific mind has already rejected so simple a solution. He prefers to risk the destruction of his gear by keeping it under his own watchful eye."

She would admit Ethan's mistake to herself but not to Jace. Instead, she offered a smile of appeasement. "A lovely morning for a river trip, is it not?"

"I find nothing pleasant about the morning, nor the weeks of travel ahead. As for Boswell, you trust him too much."

She felt a slight rebuke, and turned away, watching the manjis and Ethan. "I know him better than you do. And he saved my life at Manali."

He straightened and fixed her with an alert stare. "He did *what* at Manali?"

His response took away her casual air. "I was ill, and he treated me."

He frowned and scanned her. "At Manali? You said nothing about this before."

"No, please, you misunderstand. It was not a relapse of the fever, if that is what concerns you," she hastened. "I am strong enough for the journey."

"Then would you mind explaining what you do mean?"

She absently untied the ribbon and removed her hat. "It was all rather unpleasant, actually. I was bitten by this horrid spider. Harrington kept a collection as a hobby. . . ." She glanced about the ground, feeling a desire to lift the hem of her skirts. "I was sitting at dinner."

"How soon after you arrived?"

"A day or two later. Why? What has that to do with it?"

"I know most insects around here. What did it look like?"

"Imagining the thing makes me shudder. I would rather come face-to-face with a Bengal tiger than a long-legged hairy creature with—"

"Why do you say *imagine* it? Did you not see it?"

"No. It happened too fast," she said, remembering the spell of dizziness that had overtaken her while seated at Mr. Harrington's table. She shuddered.

"And Boswell was able to bring you out of it, is that it?"

She wondered at his flat tone of voice. "Yes. Even so, I was bedridden for the entire length of time you and Seward were gone. And now that we suspect Mr. Harrington to have been the man in the garden—" she stopped.

A breath escaped his lips. "You might have told me."

Coral replaced her hat and tied it firmly under her chin. "The opportunity did not arise until now. Besides, nothing happened after all, did it? I have my strength back, and I shall do fine on the journey."

"But you did not see it?"

"I told you. It happened too fast. Why? Is it important?"

"Because I am unaware of a spider bite that is as serious as you suggest. Tell me again how it happened."

Coral began to feel uneasy. What was Jace hinting at, if anything? He did not like Ethan; the two men were opposites in nature, and that could account for his suspicions. She slapped at an insect. "I was seated at the dinner table, and the next thing I knew I felt extremely dizzy. I remember little else, except having nightmares, until some days later. Ethan can explain what kind of spider it was."

"Is that when you both became trusted friends? During your recuperation?" he asked smoothly.

"Well, yes, you could say that. But do not forget, I have known him the last few years in London. He did save my life, Jace. And this was not the first time. I am well today because of his medical expertise while at Roxbury House."

"And of course you are very grateful."

Something in his tone put her on guard. "Why should I not feel indebted to my physician?"

"That depends."

"On what?"

"On the true cause of your illness."

She blushed. "I do not know what you mean."

"I think you do."

"I think you misjudge him. He has even suggested helping me with the untouchables. The children will need medical treatment."

"And he possesses the Christian graces of faith and charity, of course. It has nothing at all to do with pleasing a silk heiress."

Her breathing felt tight. "If he is willing to risk Uncle's ire by helping with the school, I can see no reason to doubt his good intentions."

From below on the barge, Ethan's voice was heard shouting: "Wait, you there, set the crate down *gently*! It contains medical drugs."

Jace observed her from under his hat. "Did it ever occur to you that Sir Hugo may wish Doctor Boswell to appear sympathetic to your ambitions?"

"That is too complicated," she said stiffly. "Uncle disapproves of my plans."

"It is not complicated at all. What better way to drive you to the consoling support of his nephew?"

This new thorn of suspicion only frustrated her. "The trouble with you, Major, is that you do not trust *anyone*. Sometimes I am certain you must keep steel armor around your heart."

"Never mind my heart. It is you we are discussing."

"Did anyone ever suggest to you how stubborn and domineering you are, Major?"

He smiled and looked away from Doctor Boswell to a bird winging its way across the river. There followed a moment of silence. Trying to cool her emotions, Coral focused on a pelican in the mud.

"About this spider, where was the bite?"

"My ankle."

"Did it swell?"

"No! I mean—" she stopped.

"Meaning?"

"Meaning nothing at all, Major Buckley. I was asleep during that period of time. You are not suggesting Ethan put something in my tea?"

"I did not say that. But since you mention it, it must have crossed your mind."

Coral remembered back to the night she had sat at

dinner. Sir Hugo had poured her tea, not Ethan.

She turned her head. He was still watching a fowl flying through the sky. "Very well. I had tea. But it was not Ethan who gave it to me. It was Sir Hugo."

"May I suggest your *spider* was a drug?"

She refused to shudder at the thought. She remembered the drugs she had taken in London, and how ill they had seemed to make her.

"It is to your benefit that you are not good to anyone dead," he said softly but bluntly. She winced.

"If it were a drug, what would be the reason behind it? And anyway," she added with relief, "Ethan is not to blame."

"He is a physician. A good one. Do you agree?"

"But of course."

"Then why did he not recognize your symptoms were caused by an administered drug?"

Coral was growing tense as he continued to hammer away at her foundations. "You do not know for certain that it was a drug."

"No. But if you could go back and examine that bite on your ankle, you might find that it did not exist. As for a reason, Roxbury still wants you to marry his nephew?"

"The entire family wishes it, not just Uncle," she said stiffly. "He did offer to give Ethan and me Mr. Harrington's indigo plantations for a wedding gift."

"How generous," said Jace dryly, "considering his nephew will inherit the wealth of a silk heiress. What did you tell him?"

"Do you think I would marry a man for an indigo plantation?"

He turned his head, and she felt his gaze. "No. If the choice remains your own, I doubt if you would even marry to gain the Roxbury Estate and Silk House. But you *would* marry a man like Peddington and be content to live on bread and water to translate the Scriptures."

She looked at him, speechless. It made her uncomfortable to think he could analyze her so well. To cover her embarrassment, she said lightly, "I am not that saintly, Major. I will want a trifle more than that."

"Coral, please go back to Calcutta with McKay. Wait there. When this matter in Jorhat is settled, I will discover what I can about Gem. If I have something definite before then, I will send word through Gokul."

"Jace, I do appreciate your concern." His laugh told Coral he did not believe her. She looked at him evenly. "For me to turn back now is out of the question."

His eyes measured her determination. Did she see a brief hint of admiration? It happened with such haste that she was not even certain he had responded at all.

"As you wish. We will not discuss it again. Excuse me. I need to speak with McKay about your supplies before he rides out."

22

That morning the small group boarded boats and left Manali. According to what Seward told her, the delta was a marshy mangrove jungle that would demand the full attention of the armed sowars.

"We'll not be going to the extreme south into the heart of the jungle, but heading north on the delta to the Ganges. Even so, the journey be hostile."

Standing with Seward on the barge, Coral found herself looking out over the largest estuarine forest in the world. She couldn't help but feel anticipation over the journey ahead, despite the dangers.

"I suppose after this you'll be off to the tea plantation in Darjeeling?" she asked, ready to probe for some answers.

Mention of the project was all that it took to hook Seward. His eyes brightened. "The tea plantation in Darjeeling? Aye, once the major's duty to the colonel is over, we be making a success of it. Jace and me, along with Gokul and Jin-Soo—we have large plans, if God blesses. Not that I be anxious to leave Kingscote, understand," he said. "But Jace be needing me, maybe more than your father. Jace has his mind set on making it work. I don't doubt but that he can do it. He be a hard worker, and dedicated when he believes in something." He squinted at her. "What've ye got on your mind?"

The tea plantation interested her more than she cared to admit. "I've wondered about the friendship between Michael and Jace. Michael's death on the *Madras* was an accident, and yet it did get me to wondering about their past, and something Michael once told me at Kingscote. About an accident—"

"Aye, you mean the avalanche?"

"I have wanted to ask Jace about it, but the moment never seemed appropriate. Do you know what happened?"

Seward hesitated, and Coral noticed that he appeared uncomfortable.

"I know nothing about it, lass. But if there be talk about what happened on the ship, well, I be knowing exactly what happened. I be suspecting that slander came from Sir Hugo." He paused and tried to read her expression, and when she did not deny it, he grunted. "Thought so. That being true, I don't set much mind to Sir Hugo's tongue, since it can dish out anything that pleases his aims."

Coral frowned, grateful that her uncle had chosen to ride in one of the smaller boats. "I do not doubt what you and Jace say occurred on the *Madras*. But I have been curious about a number of things. Then you were not there when this incident of the avalanche happened?"

"Nay, I know nothing of it. And since Jace hasn't seen fit to talk about it with me, I don't find it my business to ask."

"Yes, of course. But if there is nothing to the story of the avalanche, then why has Jace remained silent?"

"Good question, Miss Kendall," Jace said from behind them. "But you will not find the answer with Seward. He was not in Darjeeling. It was Michael and I, and Gokul."

Coral whirled about, her cheeks turning warm. "But perhaps you were convinced I would not tell the truth if you asked."

"No, I—" She stopped, feeling embarrassed to be caught discussing this affair behind his back.

"I suggest that any questions you have about my past be brought to me. I shall answer for my own faults."

Seward cleared his throat. "I'll be getting the kansamah to boil us up some coffee." He walked away leaving them alone.

Coral faced Jace. "I was not accusing you of wrong."

Jace said nothing, but she could see he did not believe her. "I have wanted to ask you about that avalanche ever since—"

"Ever since I was accused of losing Michael at sea?"

"No, since Michael mentioned it at Kingscote."

"But you prefer to find out about it from Seward. Perhaps you think I left Michael to die so I could latch hold of the tea plantation for myself. And when I failed the first time, I threw him overboard."

"You make it sound foolish."

"I hope so."

"I was only curious about Darjeeling."

"Then why did you not ask me?"

"I will. Would you mind telling me what happened?"

He shrugged. "We were exploring the upper mountainous region around Darjeeling years ago. I slipped and fell. There was an avalanche. It took me days to get back to the village. The truth was, I did think Michael was dead. I was surprised to find him in the village."

This, she had not expected. *Jace was the one who had slipped and fallen! What of Michael? Had he fallen also? Had he searched for Jace?*

"You said Gokul was there. He found you?"

His voice was flat. "No. He was the one who found Michael. Gokul thought I was buried under the avalanche."

"Did Michael tell Gokul that?"

"I do not remember," he said flatly. "You can ask Gokul."

In the silence that grew between them, the monkeys chattered.

There was more to the story, Coral knew that, but it was not coming from him. Perhaps Jace did not mean for it to be clear. Could it be that the story was unfavorable to Michael? If she ever met Gokul, she would ask him. It was obvious that Jace would say no more. Feeling unexpectedly tired, Coral turned away. "Excuse me, Major, but I think I will take advantage of the shade."

Jace said nothing and stepped aside.

———

They were five days into the river journey, and Coral sat with her sisters beneath the makeshift awning Seward had constructed for them on the river barge. The roof of palm fronds offered relief from the intense sun, and the curtains from Mr. Harrington could be drawn closed at night for privacy. Some simple deck chairs and cushions made the long hours more comfortable. While Marianna embroidered their mother a scarf and Kathleen resumed her dress designing in her prized portfolio, Coral continued her study of Hindi and the Hindu religion, hoping for ways to use the Scriptures on Kingscote.

Ethan had secured the use of the barge from a ferry owner in Manali, despite the fact that Jace had advised against it. But Ethan's enthusiasm for the exploration of fauna and insects had prompted him to use the barge not only to carry his medical supplies, but also to set up a tiny tent-lab. He had erected it at the back of the barge, on top of his crates and barrels. Seward called it a crow's nest. And at any hour, Ethan could be seen with his butterfly and fishing nets, making his way up the side of the crates with prized samples of plant life, fish, or insects.

But it was not the wide variety of small creatures that disturbed Coral. She guessed that they were nearing a dangerous area in the delta by the fact that Jace had unexpectedly, but unobtrusively, joined Seward to ride on the detested barge. And yet, from the casual manner in which he behaved, she had no proof that the motivation for his presence meant an increase in danger.

Marianna and Kathleen were busy with their projects, and Coral grew weary of her study. She placed her New Testament and some books into her bag, left them under her chair, and picked up her wide-brimmed straw hat. She would simply inquire of Jace if her suspicions were correct.

With that, she ventured forth from the shelter of shade into the sun. It was muggy. She had already exchanged her high-necked frocks and crinolines for the cooler muslins. Today her frock of pale yellow did little to ease the discomfort, and she was wishing for a breeze from off the river. The wood creaked beneath her slippers as she walked toward the back of the barge, and the rolling movement of the water made her grab the awning to steady herself.

"Easy, girl," warned Seward coming around the crates. He held her arm, his forehead furrowing beneath a waft of graying reddish brown hair. "Ye go falling into the river and it won't take long for them crocodiles to get busy."

She squinted beneath her hat and gazed across the water to the thick jungle growth on the river's bank, but saw nothing. Perhaps they were resting under the vines and shrubs covering the shore.

"I was not thinking of crocodiles, Seward."

Amid the thick emerald green, the shrill call of birds and the chatter of monkeys pierced the air.

Seward's scowl deepened as he looked away from Coral to scan the jungle. "Aye. I be knowing what ye think."

"Then I was right. We are entering tiger country."

"Aye," he admitted grudgingly.

Tigers . . . "I heard Jace talking to you last night at supper," she said quietly. "Is it true that fishermen are attacked frequently, and that these tigers can swim?"

"Ye ought to be ashamed, a daughter of Miss Elizabeth eavesdropping."

Coral smiled. "I was not holding my ear in your direction. But Jace had already mentioned tigers before we left Manali. And I could not help notice he came on the barge this morning. He usually rides in the lead boat. Tell me, Seward, is it because he thinks that we might be attacked?"

"No need to take the action of the major as sign of anything particular. The major and I be excellent shots, and it won't be the first tiger we brought low if it comes to that."

"Then it is to protect us that he chose to ride the barge?"

Seward rubbed a large hand over his beard and glanced upward. Coral whirled and followed his gaze, holding on to her hat. Jace was lounging on top of some of the crates. Had he overheard?

Coral's brows inched together. How could Jace remain so relaxed? The swoosh of the water could sound hypnotic as the Indian oarsmen dipped and sliced their poles through the river. But she remained alert. She swished an insect away with her hand, and stopped—a splash of water was followed by a cry, then a scream!

"That was Marianna!" she cried.

Seward hurled himself past her, and Coral caught up her skirts and stumbled after him. Kathleen came toward them at the same time, her face white, an arm across her stomach as if she wanted to gag. She pointed behind her. "It's Ethan, he fell! And there are crocodiles! I saw them!"

Seward ran to the rail, his eyes searching the river. Coral was beside him. Ethan's butterfly net floated past the barge. "Doctor Boswell!" Seward bellowed.

Sir Hugo was standing at the back of a small boat that was ahead of the barge. One hand cupped his mouth as he shouted: "Do something!"

Coral seized the rail, afraid of what she would witness. At first she saw only white egrets feeding. Then a movement caught her eye. Something slithered from the tall grasses on the bank and entered the water with a splash. The crocodile edged its way deeper into the river, its gray-green body sliding through the water, the small eyes protruding just above the surface.

Coral's heart thudded. A quick glance on both sides of the bank revealed more than one. Crocodiles! Everywhere.

Kathleen gripped her arm. "There! Look!"

On a mud flat along the riverbank there were a dozen creatures dozing in the sun. Their jaws were open wide displaying daggerlike teeth.

Sir Hugo was still shouting, trying to get the two sowars riding guard in his boat to save Ethan. Seward had grabbed the chairs from beneath the awning and tossed them into the river.

"Dear God!" whispered Coral, icy hands going to her mouth.

"Nay, lad!" shouted Seward.

Fear struck Coral's heart. *Jace! He would not!* She heard a second splash, and her heart seemed to stop. She brushed past Kathleen and ran up beside Seward.

"Shoot at anything leaving the bank!" Seward shouted to the sowars in the other boat, and had his own rifle aimed, but the uncertainty of whose movement they saw in the waters made it dangerous.

Coral's anxious gaze picked up a struggling shape some distance from the barge, and the next moment it disappeared again. Then she saw Jace swimming with strong stokes in Ethan's direction. Her eyes riveted on him as he dove beneath the water. How long? A minute? Her hands gripped the rail so tightly that her knuckles were white. *Please, Lord, protect them. Please . . .*

"Get a rope ready!" Seward was shouting to the oarsmen.

Coral saw Jace come up for air with Boswell holding on, struggling and gasping. Jace thrust him away with his foot, then grabbed the back of his collar and swam toward the barge.

"To your left!" Seward bellowed.

Coral saw the crocodile moving toward Jace. Seward raised his rifle and a shot crackled, spitting water around the head of the crocodile. Another shot pierced the water. A second and third crocodile left the banks, and the sowars riding guard in Sir Hugo's boat fired shots into the water.

A minute later Jace neared the barge with Ethan. Coral stood back to give the men room as Seward and an oarsman grabbed them by the shoulders and hauled the two of them out of the water onto the deck.

"Thank God, lad!" said Seward, thumping Jace on the shoulder. "Ye be in fine shape, but Boswell looks like a drowned rat."

Jace sat down to catch his breath, while Ethan sputtered and spat water.

"Major, I am in your debt," Ethan gasped.

Jace held up a hand. "Save your breath; we are even now." He got to his feet, swaying a little, and walked away.

Kathleen came rushing up. "Coral, come quick. Marianna's fainted. Do you have smelling salts with you?"

Coral hurried to the front of the barge where Marianna was already stirring.

"It is all right, Marianna. Ethan is alive. Major Buckley saved him from the crocodiles."

Marianna was so relieved that tears welled in her eyes. It was then that Coral saw the Hindi New Testament clutched to Marianna's heart. A wave of understanding swept over her. Marianna had turned to the Lord in the one way she knew how, by grasping His words. She could not read them, yet held them close to her heart.

Marianna looked at Coral. "Will you teach me to read Hindi? I opened the New Testament, and it was horrid! I could not read the words."

Coral smiled. "But do not forget the King James Bible Granny V gave you at Roxbury House."

Marianna looked sheepish. "I . . . I left it in the bedroom dresser drawer."

Kathleen went to her bag and pulled out a small black book edged in gold, with a bookmark made of silk, and embroidered with the Roxbury coat of arms. Her amber eyes gleamed with pride as she looked down at Marianna.

"I did not forget mine. Here," she said handing it to Marianna. "You can use it until Granny V sends yours. One of the maids is bound to find it."

"Thank you, but what will you use?"

Kathleen tilted her head and looked at her. She said nothing.

"Anyway," said Marianna to Coral. "I still would like lessons in Hindi. And so would Cousin Ethan. Maybe we could have a class. We have the time. And then I could write Mr. Peddington and tell him what I was doing."

"Charles would be pleased, indeed," said Coral.

"Count me out," said Kathleen. "I had enough difficulty with English grammar."

But Coral knew that Kathleen could speak Hindi better than she would let anyone know.

Coral looked up at the sound of bare feet on the deck to see the kansamah hurrying by. In one hand he held a pot of something steaming hot. In the other, two pewter mugs.

Coral wondered at her own action, but was on her feet and hailing him to stop. "Hot tea?"

He grinned. "No, miss-sahiba. Coffee. I made before physician fell in river. Favorite of Major-sahib."

"Yes, I know. I will take it to him. You can bring the other cup to the doctor."

How could she possibly have considered that Jace might leave Michael for dead? He had risked his life with horrible crocodiles for Ethan, a man he did not even like.

When she walked up, Jace was sprawled in the sunshine as though he had not a care in the world, his face buried in his arm, letting the heat dry him. Coral stopped, and a little breeze brushed the hem of her skirt against him. She held the coffee behind her. "Asleep already? It is not fair to the others for you to be so calm."

He moved his arm just slightly in order to peer up at her.

"I have a pleasant surprise for you," she said. "You deserve to be pampered."

He raised himself to an elbow, and a brow went up. "I am speechless."

Coral smiled and produced the mug. "Coffee. Although why you like it I cannot guess. Too bitter."

Seeing the mug, he sighed with satisfaction. "But only one cup?"

She brought the pot out from behind her.

"You are beginning to understand my weakness." He took the mug, and Coral stooped and poured, then set the pot down on the plank beside him, taking care that it not tip over. She straightened, holding her hat in place.

Jace took several gulps, then said grimly, "If you came to thank me for saving Boswell, there is no need. It was my duty."

Duty. How cool and pragmatic he deliberately made it sound. There was something else in those words. His duty on the *Madras* when Michael was lost at sea had been questioned by Sir Hugo and Ethan.

"I believe it was more than that," she said. "You would have done the same thing if you were no longer Major Jace Buckley, but captain of the *Madras*."

"If I had known there were crocodiles lurking in the waters, I would have let poor Boswell go the way of all flesh. How is he, by the way?"

Coral could not accept the glib remark. "He is fine, thanks to you. Seward is looking after him. And Sir Hugo hopes to board as soon as it is safe to do so. But Jace, you *knew* there were crocodiles."

He hesitated slightly, then finished the coffee and set the cup down. "If you see the kansamah, tell him the strength of the brew is perfect."

"The reason why I insist that you knew," said Coral, "is because you came aboard this morning knowing this is tiger country."

"Think so?"

"And, since you know that much about the area, you would know of the risk of crocodiles. It was Ethan who did not know. Marianna saw him fall in. He was trying to reach a black beetle with a red stripe, stretched too far with his net, and when he brought it down to catch it—he fell."

Jace smiled.

"Why do you wish to deliberately underestimate this deed of bravery?" probed Coral.

"You are right. Should I not wish to make myself look gallant after being accused of leaving a friend to die?"

"I do not know what happened in Darjeeling. Perhaps I no longer wish to. But I do think I know why you jumped in to save Ethan. A crisis can bring out of a man's heart what is truly there."

"Caution . . . I feel the probing fingers of a quizzical young mind. You would do best to not pry too deeply."

A strong breeze lifted her hat and sent it scuttling toward the deck. Jace reached out and caught it as it went by. He stood. "Your hat, Miss Kendall." His eyes held hers. "Perhaps you best retreat to the shade of the awning."

"You are not as cynical and pragmatic as you make out."

He said nothing and looked at her evenly.

"Are you?" she asked quietly.

He finished his coffee.

"I am beginning to think you choose the armor of a crocodile to scare people away."

"Do you have some particular person in mind?"

"It could be anyone you begin to care about."

"May I give you a word of advice?"

She smiled. "Again?"

"You might think twice before you try to remove the armor. The crocodile is even more dangerous when he doesn't want to scare away his dinner."

She felt her cheeks turning warm and took her hat from his extended hand. "Thank you for the warning, Major." She placed her hat on. "If you will excuse me."

Jace watched her walk away, the breeze catching her soft yellow skirt. *You are quite right. I would just as soon sail the Madras into battle with the French than allow your sweet fingers to meddle with my armor!* The more she thought him a risk, the more she would keep her distance.

He stood there, listening to the sounds of the jungle closing in about him. He walked over to his wet tunic and snatched it up. As he did, he felt something in the front pocket and removed it. His hand held the military medal that he had won. Gokul had placed it on his uniform jacket in Calcutta the night he became Major Jace Buckley.

"Gokul," said Jace aloud, with soft frustration, "I would not be in this predicament now if it had not been for you leasing the *Madras.*" Neither would he have come up against Kendall's daughter. The sooner he got this mission in Guwahati over, the better. He would pay the colonel, board the *Madras*, and head to sea. But then there was Gem . . .

Seward approached and Jace turned, scowling.

Seward gave him a questioning look in return. "Did the lass bring you your coffee?"

"She brought it. The kansamah will do well enough next time. Where is my gun?"

"Right here, lad. Boswell be wanting to see you to offer his thanks."

"Tell him it was nothing."

23

Coral found that the days on the river—with the heat and droning insects—inched by, but the nights with thick darkness due to the trees and vines were by far the worst. With tenacity she adhered to her Hindi New Testament. The very touch of the binding, the now-familiar pages with their underlined verses brought security.

Marianna did little to help Coral's own spiritual struggle. Receiving no sympathy from Kathleen, her younger sister leaned on her for the faith that she lacked. Marianna, who feared anything that buzzed, hissed, growled, or simply spun a web, was terrified of the jungle crawling with poisonous snakes and prowling tigers.

She and Marianna read Psalm 18, memorizing the promises together.

"The Lord is my rock," Coral began. "Now it is your turn."

"And my fortress, and my deliverer." Marianna scanned the riverbank out of the corner of her eye. "My God, my strength, in whom I will trust; my buckler, and the horn of my salvation—"

"And my high tower," Coral concluded. "Stop looking for crocodiles!"

Coral knew that her words were meant not only to comfort Marianna but also to remind herself.

On an afternoon when it was safe to disembark and allow the kansamah to cook supper on land, Ethan refused to leave the barge, and Coral began to worry about him. "Your supplies are safe enough, Ethan. Do come join us by the fire. Seward says one of the sowars will stand guard."

"I shall eat here, my dear," he insisted. "Send one of the soldiers with a dish. And do make sure the victuals are well cooked. Vermin infest the waterfowl."

Was he ill? Coral wondered. She looked for Jace, but he had gone off an hour earlier on his own. Now as she walked precariously toward the trees through which he had disappeared, she frowned. Anything could happen to Ethan alone on that barge. Suppose he fell into the river again? It was not likely, of course, but they were entering tiger country. Had not Jace said that the tigers were bold enough to attack fishermen in their boats?

It was a menacing sundown that streaked the sky red, while the jungle brush reflected the shades of flame. Coral stepped with caution across the ground, with her mind on snakes. Her ears were attentive, listening for the low rumble of a tiger, but there was nothing except the quiet chortle of jungle birds settling down in the twilight for the night.

She walked under an overhang of branches, contacting a thick, sticky web that brushed against her face. Ugh! With a swift move of her hand she brushed it aside. She was about to walk on when Jace emerged through some trees, looking sweaty and hot but merrily whistling. Dirt was smudged across one side of his face, and he was carrying wild honey and several fowl, already plucked for the kansamah to roast.

He stopped when he saw her, and Coral decided that he was not pleased.

"Careful where you wander. I came across a python. It caught a wild pig," he said.

Coral envisioned the huge viper crushing the pig as it tightened its grasp about its victim's body. She shuddered, rubbing her arms, and glanced about cautiously. "It is Ethan. He refuses to leave the barge."

Jace dangled the gaunt birds by their feet, and she watched their heads flop about.

"I thought the physician was supposed to do the worrying? If you will permit the observation, you are looking frail, even if your spirit is dauntless."

His remark made her aware that the strands of her hair had come undone from the chignon. Self-consciously she brushed them away from her cheek. A safari was not exactly the environment for careful grooming.

"Tell the doctor to forget his beetles and butterflies, and do some fussing over you."

"I prefer as little fuss as possible, thank you. What do you expect to do with those scrawny birds?"

"Treat your finicky appetite to the unforgettable delights of my cooking. What else?"

"You cook?" She was not really surprised; it was like Jace to be independent.

"My dear girl, but of course! How do you think I have managed to survive all these years? On Gokul's curry and rice? Tonight I shall dismiss the kansamah, and fix roast waterfowl glazed with wild honey and mango stuffing. How does that sound?"

Coral glanced at the birds with their flopping heads, their eyes still open and staring at her. "Thank you, but perhaps rice will do."

He laughed, then scowled at the birds. "I do not

blame you for refusing the moonlight dinner. Not much to look at, are they?"

Coral followed his scowl to the scrawny plucked birds with their long, shapeless legs suspended like puppets on a string. For no apparent reason, she began to giggle.

He looked at her for a long moment, then smiled, and when Coral could not stop, he too began to laugh. He extended the birds with an elegant bow. "After you, Lady Kendall. I shall deliver my prize to the kansamah, then proceed to rescue Boswell from the barge."

Coral curtseyed. "Thank you, Major. You are kind. What would I do without you?" She cast him a glance, wondering if he would choose to make something of her words.

With concealed relief that he had let the opportunity slip by, Coral turned to walk ahead.

"Stop. Do not move," he commanded.

His voice held a note of authority that she accepted without question. She held her breath, listening, but only the buzz of a mosquito about her ear disturbed the deepening twilight. A faint rustle of leaves stirred in a breeze. What did he hear? A tiger's pant? A cobra slithering through the grasses? Jace was in tune with the jungle and experienced with danger. Her skin tingled as she waited, but only silence surrounded them.

She heard his steps come up behind her, then pause. Coral could feel his gaze, and an odd quiver inched up her back. She tensed. "Would you mind telling me why you are staring at the back of my neck?"

She waited, but he gave no answer. She was about to turn when his hand closed firmly about her forearm. "Do not move."

It was then that she felt something tickle the back of her neck. Suddenly repulsed, she sucked in her breath. *That web!* She fought an impulse to scream.

"Stay calm," came Jace's quiet voice.

A moan escaped through her lips as the slow, ticklish movement of gentle legs walked across the back of her neck and came up to a stop below her earlobe.

A spider! The imagery that jumped into her mind sent her heart pounding. A trickle of perspiration ran down her sides. It had to be huge! She could feel the hairy, spindly legs! She would faint, she would scream, she would slap at it with her palm in hysterics—

"Easy."

"No, no, no—" came her voice, ragged with fear.

His grip about her arm tightened like iron and she winced. But it brought her mind momentarily off the spider. "In a moment it will crawl up the side of your face to your hair where I can safely knock it off."

She bit her lip and wanted to cry. *Lord, please make it crawl away.*

"Jace . . . I cannot stand it," she gritted, her fingers digging into her skirts. "I can feel it *moving!*"

His short laugh came unexpectedly, and with it came a stiffening of her back.

"And this is the little girl who boasts of warding off angry Hindus to gather children under her wings? Why, in another moment you will scream and swoon into a heap of petticoats."

She caught her breath with a gasp that wanted to choke her, but his light mockery stiffened her resolve.

"Did you not tell me you feared nothing in all India? Now you can prove it."

Coral closed her eyes, squeezing them so tightly that tears oozed from the corners. She swallowed, her throat dry, and whispered, "What is it doing?"

"It has decided to get cozy. Patience."

"Do *something!*"

"I cannot. It is in the groove of your neck."

"If you do not, I will!"

"Do not move. This is not your little spider at Manali. It's deadly. Once he moves a little more to the right, I will have it."

His hand squeezed her arm again, and his voice was kind. "Concentrate on the Lord. Isn't that what you told Marianna to do? Now the Lord has given you an opportunity to trust Him. Remember your verses?"

"I c-can't think!"

Jace let out a quiet breath. "Lord, if you would just get the thing to move a few inches."

Coral felt the perspiration dampen her forehead. It was moving again, this time from beneath her ear, up the side of her face, each leg stepping slowly, cautiously touching her cheek, her temple, and now her forehead.

She did not dare open her eyes for fear she would see it. She could hear her heart thumping.

"Just another moment, Coral. Nice and steady—" His hand struck quickly, swiping it off her hair and tossing it to the jungle floor. "There. You are safe."

Relief brought a surge of weakness. She held his arm and dropped her forehead against him with a catch in her throat. She felt his fingers touch the side of her face where the spider had been, smoothing aside the damp tendrils of hair.

"It is all over now," he said softly.

She could have stayed there with his arm about her waist and basked in the hypnotic effect of his touch, but her senses came awake. Her eyes opened and she became aware of a new danger.

Her head came up to confront his close gaze, and her emotions took a tumble. If she did not resist the beckoning enticement now, it would be too late. And then what?

His arm released her. "I think," he said, "that we best get back."

Coral felt a rush of embarrassment to think that he had been the one to suggest it. She took several steps backward, her breath short. Her eyes dropped to the ground between them. The spider was cautiously stepping its way across the ground cover, and heading toward the vines that draped from the trees. The creature was the size of a mango. It was not black as she had imagined, but chocolate brown with speckles of yellow. She shuddered. If there was one spider, there must be more. She glanced up into the tree branches, rubbing her arms as her skin prickled.

Jace stepped on the spider with his boot and something spurted. Coral nearly gagged, covered her face with her palms, and turned away.

"Alas, fair maiden! The dragon has been slain! Shall we go?" He snatched up the gangly birds with a slight smile, and the intensity of the previous moment vanished.

Relieved, yet vaguely disappointed that he could shed it so easily, she quickly turned away. "Thank you for your help, Major. I think I hear Sir Hugo calling." She gathered up her skirts and walked past the squashed spider without another glance.

Sir Hugo was coming through the trees just as Coral emerged. His countenance was hard as his eyes went past her to Jace Buckley, following leisurely behind.

"I've engaged the major to see that Ethan leaves the barge," she said.

"Ethan is not a child. I suggest you allow him his own opinion and not run to Buckley with all your grievances."

She was startled by his anger. "I don't run to the major with every petty misfortune, Uncle. But since he is in command of the trek north, it is fitting he should know about Ethan."

Sir Hugo said nothing as Jace walked up. She wondered if Jace had overheard. Embarrassed, Coral brushed past them both and returned to camp. When all was quiet about the campfire, with the guards on duty, Coral tried to sleep, listening to the breathing of her sisters lying next to her. She felt ashamed of herself. There had been a brief moment when she had felt something that she was certain no decent girl should ever experience. And she had experienced that emotion not with Ethan, but the very one she knew she must avoid! And to make it all the harder to bear, *he* had been the one to calmly draw away, reminding her, as though she were a child, that they must get back to the others.

How scandalous! Had he been able to guess? Had her uncle?

No, Jace could not have known, she decided with deep relief. It had all happened too quickly, and he had glossed over it unawares, completely absorbed with the spider. If he had not stepped on it, crushing it—well, he had, and she could only guess that he had done it deliberately. It certainly had brought reality crashing between them.

24

Jace knew the route to follow and the difficulties to be encountered. Seward was in charge of camping sites, and they were few and far between. Often Coral strained her ears to hear Seward whispering to Jace that the risk was too great to disembark, for the campfire and smell of humans would attract the tigers. On many dark nights they lit fishing lanterns and remained on board the boats rather than camp on land, and always Jace saw that Coral and her sisters had more than their share of sowars guarding the barge.

During the jungle trek, Coral often found her thoughts wandering toward William Carey. His dedication to the work of the Lord encouraged her to measure her own spiritual fervor. By enabling grace, Master Carey and his family had managed to survive the suffering of life in the jungle terrain of the Sunderbans in the heart of the delta. Somehow he had managed to build a bamboo house to live in, and had even planted his garden—something that Carey did wherever he went. How long had he and his family lived in the delta, she wondered. It took courage and commitment to stay the course. Who could fault Mrs. Carey for becoming ill? She thought of

277

herself. Did she have that measure of dedication to the One she called Lord?

"The Sunderbans is where William Carey's little boy Peter died, and Mrs. Carey became ill. She still has not recovered," Coral told Seward as they watched the sun rise over the jungle trees.

" 'Tis no wonder to me. Making a living there be hard as iron. The man had himself more than his share of courage. Would make me shudder, leaving London with a wife and children for a spot like that." He shook his head sadly.

Coral's eyes shone, and she looked out across the river. "He came, knowing the desperate need of India, knowing that there was only One who could break the chains of darkness. No sacrifice was too much to ask of himself or of his family, knowing the price the Lord willingly paid."

"Now, little lassie," he wheedled. "Ye frighten me to wit's end when ye go talking like that. 'Tis the steps of Master Carey you be willing to follow, and I don't like the looks of the way they lead."

Coral smiled up at him and looped her arm through his. "Do not worry, Seward. I could never be as brave. My steps lead to a different path. And I promise, a school on Kingscote must have Elizabeth and Hampton's approval before I ask you to lift a hand to help me build it."

His bushy brows came down, and he cocked his head, lowering his tricorn. Coral laughed at his suspicious eye.

"So ye be intending to involve poor Seward in your scheme, do you? I suspect ye intend to get a structure up before the rains. But don't go forgetting your uncle. He will have something to say to Sir Hampton about this school of yours. He be dead set against it from the start. And he won't change his mind anytime soon."

"Mother will be on my side. You wait and see. She has always had a love for the untouchables."

"Aye, that I know. And 'tis that which bothers me. She knows you grieve for Gem."

Gem. His name winged its way through her heart, bringing sweet memories. Would Jace be able to discover his whereabouts? And if he did, could she manage to retrieve him? She wanted to tell Seward, but since Jace had asked her not to mention it to anyone, she kept the secret locked within her heart. If Jace wanted to explain to Seward, he could do so himself. But she longed to share the hope with someone, and somehow Seward offered the biggest shoulder to lean on.

"What would you say if I told you Gem might come home?"

Seward's head turned, and his gaze was as sharp as a hawk's. Coral's eyes glistened, and her hand squeezed his arm.

"What's this? Gem returning home to Kingscote? Who told you such a thing? Lass, ye need be careful about dreams."

There was a movement behind them, and Coral whirled, her hand still on Seward. It was Sir Hugo. His dark handsomeness was foreboding as he stood in jungle hat and knee-length coat, a rifle in one hand and a pistol strapped about his hip.

"I think it best, my dear, you not wander the barge alone. Stay with your sisters under the awning."

"You're leaving the barge?" she asked, noting he also carried a leather satchel.

"I shall ride one of the boats in the lead. Do be cautious."

"Yes, Uncle, of course," she said, hoping her relief over his departure did not show. If he was in the lead boat, she wouldn't be under his constant eye.

"And Major Buckley?" she asked.

She felt her uncle's penetrating gaze rummage

279

through her mind, as though wondering about her motive in asking.

"The major will remain on the barge, not that I agree with the decision. He ought to be in the lead boat, but since he insists otherwise, I shall take the position."

From the corner of her eye, she could see Seward straighten a little with displeasure.

"The major be knowin' the river like you know the innards of the Company, Sir Roxbury. Rest assured he knows what he's about."

Hugo's mouth curved. "Your loyalty is undaunting, Seward." He turned to join the manji, who waited to bring him to a small boat, giving a last warning to Coral. "The river will soon be full of crocodiles. You best watch Marianna."

When he had gone, Seward looked after him with a scowl, lowering his hat. "Your uncle be good at intruding and imposing himself on others' business!"

"And rightly so," came Ethan's voice, but if he was offended at Seward's opinion, his expression did not show it. He appeared to be in a good mood as he walked up, and ignoring Seward, said cheerfully, "Good morning, Coral. Have you by chance read Marco Polo?"

Seward was silent, eying him, but Coral smiled. "Good morning, Ethan. No, I have not. I suppose you have, or you would not have inquired."

"I must say it was a fascinating read." He shaded his eyes with his hand and scanned the riverbanks. "He made mention of India, of course. Said he may have discovered the unicorn. I wonder if there are any about?"

Coral glanced at Seward who smirked beneath his beard. "There be none about these parts, Doctor. But if ye be wanting our opinion—that is, the major and me—'tis the one-horn rhino near Kingscote that be Mister Polo's unicorn."

"Indeed? Then we will see the brutes? Marvelous!"

Seward warmed at Doctor Boswell's interest in wild-life, and leaned his arm against the rail before launching into a discussion. "Now, if ye be interested in more than bugs and beetles, I can take you on a safari around Jorhat."

"Kingscote is near there?"

"Aye, the plantation be running for miles along the Bramaputra River and into the jungle. If ye wish to see the rhinos, the best way is by elephant."

"I shall take you up on that, Seward, my friend. Perhaps you can suggest the best location on Kingscote for my lab as well. I should like it away from the house. My work calls for isolation. Say, a half an hour's walking distance."

"Sir Hampton be letting you do as you wish, I am sure of that much. He be grateful if you can get Lady Elizabeth back on her feet again."

"Believe me, Seward, I shall certainly try. I could not bear to see Coral going through a summer without a smile to lighten her face."

Coral turned to him with one of her loveliest smiles just as her eyes met Jace. There was a slight turn to his mouth as he walked up to the group.

Seward said, "Morning, lad. Did the kansamah bring you some coffee?"

"Yes, Seward, thanks. Morning, Miss Kendall, Doctor," said Jace.

"Major," said Ethan. "I understand we are nearing the worst of the delta. I find it fascinating! How is it that you and Seward know so much about it?"

"The major's been in India since he was twelve," said Seward.

"You are near to being a native yourself," said Boswell. "There must be little you do not know of the land

281

or of its strange assortment of religions."

"I was raised by a guru," offered Jace flatly, folding his arms. "What would you like to know, Doctor?"

Coral guessed that he enjoyed shocking Boswell. But she remembered back to that day in Calcutta when she had stumbled upon the widow burning. Jace had appeared to know something of the person and work of Christ. As she glanced at Ethan, she read his expression, and knew that the thought of being raised by one of India's strange mystic gurus did indeed shock him.

She hastened, "Oh, do tell us about the delta, Major. Do you think we will run into a tiger?"

"After our venture with the spider, are you now anticipating more excitement, Miss Kendall?"

She was about to say something when Jace turned to Ethan. "I would be interested in knowing the kind of spider that put Miss Kendall to bed for days."

There was an uncomfortable pause, and Coral's breath paused with it.

"Ah, if only I did, Major. I am afraid I can offer little information. You see, I am not acquainted with the strange species of India. Not that I am sure this one came from India, mind you. At least Sir Hugo and Mr. Harrington had never seen this particular species before in Manali."

So, thought Coral. *That should answer Jace's suspicions.*

She looked at Jace almost triumphantly, but he was casually studying Boswell.

"Then that explains why it took so long to get Miss Kendall back on her feet," he said smoothly. "You were not quite sure how to treat the poison?"

Ethan's smile was menacing. "Quite, Major. Mr. Harrington decided the spider may have been brought unwittingly into the house in a shipment he had sent for from the jungles near Malaysia. You have been to Malaysia, I understand?"

"Yes."

"Ah, a pity I do not have the spider with me. You might look at it and enlighten us. I kept it in a bottle for several weeks until it died."

"A pity."

"I have seen one spider too many," interrupted Coral, "so I shall not mourn its absence. If you gentleman will excuse me, I have some studying to do."

"Ah, Hindi, of course," said Ethan. "Your intelligence is a treat, Coral. So many women today would prefer to read magazines from Paris offering the latest hats."

"I imagine Miss Kendall would look enchanting in a Paris hat," came Jace's resonant voice.

Coral refused to blush, although she would not meet his eyes. She imagined he had said it to rile Ethan, yet her memory ran back to their meeting in the Calcutta bazaar, when he had asked her if they had met in Paris.

Ethan turned to him, his expression cold and challenging. "And I suppose you have been to Paris as well?"

Jace smiled. "I find travel one of my most treasured pleasures."

Coral turned, relieved, as the head boatman walked up and salaamed. She took her leave, coming up to where her sisters sat under the awning. She removed her hat and fanned herself briskly.

By afternoon, the fears that the head boatman had already delivered to Jace filtered down to Coral. The water level was low in places, and this proved difficult for the village oarsmen. She heard a second discussion in progress as the boatman and Seward tried to explain the situation to Ethan.

Jace walked up, hands on hips. "Now what?" came his flat question.

"The doctor not be agreein' about the barge and the upcoming silt beds."

"What can be done, Major?" snapped Ethan, as though Seward and the boatman were both going out of their way to be disagreeable.

"As I explained earlier, we can use the barge for perhaps another day, then we must proceed without it," said Jace.

"What! I will not consider removing my supplies from the barge!"

Jace turned to the boatman and spoke in Bengali. From where Coral stood under the awning she caught snatches of the discussion. Within several hours they would come to a bad section of the river, due to the low seasonal levels of water.

"Silt very thick, sahib," the boatman tried to explain to the infuriated Boswell. "Water very shallow! No good! Barge too big, sahib!"

"Under no circumstances will any boatman remove my supplies. I hope that is clear."

More trouble, thought Coral as she walked up. Hoping to allay matters, she smiled sweetly at Jace.

Jace folded his arms and said lazily, "Perhaps you can convince the doctor, Miss Kendall."

Coral turned to Ethan, who looked in no mood to be placated. "I fear it is all our fault, Ethan. The major warned of this in Manali."

But Ethan was still glaring at the boatman as if the matter were a conspiracy against him.

"The major sent Seward and several sowars upriver this morning to check the water level," said Coral. "We have no choice."

"But leave my supplies? Good heavens, Coral! Impossible!"

"I've already spoken to the manjis," said Jace calmly.

"They will bring the rest of your equipment back to Manali on the barge. Mr. Harrington can then prepare a careful shipment to Calcutta."

"Careful? What do novices know of medical equipment and my samples? Do you realize what pains I have taken to get samples of fauna and insects?"

"Quite aware," Jace said evenly.

Ethan caught himself, apparently remembering the crocodiles. He sighed and ran a hand over his face. "Major, you must forgive me. I am overwrought."

"As soon as Plassey is under British control, Captain McKay will be able to bring your equipment."

"The major is right, Ethan," Coral interjected. "I am relieved to have taken his advice in Manali. Your equipment can be sent on to Kingscote with my school supplies."

"Doctor, you must decide what you wish to bring with you. Baggage will be kept to what you can carry," said Jace.

"This is appalling," said Ethan. He turned stiffly and walked across the barge to survey his small mountain of crates and barrels. On the peak, the tiny tent-lab stood precariously. A black and white fowl that had landed to perch squawked and flew into the jungle.

When Coral awakened that afternoon, it was to the movement of water beneath the hard planks of the barge. She stared up at the branches that extended over the river and caught glimpses of a family of monkeys swinging from limb to limb in noisy chatter. From the position of the sun she guessed that she must have dozed off after the lunch of mangoes and coconuts.

She sat up. Kathleen and Marianna were still napping. Low voices caught her attention. Jace was again on the barge, and Seward was talking to him. Looking ahead, she saw the shallow areas coming into view. Here they would board the small boats, and several of the village boatmen would bring the barge back to Manali. Coral awoke her sisters, then gathered together their baggage.

When Seward had gone, she walked up to where Jace stood at the end of the barge. His eyes were on the thicket along the waterway, dense with jungle growth and trees. She stood next to him, saying nothing, her thoughts on the danger lurking silently beyond their line of sight.

Vines wrapped about some of the branches like pythons, reaching across the river to form a woven screen, casting deep shadows on the water. Coral knew enough of Bengal tigers to understand that they lie waiting in ambush. In the heavy thicket along the water, they could stalk the slow-moving boats for some distance without being noticed.

She glanced about at the other boats. The sowars were alert, two guarding each boat with rifles. Coral could feel the tension in the air. Vines and tree branches interlaced into an arbor above them, and birds and monkeys squawked and chattered overhead. Water slapped the side of the barge. Coral was so engrossed in staring ahead that she did not even hear the insect buzzing at her ear. The barge slid across the water, the dip and slice of the poles making a rhythmic swoosh.

The head manji glanced about the riverbank with nervous eyes. "Sahib Buckley, it is here we part. Please do not wait."

"Understood."

"Seward's boat is coming," said Coral, seeing his rugged form rowing with two sowars. Sir Hugo and his servants waited for them in a clearing in one of the other boats. Jace signaled the manji to bring the barge to the bank. A minute later Seward boarded while the two so-wars kept a watchful eye on the jungle behind them. The baggage was loaded, and Kathleen and Marianna were lifted into Seward's boat.

"What about Ethan?" Coral asked, and turned to look up at the crow's nest.

Jace walked toward the supplies and shouted up. "Doctor!"

"I am coming—but I need help with the crates."

Jace said something under his breath and stood with hands on hips. Coral hurried around the supplies to the other side.

"Ethan, do hurry. It is dangerous here—"

She stopped, unable to believe her eyes. Ethan was dragging several crates behind him that he had tied to-gether with rope. Coral's heart sank. Jace would be fu-rious.

"You cannot take all that," she whispered.

"Nonsense," came his cryptic reply. "The boat can hold this without difficulty."

Coral turned as Jace strode up. He, too, stopped. She watched his annoyed expression.

"Will they fit?" she asked in a small voice.

Jace's cynical gaze held hers until she straightened her straw hat and glanced at Ethan's trunk. Jace turned to Ethan. "You may bring one crate and one bag. Even that is generous."

"How do you expect me to set up a lab with some-thing so meager?"

"Your lab, sir, is the least of my concerns at the mo-ment."

Ethan looked at him with cold anger. "No, I cannot."

Jace stepped back and gestured his arm down toward the small boat. "Allow good sense to prevail."

"Major, I—"

"If you do not move, you will take nothing. Consider that an order."

Ethan stared angrily at Jace's unrelenting features, then turned to his possessions. "Seward! If you will, I shall take this crate. Do be extraordinarily careful. And I shall carry my own bag."

As Coral waited, she glanced at Jace. A harbinger of unease crept up her spine. Her breath paused. Jace's gaze narrowed as if picking up her alarm. Suddenly he grabbed her arm and pulled her toward him. "The monkeys . . ." Jace began.

"They stopped chattering!" whispered Coral.

"What is it?" Seward called.

Coral looked up. Her throat constricted and a scream died. On the overhanging limb crouched a male Bengal tiger. Ten feet of rippling black and gold splendor tensed for the spring, his jaws partly open, his yellow eyes savage with fury. He seemed to consider his next move, lifting his head slightly, his lips drawn back, and a low rumble reverberated in his throat. The gnarl hovered above her like thunder, shaking and rattling her bones. Coral felt her body hurled to one side, and she landed on the deck, stunned, while both tiger and gun shots converged.

The shots had come from the sowars, but the beast was far from dead. One shot had missed, splintering the branch, the other grazed its shoulder, and the wound only maddened it.

The Indian manji screamed—"Save me, sahib!"—just as the tiger lunged and the splintered limb fell to the barge. A flash of yellow and black brought down the screaming boatman. Jace steadied his aim and fired. The bullet smashed into the tiger's chest. The sight nauseated Coral, and somewhere in the distance she heard Marianna's hysterical screaming.

The tiger's yellow eyes were not on her, nor on the

writing manji. It came bounding toward Jace, becoming a momentary blur of color that collided with a second blast of his gun, knocking Jace backward as they plunged into the river, sending a spray of fetid water splashing over Coral's skirt. Dazed, sickened by the moans of the manji and the smell of blood, a welcome darkness closed about her like a drawn shade upon her reason.

25

Coral awoke, aware of the anxious voices of her sisters crowded about her and a babble of men's voices in the distance. But there was something else, something stinging her nostrils as she tried to breathe . . . and she moaned, trying to turn her head. Her eyes fluttered open, and she saw Jace bending over her. Her head rested on his arm, while his other hand waved something in front of her nose.

She reached a feeble hand. "Stop—"

"She is all right now," stated Kathleen.

"I . . . w-what is that smell. . . ." murmured Coral.

"Smelling salts," said Jace. "You fainted."

She stiffened, remembering her promise to him that she would *never* faint. He obviously recalled their conversation too, for his smile was disconcertingly pleasant, and that made it worse. She pushed away the vapors and struggled to sit up.

"I am all right now, Major." It came rushing back. "The tiger! You are not hurt?"

"No."

"But the chief boatman is badly mauled," said Kathleen.

Something in her sister's tone told Coral there was cause for alarm that went beyond the unfortunate injury. Coral watched as Jace walked over to where Ethan was attending the wounded man. The rest of the hired manjis from Manali were gathered together with Sir Hugo. Jace walked up to him, and they talked in low tones.

"What is it?" asked Coral of Kathleen. "What is happening?"

"It is dreadful," whispered Kathleen. "The boatmen are blaming the misfortune on their god. Uncle Hugo insists they be allowed to placate Kali."

Kali? thought Coral, still dazed. She tried to recall what she had learned about the Hindu god. *The fiercest of gods . . . she rides a tiger and holds the weapons of destruction in her hands. . . .*

She strained to hear what Sir Hugo and Jace were saying. The manjis, along with her uncle and Seward, were preparing to leave the barge for the jungle.

Jace was reloading his gun. *What were they going to do?* Coral wondered. A terrible suspicion gripped her. She struggled to her feet.

"Coral, stay out of it," she heard Kathleen whisper, but she could not. She hurried to Jace, taking hold of his arm.

"What are they doing, Jace? Tell me."

"You're pale and shaking. Better go lie down."

"Where are my uncle and Seward going?"

"The manjis are spooked over the tiger attack. They insist on a religious ritual. They want to go ashore."

She rubbed her arms and glanced in the direction of the wounded Indian. "Kali rides the tiger because she is in control of its strength, is that it?"

"That's the idea. Kali wears a garland, but not of flowers. She adorns herself with skulls because she handles the destructive side of Hinduism and demands sacrifices." He stopped. "I think you now understand what is going on in the minds of the manjis and sowars. They spoke of it when Boswell fell into the river and the crocodiles converged on us. The fact that he was saved quieted matters down. Now there's this attack on the chief manji. Kali is vengeful."

Coral looked at him with growing alarm. "And they want to sacrifice before we go on?"

"Yes."

The thought was appalling. A sacrifice to Kali!

Jace was unreadable. She sensed, however, his veiled interest in her reaction to all of this.

But will he allow it? she wondered, recalling the incident of suttee after she had left William Carey. She also recalled that at the time he had suggested she stay out of such matters and leave the Hindu beliefs to India. Why did she expect his attitude to have changed in two months? However, he would know that in good conscience she could not leave darkness alone without trying to light a candle.

"You are not going to permit this?" she whispered.

"Believe me, Coral, I've little choice. If I do not, they will take their boats and return to Manali. That will leave us on foot in the delta. You are wise enough to know what that means."

She was. . . . Were they prepared to walk to the Bramaputra in a tiger-infested delta?

"But you have the six sowars from the troop," she argued, trying to keep her voice low. "Can you not command them to force the manjis to take us on the rest of the journey?"

"Do you think I have not thought of that? The sowars are also Hindus. After the mutiny at Plassey, I doubt very much if I can command them to do anything they find contrary to their religion. Oh, yes, they would salute, they would pretend to carry out my order. But I doubt if we could go to sleep tonight and awake with the sowars still on duty. I cannot risk the lives of you and the others."

Frustrated, Coral turned to watch her uncle and Seward rowing the small boat toward the jungle, following the manjis and sowars. They would trap a live sacrifice for Kali and offer it on a makeshift altar.

"There must be something you can do," she whispered. "Let me talk to them!"

"The way you did at the suttee back in Calcutta? I think not! You'll only make matters worse. Now go to your tent."

She stared up at him, helpless to stop it, yet knowing his course of action proved the wiser. And yet, his dismissal nettled her.

He must have noticed, for his mouth formed a wry smile. "Please."

"But, it's positively heathen to force poor Seward to attend the ritual."

"Madame, I am not forcing *poor Seward* to do anything he doesn't wish to do. I need another gun. To be frank, I don't trust Roxbury."

She drew in a breath. "What—"

"She is right, Major. We'll have none of this," Ethan's cold voice interrupted.

Oh, no! she thought, whirling around to face her cousin. Ethan's interference was the last thing they needed now!

Evidently Jace agreed, for he returned Ethan's hard stare and said flatly, "Stay out of this, Boswell; you have a wounded man to care for. No one is expecting you to involve your conscience."

"It is enough that you have asked the others to do so. And you insult the Christian sensibilities of Miss Kendall."

"That can't be helped. Interfere now, when you know nothing of what is involved, and I can guarantee that by morning you will have exceedingly more patients, and they will not all be natives."

"I will not stay out of it, *sir*. This Kali nonsense is all quite offensive to me, as well as Miss Kendall."

"I suppose you would rather see three women on foot in tiger country? Do you have any idea how far it is to Guwahati?"

"No, but I am quite certain we can find boatmen in the next village."

"The next village does not exist. It is a month till we reach Sualkashi. You will stay on the barge. You may guard the women if you can use a gun. There are still tigers in the area."

"I can use a gun, Major, and quite well as a matter of fact."

Coral saw a cold glitter in Jace's eyes that she had come to recognize as best left alone.

She said quickly, "Ethan, the major is right after all. There is nothing we can do."

Ethan stared coldly at Jace. "I fear you are quite right. There is nothing anyone with any moral sensibilities could do to convince the major of this despicable act. Perhaps he has been too long in India himself to understand those of us who are civilized and of Christian principles."

She sensed with a certain dread what was coming, but before she could act, Jace grabbed Ethan by the front of his cravat.

Jace's words came with brutal clarity. "I may take a slap across the face from a woman, but not from you. Your talk is little else but cheap hypocrisy, directed to impress Coral. It has impressed no one else. You speak of your loyalty to Christianity? You would sell your soul to marry a silk heiress!" He released him abruptly and turned to go.

Ethan said something between his teeth and grabbed Jace's shoulder, jerking him around. Ethan appeared prepared to backhand him, but Jace struck him with a savage blow, sending him crashing backward into his crates. Ethan lay sprawled, unconscious.

Coral sucked in her breath, but remained calm. Her eyes darted to Jace, and seeing his challenging expression, as if he expected her to rush to Ethan's side, her jaw set.

"That was quite uncalled for, Major," she said, surprised her voice didn't shake.

He showed no remorse, and certainly no sympathy. "He'll survive. I won't say as much for the rest of us if you insist on imposing your standards on the manjis."

She knew he was right. Jace's understanding of the Hindu people stood in stark contrast to Ethan's lack of experience. Jace had proved wiser, yet she felt irritated with both men for behaving as they had. Turning abruptly, she left him.

Jace stared after her for a moment, the blue-black of his eyes glittering; then he too turned and left for the small boat.

Coral joined Kathleen, who was kneeling beside Ethan with a wet rag, wiping his face. Her sister was pale and shaking but silent.

"Oh, I want to go home!" Marianna choked. "I hate this journey! I positively hate it!"

Coral was convinced of only one thing. If she was ever to confront India with Christianity, she would need to find another way. A gentle, loving way that did not alienate and breed confrontation. She had thought she could handle it, but she was now aware of her own weakness, failure, and fear.

"Maybe Uncle Hugo is right," said Coral wearily. "I have caused little but trouble, and no good has come from anything I have done since Jemani's baptism! Even Rajiv died—and Gem was abducted! Maybe I should forget everything! It is not worth it. Nothing is worth hate and violence!"

Surprisingly, it was Kathleen who came to her defense. "It was their angry reactions that did this. You are not to blame. It would have happened eventually anyway. And if you ask me, it had less to do with Kali or Christianity than it did with how Ethan and Jace feel about you. Besides, how can you even talk about giving up when you want to build that school for the untouchables? What do you care if others misunderstand? You cannot quit now; you have not even begun!"

Shocked, Coral looked into her sister's face, surprised at what she had heard. Kathleen's amber eyes gleamed with an emotion Coral had never seen before.

"But it is you who wish to go back to the Silk House!" said Coral.

Kathleen looked determined. "The important thing right now is that you, too, do not lose your dream. I may not go back to London—ever. I may not become a designer in the Silk House. But I shall truly be discouraged if you lose what you believe in."

"Why, Kathleen," she breathed. "I did not know; I never guessed you would come to my side like this. I thought—"

"I know what you thought. And maybe you were right. But everything that has just happened has made me think differently. I want you to win your struggle for the mission school on Kingscote, Coral. And Marianna and I are going to help."

"Oh, yes, we will, Coral," said Marianna. "We will

stand with you when you talk to Papa and Mother, and we will pray, too!"

Coral reached both arms for her sisters, hugging them to her.

Ethan was stirring. "W-what happened?"

"Some bad things worked together for good, that's what," said Marianna.

"Coming from you, Miss Pessimist, that *is* something," said Coral, laughing.

"Here, Cousin Ethan, drink some water," said Marianna. "And then you best do something about the cut on your lip. Oh, dear, you're bleeding—"

"Here, let me," said Kathleen, raising his head and bringing the canteen to his mouth.

26

The dawn beckoned with the first reddish hue of a new day of adventure. Coral heard the screech of a jungle cock, then the voice of Seward singing: "Amazing grace, how sweet the sound, that saved a wretch like me. . . ." She silenced her body's groan and forced herself to crawl out from under the bedroll she shared with Marianna and Kathleen. The relentless journey resumed.

The delta now lay behind them, and they continued the trek down the Ganges River. At the village, they had purchased supplies and rested for a day before resuming their journey. Coral thought she had never been so exhausted but was determined not to let anyone know. She had insisted to Jace that she was strong enough, and now she must not disappoint him or Seward by becoming an extra burden they did not need.

At the Ganges, the remainder of the manjis left them to return to Manali, and Jace and Seward hired other small boats to bring them down the wide river to the Bramaputra.

The long days marched on one by one. Coral felt as if she had ended up in the major's 21st Light Cavalry. He set a rigorous pace, but she did not complain, nor did

Kathleen and Marianna. They knew the reason, as did Sir Hugo. Having experienced the seasons, they understood the risk of the monsoon. The month delay at Manali had robbed them of important time. Coral tried to get Ethan to understand as the camp stirred to wakefulness, the campfire still burning red against the shadows.

"You have lived in Burma," she said. "You know what the monsoon means. If the major does not complete the journey before the rains start, we'll be forced to remain in one of the isolated villages for months. The entire Assam valley is usually flooded."

"I am aware of the danger, but I am also a doctor. You are near exhaustion. Can the major not see that?"

"Yes," came the cheerless reply from behind them. Coral turned, still in the process of braiding her hair, and saw Jace.

"If my memory serves me right," he said to Ethan, "I strongly advised Miss Kendall to return to Calcutta when we were at Harrington's."

What Jace did not say was what Coral and Ethan both knew. It had been Ethan who backed her up on her determination to come.

Ethan's cold stare riveted on Jace. Jace ignored him, turning his back toward Ethan to face Coral. Her eyes dropped to the mug in his hand.

"Coffee," he said, offering it to her.

Her lips turned up softly. "Thank you, Major." She took the cup from his hand, and a small smile played at the corners of his mouth before he turned and left.

"Arrogant—"

"Stop it, Ethan!" Turning abruptly away and taking her coffee with her, she strode off toward the river for her morning wash.

Coral shielded her eyes beneath her hat and glanced in the direction of the clouds. "How far to the Bramaputra?" she asked Seward, who was kneeling on the shore, splashing water on his dusty face.

" 'Tis my guess we've gone about a hundred kilometers on the Ganges. It be not far now."

As the sapping heat of May set in, building toward the rains, they arrived at a remote village near the junction of the Ganges and Bramaputra rivers.

"A bazaar," cried Marianna with excitement.

Kathleen, who had lost her bar of soap weeks earlier, clasped her hands together in delight.

While Jace and Seward found supplies, Coral went with Sir Hugo, Ethan, and her sisters. They bought dozens of personal items that would make their journey more comfortable, then visited the booths selling hot foods. Seward joined them, making much of the delicious meal.

"Where is the major?" Coral asked him, noticing that Jace had not joined them.

"Speaking to the tehsildar, the village headman, about hiring elephants farther ahead. Neither of us likes the feel of things," said Seward.

After replenishing their goods, they began the journey north up the great Bramaputra toward Guwahati. Coral grew more exhausted by the day and began masking spells of dizziness. Casting anxious glances in her small mirror, she was thankful that there were no dark circles beneath her eyes to give away her recurring illness.

I've got to get home. We are so close now.

Soon her appetite failed her. She thought no one noticed, for she was careful to throw her uneaten supper into the river.

"Feeding crocodiles?"

She turned, startled at Jace's voice. She refused to

show anything was wrong. "I wish you would not sneak up on me, Major."

"It's still some four hundred kilometers to Guwahati. Kingscote, two days more."

"I shall be all right," she insisted, and walked past him to where her sisters were gathered.

The heat continued to build. One morning, Coral awoke with a start to feel the bright sunlight. *Have I overslept? But why did they not awaken me?*

The campsite was nearly empty, her sisters no doubt having gone farther down the river to wash. She sat up and saw Sir Hugo standing with the major and Seward by the riverbank. Jace was talking in low tones. Hugo looked toward the distant cloud formations—harbingers of the monsoon.

It was unusual that the order to break camp had not come by now, thought Coral, glancing toward the position of the sun. The squeal of birds, sometimes shrill enough to pierce the ears, echoed in the trees. She dressed quickly and went to find the kansamah for a mug of hot tea, hoping to gain some strength.

When Seward gave the announcement, the news came as a pleasant surprise for Coral. The major believed he could procure elephants for a landward journey along the river toward Sualkashi. It would mean a less rigorous trek for the women, and Coral could lie down and sleep in the howdah if she wished.

"Elephants," said Coral with enthusiasm. "But where will you find them?"

"The major be friendly with the owner."

"I see." She was curious, glancing in Jace's direction.

"The trainer be not a man with liking for the British," said Seward in a low voice. "He deals with the maharaja at Guwahati, training elephants for battle. But Jace be knowing the man and is sure to get them since the trainer be a relative to Gokul."

The elephant trainer serves the maharaja. Thinking of Gem's royal blood, Coral met Jace's gaze and, for a moment, thought she saw a glimmer of anticipation in his deep blue eyes.

Coral heard the elephants trumpeting and stood, shading her eyes to gaze down the riverbank. The small cavalcade of brownish beasts were in view, their ears flapping, their feet stirring up the dust. They would ride on the backs of the elephants inside a howdah—the framework holding a seat large enough for several people, and decked with red and gold cloth. Astride the elephants' magnificent necks, close to their heads, rode the bronzed drivers, the mahouts. They were naked except for a cloth about their loins and the familiar dusty turban wrapped around their heads.

Coral smiled to herself and quickly tied on her hat. It had been years since she had ridden on an elephant, and she looked forward to the journey. The first elephant carrying Seward was followed by six more, with empty howdahs rocking on their strong backs.

Coral laughed at the moan coming from Marianna. "At least there are no more crocodiles. Come, elephants are the most wonderful animals in the world."

"Yes, like Rani?" said Kathleen with a wry suggestion in her voice.

Coral smiled at the mention of her pet elephant at Kingscote. Rani had become spoiled, trumpeting her disapproval if Coral ever forgot to have one of the boys lead her down to the river for her morning wallow.

Coral led her sisters to a young female, anxious to show that she knew something about the handling of her favorite animal. She gave a loving pat to the elephant's trunk, and a small, round eye looked down at her from under several long lashes, seeming to blink its approval.

303

"We will ride on this one. What is her name, mahout?"

The Indian lad smiled and stroked his hand downward across the trunk. "This is *Yakshi*, because she is a maiden who will one day be queen of the others." With a shout and a swat from his ankus, he brought the elephant down to a kneeling position. He threw down the rope ladder connected to the howdah.

Lifting her skirts, Coral climbed the ladder while the sowar held it steady. It was a long way up, and she gripped the rough rope with her gloves and tried to place her slippers into the moving rungs while the mahout leaned down to help her inside.

At last, Kathleen and Marianna were seated with her, high above the ground. Coral laughed at Marianna clinging to the side of the howdah as if the whole contraption would slide off the elephant's back.

Soon the elephant cavalcade began, with two sowars on the lead elephant followed by Yakshi. Just then, Yakshi curled her trunk, opened her mouth wide, and trumpeted her displeasure. "Behave, Yakshi!" the mahout yelled in Hindi. "You cannot be queen today!" But Yakshi's antics provoked two elephants to sidle back and offer their support. The trumpeting pierced the morning air, and the loud blast brought Marianna's hands against her ears. Coral winced at the deafening sound. But soon the elephants were on the move, and Coral focused her attention on the passing terrain. At last it seemed reasonable to dream contentedly of Kingscote. *Home!*

The days passed. The humidity continued to build toward the onset of the rains, and so did Coral's anticipation. Sunrise on the Bramaputra was rippling with golden light. Coral watched the fishermen in their small canoelike houseboats with thatched roofs. Elephantback was the best way to view the rich and diverse wild-life, and Coral wondered how Ethan enjoyed the sight of the flock of pink flamingos. Assam was home to the native muga caterpillar, better known to Coral as the humble but glorious silkworm. There were also cheetahs, sometimes called an Indian panther, lions, tigers, and golden langur monkeys—which made her wonder if Jace missed his partner Goldfish.

On the north bank of the river, Coral was watching for something else. "There! See it?"

Kathleen and Marianna looked quickly in the direction she pointed.

The famous one-horned rhino stood dark against the tall yellow-brown elephant grass. Coral turned in the howdah and waved to Ethan, who was riding with Sir Hugo. She pointed toward the magnificent animal and heard him give a shout of exclamation: "The unicorn!" She laughed at his response, but then saw Major Buckley watching her. She averted her eyes, disturbed that his gaze could make her heart beat a little faster.

Only a grouping of chital, swift-footed spotted deer, captured their attention away from Marco Polo's unicorn.

When they arrived at Sualkashi, on the north bank of the Bramaputra, Coral's excitement mounted with her sisters'. They were perhaps no more than four days from Kingscote.

Sualkashi was noted for its fashionable silk-weaving centers, and Kingscote silk was often brought here by barge.

They arrived during the fair called a *mela*, and the bazaars were busy. Coral concentrated on the thought of the white walls and blue roof of Kingscote.

At the fair, she bought presents for the female servants of the house: silk scarves and beaded slippers. She had already purchased gifts for her parents and Alex in

London. She was pretending interest in a silver bracelet when a wave of dizziness assailed her. The low table appeared to heave, then sink, and she felt herself falling with it. A firm hand closed about her arm, holding her up.

"Thank you, Seward—I am all right. The sun is a trifle hot today."

"Deception does not become you."

Her chin jerked up, and she tried to focus on Jace. "Well, you just seem to appear out of nowhere at the oddest—"

"I think it is time I had a word with your *attentive* physician." He gazed down at her from beneath his hat.

Again she was aware of how dominant he was, and when their wills clashed, he reminded her of the walls of Jericho.

"You know quite well that my uncle will look for any excuse to delay my arrival at Kingscote."

"And that is why we are not going to give him one. You are going to bed for the next eighteen hours."

"And just how, sir, do you expect to arrange all that?"

He glanced about the bazaar. "There are some cushions over there by the shop. You can sit there like a proper young English woman and have tea with your sisters until I get back."

"Where are you going?"

"I know someone here," he said evasively. "A family."

"The man who owns the elephants?"

"Yes." He turned toward a booth. "Seward!" he called.

Seward walked up.

"Put on your best manners," said Jace. "You will be taking Miss Kendall and her sisters to tea. I will return soon."

How Jace managed it, she did not know. She and her sisters arrived by rickshaw at a private residence, where doves cooed in the mango trees. As they stepped from the rickshaw, she saw Jace speaking to a stalwart Indian man in his fifties. Some minutes later a young Indian girl arrived from the back of the house, her long, dark hair falling loosely down her back. The first thing Coral noticed was that she was quite attractive; the second thing was that her smile and eyes brightened when they fell on Jace.

Coral felt an irrational sense of annoyance with the girl. It was silly to fall all over him that way! And just *why* had the major brought her *here*? Her gaze moved from the girl's face to Jace's, saw his disarming smile, then watched him say something for her ears alone. Whatever it was brought bright, melodic laughter—*like a little bird*, thought Coral. She felt the girl's eyes turn toward her and her sisters, and then back to Jace, followed by another amused laugh. *And just what did he say about me?*

Coral felt her cheeks turning warm but did not bother to analyze the reason. The familiar look that passed between the girl and Jace brought a dart of resentment. Feeling guilty, Coral turned her head away with determination. Naturally a man like Jace would know other young women. She thought of Ethan. She must apologize to him when she next saw him for running off like this on a wild scheme of the major's. Why had she even listened to Jace?

Her heart thumped irregularly, and quite unexpectedly she found the faces of those around her becoming blurred. *If I faint now, I shall seem a silly fool. A spoiled Englishwoman who melts in the harsh reality of the world around her! It will give the girl another reason to be amused, and another reason for Jace Buckley to think of me as a fragile blossom!*

Yet the more she tried to retain her balance the more she felt ill. She became aware of a small flutter about her and the voice of Kathleen as she sank to the ground.

Coral stirred and sighed. . . . Her lashes fluttered open as a breath of warm wind moved the mosquito netting. The woven-grass screen on the window was wet, offering some relief from the heat. Her mind felt clear, and physically she felt more rested than she had in weeks.

She forced herself to sit up and cast aside the cover. She glanced about the room. It was small but neat, and scrubbed clean. Outside she heard the birds chittering. Kathleen and Marianna were still asleep on mats in the corner. Beside her was the empty tea cup—at least, she had thought it to be tea, and had a memory of Kathleen feeding the liquid to her a little at a time while Jace stood by. Coral remembered nothing else. Evidently she had slept through the night.

She picked up the cup and sniffed but did not recognize the faint odor. Whatever it was, she felt no harm, and in fact, she felt a good deal better. There had been no horrid hallucinations. But what had Ethan thought of the major's whisking her off like this? How had Jace managed to win over Uncle?

The door opened and the lovely Indian girl came in, carrying a breakfast tray and a jug of steaming water. Her expression was confident, with a little sly smile on her lips.

"Good morning, sahiba. You slept well?"

"Yes, thank you."

Coral made up her mind that she would not ask the girl any questions about her friendship with Jace Buckley and, thanking her in Hindi, asked, "And when will the major and Mister Seward arrive so that my sisters and I can leave?"

She pursed her lips. "I do not know when the man named Seward will come, nor when you will leave, sahiba."

"And the major? Did he say when he would come back?"

"Jace is yet asleep. Shall I go back and awaken him to ask?"

Coral stared at her. She called him *Jace*. And he had not left the day before with Seward. She turned her head away and snatched up her brush, bringing the bristles through her long tresses. "No. It does not matter."

"Sahiba? You spoke so quietly, I did not hear."

Coral met her eyes evenly. "No. Do not waken him. That is all. You may go now."

The girl smiled and left, closing the door behind her.

Coral stood. Her eyes narrowed. She realized that she was clutching the brush. She started to throw it at the door, but caught herself when Kathleen's sleepy voice broke in: "What is it, Coral? Something wrong?"

Coral sat down quickly. "No. Nothing is wrong. Everything is just as I expected from the first moment I met him."

Kathleen raised herself to an elbow and squinted at her sleepily. "W-what?"

"Do get up, both of you. I want to leave. I want to find Ethan."

Kathleen frowned. "Ethan! Whatever is the rush?"

"Yes, Ethan," repeated Coral so quietly, so insistently,

309

that Kathleen said nothing more and simply stared at her. Finally, she tossed aside the cover, giving Marianna a shake. "Wake up. Whatever the major put in her tea last night has cured Coral of everything but impatience."

27

On the following morning, they arrived by ferry at Guwahati, the gateway to the northeastern frontier. In a few days they would be home!

Domed temples and intricately carved white and red stone buildings were everywhere. Along the river, gondola-like boats plied up and down among the more humble barges belonging to the net fishermen. Coral recognized Peacock Island sitting in the middle of the water, housing one of the historic Hindu temples.

She commented to Ethan: "The temple of the Nine Planets was the center of the study of astrology in ancient times. And over there, on Nilachal Hill, is the important Hindu temple. It was destroyed by Muslim invaders in the 1600s but rebuilt by the Hindus. In August, pilgrims come here from all over India to keep their festival."

Ethan appeared genuinely inquisitive. "Yes, Hugo mentioned it. It is the center of energy worship, is it not?"

She looked at him sideways, unwilling to explain the rest. It was also a form of Hinduism with strong sexual and occultic undertones.

Here in Guwahati, Sir Hugo Roxbury would repre-

311

sent the East India Company; and Major Buckley, between trips to the military outpost at Jorhat, would command her uncle's security force at the British residency. They were all expected to call on the maharaja that afternoon.

The white palace with intricate stonework and inlaid marble veined with blue and gold was built near the half-circle bank overlooking the wide Bramaputra. To the north, the great Himalaya mountain range gazed back majestically.

Coral grew tense at the thought of seeing the maharaja face-to-face. How could she possibly remain placid when looking upon the man responsible for Gem's abduction and Rajiv's death? Was Gem alive and somewhere in the guarded palace? The possibility that he was—that Jace may soon discover the facts—set her nerves on edge. *I must trust the outcome to God*, she repeated to herself, hoping to quell her disquiet.

When they arrived at the palace, Coral glanced about for Jace, but he had disappeared without a word shortly after arriving. As Seward waited on the steps of the palace-fortress, Sir Hugo Roxbury and his family were brought by turbaned guards carrying tulwars into the Hall of the Diwan-i-Am, the hall of public audience.

Coral's heart thumped in her throat as she stood with dignity between Kathleen and Marianna. Her eyes fixed on the raised dais where the maharaja would make his lofty appearance. *I must not hate.* But only the love of God could reach through her trembling body to feel for this man.

At this very moment Gem could be a slave in the women's quarters.

A sudden dart of fear pierced her heart as a new thought mocked her faith. *Suppose they have made him a eunuch?*

Ethan glanced at her, as if aware of the change in her mood, and his hand took hold of her elbow, giving her a gentle squeeze and a reassuring smile. He leaned over, whispering in her ear, "It will all be over soon, dear. Then you can go to your room to rest."

He had mistaken what must have been a pale and tense face for weariness. As if trying to cheer her, he whispered, "Did you ever see such marvelous patterns in marble work? King George would be envious!"

She glanced about, trying to quiet her mind, trying not to think that Gem could be so near. She concentrated on two intricately carved pillars of whitish blue stone, veined with gold. A thick crimson rug near the dais was embroidered with blossoms. The walls were inlaid with tiny marble mosaics forming a mammoth peacock with ten thousand blue eyes. The domed ceiling was inlaid with veined gold marble, and there were engraved images of the Hindu idol-gods; but Coral only recognized the popular elephant-headed son of Shiva, the god of wisdom and prosperity.

A pompous voice spoke from the step of the dais: "The maharaja, His Excellency Majid Singh himself, must send his appeasement. It is with regret that we must announce that His Excellency is not well. The maharaja sends his greetings. He hopes he will be able to receive you on the third day at the state dinner."

The sober-faced official in yellow and purple left the step and strode toward Sir Hugo, briefly touching fingertips to his forehead, stepped backward, turned toward a beaded doorway, then clapped his palms. Several Indian guards appeared with stoic faces and black beards. The official ordered them to escort the governor-general's party to the newly constructed British residency.

"A moment please," said Sir Hugo to the official. "It

is with deep concern we learn of His Excellency's health. My nephew here is a respected physician of some credential in London. If the maharaja is so inclined, he will offer his opinions of the king's health."

Coral looked at her uncle, somewhat surprised by his offer. His dark eyes turned triumphantly to Ethan. Ethan's jaw tightened.

"I shall bring him your words, sahib. It may be that he will consider them to be most generous."

The English residency was a large bungalow of red stone with ten servants. They offered a salaam to Sir Hugo from the front steps as he left the ghari.

Coral could think of little but rest and sleep, and was dismayed when a gaudy-dressed Indian official informed them that there would be a state dinner in their honor the next night at the residence of the dewan, the chief Indian official in the maharaja's royal court and council. Coral remembered that Mr. Harrington's so-called secretary Zameen had been the dewan. *Just who has taken his place in the court?*

Coral's heart thumped unevenly. At the one time when she wanted to be strong and alert, she felt the weakest. *Oh, I must not get sick now!* Gem! He may be somewhere in the palace! Could it be that her child was so near, yet so far from her touch, her protection? *Lord God, if he is here, help Jace to discover his whereabouts! Please! Let me see him! Nothing is too difficult for you!*

Their bedroom chamber in the British residency seemed like paradise. There was a huge bed with room to spare for the three of them. Soft coverlets draped the bed, and thick rugs padded the floor. A private bath of marble was built into a secluded garden with flowering vines, and—

A squeal came from Marianna. "Oooh! Look!"

Coral and Kathleen whirled, expecting to find a

314

coiled cobra or a tropical spider. Instead, Coral found Marianna pointing with triumph to what the French called a *toilet.*

Kathleen took hold of Coral's elbow. "A bath, and then you are going to bed. No state dinner tomorrow night."

"But I must go, Kathleen."

Jace might have information on Gem, she thought. And where had Jace disappeared to? Despite her intentions, Coral was too fatigued to thwart Kathleen.

An hour later, bathed and comfortable within her soft peignoir, she grudgingly swallowed the medication that Ethan had left for her to take. She could hardly keep her eyes open as Kathleen pulled the covers up over her shoulders.

"I must go," she kept murmuring, "I must."

———————

Jace drew the horse to a stop and peered into the gathering dusk. In the silence he heard a jackal howling as the first stars blossomed in the sky. On several occasions since he had first ridden from Guwahati that afternoon for the British outpost at Jorhat, he had nearly turned back. It was troubling that Roxbury had appeared so willing for him to interrogate the Burmese prisoner held for the assassination of Major Selwyn. After the interrogation, Jace was to gather soldiers to make up his security guard and return to his new post at Guwahati. He did not want to further deplete the meager forces at the outpost, already in short supply of fighting men, until the 13th arrived from Calcutta with McKay.

Riding his horse forward through the dried grasses, a red-necked duck was startled and with a flap of its wings flew to the other side of a swamp. Jace rode on and arrived at the gate of his old command post by early dawn.

The wall was breached in places and in the process of being rebuilt. The stone garrison wore the scars of blackened smoke. Barracks stood empty, a somber reminder of men he had served with who were now buried. Jace went with the young English ensign to the stables, where a dusty sepoy led out the black mare once belonging to Major Selwyn.

"She is a fine horse, Major," said Ensign Niles.

The sepoy handed Jace the reins, and as he did, Jace felt a piece of paper being tucked into his hand. He looked into the immobile black eyes, but the sepoy showed no response and walked away.

Jace, too, revealed nothing of his thoughts as he addressed the young ensign.

"I am under orders from Colonel Warbeck to interrogate the prisoner. I wish to see him now."

The ensign blanched. "Orders from Colonel Warbeck, sir?"

"Is something wrong, Ensign?"

"No, Major. That is, I did not know there were orders from Colonel Warbeck. The colonel is your father, is he not, Major?"

Jace said nothing for a moment and gave a pat to the neck of the friendly mare. "He is. Take me to the prisoner."

The ensign made no sound. Becoming aware of his anxiety, Jace looked at him. The ensign stood stiffly, and white showed around his mouth.

"Well, Ensign?"

"There appears to be some mistake in orders, Major."

"What do you mean—'mistake'?"

"The prisoner was brought to Guwahati several weeks ago," he hastened, "but I did not know that the colonel had expected you to interrogate him."

Jace was furious. "You *authorized* the prisoner to be sent to Guwahati?"

"I was told it was the wishes of the maharaja!"

"*He* ordered his transfer?"

"No, the dewan did, sir!"

"Since when, Ensign, does the dewan have authority over the Bengal army?"

"Yes, sir! I mean, I understand your concern."

"Concern? This is the British military! Neither the dewan nor the maharaja has authority over military matters. You are aware of that! Ensign, you will be called in question for releasing the prisoner to the dewan. The prisoner had important information on the attack. Do you understand that he may be dead by now? Obviously someone does not want him to talk."

The ensign swallowed and said nothing.

"Who is in command until the 13th arrives?"

The young English soldier shuffled his feet. "I am, Major. That is, I and the dewan. He—"

"You and the dewan! Where is the dewan? I wish to speak to him."

"He is at Guwahati, sir!"

Jace stopped. His fury with the ensign diminished as he contemplated his own folly. He had little doubt that Roxbury had known.

Jace led the black mare into the morning sunlight. Alone, he read the message that had been pressed into his hand in the stables.

Namaste. News, sahib. The bazaars in Jorhat prove full of talk. The raja may take sudden ill and die. The dewan was seen in a meeting in Darjeeling only weeks ago with the Raja Bundhu. And Burra-sahib Roxbury is a wor-shiper of Kali. I shall look for you in Guwahati. Gokul

Jace stood in silence. Roxbury a worshiper of Kali? No doubt he only wished others to think so. Ghazis, perhaps. Were these religious zealots planted within the palace of the maharaja of Guwahati? On Kingscote?

———

The next morning, Coral was unexpectedly summoned to see Sir Hugo. As Seward waited outside the door, Coral entered to find her uncle behind a desk. She felt uneasy as his pensive dark eyes fixed upon her, and her gaze dropped to a letter that lay on the desk in front of him. *Is something wrong?* she wondered.

"You called for me, Uncle?" she asked, keeping her voice calm.

He sighed, appearing troubled. "Yes, Coral. I fear there is disturbing news. Alex is missing."

"Alex!"

"He was last heard from in the mountainous regions of Darjeeling. Hampton has left Kingscote and is trekking west in order to try to find him and bring him home."

Alex, missing! "But what was he doing in Darjeeling?" she asked. "Alex has no interest in the area, or in travel—except perhaps returning to Vienna!"

"You might as well know that his mind has not been well recently. After what happened to Michael, Hampton seems to think he went to Darjeeling because it meant so much to his older brother. We think he was trying to locate the land holdings belonging to Buckley and got lost."

"How did my father learn about Alex?" she asked.

"A local from the area of Darjeeling arrived at Kingscote. Your father departed with him at once. I suppose the tension over Michael and the tea plantation weighed on his conscience. He felt he must go himself to find Alex."

Sir Hugo stood, the letter in hand. "I do not wish to alarm you further, but the journey will prove hazardous this time of year for Hampton. As for Alex, we can only hope he has been found by natives and is being cared for."

Coral's mind went in several directions, coming back to Jace. Jace *knew* Darjeeling. If anyone would know where to look, it would be he and Seward. But Jace was chained to the military in Guwahati!

"Is the letter from my father?"

"Yes, it arrived weeks ago."

Coral thought of the many delays in their travel. Her father may already be in Darjeeling searching for Alex. Had her father mentioned Mother in the letter to her uncle? "May I read the letter please?"

"Of course." He handed it to her.

Coral recognized her father's handwriting. The message was brief, making mention of his absence, of several skirmishes along the border with Burma, and of the few British soldiers patrolling the area.

The situation here near the borders is growing more dangerous with the passing weeks. Yet I have no choice but to leave matters here in the hand of the Almighty and take my leave. I have found it necessary to journey to Darjeeling to find Alex. Word arrived by courier that he is missing. I shall return to Kingscote as God enables and as soon as possible.

Coral stood looking at the letter, dazed.

"This changes matters considerably," said Sir Hugo. "Without your father or brother at Kingscote, I think it wise that you and your sisters remain here until more soldiers arrive from Calcutta."

Not return home? The thought was devastating! If Kingscote was not safe, she had more reason than ever to get home to her mother. Why, her father could be away in the Darjeeling area for several months. As for the regiment from Calcutta, they could only guess when Plassey would be retaken and troops arrive in the northeast!

"The dewan has proven most cooperative under the circumstances," he continued. "He has offered to let you and your sisters stay here at the residence. You will be guarded by the dewan's own men."

He must have seen her dismay for he walked toward her and placed his hands protectively about her shoulders. "I would stay myself, if I could. But business forces me to travel with the major to the outpost for a few weeks. I fear this nasty business with the death of Major Selwyn must be looked into. But do not be alarmed. Ethan will remain here."

Looking into his gaze, which showed nothing but concern, Coral wondered if she had just cause to feel so suspicious. Her alarm, however, had nothing to do with her uncle's departure. *I must resist his plans*, she told herself firmly. But exactly what did Uncle Hugo have in mind beyond delaying her at Guwahati? And for what possible reason?

"I am sorry to worry you, Uncle, but I cannot accept the dewan's invitation. If my father has left for Darjeeling, then Mother is not only ill but alone. There is even more reason for going home. She will be worried about Hampton and Alex, and will need me." She offered a smile. "Besides, I have Seward for protection."

"Ah, yes, Seward. A stalwart fellow. Well, I expected this response. I suppose there is little I can do to stop you. After all, I am not your legal guardian yet. But with the mutiny at Plassey delaying Captain McKay's troop,

I cannot help but be concerned as to where all this is leading."

Coral's mind stumbled over something he had said, and the words commanded her full attention. Yet Uncle Hugo did not seem to realize his mistake. She quelled the question forming on her tongue—"Not her legal guardian—yet?" But why would he even say such a thing? She had her father and mother, and Alex. Perhaps he had uttered a hopeful wish. In which case, it was best that she appeared not to have noticed.

He was frowning to himself, and Coral knew that without proof she must accept his behavior as genuine. It would be disastrous to come out and accuse him of manipulating the trouble with Major Selwyn and the mutiny at Plassey.

"It is you who faces trying times here at Guwahati," she said. "You have accepted a difficult position from the governor-general. With war looming, you will have enough concerns without your nieces here to impose."

"Major Buckley will prove of great assistance to me. I could have no one better to command the security force. And neither could the royal family."

Did he mean it? She recalled the dark accusation that Jace had made in Manali about her uncle plotting his death in the mutiny. Would the major be safe here in Guwahati? Coral's tension mounted.

He walked her toward the door. "I regret I must leave tonight after the state dinner to ride with the major to the outpost. We must delve into the matter of the attack."

Coral was cautious. She must speak to Jace. "The major will be at the dinner?"

"Yes, I believe the new dewan has especially invited him. I will contact you at Kingscote."

Coral dutifully kissed his bearded cheek goodbye and joined Seward outside the door.

"Take good care of my nieces, Seward," Hugo told him. "Unfortunately, I was unable to talk Coral into staying. See them safely to Kingscote. I will be leaving tonight with Major Buckley for Jorhat."

Seward's rugged face told Coral nothing of what he thought of the matter of her father and Alex in Darjeeling. Knowing his loyalty, he would be inclined to risk almost anything in order to be at her father's side searching for Alex.

Seward touched his hat with a salute in her uncle's direction. "Aye, Sir Hugo. I shall get them to Kingscote safely enough."

"Should you find it necessary to get in touch with me, do not hesitate to send a message to Jorhat," ordered Hugo.

Coral followed Seward out the hall and down the steps to the waiting ghari.

"Seward, something is very wrong!"

"I don't like none of what is happening. With Alex missing, and Sir Hampton taking his leave to go after him, Miss Elizabeth be alone. And things do not add up to me."

"How long will it take us to reach Kingscote?"

He squinted toward the bright sun. "If we leave in the morning, we can be there in two days."

"Oh, Seward! Do you think my father has located Alex?"

He frowned as he assisted her into the ghari seat. "As both me and the major can testify, Darjeeling is located near the Eastern Himalayas. It be rugged, mountainous trekking. It won't be easy for your father, or Alex. And that, lass, be what worries me most."

Coral's heart was heavy. First she had lost Gem, then Michael. . . .

Lord, please guide and protect my father. I cannot bear to lose him too.

322

28

Jace left the outpost in Jorhat and returned to Guwahati and his military quarters near the residency. A rajput guard, tough and lean, waited for him with a message from the dewan. Jace was not surprised to see the rajput here, so far from central India. Believed to be born of the warrior caste, the rajputs often served maharajas.

"His Excellency's chief minister bids that he see you before the official dinner tonight, Sirdar-Buckley."

The rajput stepped aside, allowing a lesser servant to step forward, bringing fingers to forehead. He stepped back out the door and quickly returned, holding several presents.

"The dewan requests you to accept these gifts from his hand."

Jace was skeptical of the hard look in the rajput's dark eyes. So the dewan wished to give him gifts. . . .

There was a handsome black tunic embroidered with gold, a turban, and a *tulwar*!

The sight of the curved blade strengthened his suspicions. Jace turned toward the rajput, but he was gone. He picked up the sword and tested its balance.

Arrayed in the fine clothing, Jace arrived at the palace

of the maharaja an hour before the official dinner. Two rajput guards escorted him across marble floors and up the steps between gold-embossed pillars into the Diwan-i-Khas, the hall of private audience.

Jace stopped. The dewan lounged comfortably on silk cushions, waiting. He was anything but what Jace had expected. Unlike Zameen, *this* man was young and darkly handsome, with an arrogance in his black eyes. He was lean and tough, and a deadly ruthlessness cloaked his smile, showing even white teeth. He wore the garb of wealth, his fingers winking with gems as he played with the hilt of his tulwar sheathed in a jeweled scabbard.

Caution. Jace's hand moved slightly toward his blade. The man he faced was now all too familiar.

The dewan produced what was meant to be a pleasant smile. "Greetings, friend Jace. I am surprised to see you are bold enough to come to the royal residence of my father. And as Roxbury's security guard!" He gave a laugh. "What I have always respected about you is your reckless humor."

Why would the nephew of the maharaja wish to be the dewan?

"We meet again, Sunil," said Jace.

"We had to meet again. It has been too long since the missing temple treasure of Kali."

"Ah. The idol of Kali. His Excellency is convinced I am a robber of temples. I often wondered who told him so."

Sunil spread his hands. "And you are assuredly innocent."

"I may acclaim merit for boldness, friend, but I am not a fool. Would I risk my head in serving the governor-general's resident to the maharaja if I were not?"

"I agree it would be most unwise."

"I will speak to His Excellency in private audience," said Jace. "It may be that the temple treasure will soon be returned."

Sunil gestured toward the cushions. "Sit down."

As Jace seated himself, a servant appeared with a glass of wine. Jace noticed that Sunil's gaze dropped to his sword hilt.

"You will not need that—not now," said Sunil. "As you said, you would not risk coming here unless you were innocent—or know where the treasure is."

Jace thought better than to let him know that he had the statue. He had never trusted Sunil. The young man was too ambitious, more so than his older brother, Rajiv. Sunil was likely to have a number of guards in the palace who were more loyal to him than they were to other members of the royal family.

Did he have his eyes upon a more powerful position?

Jace studied him. "So you are now the dewan of His Excellency. What happened to Zameen?"

He hoped Sunil would offer information, but the haughty young nephew of the maharaja was too cautious for that.

Sunil smiled and said easily, "You have already seen in Manali that Zameen has retired, along with Harrington."

"Who told you of Manali?"

Sunil smiled. "Roxbury. Who else?"

Jace, too, smiled. "Somehow I thought it might have been Sanjay." He watched Sunil over his glass, but the man was too clever to give himself away.

"Sanjay, Sanjay," he repeated thoughtfully. "No, I have not heard of him. A friend of yours?"

"I intend to bring him back to Calcutta to be shot for treason."

Sunil refilled Jace's glass, showing nothing.

"Sanjay planned the mutiny of the 17th near Plassey."

"Ah, yes. I have heard. A grief, a tragedy."

Is Sunil the power behind Roxbury? Or are they working together toward some compatible goal?

"His Excellency does not yet know of the mutiny at Plassey," Sunil said.

"It is not Plassey I wish to speak to him about, but the attack on the outpost at Jorhat. You have a prisoner who belongs to the British government. I would like him turned over to me at once."

Sunil smiled. "I am afraid that is out of the question. As to the attack on the British outpost, you will find that infiltrators from Burma hosted the killing of Major Selwyn. My family welcomes the English presence, do we not? His Excellency has signed a treaty with the East India Company."

Jace wondered if Sunil's own feelings corresponded with his uncle's. Rajiv had mentioned that his brother, Sunil, resented the East India Company.

"As for my position as dewan, it was the will of His Excellency."

"The raja needed a man of wisdom. One he could trust," said Jace smoothly.

"His Excellency trusts few these days."

"Was it also the raja's will that you take over the command of the British outpost?" Jace said dryly.

Sunil smiled. "No. That was my idea." He spread a hand. "It is nothing. Your English ensign was young and inexperienced in such matters, so I have been assisting him."

"The treaty between the raja and England grants the Company control over disputes that arise with neighboring states. That includes Sikkim, Bhutan, and Burma. Until troops arrive to take their positions, the ensign is in command, inexperienced or not."

"Ah, but now that you and the Resident Roxbury have arrived, I shall be most pleased to leave military matters in your hand. However, I cannot turn the prisoner over to you."

"Of course, he is dead," said Jace bluntly.

"A tragedy. Hung himself in the dungeon. He served a warlord named Zin in Burma. I understand Zin is also your friend."

Jace said nothing. Zin could not truly be called a friend. That would be like keeping a python for a pet.

"Naturally," said Sunil, "you are free to conduct your own investigations. But a private audience with the maharaja?" He dismissed the idea with a gesture. "What you wish to say to my uncle, you can say to me. He is a busy man."

As he watched Sunil, Jace became convinced that it was even more important to speak alone with the raja. He deliberately changed the subject to measure his response. "I see you carry your brother's tulwar."

Sunil touched the curved sword. "Yes. It belonged to Rajiv." His expression sobered, and he finished his glass of wine in one swallow. "My brother was a fool to marry that woman." He set the glass down harshly. "Jemani was wrong for him."

"Then you knew the peasant girl?" Jace felt his gaze and reached for a fig from the basket of fruit.

"I did not know her. She was of a lower caste. I knew that His Excellency could not accept the marriage. Caste cannot be broken."

"Then Rajiv must have told you of Jemani?"

Again he felt his granite gaze. "Yes. He told me. She worked in the silk hatchery at Kingscote."

Jace knew that Jemani had not worked in the silk hatchery. Then why did Sunil find it necessary to lie?

"A pity your brother had to die for breaking caste."

"You assume his death was the punishment of our uncle?"

"Who else?" said Jace smoothly.

Sunil stood. "I suppose you are right. The royal family could not accept Rajiv's marriage. Nor the son born from the untouchable."

Jace affected indifference. It was unwise to mention the abduction of Gem, or anything about the boy. He must speak first to the maharaja.

"Now that Rajiv is dead, you will reign after your uncle?"

Sunil smiled condescendingly. "No. There is another heir closer than I. At the moment I am content to be his dewan."

The question had accomplished its purpose. At the mention of power, the dark eyes came alive. If Rajiv had lived, he would have been heir. Now that right went to Sunil. But who was this heir who was closer than Sunil?

To a man like Sunil, even Gem would be seen as a threat.

"It is time," Sunil said. "The official guests arrive for the maharaja's state dinner. We will talk again."

Jace now believed the maharaja had no part in the mutiny, and that the maharaja knew nothing of his nephew's drive for power. The question was, what did Sir Hugo expect to receive by helping Sunil? Whatever was planned, it was intended to happen before British reinforcements arrived under McKay.

Jace had been able to take fifteen men with him from the outpost and still leave some measure of fighting force intact. Fifteen soldiers were not enough to protect the maharaja if it came to that. But then, that may have been someone's intention all along.

———

Seated on a dais, the maharaja was a glitter of jewels and silks, as were his politically powerful Indian guests and the dewan himself. Among those who were there to pay tribute to the governor-general's resident were several Portuguese representatives and some English from elsewhere in the northern frontier; men whose sharp eyes and hard faces bespoke the reason for their presence in India—the wealth of trade that reached to Calcutta in the south, and China and Burma in the east.

A lovely image in her exquisite frock designed by Jacques, Coral's gaze swept the grand hall hoping to see the major. She must discuss her father and Alex with him before she left for Kingscote in the morning. Instead, her gaze confronted the dewan, and she tensed. Rajiv appeared to be standing across the hall from her, garbed in royal Indian fashion, but that was impossible. The husband of Jemani, the father of Gem, was dead. But the dewan bore the same bronzed good looks and could easily pass for Rajiv's twin. The cool black eyes stared at her without the customary deference offered a white colonial woman. Coral turned her head away. Was this the new dewan who had taken the place of Zameen?

Coral looked about for Ethan and saw that he, too, was absent. A minute later she turned as Uncle Hugo walked up with the dewan. Coral behaved as though she were unaware of his alert appraisal.

"The Maharaja Majid Singh sends his greetings, Miss Kendall," the dewan said. "I, too, wish to assure you and your family that any infringement on Kingscote plantation by Burma will evoke my highest displeasure."

His highest displeasure?

"My family also sends good wishes to His Excellency, the Maharaja," she said.

She found the dewan's military offer disturbing but

noticed that her uncle showed no curiosity over the surprising overture.

For a century, Kingscote had been recognized by the Assam rulership to be private territory, isolated from the all-too-frequent squabbles of Hindu maharajas, Muslim nawabs, and Buddhist warlords from Sikkim and Burma. Any territorial infringements on Kingscote by warring factions were handled by her father and hired mercenaries. Sir Hampton, like his father before him, had fought to protect his holdings and had won the respect of the governing province. But now that the maharaja had signed a treaty with the East India Company, Coral suspected that her uncle would begin to insist that the mantle of Kingscote's safety fall under Company jurisdiction.

When Jace did not arrive, Coral's unease mounted. Where was he? Who knew when they would see each other again? She was certain that by now Seward would have told him about her father and Alex, but she must be positive. And what of Jace's promise to inquire of the maharaja about Gem?

Guarding her feelings, she found it uncomfortable to look at the maharaja, who had not yet descended from his dais to grace his guests with his presence. Mingled pain and bitterness welled up in her heart. Could this detached and indomitable man, glittering with jewels, have ordered his nephew killed for breaking caste?

The thought that she stood in the same room with those who had killed Rajiv and abducted Gem took away her appetite. *I cannot bear to look at him*, she thought. And Gem, where was he? Somewhere in the palace? Was he dead? Could he have been sent to some warring maharaja or nawab as a slave? Suppose . . . suppose they had tortured him, or thrown him to the tigers?

Did the dewan or the maharaja know that she was

the woman who had adopted Gem and baptized Jemani? She decided that His Excellency *must* already know. And yet his detached gaze never once glanced in her direction. Only the dewan stared at her, and Coral was becoming more concerned by the moment.

If Jace does not come soon, I must make some excuse and leave.

Perhaps he would not come. She glanced about the large room again then stopped short. Her eyes collided with a handsome Indian warrior who stood in the open arcade leading off into the garden.

Confused, she thought, *Javed Kasam! What is he doing here?* Then quickly she caught herself. Jace Buckley was not in tunic and buckskin trousers, nor in uniform, but dressed in handsome black and gold Indian garb. His steady gaze was fixed not on her, but on Dewan Sunil.

With relief, Coral picked up her skirt to cross the floor in his direction when Ethan walked up and took her elbow.

"My dear, I apologize for my tardiness. But something important came up to delay me."

At the concerned edge to his voice, she looked at him, and saw that his gray eyes were troubled.

"Uncle did not explain?" he asked.

"Explain?"

"I must talk to you alone." He glanced about, as though searching for the appropriate place, and before Coral could respond, he escorted her across the floor to an alcove screened by cascades of vine, where stone bowls were filled with floating orchids.

Ethan's expression of alarm increased her own. "What is it, Ethan?"

"A disappointment on my part. I cannot leave with you in the morning for Kingscote. Hugo needs me here at Guwahati for a time."

"I do not understand. You do not serve the Company."

"No, but the maharaja is ill. He has asked for my help."

"The maharaja?"

"Hugo agrees my cooperation will be beneficial, not only to His Excellency but to the East India Company. The king is apparently upset with his own physicians." Ethan frowned. "I cannot refuse a man of his position. And Hugo has asked me to stay on for a few months—"

"A few months, but, Ethan! What about my mother? She is very ill!"

He took hold of her shoulders and looked so unhappy that Coral restrained her disappointment.

"Believe me, Coral, this is not my wish. I have already arranged for the medicine your mother will need and sent it to your chambers by route of Seward. If you need more, you have only to send someone to me."

Coral had not noticed the maharaja looking ill, but public appearances meant little.

"It may be that I will decide to stay until the troops arrive from Calcutta," he said. "I prefer my supplies to be hauled to Kingscote under my supervision."

"As long as I have the medication for my mother, my sisters and I can manage. It is good of you to treat His Excellency. Have you any idea what is ailing him?"

"No, but I shall see him first thing in the morning. He will eat nothing tonight, so he has told me."

Coral glanced through the vines toward the dais. The maharaja had unexpectedly left the hall.

"He is gone," she said, surprised.

As Coral glanced in the direction of the dewan, she saw that he stood, unsmiling, beside Sir Hugo.

"I must say it is dreadful news about Alex," Ethan said. "Uncle, however, assures me your father is acquainted with the area of Darjeeling."

Coral wondered. No one knew the mountainous region as well as Jace. If only he were not obligated to the military, he and Seward could go in search of them! Suppose the monsoon arrived before her father found Alex? The tumultuous rivers and the mountain slides could put both their lives at risk.

"Poor Alex," murmured Ethan.

Poor Alex? Something in Ethan's voice caused her to study his face. He appeared thoughtful, and with a hint of pity, which seemed a little odd to her.

"Alex will not be the first man to lose his way in the mountains," she replied. "But he should not have gone without a guide. Losing one's way is a common problem with trekking. It could happen to most anyone, even my father."

Coral glanced toward the garden where she had last seen Jace, but he was gone and nowhere visible in the hall.

The dewan had come to stand beside her. "You will reconsider, and stay in Guwahati, Miss Kendall? Why not remain with Doctor Boswell until British troops arrive?"

"Your invitation is most generous, Dewan. But circumstances will not afford the ease. My mother is quite ill with the fever, and I am anxious to be home."

"I quite understand," he said, his handsome face too grave. "It is unceremonious of us to ask the physician to stay, yet generous on your part, Miss Kendall, and yours, Doctor Boswell."

"Have you any notion what is ailing His Excellency?" Ethan asked.

The dewan showed no expression. "Age perhaps. We trust you will do what you can, Doctor Boswell."

"I assure you, Dewan, I shall do my best."

As Ethan discussed medicine, Coral inched away until she came up beside Kathleen and whispered behind her peacock fan, "Keep the dewan and Ethan occupied. I must speak to the major alone."

"I saw him leave a minute ago."

"Which direction?"

"The garden."

Coral unobtrusively retreated across the polished floor toward the wide-open doors leading out into the parklike garden. She glanced backward and saw that everyone was occupied. She caught up her skirts of amber taffeta and, once out of sight, sped into the fragrant garden with its colored glass lanterns. He could not have gone yet, not without at least telling her goodbye.

She had not gone far into the pillared pavilion when she saw him. He was standing a short distance away by the steps that led to a lower tiered garden leading down toward the Bramaputra River. He must have heard her footsteps for he turned. Coral paused, glancing back over her shoulder. No one had followed her. She walked quickly toward him, hearing the musicians playing their *sitars* from the upper gallery. The stringed instruments played a haunting *ghazal*—music derived from poetry, always a hopeless love theme. She hurried toward Jace in a rush of slippers and silk.

29

This is not going to be pleasant, thought Jace.

The music from the sitar did not soothe but was irksome. What had come over him? Why did he let a feeling of responsibility toward her divide his mind? This was no time to let emotion come between him and the work the colonel had sent him here to do. He would pointedly tell her his concerns about Gem and say goodbye.

Coral stood before him for a moment staring at him, and he wondered what thoughts were running through her mind. He rejected what was racing through his own.

Jace believed he understood what she thought of him. He was the sometimes arrogant man who cared little about anyone or anything except completing his mission for the colonel, returning to Calcutta for the *Madras,* and disengaging himself from any emotional ties or bonds. She was more right than wrong.

"Did you hear about Alex?" she asked.

Seward had explained everything, but Jace was reluctant to tell her of his concerns, although he had shared them with Seward.

"Yes, Seward told me," he said briefly.

She came closer. The wash of moonlight fell upon her,

sending tiny shimmers through her golden tresses and lending softness to the lines of her gown.

Jace put an iron clamp about his emotions. *Not this* . . . He did not want it.

"Sir Hugo asked me to stay here until Captain McKay arrives, but I refused. I am leaving in the morning with Seward," she said.

"Yes, I know."

He saw her hesitate at his briefness, and he reinforced his action by turning away to look out at the river, as though preoccupied with more important matters.

"How long will you be in Jorhat?" she asked.

"I do not know. Longer than I first thought."

A long time, he wanted to say. *Perhaps it is best we do not see each other again.*

"There is something I want to say before I leave," Jace said.

He saw her hesitate, as though retreating emotionally. Was she misguided enough to think that he would become a romantic fool? He folded his arms. It was best that she knew who the dewan was. He had seen the way Sunil looked at her. One man knew the thoughts of another man when it came to a woman as lovely as Coral.

"Stay away from the dewan. He is the younger brother of Rajiv. He cannot be trusted."

"Then I was correct when I told you that years ago I saw two young men riding on the royal elephant with the maharaja!"

"He is ruthless. He may be the one behind the trouble at Plassey and the attack on Major Selwyn. Your father would do best not to trust him where Kinscote is concerned."

"The dewan mentioned Kingscote to me tonight. He said he would do what he could to protect the silk enterprise from Burmese soldiers."

"He wishes to appear friendly for his own reasons. I am convinced he is working with your uncle." He saw the veiled flicker of pain. "I am sorry. . . . I believe they have some plan that will benefit both of them. I have informed Seward. And when your father returns, Seward will explain."

Again she hesitated, as though wanting to avoid a decision.

"Yet there is no proof of your suspicions that my uncle is involved," she stated.

"No, but I am certain that the dewan is a man of whom to be cautious."

"My father would find the dewan's offer of protection for Kingscote suspicious," she said. "He has had a good relationship with most of the rulers here in the northeast and would not believe an attack on us likely. They call him the Burra-sahib, the '*Great Man.*' "

Jace hoped that she did not notice his reaction to the description she had offered of her father. The garden at Barrackpore . . . what had Marianna overheard? *"An accident of one so great would not be as easy. He is a respected man."*

Could Sir Hampton Kendall be that man? Was the message that Alex was missing intended to be a trap?

Reluctant to alarm her, he said nothing. Whatever was happening, he could not stop it now. Sir Hampton Kendall was three weeks into his trek to Darjeeling. He must warn Seward—

"Major, is something wrong?"

He came back to awareness. "You were saying about the dewan?"

"My father has always hired mercenaries to protect the plantation. He would not accept help from the dewan."

"Yes, of course. A wise move. Sir Hampton would do

well to be suspicious, and so would you. Listen to me. I cannot prove it yet, but I think Sunil was involved with others on Kingscote to have Gem abducted."

He saw her tense, but she made no sound. He respected her for that. Her innocent appearance was an asset in confronting men like Roxbury and Prince Sunil. They underestimated her. Jace did not. Not anymore.

"But what motive would he have to abduct Gem?"

He paused, reluctant to hurt her. "You should know the answer to that."

She must have shivered, for she held her arms and glanced back toward the lighted hall.

"The ritual killing of Rajiv—you think Sunil had his own brother killed?" she whispered.

"Yes. Rajiv was a threat to his ambitions. The marriage to Jemani might have offered the excuse to destroy him. Sunil desires to be the raja after his uncle. Gem, too, could have been a threat to Sunil's royal ambitions."

"The caste system would shut Gem out," she insisted.

"You are right. Unless—" and he looked at her. "You once told me you knew very little about Jemani. Is that true?"

She hesitated. "Yes, I was only fifteen when she and Rajiv arrived. They only said they were from Rajasthan, that they were escaping a famine."

"Rajasthan," he repeated to himself. He allowed his mind to wander into a path that neither he nor Coral had ever considered. What if Jemani had not been born an untouchable? It could be true that she had come from Rajasthan, but was it also possible that she too had come from a royal line? Perhaps a faction at war with the maharaja here at Guwahati? That would explain her disguise.

That would make Gem royalty, an heir to two thrones. . . . And if peace ever came between the two warring houses he could rule either, or both. *Had Sunil somehow known this?*

Jace recalled Sunil's expression when he had asked him if he knew Jemani.

Because of Jemani's Christian baptism, and the resentment it brought to the Hindus on Kingscote, it would have been easy for Sunil to have gotten the support of someone on the plantation. That someone may have delivered the message to Rajiv to meet his brother in the jungle.

Perhaps Sunil had written a false conciliatory message from their uncle. If that were true, it would account for Rajiv's willingness to meet in secret and yet not suspect danger.

"Then Sunil may know where Gem is," Coral said.

Jace was beginning to think that Sunil did not know, not yet, but was intensely looking for the boy. Had the trail led him into Burma? Yet he did not wish to raise her hopes. Gem's danger remained real. Sunil would have no reason to leave the child alive if he found him. Jace knew he must find him first.

Perhaps he would not tell her now, not with Sunil in the palace. After she arrived at Kingscote, when her father had returned—yes, then he would send a message through Gokul.

"You must say nothing to the dewan," he demanded. "Be polite but distant. Do not mention Gem. I will first speak with the maharaja before I leave Guwahati, and learn what is possible. It is also important he understands his nephew's ambitions for the throne."

"The raja is ill. Ethan was asked to stay and treat him." She said swiftly, "Do you suppose—?"

"Poison?" Jace asked bluntly. "It is my guess. Then I must see the raja tonight."

"But how?"

"I do not know yet. . . . Who asked Boswell to stay?" He saw her falter.

"My uncle mentioned to the maharaja that Ethan was a physician."

It did not surprise him. Did Roxbury believe he could manipulate Boswell's medicine to accomplish the raja's death? Jace did not doubt that he had used Boswell to accomplish his purposes in London with Coral, but murder? Just how far would Boswell go?

"Something else," he said. "I want you to delay your mission school until your father returns with Alex. Will you do that?"

"I . . . I will think about everything you say, and I will pray for guidance and wisdom. It is the best I can do, the wisest."

As he looked down at her, he had the disturbing notion that Coral prayed about everything. Did she ever pray for the scoundrel Jace Buckley? Thinking that she might made him uncomfortable.

"Wait until Sir Hampton returns," he repeated. She did not answer him, and the silence grew until he caught his breath with exasperation. "That I find you frustrating, yet still admire your spirit, is beyond sound reason. Nevertheless I do."

"I find your admiration a compliment, Major."

His eyes narrowed. "Will you do as I say?"

Her chin lifted slightly, and her eyes met his evenly. He read that expression and smiled for the first time. "All right. Will you 'consider' my advice?"

He saw her expression soften, and a little smile touched her lips, but it was gone as swiftly as it came.

"I always take your advice seriously, Major. After saving me from both tiger and spider, how could I not?"

His brow slanted. "And yet, you will press ahead. I will say it anyway. Take extra precaution about doing

anything that would provoke the religious ire on Kingscote. Watch your servant Natine. I think he is a ghazi."
She tried to interrupt. "No, do not protest. Be cautious
around him, and depend on Seward."

"You are leaving for the outpost tonight with my uncle? How long will you be there?"

"For as long as it takes to inquire into the death of
Major Selwyn. The Burmese prisoner is dead. Somehow
I must make a trip into Burma. How to accomplish it
without Roxbury's suspicions will prove difficult."

She looked at him with surprise. "Burma?"

Jace thought of the local warlord, Zin. Did he know
anything about Gem's abduction? If he did, it would
prove the motive for Sunil's visit. The question was, what
had the warlord been willing to tell Sunil?

Zin was a crafty man who would bargain for political
favor and wealth. Jace had little to bargain with except
the stolen idol of Kali, and in order to use it, he would
first need to speak with the maharaja and gain his support. That would mean confiding in him about Gem.

"I expect to discover information in Burma that may
prove useful," he said simply.

"And after Burma, when your duty to the colonel and
my uncle is complete? Then what?"

After his military duty. . . ! He folded his arms across
his chest and tilted his head to look at her. Her question
was not flirtatious, he knew her too well for that. But he
could almost read something into it. He knew an invitation when he heard one, even when it was disguised.
Did this mean she would miss him when he disappeared
out of her life once and for all? He felt some solace for
his frustrations. He hoped she would think about him as
much as he would remember her. He smiled to himself.
The memory of Miss Coral Kendall in the bazaar of Calcutta, confronting a guru and his trained crows for a

group of half-naked children, would remain with him wherever he went.

They both knew there was no possibility of a relationship. She was a *silk heiress*. He had nothing. He would not accept wealth and prestige from her hand. He must make his own success in the tea plantation in Darjeeling. Even if they admitted the attraction between them, his success could take years. Ethan, if he was smart, would not wait that long. Nor could he imagine the Kendall and Roxbury families waiting.

"After my service here," he repeated as though deep in contemplation, "I shall resume where I left off, before Gokul and the colonel trapped me back into wearing this uniform." He could have added, *And before I met a certain young woman who was out to take on the world* . . . "I shall never suddenly emerge a saint, Miss Kendall, if that is your hope."

"You misunderstand me," she said quietly. "What my expectations are for your future does not truly matter. It is not for me to choose, but what God asks of you, and what He wants to make of you. He does not make mistakes. What about you, Jace? Do you trust Him? With the *Madras,* the tea plantation, your dreams? Or do you think He wishes to destroy them, turn them into ashes?"

"A missionary to the very end. I shall keep your fair words in mind," he said with a smile. "As for your future, you will make the perfect helpmeet for the gentleman Charles Peddington. He is worth two of Boswell."

She spoke in a whisper. "I think you know the Lord better than you wish to admit. Why do you hide it?"

"Your questions have a way of backing me into a corner. I do not take well to retreating from beautiful women. It has always been the other way around."

This was unfair, he decided—a beautiful young

woman whose religion was a constant goad to his conscience.

"I think I have been honest with you about what I believe," he said quietly. "I have never tried to mislead you. It is Boswell's new interest in the Scriptures that you should question."

Her confusion was evident, and her eyes searched his. "Ethan? He has nothing to do with this—"

"I think he has quite a lot to do with this. Unlike his glib manners, I have not pretended to be something I am not."

"You are unfair, Major. He does have a concern for the things of God."

"Maybe. But not in the way he has wanted you to think. With men like Newton and Carey, Christianity is their life. They go to sleep with God's name on their tongue, and they awake in prayer. Boswell's consecration is a jest. I shall let you decide why he behaves so."

"Seward said you have met John Newton?"

"In London. Seward arranged the meeting. And at risk of dashing any new ideas you may have about Jace Buckley, I will hasten to say that I have had no spiritual experience like that of he or Wesley. Newton speaks of God as though he knows Him. If I were you," he said calmly, "I would make careful inspection of what is beneath that pious mantle Boswell is wrapping himself in."

She looked up at him, troubled, and he guessed from her eyes that it was not over Ethan.

"Meaning, of course, that my cousin wishes to deceive me? Major! I think it is highly inappropriate to say he is a hypocrite."

He refused to back down and stared at her evenly. "Nevertheless, Miss Kendall, that is what I am doing. The dewan is not the only man of whom you need to be cautious."

She hesitated, and her breath came quickly. "You—you would dare compare Ethan to—"

"No," Jace said flatly, feeling irritated because she insisted on defending him. "Ethan is not as cold and clever in his ambitions as Sunil or Roxbury. I suspect he merely follows his uncle's orders. As I see it, that too is a danger. He is a compromiser."

She said quickly, "I know you do not like him. And I cannot understand why it should be so. But I can assure you that Ethan can be trusted. And I will not look narrowly on his motives just because he is your opposite and—"

"I can take most any of your deductions, but I will not go so far as to let you think I envy his noble character, so opposite mine. That is not why I question his motives, and warn you to be cautious—" He caught himself from going further in his frustration and put another clamp on his emotions.

Her features showed that his words had hurt her, although she seemed to struggle to mask them. She obviously felt strongly about Boswell.

"I am sorry," he said quietly, bothered because he had brought her pain. "As you wish, we best drop the subject. I have much to do before I ride out tonight with Sir Hugo. I must see the raja. I wanted to speak to you only because of my concern about the dewan. Now that I have done so, I must go."

"Yes," said Coral, "you are right, of course, I will not keep you. As you say, you must get ready to leave."

He wanted to frown at the silence between them. It was worse than all the noisy but simple chatter of the dewan's dinner guests, and much more painful.

The music coming from the sitars filled the garden.

She spoke with a little rush. "I'd better go back before I am missed. Goodbye, Major."

He said nothing. At the moment, the word *goodbye* might have weighed as much as the *Madras*.

She turned to walk back to the lighted palace hall, then paused. Her eyes came swiftly back to his, searching one last time.

"And Gem? You will. . . . Will you speak to the maharaja?"

He said evasively, "I will speak to him."

"You will come to Kingscote to let me know?"

He felt the tension of her persistence. Did he truly want to see her again? Even if her dreams came true and he was able to rescue Gem—did he want to be the man to return him, or was it safer for his own emotions to send the child back to Kingscote through Gokul?

"I do not know," he said stiffly. "As I said, it is necessary that I visit an acquaintance in Burma. He is the friend of a 'certain Indian mercenary' you met in Calcutta, a man involved in intrigue. I think he can offer me important information on the mutiny here and at Plassey. I could be gone six months, a year, even longer."

"I see."

"But I will send Gokul with whatever news I can discover about Gem."

She stared at him, her expression strained in the pale moonlight. Hoping to ward off any further questions, he said: "You will be missed by the guests."

She stood there watching him. Suddenly, her voice tense, she whispered, "You think Gem is no longer alive."

He said nothing. He turned to lean against the garden rail, noticing the dancing glimmer of moonlight on the river. He had hoped to avoid this moment, but she persisted. He heard her hesitant steps come up behind him and felt her nearness.

"I find it painful to caution you. I wish for your hopes

and joys to come true. We both know life does not always work that way."

She paused for only a moment, and he guessed she was holding back her emotions. "You have been the only one who has understood about Gem, about how desperately I want—"

Her voice broke, and Jace knew if he did not reinforce his own feelings and remain aloof, he would be tempted to draw her into his arms and comfort her. "I will keep the promise to discover his whereabouts. But as I told you before, I cannot promise a joyful outcome. I would give anything if I could."

She did not answer him, and he saw her swallow back her disappointment. He found it difficult to bear, and looked out across the gallery rail into the shadowy garden. He was conscious of a bewildering pain that he did not want, and he tried to smother it, to reject it. His fingers clamped about the rail.

"All this time I believed that he had to be alive," she said, and her voice broke. "I was so certain. Jace—"

He felt her hand clutch his tunic in a desperate move, as if somehow he had only to say he was mistaken, and hope would rise from the ashes with a flutter of golden wings and soar. He turned to look down at her, and as he did, her eyes filled with tears, as soft as liquid jewels in the moonlight, and he became too aware of her closeness, of her touch. Despite his caution, he knew he could no longer deny the kindled flame burning in his heart. . . .

———

Coral was too surprised to react. One moment she felt pain and loss over Gem; the next, her thoughts were filled with the man who held her in his arms. The same man whom she had for so long denied access to her affections.

His voice was so soft, she wondered if she imagined the words whispered in her ear: "The game is not played fairly, Coral. I could love you so easily."

All ability to reason dwindled into something wild, sweet, and dangerous—the warmth of his lips on hers, the feel of his rugged tunic beneath her palms, the fragrance of spice as he held her tightly.

"Coral? Are you out here?" Ethan's voice shattered the stillness like the crack of a whip.

Jace breathed something in exasperation.

For Coral, reality rushed in with a flood of guilt. She wrenched free, her heart pounding in her ears, and backed away, her hands pressed hard against the sides of her skirt. She stood shaking.

Jace seemed neither intimidated by the sound of Ethan's steps approaching on the stone nor the least bit ashamed for his action.

"Coral?" Ethan called again.

She thought briefly of the perfunctory slap that society demanded of a lady on such occasions but could not bring herself to do it.

"I am waiting for my just retribution," came Jace's dry voice.

She managed a calm whisper. "I am certain it would not be worthy of either of us."

"But that cannot be said of kissing you goodbye. I found it worthy of my fondest memory."

Merely a memory? After he had *dared* to hold her in his arms and kiss her?

Her emotions took another tumble, hitting bottom with harsh cruelty. There was no doubt but that he had held other women in his arms and kissed them goodbye. How many women? What to her was the rainbow after a storm, the crown jewel of emotional commitment, meant little to a man like Jace Buckley. But of course she had known that all along and had been cautious to avoid this very moment. And he had dared to ignore her boundaries!

As though conjured up in the mocking mist, the smug young face of the beautiful Indian girl in Sualkashi flashed before her, evoking vivid scenes that lit an angry spark. Her palm was across his face before she even realized she had slapped him.

It took him by surprise, for he took a small step back.

With more dignity than she thought she possessed, Coral picked up her skirts, whipped around, and walked quickly toward the lighted banquet hall.

After she was out of his view she ran into the lighted courtyard, nearly colliding with Ethan.

He caught her by both arms, and when she looked at him, his eyes scanned her face, then hardened. He looked over her shoulder in the direction from where she had come.

"Is Buckley out there? What has he said to you, what has he done? I shall—"

"No, please, Ethan, I want to go inside. I am not feeling well."

And as Coral took an unsteady step, he led her gently toward the lighted salon.

———

The evening wore on miserably. Coral was seated at a grand table between Sir Hugo and Ethan, but she could not concentrate on either of them. Kathleen and Marianna sat beside attentive escorts. The conversation and the music from the sitar all went unnoticed by her, while she struggled to keep her frayed emotions behind a proper demeanor. The rich assortment of dishes from the maharaja's kansamah were tasteless and dry in her mouth, and she could hardly swallow. She dare not look at the dewan, for fear she would think of Gem. With every moment that dragged by she wondered what time it was, and how much longer she must stay.

One thought rekindled the smoldering flame in her heart: Tomorrow she was going home, home to Kingscote and to her mother.

From her memory, the little song she had taught Gem came back, haunting her emotions above the festive din:

Shepherd, Shepherd, where be your little lambs?
Don't you know the tiger roams the land?
Softly, little lamb, softly, I AM always here.
My rod is your protection, My arm will hold you near.

Oh, Lord, prayed Coral. *I cannot stand it. I am going to cry. Please, not here, not now, not in front of them! And Jace—*

The glass slipped from her fingers and came splashing down in her lap, soaking the lush silk skirts. "Oh!"

There was a rush by Ethan to offer her his napkin, and even the dewan stood, calling for a servant. Horrified, Coral apologized for the disturbance and murmured something about excusing herself.

Somehow she reached the stairs that led up to her bedchamber. Climbing the steps, she blinked back the tears and clamped her jaw. She refused to permit her mind to find its way back to Jace.

Cold fingers of pain squeezed about her heart. She could feel, if she permitted herself to do so, an odd feeling of emptiness, a void that was left to stand stark and bare. Unsatisfied, unfulfilled. Jace was forever gone. And now?

She was certain of one thing: He had kissed her only because he thought he might not see her again. He was indeed a rogue! She had understood that he was not the manner of man to be content with the dreams of Miss

Coral Kendall. Neither her wealth nor her beauty would lure him to Kingscote. No. He had deliberately kissed her because he knew it was goodbye.

Feeling emotionally spent, Coral paused on the stairway, and looked back in the direction of the open doors that led out into the garden.

Gone. First Gem, and now this illusive man who came and went in the masquerade of three men, none of whom she truly understood. He would not remove his armor for anyone, especially her.

No, she would not think about him anymore. She forced herself to whisper aloud, "The Lord is my high tower."

Her back stiffened as her thoughts continued to be consumed with Jace. She tried futilely to erase from her memory the feel of his lips.

Maybe, yes, just maybe—I should go ahead and let Ethan know that I am ready to become his betrothed, she thought angrily. How could Jace simply say goodbye?

And just whom had she said goodbye to? Major Buckley? Javed Kasam? Or was it the captain of the *Madras*?

Coral sighed audibly, wearily, as she reached the second-floor landing and crossed to the door of her chamber.

I have work to do on Kingscote, she thought. *I have a school to open, children to teach, and Ethan . . .*

Coral straightened her shoulders, turned her back, and entered her room, shutting out the world behind her.

30

Even before the mansion's white walls and blue stone roof came into view, Coral felt the anticipation swelling within her soul. Home at last!

When Seward stepped from the boat onto the ghat steps with Coral and her sisters, a Kingscote ghari was waiting near the river. Two white-clad bearers stood to greet them, extending palms to forehead. "Welcome home, Missy Coral! Missy Kathleen! Missy Marianna!"

From the main landing on the Bramaputra River where the elephants hauled the precious cargo down to the boats, Kings Road ran northeast through the tropical forest into the massive holdings of the Kendall silk plantation. The road, named after great-grandfather Kingston Kendall, was wide enough for four elephants to pass side by side. Although the plantation road had existed for seventy years, well-beaten by elephant feet and the wheels of wagons, the jungle creepers and ferns were in need of constant vigil to hold back their rapid growth. Tall trees arched their branches overhead, exotic leaves blocking the sunlight, while on either side of Kings Road, the dense tropical forest of northeastern Assam surrounded them.

The afternoon was hot, and Coral and her sisters swished their fans in excitement. The horses' hoofs clopped forward up the wide two-mile road toward the Kendall mansion.

"Orchids," gasped Marianna. "I'd forgotten them. Oh, stop the ghari, Mister Seward." She turned to Coral and Kathleen. "Let's pick an armful for mother!"

Coral could imagine Ethan's delight when he discovered that the orchids grew wild. The small white and lavender jewels twining about the trunks of trees reminded Coral of the decorative garlands of Christmas festoons. She offered her wide-brimmed hat, and the three of them filled it while the giant scarlet butterflies flitted from blossom to blossom. Even Kathleen was moved, and paused to look about in reverie. "I'd forgotten all this," she said simply.

Coral understood her emotion, and a melancholic hush descended upon the three of them.

Soon the ghari emerged from the steamy shadows into a wide clearing confronting the mansion that sprawled along a sloping expanse of emerald-green with sunlight gazing down upon white marble from Rajasthan. The domed roofs made of small blue mosaics glistened against the distant backdrop of the massive mulberry orchard.

Coral's heart swelled with longing. Memories of her mother seemed to rush down the wide steps. Her father, Michael, Alex, and a host of remembered family servants all seemed to move toward her in a memory-inspired homecoming. And Gem . . . Gem was always there waiting in the rose garden of her mind.

Marianna was already running toward the steps, Kathleen coming behind, but Coral stood in grateful praise to the Lord who had brought her home again.

With anticipation Coral began walking, then running, toward the verandah.

The house servants were all assembled to welcome them, and Coral smiled and called to them in greeting. But it was her mother she wished to see!

A man emerged from the others and came down the steps to greet them. He stood dressed immaculately in a blue silk three-quarter-length jacket. He wore white leggings and small woven shoes, and his turban was white cotton, embroidered on the edges with blue. His face was expressionless, but the dark eyes glinted like rippling pools as they fixed upon Coral.

"Natine," she said gently.

Then he smiled, his eyes crinkling at the corners, and he came to life. "Miss Coral, welcome, welcome!"

Looking into the eyes of Natine, Coral thought she could see her own reflection as she greeted the man she had known since she was a toddler. "*Jai ram*, friend Natine! How good to be home again."

"You look well after your sickness. You are strong again?"

"Much stronger, and delighted to be home in India."

It was Natine who ended the conversation. He brought his fingers to his forehead then turned toward the servants. He clapped his hands, and one by one the others stepped forward to greet them.

She must tell Natine not to clap at the others. He could be pretentious, but she told herself that it was his commanding way and had been for as long as she could remember. She recognized most of them and smiled her greeting to each one, speaking their names. She went out of her way to try to show respect and warmth, knowing that it was these people that she hoped to win to her cause. The Kendall family had always been informal with the workers, but to her mild surprise they remained grave, murmuring the correct response. *As though I am a stranger,* she thought. *More of Natine's rules,* she decided. She must change all of this.

She noticed a young woman standing behind the others. There was something familiar about her. Then she remembered and smiled. "Preetah?"

Natine's niece stepped forward. The girl had not been working at Kingscote when Coral left for London, but lived with relatives in the village farther north. She was pleased to see her among the house servants. Looking into the young woman's eyes, Coral thought them to be joyless.

Preetah gestured her greeting and murmured Coral's name.

"And the memsahib?" Coral asked Natine, glancing up the wide stairway. "Is she well enough to see us now?"

"Oh, we must see Mother!" cried Marianna.

Natine retained his dignity. "Memsahib is recovering but now asleep," came his faultless voice. "Her daughters are much on her mind."

"Asleep? Is that all," said Kathleen with relief. "Then we'll awaken her, won't we, Marianna? Come, Coral, let's surprise her!"

Marianna raced Kathleen to the top of the landing. Coral remembered that with her mother ill and Sir Hampton and Alex gone, she and her sisters were in command of Kingscote. Restraining the desire to run into her mother's arms, she turned and spoke quietly to Natine. "I want you to give Seward a full report of how everything on Kingscote is progressing in my father's absence. Seward will sit at the head of the table tonight in Sir Hampton's place."

"As you wish, Miss Coral."

Coral walked back to the verandah, where Seward still waited, and looped her arm through his. She smiled up at him but noticed he wore a tinge of frown. "We're home, Seward, thanks to you and Major Buckley. Learn everything you can about Father and Alex. I will speak to you alone after dinner in Hampton's office."

"Aye, lass, and give Miss Elizabeth my regards. Here be the medicine from Doctor Boswell."

With a smile Coral rushed up the stairs so swiftly she had to pause on the top landing to catch her breath. She hurried down the hall past her own room and the adjoining chamber that had once belonged to Gem, pausing only briefly to touch the door. She stopped near her parents' chambers.

The door stood wide open, and outside in the hall Jan-Lee was seated on a chair. Seeing Coral, she stood, her eyes flickering in the ageless face beneath rich black hair touched with white.

"Jan-Lee."

The Burmese woman stared at her, then her lips turned up at the corners. "Welcome home, Miss Coral." Swiftly, Coral was in her arms, and for a moment a silk heiress and a servant stood bonded in no other thought but love.

Coral pulled away. Brushing the tears from her cheeks, she looked toward her mother's bedroom. She hesitated, bringing her emotions under control; then clutching the bottle of medicine to her heart, she entered with a soft rustle of skirts.

The familiar room was rich with mahogany furniture, thick Afghan rugs, and heavy gold-braided drapes that were drawn across the verandah doors to shut out the heat. An Indian child worked the fans, her wide, curious eyes on the scene before her as Kathleen and Marianna bent over their mother beside the large bed.

Coral tiptoed to the side of the bed, and Kathleen moved away, wiping her eyes. At the sight of her mother, Coral stood transfixed, still gripping the bottle. Two black braids rested on the lace pillow-cover beside the thin face. Dark circles ringed her brown eyes, and as they came to rest upon Coral, moisture oozed from their corners and ran down her cheeks. Her fever-cracked lips quivered as she tried to speak her daughter's name. A limp hand reached out for her. In a moment Coral was in her arms.

"My Coral . . ."

Coral could not speak. Her throat cramped, and she simply clung to her.

Her mother's prolonged suffering spurred Coral to action. Bringing herself under control, she prepared Ethan's prescription, believing that God would bless the results.

"Mother," she whispered. "I've brought you medication. It will help make you stronger, just as it helped me in London."

She and her sisters stayed until the medication brought her into restful sleep, then Jan-Lee spoke. "I'll look after Miss Elizabeth now. She would want her daughters also to rest."

Her sisters showed their weariness, and they tiptoed across the polished wood floor to the door. Marianna cast a wistful glance back before reluctantly leaving.

Coral remained seated on the side of the bed, and when the sound of their steps faded, she quietly rose and stood, looking down at her mother. Despite the long battle with burning heat and hallucinations, her mother's face reflected the inner composure of her deep faith in the Scriptures. She was graying at the temples and hairline, her cheekbones prominent due to the loss of weight, but still her mother looked much like the image Coral had carried in her memory.

Jan-Lee stood at the open doors leading onto the verandah, watching Coral steadily. Her features were quiet but showed concern. Coral wearily walked up beside her. Together, they looked out into the twilight settling over the distant jungle. The smooth lawns and trees lining the drive were beginning to darken. How hushed the coming of evening was! Even the usual clamor of birds only whispered in Coral's ears. Here in this comforting interlude, she stood beside Jan-Lee, her mother's most intimate servant—her own as well. Coral laid her head against her arm and Jan-Lee held her in silence.

A peacock's shrill call pierced the oncoming shadows. Coral stirred. "How is little Emerald?"

Jan-Lee's mouth turned into a pleased smile. "She is a good child. She remembers you and the songs you teach her back then."

Back then ... when Emerald had played with Gem. . . . Inevitably, her heart drawn down the path of warm memories, she found herself recalling the night she had brought Gem home from Jemani's hut near the silkworm hatcheries. Coral had given the tiny infant to Jan-Lee to nurse along with her own newborn daughter, Emerald. How long ago that all seemed now!

The violet dusk was losing color over the darkening jungle trees. "Tell me about Mother. Does she know that my father went to find Alex? That there is danger?"

"She knows. Each time she wakes she asks if there is word."

"The message, how did it arrive?"

The woman's eyes hardened. "It was a man of my ancestry who brought your brother's ring. The one your father gave him before Mister Alex went to study music. Said he was very ill. Your father look at ring, and his face grow sad. Then at once he gathered group of men and prepared for trek to Darjeeling. They leave the next morning while it was yet dark."

"He took men with him? From the village?"

"No, Natine was unable to find the men to go so quickly. So Mister Hampton took volunteers from the silk workers. Twelve went with him by boat, carrying guns."

"Guns?" gasped Coral, her tired mind at once alert.

Jan-Lee nodded. "For protection. There is talk of marauders from the border."

Seward would have the latest information on any infringements from the Burmese warlord, if there were any truth to the rumors from Sir Hugo, and she would speak to him later that evening.

"Has there been any trouble recently?" she asked.

Jan-Lee shook her head. "No trouble except the illness."

"Are there many sick on Kingscote?"

"Yes, women, children, the old men. Yanna and I attend them as best we can since your mother became ill."

Yanna. By now, thought Coral, the girl would be of marriageable age. She wondered how Yanna would find a Christian husband, since Coral's mother had written that Yanna had been baptized.

"Natine is displeased that his niece Preetah was helping Yanna and me with some of the sick. He threatened Preetah. Miss Elizabeth had to get up from her sickbed to speak to him. And this when she was very ill. She collapsed after that and did not come awake for many hours."

Coral felt a quiet indignation that Natine would cause her mother such trouble when she needed complete rest.

"I'll see to Natine, and to the sick," she stated. "There's little I can do about his niece, but he cannot interfere with you or Yanna. I wish to see the ill for myself. Will you take me tomorrow, Jan-Lee? I want to make a full inspection."

Jan-Lee glanced toward Elizabeth, who was moaning softly, and she leaned down to pick up the bucket of cool, scented water. She carried it to the side of the bed and Coral joined her, wringing out the cloths and handing them to Jan-Lee, who wiped down her mother. Her fever-racked body was gaunt, and Coral's heart wrenched with anxiety. Would the medicine cure her mother? And what of herself? Had she looked this bad in London? Sir Hugo insisted she had almost died. Perhaps his words had not been far from reality.

"Miss Coral, you must not take on all the burdens at Kingscote in your mother's place. If you do, you will weary yourself and get sick again. Then what?"

"Did my mother do too much, Jan-Lee?"

"She works too hard for untouchables. Mister Hampton was upset, but she would not listen. We buried three infants, and mothers, and old men, old women, all too tired to fight on. It was after that that she got very sick too. Now Yanna does what she can, and Emerald helps, but I cannot leave Miss Elizabeth for long."

"I'm feeling strong. And Kathleen and Marianna can help me."

Jan-Lee cast her a silent glance, seeming to question her sisters' willingness. Coral told herself she would send for Yanna first thing in the morning. She must also speak to Natine about his bullying ways with the other workers, but perhaps it was wiser to wait until they were home for a few days. Somehow she knew that the dignified man would not take her words as anything less than meddling. He would still see her and her sisters as mere girls who should occupy their time in frivolous activities.

Coral drew in a little breath. It was not going to be easy to put a curb on him in the absence of her father. She would also speak with Kathleen, who was the eldest.

Together, the two of them must stand shoulder to shoulder, representing the Kendall authority, until their father returned with Alex.

"Thank heaven we have Seward!" she murmured.

———

Coral took after-dinner tea with Seward in the comfortable but overcrowded office that belonged to her father. Books lined the wall, stacked knee-high on both sides of the mahogany desk, and papers and parchments concerning the business of Kingscote were piled in disarray. The room with its many trinkets gathered haphazardly from his far-reaching travels told much of Sir Hampton Kendall's rugged personality and colorful past. Her eye fell on a carved elephant that she remembered from her childhood, for it held a special enchantment, and she had named it after her pet elephant, Rani. Somehow the miniature brought Jace to mind.

Where is he now? What is he doing? Coral stirred uneasily and tried to dismiss him from her mind.

"Like I said, lass, it's a feeling inside that bothers me. And Jace has his suspicions too."

"He said nothing of them to me!"

"He wouldn't. And he wouldn't care for me mentioning it to you now. But seeing as how I'm asking my leave to go to Darjeeling, it's only right I tell you why. But I be distressed over leavin' you and your sisters and Miss Elizabeth alone here."

"We're not alone," she hastened. "I'm sure there is little to worry about. I want you to go to my father. By now he and Alex may need you."

She leaned toward him and said quietly, "But why did Jace think the message brought to my father could be deceptive?"

Seward rubbed his bearded chin, watching her

thoughtfully, as though wondering how much he should reveal. He glanced toward the closed office door. "Jace be thinking Alex could not have the fever."

She was alert. "Why not?"

"It is very uncommon to the climate of Darjeeling. It's cool in the mountainous region."

She felt her skin prickle. "Then what could possibly lie behind the message? And who would send it? According to Jan-Lee, the messenger gave my father Alex's ring as proof."

"Aye, 'tis what bothers me."

"Did—did Jace say anything else?"

Seward frowned at her, and his eyes drifted to the elephant in her hand. She decided from his expression that Jace had said more, but Seward was sworn to silence.

"There be no proof of anything," he cautioned. "Let me worry about your father and Alex. You take care of Miss Elizabeth. So with your leave, I'd like to take out on my own."

"Go at once," she said swiftly, setting the elephant down and standing to her feet. "I wish Jace would have told me at Guwahati."

"He wanted me to see you here safely. He also expects me to stay, and he won't be liking this. But I be more worried about Sir Hampton than an attack on Kingscote. Besides, I've a few good men on Kingscote I'd trust my life to, and I know they be risking themselves to protect you and your sisters and Miss Elizabeth. They be loyal, but I can't say as much for some others," he suggested darkly.

Coral knew that he meant Natine. Somehow she could not agree. "We have Madan and Thilak, and their sons."

"Good men, all. Should you be needing any help, they

be at hand. And I'll be back with Sir Hampton and your brother as soon as I can."

Coral nodded, feeling suddenly jittery.

Seward stood, as if in spite of all his words to the contrary, he did feel concern about leaving them. He fingered his tricorn. "Jace not be liking this," he repeated.

"We're home, among people we've known since we were children."

She smiled, even though she was tense with mounting alarm. She knew Seward too well. If he wasn't convinced that her father could be in trouble of some sort, there would be little that could budge him from her side. She had long depended upon Seward, not only for physical protection, but in being the uncle to her that Sir Hugo was not.

If Seward was convinced, his frown did not lessen. She saw that his emotions were torn in two directions at once. "Go in peace," she said softly. "You and Jace won't tell me, but it's my father who is in danger. You must find him, Seward! If something should happen to him—" Her voice broke.

"Aye," he said huskily.

"—Uncle Hugo would become my guardian, controlling Kingscote."

"That be the part that's been eating at me . . . and Jace. So you know."

"But Sir Hugo wouldn't be involved in . . . in—" She couldn't speak the words.

Seward's eyes hardened like ice. "In harming Sir Hampton? Who knows what grows like jungle creeper in a man's heart. In the end I suppose a man could do anything if his greed is not rooted out. Mind me now, I am not saying that it's so," he hastened. "You best keep all this to yourself."

"Yes, Seward. You'll be careful on the trek?"

"Don't be worrying about me. Me and Jace been there more than a dozen times." He put his hat on and turned to leave. He smiled kindly, affection warming his eyes. "The Lord be your stay, lass."

He went out, shutting the door behind him. She was left alone.

A few minutes later she heard him mount a horse outside on the carriageway, and the sound of hoofs riding away were lost in the darkness of the night.

Coral stood without moving, wrestling with the loss. "Bring them home safely, Lord. All of them."

Coral refused to give in to a nag of doubt and fear, and instead walked behind her father's sturdy desk. She sank into the leather chair, feeling small in comparison to its size. She opened a top drawer where she knew he kept the small Bible that Elizabeth had given him one Christmas when Coral was still a child. It was gone. Her father had taken it with him before his hasty departure to search for Alex in Darjeeling. The realization brought a smile to her lips. Perhaps the difficulty facing them would end well.

Kathleen and Marianna had already gone to bed when she climbed the darkened stairs in the silent mansion. At the landing, she stopped, feeling as though she were being watched.

She turned and looked down into the Great Hall, but there was no one there.

In her room, she stood in reflective silence, trying to sweep her mind clean of everything but the satisfaction of being home where she belonged. She took a moment to drink in the familiar setting. Only the tension of the problems at hand sapped the moment of a joy-filled homecoming.

Everything appeared just as she had left it some years earlier. The four-poster bed with its mosquito netting, the brightly scattered rugs on the polished wood floor, the wide verandah that overlooked the Bramaputra River. Crossing the floor in the lantern dimness, she stepped out onto the verandah into the warm night.

There in the shadows she stood for a quiet minute and tried to calm her anxious spirit. The Lord did not slumber nor did He sleep, she repeated to herself. He knew. Whatever the future held, the promise of His strength and purpose would also be there to guide their steps.

"One day," Coral murmured, "we will understand that without the storm, there would not be the beauty of the rainbow."

Above and toward the river, the sky held a dusky hue of rose. Beneath its glow, the water appeared to sit like glass. The distant fringed tops of the palm trees stood motionless. *Home.*

"What I need is the luxury of soaking in a cool scented bath," she told herself with deliberate joy. "No crocodiles . . . no snakes . . . no spiders. . . . And after that? The feel of silk!"

31

In the days that followed, Elizabeth did not recover her strength. She spent much of her time between wakefulness and sleep, her body growing more gaunt, eaten away by fever. The medication that had helped Coral in London appeared to have no more effect than sugar-water. The sickness and hallucinations continued.

Coral decided that if any good was born from this trying time—with their father and Alex missing, and their mother slowly slipping from their grasp—it came from the effect that uncertainty and sorrow had on Kathleen. Her sister had grown sober, more reflective, and more patient with Marianna.

The three of them took their nightly vigil by their mother's bedside, while either Jan-Lee or Mera joined them. Since Coral had offered to take the late-night watch after Kathleen, she often entered their mother's room to find her sister seated in the chair reading from the worn King James Bible that rested on the bedstand. Kathleen never mentioned her new study of the Scriptures, and neither did Coral make a point to ask her, feeling it wiser to say nothing. The evidence of Kathleen's seedling faith brought the one joy to Coral's heart during this time. Indeed, God was in control, bringing His peace to Kathleen's turbulent life.

Kathleen took her by surprise one morning after tea when she announced, "I think the three of us should hold a prayer vigil for Mama. It's the one thing we haven't done. We've prayed separately but not together."

Marianna nearly spilled her tea, but Coral said smoothly, "You are right. Why didn't we think of it sooner? When should we start?"

Kathleen hesitated, accustomed to leaving such decisions to Coral.

"Well . . ." She looked from Coral to Marianna, then cleared her throat. "Tomorrow is Sunday. We could dedicate the entire day to prayer. Maybe—maybe even fast. We've so much to pray about. Not only Mother, but Father, Alex, and the mission school."

"Why Kathleen—" began Marianna in awe but stopped short when Coral nudged her beneath the table with the toe of her shoe.

With Sunday given over to prayer and Bible reading, the next weeks passed without disturbance. The answer came gradually, like the buds slowly turning into blossoms. Their mother's hallucinations grew further apart, the fever ebbed, and she became mentally alert for longer periods of time. She was able to keep warm broth down without vomiting, and within another week was eating scrambled eggs and enjoying hot tea.

As the days continued to pass, Elizabeth was able to sit up with pillows propped behind her, smiling weakly at her beaming daughters. It was during these precious times of mother-daughter fellowship that Coral became certain their mother would recover. Already there was new color in her cheeks, and though terribly thin, Elizabeth Kendall was heedful of all that was going on and able once more to pass on her commands as mistress of Kingscote.

As yet, Coral had not spoken to her about the mission school, for the opportune time did not appear to be at hand. She waited for the moment when they could speak alone.

It was ten o'clock Saturday morning when Marianna, donned in bright flounces of pink, faced Kathleen at the bottom of the stairway. "I tell you it's true. I saw the letter and asked mother."

"When! Where is it?"

Coral, hearing their excited voices, left the dining salon where she had been reading the Hindi New Testament. From the arched doorway she saw her sisters. Marianna looked pleased to have unearthed some astounding secret.

"Are you certain? Why didn't mother tell me?"

"How could she when she's been so ill? I saw the letter, I tell you. It was in Mother's sewing basket."

Kathleen groaned and raced up the stairway to her mother's room. "And to think I passed that basket every day for a month!"

"What letter?" called Coral.

Marianna whirled to follow after Kathleen, calling over her shoulder, "A letter from Granny V! She wrote Mother as soon as we left London! She's asking for both Kathleen and Mother to visit Roxbury House and settle Kathleen's future!"

"A letter! But how did it get here so soon?"

"By ship by way of Rangoon and into Assam by river," called Marianna, as though Coral should have guessed, and disappeared down the hall.

When Coral arrived at her mother's room, the door was standing open and Kathleen was speaking to her in a high state of emotional excitement. "Mother, you will let me go back to Roxbury House, won't you? You will come with me for a visit as Granny V asked?"

Elizabeth cupped her daughter's chin and looked at her sadly, as though the pleading amber eyes pricked her heart.

"Kathleen, I cannot promise now. It depends on your father and Alex."

"But Mother! I'll die if we don't go!"

Elizabeth smiled. "I don't think so; you look quite healthy to me. And you've only now come home to Kingscote. If you go running off to London so soon, what will Gavin think? Didn't you tell me he will be stationed at the Jorhat outpost as soon as he gets through Plassey? Darling, you must be fair with your cousin and not keep holding him off this way."

Kathleen kneeled beside her bed, clasping her mother's hand. "What did Granny V say to you? May I see the letter? Marianna says it arrived months ago!"

"Marianna, you should have asked my permission to tell your sister. I intended to speak to her at the proper time."

Marianna looked guilty. "Yes, Mother."

Coral watched them, saying nothing.

Elizabeth looked back at Kathleen, searching her eldest daughter's face. Evidently she saw something that disturbed her for she said quietly, "I suppose times are changing. A girl can wait until she is in her late twenties to marry, but eyebrows will be raised."

"I don't care. It is my life!"

"No," corrected Elizabeth softly. "It is God's."

Kathleen bowed her head. "Yes, I understand, and I do want His will. Only—the Silk House."

"He understands your heart."

There was a moment of silence. Coral held her breath.

"I agree, it is wise not to rush the matter with Gavin

if you're not certain. But both of you must come to some mutual agreement with your father upon his return."

"I will, I promise. Then you do understand? It's not that I don't care for him, it's just . . ." She stopped, as though her confusion made it impossible to say more. "Say you'll come with me. You know how much Granny V wishes to see you. Why it's been years since you've seen your own mother."

Coral looked at her mother and saw the wistfulness on her face.

"Yes, too long . . . I would love to see her again, and London."

"Then we'll go?" cried Kathleen with a squeal.

"We will see what happens in the coming months. First your father must approve, and we must be sure it is safe to travel, because of the fighting, and of course I'll need to regain my strength for a journey to Calcutta and a long voyage. If matters progress, and it appears as though God is leading us that way, then yes, we'll visit Roxbury House, but I cannot say when."

Kathleen threw her arms around her mother's neck. "Thank you for understanding!"

"Oh, we must write Aunt Margaret and Belinda," cried Marianna. "They'll be at Roxbury House too!"

"Yes, it would be nice," said Elizabeth. "I'll write Margaret and congratulate her on Belinda's engagement to Sir Arlen George. I am certain your grandmother will heartily approve of the choice. He comes from a good family. And that reminds me, Coral, we need to discuss Ethan."

Coral's eyes lowered, and she felt her sisters discreetly leave the room. Her heart pounding, she decided this was the moment to steer the discussion away from Ethan to the mission school.

"First, Mother, I have something to show you," Coral

said with a smile, her hands hidden behind her back.

Elizabeth's eyes warmed as they fixed on Coral. "A surprise?"

"One you will appreciate." She carefully handed her the Hindi New Testament and watched her mother's expression turn to awe.

"Why, it is written in Hindi. Where did you get this?"

"William Carey. He's also translating into the language of Assam, and Charles Peddington will send me a copy when it's ready."

Coral explained about William Carey, and the work he was doing in Serampore. "He will translate the Bible into six languages, imagine! And portions into many others. I've met all the missionaries laboring with him at the station—Mr. Ward and the Marshmans. It was Hannah Marshman who advised me on starting a mission school. And Master Carey is a man who loves India. I wish you could meet him, Mother! He will do more for the people in giving them the Bible in their own tongue than anything the East India Company could do! Uncle Hugo is against him. He insists I must not put Kingscote in jeopardy by wishing to follow Master Carey's vision and starting a school, but Uncle is wrong!"

Elizabeth did not appear surprised over her daughter's zeal. "I've been expecting as much," she said, holding the New Testament.

Coral knelt beside the bed. "I wrote you about the school from London. Margaret said you mentioned it to her in your letter before you became ill. Mother, the need for the children is so great."

When Elizabeth said nothing and the silence grew, Coral took heart. "We have over a hundred children working the hatcheries. Mother, we could teach them to read, to write, and tell them the stories about our Lord from the Gospels." Her eyes shone. "We could teach them in their own tongue. Think what it would mean to them to hear of Him in their own language."

Elizabeth stared at the words in Hindi. The moments dragged on, and Coral bit her lip to keep silent.

"Your uncle is right. There would be much opposition to building a mission school. And a good deal of hard work."

"But I'm willing to work hard. It's my calling, Mother. It's the main reason why I've wanted to come home. To start a school in the memory of Gem, to reach a hundred boys and girls like him with the truth of the Shepherd!"

Her mother touched the side of Coral's face.

Coral paused for a moment, then in a rush told her about Jace Buckley and the possibility that Gem could yet be alive. "The major has promised to help me discover the truth. And I feel certain the Lord is asking us to build the school. But without your support it will never happen. Only you can convince Father of the need, and we must stand together against Sir Hugo's opposition."

"I do not know, Coral . . . Hugo is right on one thing. Teaching the Scriptures so openly to the children would anger many. I've done what I could, but what you desire to do on Kingscote is far more involved."

"Have you mentioned it to Father?"

Elizabeth sighed. "Yes. He is quite concerned about the idea, but he promised to pray about it."

Coral's heart pounded. If her father promised to pray about the matter, then he was open to the suggestion, no matter how risky.

Coral wanted to press for a decision, but she knew her mother already understood her passion and was aware of the personal cost.

"Keep the Hindi New Testament, Mother. Read it and pray about what I've asked."

Elizabeth searched her face and laid a weak hand on her arm. "You are willing to accept my decision?"

Coral tensed. Her eyes searched her mother's. It was time to remove her hands from the project and depend completely upon God. "Yes."

"I'm thinking of you, too, Coral. If your father were to allow you to build the school, and teach, it could cost your best years in dedication to service."

"I've already thought that through. It is what I wish to do with my life."

Elizabeth looked pained. "What of marriage to Ethan? Children?"

"Ethan knows how I feel. He has his own work, and he will be starting his medical lab on Kingscote."

Elizabeth studied her, and Coral suddenly wanted to lower her eyes.

"I've heard the colonel's son is no longer serving the Company."

"He . . . he is in the military but serving reluctantly. The colonel managed to lure him back because of his ship."

"Seward says Jace Buckley is still determined to build the tea plantation at Darjeeling. I believe he'll be going with Major Buckley, along with an Indian friend named Gokul, and an old Chinese man," said Elizabeth.

Coral said nothing. The unexpected discussion about Jace made her feel uneasy.

"How well have you come to know the colonel's son?"

The question was simply put, not one that should have troubled Coral so deeply, nor brought warmth to her cheeks, but she stammered, "Well enough, I suppose."

"Suppose? You must know him well indeed, if he will risk so much to see if he can locate Gem."

"He has proven a friend."

"A friend," Elizabeth repeated. "Is he also a Christian?"

"He is searching, but I believe his faith in God is strong." Coral paused. "But his future plans are his own. And he remains an adventurer."

"I see."

Coral stood. "You'll let me know about the school?"

"Yes, but at the moment, it is you I shall take to heart. Are you in love with the colonel's son?"

Stunned by the blunt question, Coral blushed under her mother's gaze. "No."

Coral couldn't tell if her mother was convinced or not. She heard her sigh and look down at the Scriptures again. "How different you are from Kathleen. I'm proud of you, Coral. And pleased that the Lord means so much to you. But perhaps you are not so different from your sister." She looked up at Coral.

Coral wondered what she meant. How was she like Kathleen?

"For Kathleen it will mean another journey to the London Silk House to discover what she truly wants. Marriage to Gavin, or a career in silk. And for you it means a mission school and danger."

Coral smiled. "But I do know my heart."

Elizabeth said no more. She smiled suddenly. "I shall let you know my decision."

The decision came unexpectedly and sooner than Coral had hoped. On Sunday morning Coral was seated at the breakfast table with her sisters when, to their surprise, Elizabeth entered, dressed. Although pale and thin, she looked stronger.

They stood to their feet as she was assisted to her seat by Natine. The girls looked at one another and smiled.

"You may pour the tea, Preetah," she said brightly. "Natine, you may commence to serve."

"Yes, memsahib."

They ate cheerfully, and after breakfast Elizabeth looked across the table at Coral and smiled. "As soon as your father returns from Darjeeling, we shall discuss the building of the school. If he agrees, you may have your desire."

There was a delighted gasp from Marianna, and Kathleen looked at her. Coral sat motionless, staring at her mother.

"I can't promise you, Coral. But I think I can convince your father of the need, and the spirit which prompts you to do something so difficult. It is a noble cause, one worthy of the Kendall name."

Coral remembered little else except that she was on her feet. A moment later she was in her mother's arms as Elizabeth whispered, "In the memory of Gem, we shall build. And may God be pleased to prosper our way."

The thud of horse's hoofs sounded on the drive outside the dining-hall window, and Kathleen was the first to draw aside the curtain.

"A sepoy!"

"Natine, bring him into the sitting room and serve him refreshments," called Elizabeth.

"Yes, memsahib."

Marianna stood. "Perhaps Captain McKay has arrived at Guwahati with troops for the outpost."

"I'll see," cried Kathleen, and sped ahead of Natine to meet the Indian soldier.

Coral went to the window and looked out. Kathleen stood on the porch, and the sepoy handed her something, but Coral was thinking only of her mother's fair words.

A mission school for the children! The Lord had answered her prayer. She had little doubt that her mother would convince Hampton of the need.

A minute later Kathleen came rushing in waving a

white envelope. "It's for you, Coral. From Major Buckley."
Jace!

Coral felt her heart wrench. She tore it open and her hand shook as she read the bold, black writing:

I would not write you this brief message unless I had certain proof. Gem is alive. Gokul has discovered his whereabouts. It is not safe to say more in writing. If all goes well, I shall return him to you by Christmas.

J. Buckley

Coral stood transfixed. Gem was alive!

"Darling, what is it?" asked Elizabeth, rising to her feet but holding to the side of the table.

"Is it F-father?" Marianna stammered. "Something happened to him!"

"No, no," said Coral, her voice shaking with happiness, and she turned to her mother with a beaming smile. "Gem is alive!"

Elizabeth turned pale.

"Jace will bring him home in time for Christmas!" Coral said, embracing her mother. "Gem, and the mission school. What greater gifts could the Lord give me?"

She looked again at the message, her eyes resting on something she had not noticed before in the excitement. Jace Buckley had said that *he* would bring Gem to Kingscote.

Her heart skipped a beat. *Jace is coming.*

"This is a day of celebration," announced Elizabeth, a smile flooding her features.

"But the best is yet to come," whispered Coral.

GLOSSARY

ASSAM: Northeast India, location of Kingscote.

AYAH: A child's nurse.

BRAHMIN: Highest Hindu caste.

BURRA-SAHIB: A great man.

CHUNNI: A light head covering; a scarf.

DAFFADAR: A native cavalry sergeant.

DAK-BUNGALOW: A resting house for travelers.

DEWAN: The chief minister of an Indian ruler.

FERINGHI: A foreigner.

GHARI: A horse-drawn carriage.

GHARI-WALLAH: A carriage driver.

GHAT: Steps or a platform on the river.

GHAZI: A fanatic; usually with religious overtones, but also referring to political beliefs.

HOWDAH: A framework with a seat for carrying passengers on the back of an elephant.

HUZOOR: Your honor.

JEMANDER: A junior Indian officer promoted through the ranks.

JOHNNY SEPOY: Nickname for a common native soldier.

KANSAMAH: A cook.

KOI HAI: A call for service

MAHARAJA: A Hindu king.

MAHARATTA: A warlike central Indian kingdom.

MAHOUT: An elephant driver.

MAIDAN: A large expanse of lawn; a parade ground.

MANJI: A boatman.

MUNSHI: A teacher and writer.

NAMASTE: A respectful gesture of fingers to the forehead with palms together.

NAWAB: A Muslim ruling prince or powerful land owner.

RAJA: A king.

RAJPUTS: A warrior caste of the Hindus, a rank below the *brahmins*.

RANI: A queen.

SEPOY: A native infantry soldier.

SHAMIANAH: A large tent.

SOWAR: A cavalry trooper.

SUTTEE: The religious act of burning alive a widow on the funeral pyre of her deceased husband, based on the belief that by so doing she will attain eternal happiness and bring blessings on her family.

TEHSILDAR: The village headman.

TULWAR: A curved sword.

UNTOUCHABLE: One that is below the Hindu caste system, condemned as unclean in this life.